LAWRENCE BLOCK

a k a

CHIP HARRISON

including:
MAKE OUT WITH MURDER
and
THE TOPLESS TULIP CAPER

Introduction by the author
Afterword by
John McAleer

THE COUNTRYMAN PRESS / WOODSTOCK / VT.

for
KNOX BURGER
editor then, agent now
with respect, admiration and friendship
all in lieu of a commission

introduction

Back in 1969 I wrote a picaresque tale of a young man's efforts to make his way in the world and cure his virginity. I called it *Lecher in the Rye,* which should give you an idea, and used the lead character's name as the by-line. The following year Fawcett issued the book, called it *No Score,* and launched Chip Harrison upon an unsuspecting nation.

No Score sold well, perhaps because of its cover, which showed a winsome young innocent. I decided I liked the character enough to write another book about him, and Fawcett liked the book enough to publish it. (I called it *Below the Belt,* they called it *Chip Harrison Scores Again.* Call it a flatfooted tie for lack of inspiration.) *No Score* drew a lot of fan mail from teenagers who believed, or elected to believe, that it was the genuine autobiography it purported to be. *Scores Again* drew less mail, and didn't sell as well, partly because the artist depicted Chip as larger, older, and more knowing. (Her original model, she explained, was no longer available. Go figure these things.)

I wanted to take Chip further, but how and where? There's a limit, it would seem, to the length of time anyone can remain seventeen years old. There's a maximum number of times a youth can lose his virginity. What could I do with young Chip? Marry him off? Put him to work for General Foods?

Inspired, I put him to work instead for Leo Haig, converting a series of presumably amusing sex capers into a series of presumably amusing and sexy mysteries. I called the first book *The Cornish Chick Score,* since Score seemed to be a word the publisher liked, and it was issued as *Make Out With Murder,* and I haven't space to tell you everything I don't like about that title. I called the second one either *The Topless Tulip* or *The Topless Tulip Score*—who remembers?—and it wound up as *The Topless Tulip Caper*. No complaints.

I had as much real fun writing these books as I've ever had with my clothes on. (I *think* I wrote them with my clothes on.) The first was dedicated to Rex Stout, to whom my debt is obvious. The second was inscribed to three prominent mystery reviewers and the Edgar Awards committee of the Mystery Writers of America. Listen, you never know what'll work.

It gladdens me no end to have these two books back in print. Will there ever be another Chip Harrison mystery? It seems unlikely, but it's a possibility I can't rule out altogether. I know the characters are available, and I had this just the other day from Chip:

"This is to assure you that Haig and I are alive and well on West Twentieth Street. We haven't been remaindered or pulped or anything unpleasant like that. In fact, just this morning Haig looked up from the Rasboras and told me I'd live forever. 'You achieve immortality when you become a private detective, Chip,' he assured me. 'You'll remain seventeen years old forever while the universe ages around you. Like the lad on the Grecian urn, forever will you love and she be fair.' I don't know which she he's referring to, and I don't know about this eternal youth bit, but you can't knock his timing. I'd been angling to ask for a raise and he stopped me dead in my tracks. I tried to get back on course by asking him how much does a Grecian earn, but he wasn't playing."

—Lawrence Block
Greenpoint, Nov. 82

make out
with
murder

one

The man was about forty or forty-five. I guessed his height at five-seven, which made him about four inches too short for his weight. He was wearing a brown suit, one of those doubleknit deals that are not supposed to wrinkle. His was sort of rumpled. He was wearing gleaming brown wing-tip shoes and chocolate brown socks. He wore a ring on his left pinky with what looked like a sapphire in it. Anyway, it was a blue stone, and I figure any blue stone is either a sapphire or trying to look like one.

I don't know all this because I have some kind of terrific memory or anything. I know it because I wrote it all down. Leo Haig says that ultimately I won't have to write things down in my notebook. He says I can train my memory to report all conversations verbatim and remember photographically what people are wearing and things like that. He says if Archie Goodwin can do it, so can I. It's a matter of training, he says.

Maybe he's right. I don't know. If so, I need all the training I can get. I figure it's going to be a good day if I remember in the morning where I put my wristwatch the night before.

Anyway, there's something we'd better get straight right

in front. In the course of writing all this up for you, some of the facts will be as I've jotted them down in my notebook, and some will be as I happen to remember them, and things like conversations are as close as my memory can make them to how they happened originally. I don't have a tape recorder in my head, but I do tend to listen to people and remember not only what they said but how they said it. I suppose that's as close to the truth as you can generally come.

The guy in the brown suit was very boring to follow. I picked him up outside of the Gaily Gaily Theater on Eighth Avenue between 45th and 46th. That was 1:37 in the afternoon, and the particular afternoon was the third Wednesday in August. He emerged from the theater (*All-Male Cast! XXX-rated! Adults Only Positively!*) making those hesitant eye movements that you would expect anybody to make under those circumstances, as if he wanted to make sure that nobody he knew was watching him, but without making it obvious that he was looking around.

I picked him up because I liked the idea that he was already behaving with suspicion. It seemed likely that he would be more of a challenge.

See, I had no real reason to follow this man in particular. This was what Leo Haig calls a training exercise. We didn't have a case at the time, and while he enjoyed having me hang around and listen to him talk while he played with his tropical fish, we both eventually felt guilty if I wasn't doing something to earn the salary he paid me. So he sent me out to follow people. I would do this for as many hours as I could stand, and then I would go back and type up a report on my activities as a shadow. He would then read the report very critically. (I'm surprised he managed to read these reports at all, to tell you the truth. When all you do is follow a woman from her apartment building to Gristede's and back again, there is

not a hell of a lot of excitement in a detailed report of
what you have seen.)

But all of this would develop my powers of observation,
he said, plus my skills in following people, in case we got
a case that demanded that sort of thing. And it would also
point up my journalistic talents. Leo Haig is very firm on
this last subject, incidentally. It's not enough to be a great
detective, he says, unless somebody writes about it well
enough to let the world know about you.

Well, the guy in the brown suit certainly moved around
enough. From the theater he went to a cafeteria on Broadway and had a cup of coffee and a prune Danish. I sat half
a dozen tables away and pretended to drink my iced tea.
He left the cafeteria and walked around the corner onto
42nd Street, where he entered First Amendment Books, a
hole-in-the-wall that specializes in reading matter that
abuses the amendment it's named after. I don't know what
he bought there because I didn't want to go in there after
him. I loitered outside, trying not to look like a male
hustler. By concentrating on Melanie Trelawney, I figured
it might be easier to project a determinedly heterosexual
image.

Thinking about Melanie Trelawney may not have made
me *look* more heterosexual, but it certainly made me *feel*
heterosexual as all hell. And thinking about Melanie
came fairly easily to me because I had been thinking of
very little else for the past month. In a sense, thinking
about Melanie was more rewarding than spending time
with her, because I allowed myself to play a more active
role in thought than I did in life itself.

In the little plays I acted out in my head, for example,
Melanie did not deliver lines like, "I think we should wait
until we know each other better, Chip." Or, "I'm just not
sure I'm stable enough for an active sexual relationship."
Or, "Stop!"

My mental Melanie, my liberated, receptive Melanie
was purring like a kitten while I stroked the soft skin of

her upper thigh, when the man in the brown suit picked that moment to emerge from First Amendment with a parcel under his arm. Magazines, by the size and shape of the parcel. I had a fair idea what kind of magazines they were.

He headed west and walked briskly to Eighth Avenue. Just before he reached the corner he stopped in a doorway and talked to a tall slender young man wearing faded jeans and brand-new cowboy boots. They talked for a few moments and evidently failed to come to an agreement. My target heaved his shoulders and lurched away, and the kid with the boots gave him the finger.

On the other side of Eighth he had better luck. He stopped again in a doorway, and I loitered as unobtrusively as possible while they got it together. Then they walked side by side over to Ninth Avenue and two blocks north to something that was supposed to be a hotel. That's what the sign said, anyhow. From the looks of it I got the feeling that if you ever needed a cockroach in a hurry, that was the place to look for one.

There was a liquor store next to the hotel, and they stopped there first, with the hustler waiting outside while Brown Suit bought a bottle. He came out with a pint of something and they went into the hotel together.

I was going to leave him there and say the hell with it, and either follow somebody else or call it a day, but Haig had told me just a couple of days ago that the attribute of a successful surveillance man most difficult to develop was patience. "You must cultivate *sitzfleisch,* Chip. Sitting flesh. A mark of professionalism is the ability to do absolutely nothing when to do otherwise would be an improper course of action."

I went into a coffeeshop across the street and settled my *sitzfleisch* on a wobbly counter stool. The special of the day was meat loaf, which suggested that the activity of the night before had been sweeping the floor. I had a glazed doughnut and a lot of weak coffee, and concentrated on developing the ability to do absolutely nothing.

While I worked on this I did a little more thinking about Melanie Trelawney.

I had met her about a month ago. I was in Tompkins Square Park trying to decide whether or not I wanted a Good Humor. The Special Flavor of the Month was Chocolate Pastrami and I wasn't sure I could handle it, but it did sound off the beaten track. Somebody came by that I knew, and then someone else materialized with a guitar, and eventually a batch of us were sitting around singing songs of social significance. After a while somebody started passing out home-made cigarettes with an organic and non-carcinogenic tobacco substitute in them, but I just passed them up, because by this time I had seen Melanie and I was high already.

We got to talking. Nine times out of ten when I meet a really sensational girl it takes an exchange of perhaps fourteen sentences before one or both of us realizes we could easily bore each other to death. Sometimes, say one time in ten, it doesn't happen that way. In which case I tend to flip out a little.

I'll tell you something. Sometimes when two people meet each other, the best thing that can happen is that they go directly to the nearest bed. Other times the best thing can happen is that they take their time and really get to know each other first. Either way is cool. The problem comes when the two people perceive the situation differently.

Not that she was precisely driving me up a wall. There were times when it felt that way, I'll admit, but basically it was a question of Melanie's feeling it was very necessary for us to take our time, while I felt that all the time we had to take was whatever time it took to get out of our clothes. Since Melanie always wore jeans and a tie-dyed top and sandals, and nothing under any of those three articles of clothing but her own sweet self, and since I was sufficiently motivated to take off my shirt without unbuttoning it, this process would not have taken much time.

It probably wasn't as bad as I'm making it sound. I mean, I'm not Stanley Stud who has to have a woman every night or his thing will turn green. I *want* a woman every night, but I've learned to live with failure. We were getting to know each other, Melanie and I, and we were getting to know each other slightly in a physical way, and eventually things were going to work out. Until then I wasn't sleeping very well, but I had decided I could put up with that.

I sat at the counter and stirred my coffee, trying to convince myself that I wanted to drink it. Every few seconds I would glance out through the window to see if the man in the brown suit was finished and ready to lead me off to still more exciting places. Every once in a while someone with the same general orientation as Brown Suit would give me a sidelong glance. Which made me think defensively again of Melanie.

One thing had been bothering me lately. I couldn't escape the feeling that Melanie might be a little bit out of touch with reality.

For maybe the past ten days she had been behaving strangely. She would laugh suddenly at nothing at all, and then a few minutes later she would start crying and not say what it was about. And then a couple of days earlier she explained what it was. She was convinced she was going to die.

"Two of my sisters are already gone," she said. "First Robin was killed in a car accident. Then Jessica threw herself out the window. There's just three of us left, Caitlin and Kim and me, and then we'll all be gone."

"In seventy years, maybe. But not like tomorrow, Melanie."

"Maybe tomorrow, Chip."

"I think maybe you do drugs a little too much."

"It's not drugs. Anyway, I'm straight now."

"Then I don't get it."

Her eyes, which range from blue to green and back again, were a very vivid blue now. "I am going to be killed," she said. "I can sense it."

"What do you mean?"

"Just what I said. Robin and Jessica were killed—"

"Well, Jessica killed herself, didn't she?"

"Did she?"

"Jesus, Melanie, that's what you just said, isn't it? You said she threw herself out a window."

"Maybe she did. Maybe she . . . she was pushed."

"Oh, wow!"

She lowered her head, closed her eyes. "Oh, I don't know what I'm talking about. I don't know anything, Chip. All I know is the feelings I've had lately. That all of the Trelawney girls are going to die and that I'm going to be next. Maybe Robin's accident really was an accident. Maybe Jessica did kill herself. She wasn't terribly stable, she had a weird life style. And maybe Robin's accident really was an accident. I know it must have been. But—I'm *afraid,* Chip."

I saw her a couple of times after that, and she was never that hysterical again. She did mention the subject, though. She tried to be cool about it.

"Well, like it's a good thing you're working for a private detective, Chip. That way you can investigate the case when I'm murdered."

I would tell her to cut the shit, that she was not going to be murdered, and she would say she was just making a joke out of it. Except it was only partly a joke.

I guess that coffee shop wasn't the best place to pick for a stake-out. Not just because the coffee was rotten, but because the clientele was largely gay.

Which is all right as far as I'm concerned. I don't get uncomfortable in homosexual company. I have a couple of gay friends, as far as that goes. But the thing is this: if you sit in a place like that, just killing time over a cup of coffee, and if you're young and tallish and thinnish, which is to say the general physical type which is likely to hang out in such a place for a particular purpose, well, people come to an obvious conclusion.

It was getting a little heavy, so I paid for my coffee and went out to wait outside. I guess that turned out to be worse. I wasn't outside for five minutes before a heavy-set man with a slim attaché case and a neatly trimmed white moustache asked me if he could buy me a drink.

I took my wallet out and flipped it open briefly. "Police," I said. "Surveillance," I said. "Scram," I said.

"Oh, dear," the man said.

"Just go away," I said.

"I didn't actually do anything," the man said. "Just an offer of a drink, all in good faith——"

"Jesus, go away," I said.

"I'm not under arrest?"

Across the street, the man in the brown suit emerged from the hotel. He still had his package of magazines with him. I told the idiot with the moustache that he was not under arrest, but that he would be if he didn't piss off.

"You're not Vice Squad?"

"Narcotics," I said, trying to get past him.

"But you should be on the Vice Squad," he insisted. "You'd fool anyone."

I've decided since that he must have intended this as a compliment. At the time I couldn't pay that much attention to what he was saying because Brown Suit was on his way into a subway kiosk and I had to hurry if I didn't want to lose him. It occurred to me that perhaps I did want to lose him, but I wanted to get away from the creep with the moustache in any case, so I charged down to the subway entrance and caught sight of the man in brown just as I dropped my own token into the turnstile. Actually, it was his turn to follow me for the next little bit, because he had to buy a token. I always have a pocket full of them.

Leo Haig believes his right-hand man should be prepared for any contingency.

I bought a paper to give myself something to hide behind and to kill time so that he could let me know which train we were going to ride. It turned out to be the downtown A train and we rode it to Washington Square. Then we went up and around and caught the E train as far as Long Island City. This puzzled me a little because he could have caught that same E train at 42nd Street and saved going out of the way a couple of miles, but I figured maybe he changed his mind and had some particular last-minute reason to go out to Queens.

At Long Island City he got out of the train just as the doors were closing, and if I hadn't been standing right next to the door at the time I would have gone on riding to Flushing or someplace weird like that. But I got out, and I immediately began walking off in the opposite direction from him. After I had gone about twenty yards I turned and looked over my shoulder and there he was. I started to turn again, but he was making motions with his hands.

I just stood there. I didn't really know what else to do.

"Look," he said. "This is beginning to get on my nerves."

"Huh?"

"You've been following me all afternoon, son. Would you like to tell me why?"

Leo Haig always tells me to use my instinct, guided by my experience. He stole this bit of advice from Nero Wolfe. My problem is, I haven't had too much experience and my instincts aren't always that razor-sharp.

But what I said was, "I have to say something to you."

"Well, you could have said it back on Ninth Avenue, son. You didn't have to wait until we both rode back and forth underneath Manhattan Island."

"The thing is, I don't know if you're the right man."

"What right man?"

"The married man who's been running around with my sister, and if you are—"

Well, he damned well wasn't, and that was a load off
both our minds. He laughed a lot, and he did everything
but explain to me precisely why he was extremely unlikely
to be running around with anybody's sister, or to be married, and we went our separate ways to our mutual relief.
I got another E train heading back in the direction I'd
come from and he went somewhere else.

At least he hadn't made me until I'd tailed him to
Ninth Avenue. I suppose that was something.

There's probably a good way to connect from the E
train to something that goes somewhere near the Lower
East Side, but I'm still not brilliant about the subway
system and the maps they have there are impossible to
figure out, especially when the train is (a) moving and
(b) crowded, which this one certainly was. So I rode
down to Washington Square again, feeling a little foolish
about the whole thing, and then I got out and walked cross-
town. I called Melanie a couple of times en route, but the
line was busy.

Melanie's place was on Fifth Street between Avenue C
and Avenue D. I could never figure out why. I mean, I
could figure out why the building was there. It had no
choice. Buildings tend to stay where you put them, and
nobody would have allowed this building in a decent
neighborhood anyway. But Melanie did have a choice.
She wasn't wildly rich, and I don't suppose she could have
stayed at the Sherry-Netherland, but she could have had a
better apartment in a safer neighborhood with the income
she got from her father's estate. Instead she lived on one
of the most squalid and unsafe blocks in the city.

"You know," I'd told her a day or two ago, "if you
really insist on having this irrational fear of being murdered, you ought to move out of this rathole. Because when
you live here, being murdered isn't an irrational fear. It's
a damned rational one."

"I feel secure here," she said.

"The streets are wall-to-wall junkies and perverts," I said. "The muggers have their own assigned territories so they don't mug each other by mistake. What makes you feel secure?"

"It's a settled neighborhood, Chip."

I walked through it now. It was at its very worst in the afternoon because the light was bright enough to see how grungy it was. It was also bright in the morning, but there was no one around. Starting a little after noon, the rats would begin to peep out of their holes.

I got to her building. They still hadn't replaced the front door. No one knew who had taken it, or why. I walked up four very steep flights of stairs and knocked on her door.

There was no answer.

I knocked a couple more times, called her name a lot, and then tried the door. It was locked, and that worried me.

See, Melanie would only lock her door when she was home. I know most people do it the other way around, or else lock it all the time, but she had a theory on the subject. If a junkie burglar knew she wasn't home, and found the door locked, he would simply kick it in. This would mean she would have to pay for a new lock. If, however, she left it unlocked, he would come in, discover there was nothing around to take, and finally settle for ripping off her radio. Since the radio had cost fifteen dollars and the big cylinder lock had cost forty, it was clear where the priorities lay.

I knocked again, a lot louder. She would not be asleep at this hour. And her telephone had been busy just a few minutes ago. Of course telephones in New York are capable of being busy just for the hell of it, but—

I got this sudden flash and didn't like it at all. So I did something I've wanted to do for years. I think it's something everybody secretly wants to do.

I kicked the door in.

You'd be surprised how easy that is. Or maybe you wouldn't when you stop to think that some of the most decrepit drug addicts in the world do it a couple of times a day. I hauled back and kicked with my heel, hitting the door right on the lock. On the third try the door flew open and the forty-dollar lock went flying, and I lost my balance and sat down without having planned to. I suppose a few tenants heard me do all these things, but they evidently knew better than to get involved.

The apartment was a rabbit warren, a big living room and a long hallway that kept leading to other rooms, some of them containing Salvation Army reject furniture, some of them papered with posters of Che and stuff like that. Actually I think Melanie paid as much rent for the place as I paid for a room in a decent neighborhood. She said she liked having plenty of space. Personally, considering the condition of the rooms, I would think that a person would pay more for less space. One room in that building would have been bad enough. Five rooms was ridiculous.

The telephone was in the living room. It was off the hook. I worked my way through the apartment, calling out her name, picking up more and more negative vibrations and getting less and less happy about the whole thing.

I found her in the back room. She was spread out stark naked on her air mattress, which is just how I had always hoped to find her.

But she was also absolutely dead, and that was not what I had had in mind at all.

two

She wasn't the first corpse I
had ever seen. One summer I picked apples for a while in
upstate New York, a job which consisted largely of falling
off ladders. The other pickers would go out drinking when
they were done, and sometimes I would tag along. There
was usually at least one fight an evening. Sometimes somebody would pull a knife, and one time when this happened
it wound up that one guy, a wiry man with a harelip,
caught a knifeblade in his heart and died. I saw him when
they carried him out.

The first book I wrote, I covered my experiences apple-
picking, but never put that part in. God knows why.

So she wasn't the first corpse I ever looked at, but she
might as well have been. I kept thinking how horrible it
was that she looked so beautiful, even in death. Her pale
white skin had a blue tint to it, especially in her face. Her
eyes were wide open and I could swear they were staring
at me.

I knew she was dead. No living eyes ever looked like
that. But I had to reach down and touch her. I put one
hand on her shoulder. She'd been dead long enough to
grow cool, however long that takes. I don't know much
about things like that. I'd never had to.

I almost didn't see the hypodermic needle. She was on her back, legs stretched out in front of her, one arm at her side, the other placed so that her hand was on her little bowl of a stomach. That hand almost covered the hypodermic needle. After I saw it, I picked up her other arm and found a needle mark. Just one, and it looked fresh.

I put her arm back the way I had found it. I went to the bathroom and threw up and came back and looked at her some more. I must have stood there staring at her for five minutes. Then I paced around the whole apartment for another five minutes and came back and stared at her some more.

This wasn't shock. I was in shock, of course, but I was being very methodical about this. I wanted to notice everything and I wanted to make sure I remembered whatever I noticed.

I left her apartment, closed the door, walked down the stairs and out. I walked all the way over to First Avenue before I caught a cab. The cab dropped me at 14th Street and Seventh. I walked quickly from there to my rooming house on 18th Street, a few doors west of Eighth.

When I was in my own room on the third floor, the first thing I did was lock the door. The second thing was to go into the bathroom and remove the towel bar from the wall. It's a hollow stainless steel bar, and there was a little plastic vial in it that contained several dollars' worth of reasonably good grass. I poured the grass in the toilet and flushed, rinsed out the vial, and tossed it out the window. Then I went through the medicine cabinet. I couldn't find anything to worry about except for a few codeine pills that my doctor had prescribed for a sinus headache. I thought about it and decided to hell with them, and I flushed them away, too. That left nothing but aspirin and Dristan, and I didn't think the cops would hassle me much for either of those. I put the towel bar back and washed my hands.

I looked in the mirror and decided I didn't like the

way I was dressed. I put on a fresh shirt and a pair of slacks that didn't need pressing too badly. I traded in my loafers for my black dress shoes.

Then I went downstairs to the pay phone in the hall. I dropped a dime in the slot and dialed the number I know best.

Haig answered the telephone himself for a change. We talked for a few minutes. Mostly I talked and he listened, and then he made a couple of suggestions, and I hung up the phone and went off to discover the body.

I guess I'll have to tell you something about Leo Haig.

The place to start, I suppose, is how I happen to be working for him. I had been looking for a job for a while, and things had not been going particularly well. I got work from time to time, washing dishes or bussing tables or delivering messages and parcels, but none of these positions amounted to what you might call A Job With A Future, which is what I have always been seeking, though in a sort of inept way.

My problem, really, was that I wasn't qualified for anything too dynamic. My education stopped a couple of months before graduation from Upper Valley Preparatory Academy, which is to say that I haven't even got a high school diploma, for Pete's sake. And my previous work experience—well, when you tell a prospective employer that you have been an assistant to Gregor the Pavement Photographer, a termite salesman, a fruit picker, and a deputy sheriff in a whorehouse in South Carolina, well, what usually happens is his eyes glaze and he points at the door a lot.

(I don't want to go into all this ancient history now, really, but if you're interested you could read about it. My first two books, *No Score* and *Chip Harrison Scores Again,* pretty well cover the territory. I don't know that they're much good, but you could read them for background information or something. Assuming you care.)

Anyway, I was living in New York and doing the hand-
to-mouth number and reading the want ads in *The Times,*
and there were loads of opportunities to earn $40 a week
if you had a doctorate in chemical engineering or something like that, but not much if you didn't. Then I ran
into an ad that went something like this:

> RESOURCEFUL YOUTH want-
> ed to assist detective. Low pay,
> long hours, hard work, demand-
> ing employer. Journalistic experi-
> ence will be given special
> consideration. Familiarity with
> tropical fish helpful but not ab-
> solutely necessary. An excellent
> opportunity for one man in a
> million. . . .

I didn't know if I was one man in a million, but it was
certainly one advertisement in a million, and nothing could
have kept me from answering it. I called the number listed
in the ad and answered a few questions over the phone.
He gave me an address and I went to it, and at first I
thought the whole thing was someone's idea of a joke, because the building was obviously a whorehouse. But it
turned out that only the lower two floors were a whorehouse. The upper two floors were the office and living
quarters of Leo Haig.

He wasn't what I expected. I don't know exactly what I
expected, but whatever it might have been, he wasn't it.
He's about five-two and very round. It's not that he's terribly heavy, just that the combination of his height and
girth makes him look something like a beachball. He has
a head of wiry black hair and a pointed black goatee with
a few gray hairs in it. That beard is very important to
him. I've never seen it when it was not trimmed and

groomed to perfection. He touches it a lot, smoothing and shaping it. He says it's an aid to thought.

I spent three hours with him that first day, and at the end of the three hours I had a job. He spent the first hour pumping me, the second showing off his tropical fish, and the final hour talking about everything in the world, himself included. I went out of there with a lot more knowledge than I had brought with me, A Job With A Future, and a whole lot of uncertainty about the man I was working for. He was either a genius or a lunatic and I couldn't make up my mind which.

I still haven't got it all worked out. I mean, maybe the two are not mutually exclusive. Maybe he's a genius *and* a lunatic.

The thing is, the main reason I got the job was that I had had two books published. You may wonder what this has to do with being the assistant of a private detective. It's very simple, really. Leo Haig isn't content with being the world's greatest detective. He wants the world to know it.

"There are a handful of detectives whose names are household words," he told me. "Sherlock Holmes. Nero Wolfe. Their brilliance alone would not have guaranteed them fame. It took the efforts of other men to bring their deeds to public attention. Holmes had his Watson. Wolfe has his Archie Goodwin. If a detective is to make the big time, a trustworthy associate with literary talent is as much a prerequisite as a personality quirk and an eccentric hobby."

Here's something I have to explain to you if you are going to understand Leo Haig at all.

He believes Nero Wolfe exists.

He really believes this. He believes Wolfe exists in the brownstone, with the orchids and Theodore and Fritz and all the rest of it, and Archie Goodwin assists him and writes up the cases and publishes them under the pen name of Rex Stout.

"The most telling piece of evidence, Chip. Consider

that *nom de plume,* if you will. And of course it's just that; no one was ever born with so contrived a name as Rex Stout. But let us examine it. Rex is the Latin for king, of course. As in *Oedipus Rex.* And Stout means, well, fat. Thus we have what? A fat king—and could one ask for a more perfect appellation to hang upon such an extraordinary example of corpulence and majesty as Nero Wolfe?"

Haig hasn't always been a detective. Actually he's only been a detective about a year longer than I've been an assistant detective. Until that time he lived in a two-room apartment in the Bronx and raised tropical fish to sell to local pet shops. This may strike you as a hard way to make a living. You'd be right. Most tropical fish are pretty inexpensive when you buy them from the pet shop, and even that price has to be three or four times what the shopkeeper pays for them, because he has to worry about a certain percentage of them dying before he can get them sold. Haig had developed a particularly good strain of velvet swordtails—the color was deeper than usual, or something—and he had a ready market for most of the other fish he raised as well, but he was not getting rich this way.

The way he got rich took relatively little effort on his part. His uncle died and left him $128,000.

As you can probably imagine, that made quite a difference in his life. Because all of a sudden he didn't have to run around New York with plastic bags full of little fishes for sale. He could do what he had always dreamed of doing. He could become the World's Greatest Detective.

Raising fish had been Leo Haig's only way to make a living, but it had not been his only interest. He has what is probably the largest library of mystery and detective fiction in the world. I think he has just about everything ever written on the subject. The Nero Wolfe novels, from *Fer-De-Lance* to the latest one, are all in hard cover; after he received his inheritance he had them all rebound in hand-tooled leather. He's been reading all of these things since he was a kid, and he remembers what he reads. I mean, he can tell you not only the plot, but the names of all the characters in some Ngaio Marsh mystery that he read fifteen years ago. It's pretty impressive, let me tell you.

The house is pretty impressive, too, and he has emphasized that he wants me to write about the house, but I'll wait until I come to the part about going there and then I'll describe it for you. I'll just say now that he picked it when he had collected his inheritance and started to set up shop as a detective. He moved in with his books and fish tanks, he managed to get a license as a private investigator, he listed himself in the Yellow Pages, and he sat back and waited for the world to discover him.

The trouble is that he's too rich and he's not rich enough. If he had more money, like a couple of million, it wouldn't matter if he ever worked or not. If he had less money, like nothing substantial in the checking account, it would mean that he'd have to take the few cases that come his way. But he's got just enough money to let him maintain high standards. He won't touch divorce work, for example. He won't do any sort of snooping that requires electronic gear, which he regards as the handtools of the devil. And he won't accept anything routine. What he wants, really, is to handle nothing but baffling murder cases that he can solve through the exercise of his incredible brain, with the faithful Chip Harrison doing the legwork and writing up everything afterwards.

I know his secret hope. Someday, if he makes enough of a name for himself, if he keeps his standards high, develops just the right sort of eccentricities and idiosyncrasies, possibly someday Nero Wolfe will invite him over to the house on 35th Street for dinner.

That's really what he lives for.

I suppose my civic duty called upon me to phone the police as soon as I discovered Melanie's body. I'm glad I didn't let my civic duty interfere with my instinct for self-preservation, because it turned out that Detective Gregorio took my towel bar off the wall and checked it out to see if I had drugs stashed in it. That was just about the first place he looked. I'm never keeping anything incriminating in there again, believe me. Pick a place that you figure is the last place the police would think of looking, and that's the *first* place they think of looking. It's the damnedest thing.

But I'm getting ahead of myself. What happened was, I went back to Melanie's place, figuring it was possible that the police had already found her without my help, but they hadn't. I had left a book on the floor so that it would be moved if anybody pushed the door more than a third of the way open, and it was still in its original position, so it seemed unlikely anybody had been in the apartment since I'd left it.

I went on inside, and I had an irrational hope that I had been somehow mistaken and Melanie would turn out to be alive after all, which is pretty stupid to write down and all, but impossible to avoid wishing at the time. Of course she was still there, and of course she was dead, and of course I felt sick all over again, but instead of throwing up any more I went into the living room and called 911.

The person who picked up the phone put me on HOLD before I had a chance to say anything, which would have been aggravating if I'd been bleeding to death or something, but then a couple of seconds later a cop came on the line and I gave him the story. They were fast enough after that. It was 5:18 when I placed the call and the first two patrolmen arrived at 5:31. You would have thought it would take them almost that long to climb the stairs. They spent most of their time walking around and opening drawers and telling me not to touch anything. They were basically waiting for the detectives but they didn't want it to look as though they were waiting for the detectives, so they asked me a lot of boring questions and sneaked a lot of peeks at Melanie's body. This seemed very disrespectful to me, but I didn't think they would care to hear my feelings on the matter so I kept them to myself.

The detectives got there before very long and took over. There was Detective Gregorio, whom I mentioned before, and his partner Detective Seidenwall. Gregorio is tall and dark and handsome, and he has one of those twenty-dollar haircuts, and he didn't like me much. Seidenwall is older, say fifty, and his name is easy to remember because he looks like the side of a wall, and he didn't like me at all.

They both seemed to despise me, to tell you the truth.

The trouble started with my name. They said they wanted a full name, not a nickname, and I explained that Chip was my legal first name, and eventually I had to show identification to prove it. They wanted to know what I was doing in Melanie's apartment and I said she was a friend and had invited me to stop in after work.

"Oh, you work, huh?" said Seidenwall.

"I work for Leo Haig. The detective."

"You mean some kind of a private cop? You on some kind of a case?"

"No. Melanie was my friend."

"Uh-huh. You a junkie too?"

"Of course not."

"Roll up your sleeves, punk."

This struck me as silly, since I was wearing a short-sleeved shirt, but I rolled up what little sleeves I had. Gregorio got a little suspicious over a mosquito bite, but turned his attention to other things. He and Seidenwall asked me approximately seven million questions, many of them consisting of the same ones over again. How long had Melanie been a junkie? How long had I been sleeping with her? Had she died right away, or was it gradual?

This last question was a trap, of course. There were a lot of questions like this, designed to trick me into admitting I had been with her when she died. There were other trick questions, geared to establish that I had sold the heroin to her. They seemed to take it for granted that it was heroin, and she had died of an overdose of it.

The questions went on for a while. They probably would have asked me fewer questions if they hadn't hated me on sight, and they would have gone on hassling me longer except they were bored with the whole thing. It was all pretty obvious to them. Melanie had overdosed herself with heroin and that was why she was dead. When I pointed out that she had never to my knowledge been a drug addict, had never used a needle, they nodded without much enthusiasm and said that made an OD that much more likely. She wouldn't know about the proper dose, for one thing. And she would have had no time to build up a gradual tolerance to the drug. Finally, some people go into something called anaphylactic shock the first time they try certain substances. Penicillin, for some people. Or a bee sting, or heroin.

Anyway, she was dead, and as far as they were concerned it was an accidental drug-related homicide, and they got too many of them to be terribly interested in each new one that came along. So they asked me all their questions and took a short statement from me, and then they asked me for permission to accompany me to my own residence and search the premises, and of course I could have refused because they didn't have a warrant. But they already hated me enough for one day, I figured, and besides I had thrown away not only the illegal marijuana but the legal codeine tablets, so in a way I was almost glad they wanted to search my room. I mean, I'd have felt a little foolish if I had gone through all of that for nothing.

Gregorio and Seidenwall seemed unhappy when they didn't find anything. They held a whispered conversation by the bathroom door, and I caught enough of it to get an idea what it was about. Seidenwall wanted to plant some drugs so they would have an excuse to arrest me. Gregorio talked him out of it, not out of fondness for me, but because he felt I wasn't worth the trouble.

"I'll tell you, Harrison," he said on his way out. "You're the only thing in this that doesn't make sense. Everything else is pretty open and shut. But you don't figure."

"Why?"

"You swear it's not a business thing with the girl. That she's a friend. And then you tell us you've known her for a month and you weren't balling her."

"I wasn't."

"You a faggot?"

"No."

"Everybody knows those hippie chicks go like rabbits. It's what you call common knowledge. But you knew her for a month without getting in her pants. It don't add up."

I didn't say anything.

"Number two. You go to her apartment and find her dead with a needle in her arm." The needle was not in her arm, but I let it pass. "And what do you do? You call the cops."

"Isn't that what a person is supposed to do?"

"Of course it's what a person is supposed to do. Nobody in this fucking city does what he's supposed to do. Nobody wants to get involved. Nobody wants to call himself to the attention of the police, especially in a drug-related homicide, especially when the person in question is a hippie punk that probably uses drugs himself."

"I don't."

"Yeah, you don't. And you're not a hippie punk either, are you? You're some kind of a cop."

"I work—"

"Yeah, I know. You work for this Haig, who's some kind of private cop that I never heard of. You're his assistant. What do you assist him with?"

"Cases."

"Uh-huh. I'll tell you one thing, Harrison. I hope this Haig character looks more like a cop than you do. Because you just don't fit the image of a cop, Harrison. Private or otherwise, you're not my idea of a cop."

I pictured Leo Haig and tried to decide which of the two of us looked more like a cop. I gave up thinking about it because it made me feel like giggling and I didn't want to giggle. I had the feeling that one giggle from me was all Seidenwall would need.

I wasn't sleeping with Melanie, I had done my civic duty and called the police, and I didn't look like any kind of a cop. Those were the three things about me that made Gregorio and Seidenwall suspicious. I couldn't quite follow their reasoning on this, but then again I didn't have to.

Suspicious or not, they walked out my door and down the stairs without even telling me not to leave town. So their suspicion was evidently just on general principles, coupled with instinctive dislike.

I suppose they would have given me a much worse time if they'd had the brains to realize Melanie had been murdered.

three

"It was definitely murder," I
said. "First of all, Melanie would never give herself a shot
of heroin. She told me she tried heroin once, she snorted
it, and it made her nauseous without giving her any kind
of a high at all."

"She might try it a second time."

"She might, but there were too many other things she
liked better. And if she did try it again, it wouldn't be with
a needle. She's terrified of needles. Some nurse had to give
her an injection once and botched it, kept stabbing around
trying to find the vein, and she still has nightmares about
it. Still *had* nightmares about it. Oh, shit."

"Settle yourself, Chip."

I nodded across the desk at him. It's what they call a
partners' desk, with drawers and stuff on both sides so
two people can use it. I was on my side of the desk. I was
very flattered to have a whole side of a desk to myself, but
I really didn't have much of anything to keep in the
drawers.

Haig took a pipe out of a little wooden rack on his side
of the desk. This was during his pipe period. He had
trouble keeping them lit, and they kept burning his mouth.
He was convinced that he would sooner or later break a

31

pipe in, and sooner or later find a mild enough tobacco, but in the meantime he was doing his best. He thought pipe-smoking might be good for the image. He took the pipe apart and cleaned it while I settled myself. He never did get around to smoking it that night.

I said, "Another thing. Melanie was extremely careful about that air mattress. You had to take your shoes off before you sat on it, and she would make me check to see if I had anything sharp in my pockets. She was very nervous about puncturing the thing."

Haig nodded. "The syringe."

"Right. Even assuming she decides to take heroin, and even assuming she's going to shoot it, the last place in that apartment she'd pick to use a hypodermic needle is the air mattress."

"You didn't point this out to the police."

"No. I didn't point out anything to them, like telling them how she was afraid she was going to die."

"Perfectly within your rights." He touched his beard, stroked it with love and affection. "A citizen is under no compulsion to volunteer unrequested information to the police. He is merely obliged to answer their questions honestly and completely, and make no false statements."

"Well, I fell down there."

"The lock."

"Right. They asked how I got in and I told them the lock was wrecked a couple of weeks ago in a burglary and she hadn't got around to replacing it yet."

"And of course you didn't tell them you had been there once before."

"No. I, uh, more or less gave them the impression I spent the past four hours with you."

"I think that was wise," he said. "They should have noticed the syringe and the air mattress. That should have been as obvious as a third nostril." He closed his eyes for a moment and his hand worked on his beard. "You should have told me of Miss Trelawney's fear of death."

"What could you have done?"

"Probably nothing. Hmmm. There were five girls altogether, I understand. Five Misses Trelawney."

"That's right. And now three of them are dead."

"And two alive. Are the survivors living here in New York?"

"I don't know. I don't really know anything about them."

"Hmmmm. Perhaps you know more than you think. Melanie must have talked about them."

"Actually, she didn't talk too much about anything. She wasn't very verbal."

He nodded approvingly. "I've never felt loquacity is a mark of excellence in a woman. Nevertheless, she no doubt mentioned something about the girls who died. Their names, if nothing else."

"Robin and Jessica."

"One died in an auto wreck and the other fell from a window?"

"Yes. Let me think. Jessica went out the window and Robin died in the car accident."

He pursed his lips. At least he did something weird with his lips, and I have never quite known what it is that you do when you purse your lips, but this was probably it. "Let's not call it an accident, Chip," he said. "Let's merely call it a wreck, just as we'll say that Jessica fell from a window, not that she threw herself out."

"You think they were both murdered?"

"I think we ought to take it as a postulate for the time being. And we have to assume that whoever had a motive for murdering three of five sisters is not going to discontinue his activities before he has done for the remaining two into the bargain. Which of the sisters was the first to die?"

I had to think. "Robin first, then Jessica. I don't know about the timing, though. All of this happened before I met Melanie. I have the impression that Jessica died two or three months ago, but I really don't know how long before then Robin died."

He closed his eyes. "That's very interesting," he said.

"What is?"

"First an auto wreck," he said. "Then a fall, then an overdose of heroin. Assuming that an autopsy reveals that was indeed the cause of death. Which would seem a logical assumption at this stage of things. There were no signs of struggle?"

"None that I could see. Uh, in Melanie's apartment, you might say there were always signs of struggle. I mean, she wasn't the world's most fanatical housekeeper."

"But nothing out of the ordinary? And no sign of another person's presence?"

"No. Except the phone off the hook, of course. I hung up myself after I called the police."

"And neglected to mention to the police that it had been off the hook when you arrived?"

"I felt they would wonder why I happened to notice it."

He nodded. "And they'd resent you for it. It's infinitely simpler for them to process this as an accidental overdose than as a murder, and a loose end like a telephone off the hook would only impress them as a complication. They'd file the case the same way, but they would be annoyed with you for bringing up irrelevancies and inconsistencies. They would have been happiest if you could have told them Melanie had been planning on trying heroin. It's as well you didn't, but that's how any bureaucratic mind works."

He spun around in his swivel chair and gazed into the fishtank at eye level. The entire room, and it is a large one, is paneled in English oak and lined from floor to ceiling with shelves. Most of the shelf space is devoted to books, the overwhelming majority of them detective stories, but fish tanks are spotted here and there on the shelves. There are a dozen of them. They are all what Haig calls recreational aquariums, as opposed to the breeding tanks and rearing tanks on the top floor. Actually, to tell you the truth, they're what Haig calls recreational *aquaria*. I call them aquariums because I'm not entirely literate yet.

This particular tank was very restful to look at. It was a fifteen-gallon tank, which means it was one foot deep by one foot wide by two feet long, and its sole occupants were eleven *Rasbora heteramorpha*. I have a feeling that you either know what they are or you don't, and a description won't help much, but Haig wants me to make an effort on matters like this. Rasboras are fish about an inch long, a delicate rose pink with a blackish wedge on their sides. They're pretty, and they swim in schools, and in this particular tank they swam in and around a dwarf amazon sword plant and a piece of crystalline quartz. The tank was top-lighted, and if you watched the fish for a while you got a happy feeling.

At least I did. Haig watched the fish for a while and stroked his beard a lot and turned around in the swivel chair with a thoughtful expression on his face.

"How old was Melanie?"

"I don't know. A little older than me. I guess about twenty-one."

"And Jessica?"

"Older, but I don't know by how much. Wait a minute. Melanie was the second youngest. And Robin was older than she was, so one of the girls still alive is younger than Melanie."

"Were any of them married?"

"Yes, but I don't know which ones. Obviously Melanie wasn't married." And never would be, I thought, and something vaguely resembling a lump formed in my throat, but I swallowed and it went away.

Haig said, "Hmmmmmm." He turned and looked at the rasboras some more. I watched him do this for a while and saw that it was going to be an extensive thing, so I got up and went over to the wall and looked at some fish myself. A pair of African gouramis, two very beautiful fish, ren-

dered in shades of chocolate. I'm not putting down the
Latin name, because there's no agreement on it yet; the
species was just discovered a couple years ago and has
never been bred in captivity, a state of affairs which Leo
Haig regards as a personal challenge. I stared into the
tank and decided that I had never seen two living creatures
display less interest in each other. We will breed the
damned things sooner or later, but we were not going to
accomplish it that particular evening.

Nor were we going to accomplish much else. Haig
swung around and said as much. *"Sitzfleisch,"* was how he
put it. "We have to let the newspapers do some of our
work for us, and then you can go to the public library and
do some of the rest. At the moment the library is closed
and the newspaper has not yet materialized, so we exercise
our sitting flesh. Get the chessboard."

I got the chessboard. I didn't much want to get the chessboard, but I could see no way out of it. Leo Haig was
about as effective at chess as he was at smoking a pipe.
Whenever there was nothing to do he was apt to want to
play. I'm not very good myself. When I worked in the
whorehouse in South Carolina, most of my job consisted
of playing chess with Geraldine. She almost always beat
me, and I in turn almost always beat Leo Haig.

We played three quick games, and they went as they
usually did. I exchanged a knight for a rook in the first
game and wore him down, and in the second I put a
strong queen-side attack together and more or less lucked
into a mating combination. In the last game he left his
queen *en prise,* and when I pointed it out to him he tipped
his king over and resigned gracefully.

"I've a feeling," he said, "that I shall never be a satisfactory chess player."

I didn't want to argue and knew better than to agree.

"I don't think the character tag of being a hopeless
chess player will endear me to the reading public," he continued.

I still didn't say anything.

"We shall pursue this a bit further," he went on. "But I think we must ultimately find another sport. In your spare moments, Chip, you might compile a list of sedentary sports requiring a certain degree of mental dexterity."

We had coffee together, and then he went upstairs to discuss chess openings with the upstairs fish. I wandered into the front room and played a quick game of back-gammon with Wong. He said, "Ah, so," a lot, which I think is why Haig hired him, and he beat the hell out of me. Then I went downstairs and around the corner for a beer.

Leo Haig's house is on West 20th Street between Eighth and Ninth Avenues, which puts it just two blocks away from my rooming house. (Which is why I selected the rooming house in the first place; before I went to work for Haig I was living on the Upper West Side, near Columbia University.) I promised I would tell you about Haig's house, and I guess now is as good a time as any.

The address is 311½ West 20th, and the ½ is because it does not front on the street. There's a house out in front, and there's an alley next to it, and if you buzz the buzzer a door opens and you can walk down the alley to the house in back, which is half Leo Haig's and half a whorehouse. It started off life as a carriage house. Many years ago, rich people lived in the house on the street and had the one in back for their horses and servants. The horses lived on the bottom and the servants on top. Now the horses have been replaced by Puerto Rican prostitutes and the servants have been replaced by Leo Haig and Wong Fat.

My rooming house is a compromise. Haig wants me to live in the carriage house. There's an extra room on the lower floor that's at least as spacious as the one I pay twenty dollars a week for, two blocks to the south. It's furnished nicely and it's reassuringly devoid of cock-roaches, which are fairly abundant in my place on 18th

Street. He keeps trying to move me in there and I keep resisting.

"The thing is," I told him finally, "I'm sort of, uh, interested in girls. I mean, sometimes something comes along that looks like the foundation of a meaningful relationship, uh, and, uh—"

Haig's spine stiffened, which doesn't happen often. "Your friends would always be welcome in my house," he said.

"It's not that, exactly."

"Your relations with women are your own business. It's been my observation that the great detectives are inclined to be celibate. Not through inadequacy, but because they have passed through the stage of sexual activity before developing their highest powers. Wolfe, of course, fathered a daughter before embracing misogyny wholeheartedly. Holmes was devoted to The Woman but lived alone. Perry Mason never so much as took hold of Della Street's hand. Poirot always had an eye for a pretty figure, but no more than his eye was ever engaged. Their assistants, however, were apt to go to the opposite extreme. I don't want to put too fine a point on this, but I would have no objection to your leading an active sexual life. You could bring women here, Chip. They could attend the breakfast table with no embarrassment."

But of course the embarrassment would come long before they got to the breakfast table. Because you cannot make an initial pitch to a girl and lead her up an alleyway and into what is unmistakably a Puerto Rican whorehouse without creating an atmosphere which is not precisely perfect. So I keep my room on 18th Street, and consistently fail to lure girls to it anyway, and Haig and I maintain this running argument.

I drank two beers at Dominick's and hung around there until the late news came and went. There was nothing about Melanie, which wasn't all that surprising. If every drug overdose made the eleven o'clock news, they wouldn't have time for wars or assassinations. I threw darts at Dominick's dart board without distinguishing myself. I thought a lot about Melanie, and I remembered what she'd been like alive and how she had looked in death, and all of a sudden I was very damned glad I was working for Leo Haig, because we were going to get the son of a bitch who killed her and nail his hide to the wall.

four

In the morning the man next door had a coughing fit, and I woke up before the alarm clock went off. I picked up a *Times* on the way over to Haig's house. In the courtyard, Carmelita was hanging out underwear on a clothesline running between two ailanthus trees. I have a lot of respect for those trees; anything that can come up out of a crack in a New York sidewalk deserves a lot of credit.

"You up early," she said.

"So are you."

"I am not go to bed yet. Busy night."

"Business is good, huh?"

"All time sailors. Want to fock like crazy. Drink and fock, drink and fock."

"Well," I said.

"Margarita, she so sore. Fockin' sailors. Mos' tricks, all they want is the blow job. Get the other from their wife. Fockin' sailors, they get blow job alla time on the boat, alla they wanna do is fock. So everybody gets sore."

"Oh," I said.

I went upstairs and into the office. Haig was busy playing with his fish tanks. I opened the paper and found the article about Melanie and started reading it. Wong came in on tiptoe with a couple of cups of strong coffee. He and I smiled at each other and he went away. Haig went on feeding the fish and I went on reading. A couple of paragraphs from the bottom I must have voiced a thought without realizing it, because Haig turned to face me and said, "Why?"

"Huh?"

"You said you'll be a son of a bitch. I was wondering why."

"I knew she had some income," I said. "But I never thought it amounted to that much. I mean, she never even offered to pay for her own brown rice, for Pete's sake."

"Make sense, Chip."

I blinked at him. "I was right about her age," I said. "She turned twenty-one in May and came into the principal of her inheritance. According to the *Times* her share came to a little over two million dollars."

"Interesting," he said.

"But then, why did she live like that? Suppose she didn't want to touch the principal, what would the interest be on two million dollars?"

"Well over a hundred thousand dollars a year."

"I'll be a son of a bitch."

"So you've said."

"I used to buy subway tokens for her. She could have gone home in a limousine. It's unreal."

He seated himself on his side of the desk and held out his hand for the paper. I gave it to him and he read the article through several times, pausing to stroke his beard between paragraphs. Now and then he made a sort of clicking sound with his tongue or teeth. I don't know how he makes that sound exactly or just what it's supposed to indicate. When he had read most of the print off the page he set the paper down and closed his eyes for a moment.

Then he said, "You have your notebook? Good. There are several things you have to do. The funeral is at two tomorrow afternoon. Had you planned to go?"

"I hadn't even thought about it. Of course I'll go."

"I think you should, for reasons in addition to your feelings for Miss Trelawney. In the meantime, there are places you should go and people you might profitably meet."

He talked for a while, and I wrote things down in my notebook.

I got to the library at 42nd and Fifth a little before the lunch crowd took over the steps. I went through the *New York Times* Index for the past three years and made a lot of notes, then headed over to the microfilm room and filled out a request slip. A girl with Dick Tracy's chin brought me little boxes of film and showed me how to use the viewer.

At first it was slow going because I tended to get side-tracked. I would be scanning my way through back issues and happen to hit an article that looked interesting, so I would stop and read it. After this happened a couple of times I realized what was going on and kept my mind on what I was there for.

Cyrus Trelawney had died three years ago. A combination of heart trouble, cirrhosis of the liver and general cussedness had taken him out five days after his eighty-first birthday. He was a widower at the time, and he left five daughters. The eldest, Caitlin, was then thirty-three. The others were Robin (twenty-seven), Jessica (twenty-one), Melanie (eighteen) and Kim (fifteen). It seemed to me that there ought to have been a thirty-year-old between Caitlin and Robin, just to preserve the symmetry. Maybe he'd had financial reverses around that time.

Although he didn't seem to have had many financial reverses generally. The *Times* obit must have been an easy one to write, because Trelawney seems to have been a properly crusty old pirate. He had come to the States from Cornwall at the age of sixteen with a couple of silver shillings in his shoe, and I guess he was better at finding

A Job With A Future than I'll ever be, because in the next sixty-five years he parlayed those shillings into almost eleven million dollars, after taxes. He did most of this in ways that I'm not equipped to understand, financial transactions and mergers and takeovers and all those words you find in the business pages of the newspaper.

Trelawney used to claim he was descended from Cornish pirates, and the *Times* writer sort of implied that no one had any reason to doubt his claim on the basis of his performance in the world of finance. He was past forty before he married, and shortly thereafter he sat about producing daughters at three-year intervals, except for the one gap of six years. He was twenty years older than his wife and he outlived her by eight years.

I got a lot of information from the obituary notice and more information from various social page articles and the stories about the deaths of Robin and Jessica, but there's no particular point in saying just what I learned where. I had to report it that way to Leo Haig, but I'll just sketch in the general facts here.

Caitlin, the firstborn, was thirty-six now. She had been married at sixteen, but old Cyrus had it annulled. She was married again six years later, divorced two years after that, married again the following year and divorced again within a year. Now she was married for the fourth time—unless there had been a divorce since then that hadn't made the papers. A couple of months before her father's death, she'd exchanged gold bands with Gregory Depew Vandiver, of the Sands Point Vandivers, whoever the hell they are. The wedding announcement told all the schools he had attended and all the clubs he belonged to and described him as connected with a Wall Street firm with half a dozen very Protestant names in its title. After a honeymoon in Gstaad, *The Times* said, the Vandivers would make their home on the North Shore of Long Island.

Robin had been married twice. When she was twenty-three she married Phillip Flanner, a man twice her age who had been her psych professor at Sarah Lawrence. Two years after the wedding, Flanner fell in front of a subway train. If your wife's that rich, what are you doing in the subway? Robin remarried three years after that. Her second husband was Ferdinand Bell. (I kept writing this down as Ferdinand Bull, by the way.) The article described Bell as a professional numismatist, which is what a coin dealer becomes when he marries an heiress.

Robin's auto wreck—Haig said not to call it an accident —took place in Cobleskill, New York, in January. She and her husband were returning from a three-day convention of the Empire State Numismatic Association held in Utica. There was a patch of ice on the road and Bell lost control of the car. He was wearing his seat belt and sustained superficial injuries. Robin was in back taking a nap and was not wearing a seatbelt. She broke her neck, among quite a few other things, and died instantly.

Jessica went out the window three months after Robin's death. The window she went out of was in the penthouse of the Correggio, one of the more desirable high-rise apartment buildings in the Village. She had lived in the penthouse with a girl named Andrea Sugar, who had been working at the time of the fall at Indulgence, which was described as an East Side massage parlor and recreation center. Jessica also worked at Indulgence as a recreational therapist, but had taken the afternoon off.

Jessica had never been married, and by reading between the lines I developed a fair idea why.

Melanie you know about.

I couldn't learn very much about Kim. She had been only fifteen when her father died and was only eighteen now. I could tell you what high school she attended but I don't think you'd care any more than I did. The items I turned up through the *Times Index* were not much help by the time I found them on microfilm. They just mentioned her as "also appearing" in a variety of off-off-Broadway shows. The shows in which she also appeared got uniformly rotten reviews. In one review, a brief pan of something called *America, You Suck!* the critic wrote: "Young Kim Trelawney constitutes the one bright spot in this otherwise unmitigated disaster. Although not called upon to act, Miss Trelawney is unquestionably an ornament to the stage."

By the time I left the library I had sore eyes from the viewer and a sore right hand from scribbling in my notebook. I also had the name of the lawyer who had handled Cyrus Trelawney's affairs. I called him from a phone booth and learned that he was out to lunch, which reminded me that I ought to be out to lunch myself. I went to the Alamo and had a plate of chili with beans. They charge an extra fifteen cents for any dish without beans. Don't ask me why.

The pay phone at the Alamo was out of order. So were the first two booths I tried, and before I found a third one I decided not to call him anyway. It wasn't likely he'd be desperately anxious to see me, and it's always easier to get rid of a pest over the phone than in person.

His name was Addison Shivers, and if I was making this up I wouldn't dream of fastening a name like that onto him, because it didn't fit him at all. I expected someone tall and cadaverous and permanently constipated. I can't tell you anything about the state of his bowels, actually, but he was nothing like what I had anticipated. To begin with, it wasn't hard to get to see him at all.

His office was on Chambers Street, near City Hall. I took the subway there and found the building and was elevated to the sixth floor, where a frosted glass window said *Addison Shivers / Attorney-at-Law.* Then there were half a dozen other names in much smaller print underneath. I don't happen to remember a single one of them.

I told the witch at the desk that my name was Harrison and I worked for Leo Haig. (If you give that the right inflection, people think they've heard of Haig even though they haven't.) I said I wanted to see Mr. Shivers. She went through a door and came back to ask what my visit was in reference to.

"Melanie Trelawney," I said. She relayed this and came back with the news that Mr. Shivers would see me. She seemed even more surprised than I was.

His office was very simple, very sparsely furnished. I guess you have to be richer than God to have the confidence to get away with that. All the furniture was oak, and you could tell right away that he hadn't bought it in an antique shop; he had bought it brand-new and kept it for fifty years. The only decorative things were a couple of sailing prints in inexpensive frames and some brass fixtures from ships. I think one of them was what is called a sextant, but I honestly don't know enough about that sort of thing to tell you what the rest of them were. Or even to swear that the one was a sextant, for that matter.

He looked old enough to be Cyrus Trelawney's father. He had a little white hair left around the rim of his head. His face was sort of red, and his nose was more than sort of red. He was well padded, although you couldn't call him fat. The strongest impression I got from him was one of genuine benevolence. He just plain looked like a nice man. Sometimes you can't tell, but then again, sometimes you can.

"You'll excuse me if I don't stand," he said. His voice was dry but gentle. "I read about Melanie, of course. When that sort of thing happens I merely wish they could hold off until I either die or become senile. I've given up asking that tragedy be averted entirely. I merely wish to be spared the knowledge of it." He looked off into space for a moment, then returned his eyes to mine. "I didn't see Melanie often after her father's death. But I always liked her. She was a good person."

"Yes, she was."

"Your name is Harrison, I believe. And you work for a man named Haig, but I don't believe I know him."

"Leo Haig," I said. "The detective."

"No, I don't know him. I don't know any detectives, I don't believe. Any living detectives. What's your connection with Melanie Trelawney?"

I'd had a whole approach planned, but it didn't seem to fit the person Addison Shivers turned out to be. "It's not much of a connection," I said. "I knew her for the past month; she was my friend."

"And?"

"She was murdered," I said. "Leo Haig and I are trying to find out who killed her."

This, let me tell you, was not part of the original game plan. Haig had emphasized that there was no need to pass on our suspicions and convictions to anyone else for the time being. But he had also always told me about instinct guided by experience, or intuition guided by experience, or intelligence guided by experience, and that's what I was using.

Mr. Shivers sat there and listened while I told him all the reasons why Leo Haig and I knew Melanie had been murdered. He knew how to listen, and his eyes showed that he was following what he was hearing. He heard me all the way through and then asked a few questions, such as why I had not mentioned any of this to the police, and when I answered his questions he nodded and sat forward in his chair and folded his hands on the top of his old oak desk.

After a moment he said, "You'll want information, of course. About the will, about the disposition of funds. I can tell you all that." He got a remote look in his eyes again. "Poor Cyrus," he said. "He was my client for fifty years, you know. Needless to say he employed a great many other attorneys, but I was his lawyer in all personal matters. And he was my friend for as long as he was my client. He was a very great man, you know."

"He must have been."

"A great man. I'm not sure that he was a *good* man, mind you. Goodness and greatness rarely keep house together. But I can say that he was a good friend. And now three of his daughters are dead. And his only son."

"His son?"

"Cyrus, Junior. He was the second born, he died in infancy. Cyrus never ceased to mourn him, especially when it became evident that he would not be fathering any more children. He wanted the name continued, you see. He was resigned to the fact that it would not be, ultimately, and felt it would be sufficient that his seed would endure through his daughters." He cleared his throat. "And now three of his daughters are dead in less than a year."

Cyrus, Jr. That explained the six-year gap between Caitlin and Robin.

"I respect your logic concerning Melanie's death," he said. "I agree that she must almost certainly have been murdered. You realize, of course, that this does not call for the conclusion that Robin and Jessica were murdered as well."

"I know."

"Though one cannot deny the possibility. Or the danger to the two remaining Trelawney girls."

I nodded.

"What do you and Mr. Haig intend to do?"

"Try to warn Mrs. Vandiver and Kim. And try to figure out who killed Melanie and how to prove it."

"You ought to have a client," he said. He opened his desk drawer and took out a large checkbook, the kind with three checks on a page. He wrote out a check, noted it on the stub, and handed it across the desk to me. It was made out to Leo Haig and the amount was a thousand dollars.

"I don't know what your rates are," he said. Neither, to tell you the truth, did I. "This will serve as a retainer. Note that I am engaging you to look out for the interests of Cyrus Trelawney, deceased. That leaves you a considerable degree of leeway."

"I think I understand."

He had one of his junior clerks find various papers about

the Trelawney estate. He went over them with me and explained the parts I couldn't understand, and I filled the rest of my notebook. He poured himself a large brandy in the course of this, and asked me if I wanted anything myself. I told him I didn't.

When I had everything he could give me, he excused himself again for not getting to his feet. He leaned across the desk and we shook hands.

I asked if I would be seeing him the following day at Melanie's funeral.

"No, I don't go to funerals any more," he said. "If I did, I shouldn't have time for anything else."

five

I had never been to a funeral
before. When my parents committed suicide, I was away
at school. I suppose the funeral took place before I could
have gotten to it, but I have to admit I never even thought
about it. I just packed a bag and started hitchhiking.

If Melanie's funeral was typical, I'm surprised the
custom hasn't died out. I mean, I can sort of understand
the way the Irish do it. Everybody stays drunk for three
or four days. That makes a certain amount of sense. But
here we were all gathered in this stark, modernistic, non-
denominational cesspool on Lexington and 54th in the
middle of the afternoon, listening to a man who had
never met her say dumb things about a dead girl. One of
the worst parts was that the jerk was sort of glossing over
the fact that Melanie was either a junkie or a suicide, or
both. He didn't come right out and say anything about
casting first stones, but you could see it was running
through his mind. I wanted to jump up and tell the world
Melanie was murdered. I managed to control myself.

I wouldn't have been telling the world, anyway. Just a
tiny portion of it. There were none of Melanie's friends
there except me. Her relationships with the people in her
neighborhood had been deliberately casual, and even if

some of them had decided to come to the funeral, they would have been too stoned to get it all together. *"Hey, man, like we got to go see them plant old Melanie."* *"No, baby, that was last week."* *"Far out!"*

I recognized Caitlin and Kim with no trouble. I would have figured out who they were anyway since they were seated in the front pew, but the family resemblance was unmistakable. They didn't exactly look alike, and they didn't look like Melanie exactly, but all of them looked like old Cyrus Trelawney. Except on them it looked becoming. They had what I guess we can call the Trelawney nose, strong and assertive, and the deep-set eyes. Caitlin was blond and fair-skinned, a tall woman, expensively dressed. The man beside her wore a tweed suit that didn't have leather elbow patches yet. His nose and lips were thin and his expression was pained. I didn't have much trouble figuring out that he was Gregory Vandiver. Of the Sands Point Vandivers.

Kim was very short and slender, also fair-skinned, but with hair as dark as Melanie's. She seemed to be crying a lot, which set her apart from the rest of the company. Crying or not, I could see what the theater critic meant; she would have been an ornament to any stage. The guy next to her, on the other hand, had no decorative effect whatsoever. He kept reaching over and patting her hand. He looked familiar, and I finally figured out where I had seen him before. He played the title role in *King Kong*.

Kim was wearing a simple black dress, and she managed simultaneously to look good in it and to give the impression that she didn't generally wear dresses. The ape was wearing a suit for the first time in his life.

There was a handful of other people I hadn't seen before and couldn't identify. I guessed that the plump, boyish man in the gray sharkskin suit might be Ferdinand Bell, Robin's husband. If there was a professional numismatist in the room, he was likely to be it. And a girl off to one side was probably Andrea Sugar, if Andrea Sugar was there at all, because nobody else around could possibly have been a recreational therapist at something called Indulgence. The rest of the crowd was mostly old, and you sensed somehow that they were there because they liked funerals better than daytime television. I understand there are a lot of people like that. Every couple of days they trot down to the local mortuary to see who's playing.

The casket was open. I guess they do this so that the more skeptical mourners can assure themselves that the person they're mourning is genuinely dead. And so that the undertaker can show off his cosmetic skill.

I wasn't going to look. But then I decided that was silly, and I went up and looked, and it wasn't Melanie at all. There was rouge on her cheeks and lipstick on her mouth and eyebrow pencil on her eyebrows and some tasteless shit had cut her pretty hair and styled it, if you could call it that. Melanie never wore makeup in her life. This wasn't Melanie. This was a reject from the waxworks.

I really felt like hitting somebody.

Haig had told me to approach one of the sisters after the funeral. It was up to me which one I chose. "The older girl is probably better equipped to make a decision," he said, "while the younger one would probably be more receptive to overtures from someone your age. Use your judgment."

I used my judgment, and decided Kim might well be more receptive to overtures from someone my age, especially in view of the fact that I was more receptive to the idea of making them to her than to Caitlin. But I used a little more of my judgment and came to the conclusion that I would rather talk to Kim without that Neanderthal of hers hulking nearby. The idea of trying to Broach A Serious Subject to her while she was intermittently dissolving in tears also left something to be desired. So it was Caitlin by default.

If you don't mind, I won't go into detail about the trip

to the cemetery or the burial. I rode out in a car full of old ladies talking about convertible debentures. There was a machine at the graveside to lower the casket, untouched by human hands, and off in the distance a couple of old men stood leaning on their shovels. They reminded me of the vultures in cartoons about people lost in the desert.

Anyway, the same limousines drove everybody back from Long Island and deposited us in front of the mortuary, and I managed to walk over to Caitlin Vandiver and her husband. I introduced myself and asked if I could talk with her about Melanie.

I got a smile from her and a blank look from him, and I also got the impression that she smiled a lot and he looked blank a lot. "So you were a friend of Melanie's," she said. "Well, I don't know that I can tell you very much about her. I don't even know what you would want to hear. We were never terribly close, you know. I'm several years older than she was."

She paused there, as if waiting for me to express doubt. She didn't look old by any means. I'm a terrible judge of age, but I probably would have guessed her at thirty and I knew she was six years older than that.

"There are a couple of things," I said. "I think it would be worthwhile for us to talk."

Her smile froze up a little, and at the same time her eyes showed a little more than the polite interest they had held earlier. "I see," she said.

I don't know what she saw.

"Well," she said, the smile in full force again, "actually I could use some company. I hate to eat alone and funerals always make me ravenous. Is that shameful, do you think?"

I mumbled some dumb thing or other. Caitlin turned to her husband and put her cheek out for a kiss. He picked up his cue and kissed her.

"Greg always plays squash on Fridays," she said. "Neither rain nor snow nor heat nor gloom of night, you understand." The two of them said pleasant things to one another and Vandiver strode athletically down the street, arms swinging at his sides. I decided that he probably jogged every morning.

"He jogs every morning before breakfast," Caitlin said. It unsettles me when people do this. I feel as though I must have a window in the middle of my forehead. "He's keeping himself in marvellous physical condition."

"That's very good," I said.

"Oh, it's simply great. I wonder what he thinks he's saving himself for. I haven't had a really decent orgasm with him since the first time I saw him in his jogging suit. Romance tiptoed out the window. Shall we eat? I know a charming little French place near here. Never crowded, quite intimate, and they make a decent martini; and if I don't have one soon—fellow me lad—I shall positively *die*."

And, after we had walked about a block, she said, "I pick the wrong words sometimes, damn it. I shouldn't have said that about positively dying. Too many people are doing it lately. Robin, Jessica, now Melanie. It's scary, isn't it?"

She took my hand as she said this and gave it a squeeze. I gave a squeeze back, and I think she smiled when I did.

We went to restaurant on 48th Street. It was empty, except for a couple of serious drinkers at the bar and a couple at a side table trying to stretch out lunch so that it reached all the way to quitting time. We walked through to the garden in the rear and took a table.

"Tanqueray martini, straight up, bone dry, twist," she told the waiter. It sounded as though she'd had practice with the line. To me she said, "Do you drink? I know so many people your age don't these days."

I'd been trying to decide between a Coke and a beer, but that did it. "Double Irish whiskey," I said. "With water back."

Her eyebrows went up, but just a little. She told me I

was to call her Caitlin. I was not certain that I was going
to do this, and supposed I would sidestep the issue by not
calling her anything at all. She seemed to think Harrison
was my first name and wanted to know what my last name
was, and I told her, and she got a little rattled and said that
Harrison Harrison was unusual, to say the least, and ultimately we got that straightened out. She didn't ask me
what Chip was short for, which was one strong point in
her favor.

There were other points in her favor. Maybe her husband jogged every morning before breakfast because he
was trying to catch up with her. The money she spent on
her clothes and her hair didn't hurt, but it didn't account
for her figure or the general youthfulness of her appear-
ane. She was tall for a woman, and quite slender, and her
breasts were not especially easy to ignore.

There was more to it than all that, though. She was
damned attractive and damned well knew it, and she knew
how to play off this attractiveness and, oh, hell, there's
only one way to say it. She was very good at getting people
horny.

She ordered mussels and a glass of white wine and another martini. I didn't want anything to eat, which surprised her but didn't seem to annoy her. She made a lot of
small talk during her meal, and when I would start to turn
the conversation around to Melanie she managed to side-
track it. After this happened a few times I stopped thinking
that she was more shook up then she was showing and
Got The Message.

What I remembered, actually, was one time when I
was taken out to lunch by Joe Elder, who is my editor. We
went to a place around the corner from his office where
they have a working antique telephone on each table. The
food is better than you'd expect. The only thing wrong with
Mr. Elder is that he can actually drink a Daiquiri without
making a face. God knows how. But all through lunch I
kept trying to talk about an idea I had for a book, and he

kept changing the subject, and later they brought the coffee and he started talking about the book, and it was the
same way now with Caitlin Vandiver. She had decided
that we were having a business lunch and she knew that
meant not saying a word about business until we were done
with the lunch.

She finished her mussels about the same time I ran out
of Irish to sip at. When the coffee came she settled herself
in her chair and came in right on cue.

"You were a friend of Melanie's," she said.

Which was my cue, so I picked it up. "I was the one
who discovered the body," I said.

"Oh, dear. That must have been awful for you."

It had been, but that wasn't what I wanted to talk about.
I told her I was concerned professionally, which brought
that tension into her expression, which I later realized was
because she thought I might be working up to some sort of
blackmail pitch. But I went on to say that I worked for
Leo Haig. "The prominent detective," I said.

"Oh, yes."

Sure, lady. "I have to tell you this in confidence. We
have grounds to believe that Melanie was murdered."

"But I thought it was an overdose of heroin."

"It was." The autopsy had confirmed this. "That doesn't
mean she gave it to herself."

"I see." She thought for a minute. Then she said, "Oh."

"I'm afraid so. It puts things in sort of a different light.
Jessica's suicide and Robin's accident—"

"Might not be a suicide and an accident. Well, Robin's
certainly was, although I suppose someone could have
tampered with Ferdie's car. Do those things happen? I
know they do in books, but my God, if I were going to kill
someone I would take my trusty little gun and shoot him
in the back of the head." She was silent for a moment, and
I wondered who she was killing in fantasy. (Whom, I
mean.) Then she said, "I never thought Jessica was the
type to commit suicide. She was always a tougher and

bitchier broad than I am, and that's going some. And she was a dyke, too."

I had sort of assumed this, but I still didn't have a reply worked out.

"Of course she might have grown out of that," Caitlin went on. "I did, you know. Although I never embraced lesbianism as wholeheartedly as Jessica did. I never stopped liking men, you see."

"Uh," I said.

"Do you want to know something interesting? When I was a girl, oh, way back before Noah built his ark, I always had a special preference for older men."

"Er."

"But now that I've slithered onto the dark side of thirty, I find I've done an about-face. I have a thing for young men these days."

"Uh."

"I've noticed, Chip, that some young men have a thing for older women."

I don't have a thing for older women, but I certainly haven't got anything against them. Actually, I don't suppose chronological age means very much. There are women of thirty-six who are too old. There are other women the same age who are not. Caitlin was in the second category, and I was becoming more aware of this every minute.

Her perfume may have had something to do with this. Her leg, which had somehow moved against mine under the table, may also have had something to do with it.

"Well," I said. "About Melanie—"

"Were you sleeping with her, Chip?"

Everybody wanted to know if I was sleeping with Melanie. First those cops, now Caitlin. I said, "We hadn't known each other very long."

"Sometimes it doesn't take very long."

"Er. The thing is, you know, that someone killed Melanie. And if someone also killed Jessica, and if it's the same someone—"

"Then Kim and I might be on somebody's Christmas list."

"Uh-huh. Something like that."

She lit a cigarette. She had been lighting cigarettes all along, but I don't think it's absolutely essential to call it to your attention every time somebody lights a cigarette. This time, though, she made a production number out of it, winding up taking a big drag and sighing out a cloud of smoke.

She said, "You know, Chip, I do have a little trouble taking this seriously."

"There may not be anything to it."

"But there also *may* be something to it, is that what you mean? Assuming there is, what do I do about it? Put myself in a convent? Hire around-the-clock bodyguards? Quickly marry the president so I qualify for Secret Service protection?"

"The most important thing is to find Melanie's killer."

" 'Catch him before he kills more?' That makes a certain amount of sense." She studied me for a moment. "The man you work for," she said.

"Leo Haig."

"He's really good?"

"He's brilliant."

"Hmmm. And what do you do for him exactly? You're a little young to be a detective, aren't you?"

"I'm his assistant. That doesn't mean my job is taking out the garbage." Actually, I do take the garbage out of the fish tanks some of the time. "I work with him on cases."

"So you'd be working on this, too."

"That's right. I do the leg work." I regretted saying that because she sort of winked and did some leg work of her own.

"I'll just bet you do, Chip."

"Uh."

"I'd like to see you devote all your energies to my case," she said. As I guess you've noticed, she tended to say things with double meanings. "I'd like you working hard on my behalf. You don't have a client, do you? You're just investigating because of your friendship for my sister?"

We had a client but he didn't want his name mentioned, so I didn't mention it. I agreed that we were involved in this out of friendship for Melanie. Which was true—I would have been working every bit as hard without Addison Shivers as a client.

She opened her bag and found a checkbook. She wrote for a minute, tore out a check, folded it in half and slipped it to me. "That's an advance," she said.

I took the check.

"An advance," she repeated. "Actually this is no day to be making advances, is it?"

"Uh."

"It's about that time, isn't it? I have to pick up my darling husband at his club. On the way home I can hear how good it is to work up a sweat. That depends how you work it up, don't you think?"

"I guess."

"Do you? I suspect you do. I have that feeling about you, Chip. And I'm sure we'll see a lot of each other in the course of your investigation of the case."

"I'm sure we will, Mrs. Vandiver."

"Caitlin."

"Caitlin," I agreed.

"It's a difficult name to remember, isn't it?"

"No, but—"

"Some of my best friends call me Cat. Just plain Cat. You know, as in pussy."

The waiter brought the check. She put money on the table and we left. I was really in no condition to walk, to tell you the truth, and I think she noticed this, and I think she was pleased.

On the street she offered me her cheek as she had offered it to her husband, but when I went to kiss her, she turned her head quickly and my mouth landed on hers. She did something very nice with her tongue, then drew quickly away, an amused light in her eyes.

"Oh, we'll get along," she said.

I felt like springing for a cab, so of course there weren't any around. I took the subway. It was hot and crowded and smelly and I wound up pressed up against a home-bound secretary. I was in the wrong condition to be pressed up against anyone and the secretary noticed it. She gave me the look people give when they find a cock-roach in their oatmeal.

When I got off the train I finally looked at Caitlin's check. It was for five hundred dollars and it was made out to me rather than to Haig. She'd spelled my first name Chipp, which explained why she hadn't asked me what my real name was. She was probably used to people with first names like that.

Actually, it would simplify my life in a lot of ways if I spelled it with two p's. I should have thought of that years ago.

Haig didn't see anything wrong with accepting retainers from both Addison Shivers and Caitlin Vandiver. "Our work will be in both their interests," he said. "I see no likely conflict. And there's certainly precedent for it. Nero Wolfe frequently represents more than one person in the same matter, and does so without either party being aware of his association with the other. In the case that was re-ported under the title *Too Many Clients,* for example—"

I had just read *Too Many Clients* a month or so ago, but there was no point in telling him that. You might as well try telling Billy Graham you read the Bible once, for all the good it would do you.

six

I was upstairs until six-thirty, helping Haig with the fish. He had a strain of sailfin mollies he was trying to fix. The object was to develop the dorsal fin to the greatest possible size through selective breeding and inbreeding and by giving the young the best possible nutritional start on life. One of the molly mothers had dropped young earlier in the day and we had to net her and remove her from the breeding tank. Mollies are less likely to eat their young than most livebearers, but every once in a while you get a female who hasn't read the book, and she can polish off an entire generation in a couple of hungry hours.

We gave the babies a heavy feeding of live brine shrimp. Haig buys enormous quantities of frozen brine shrimp for general use, but hatches his own for feeding young fishes. He tends to be a fanatic about things like this, and while he fed live brine shrimp to a few dozen tanks of young fish, I hosed out one of the tubs and prepared a brine mixture and sprinkled the little dry eggs on it.

Then we went downstairs and Wong announced that dinner was ready, and it was a Szechuan shrimp dish with scallions and those little black peppers that it is a terrible idea to bite into. Wong's shrimps had very little in com-

61

mon with the ones I had been feeding to our fish. He's a
fairly sensational cook, and never seems to make the same
thing twice.

I stayed around long enough to win a few games of
chess. Then I went downstairs and said polite things to
Consuela and Carmelita and Maria and some other girls
whose names I didn't know, and let Juana the Madame
pinch my cheek, which I wish she would stop doing, and
then I started walking downtown.

The Cornelia Street Theater was located in a basement.
You can probably guess what street it was on. There was
a banner outside at street level announcing that they were
doing *Uncle Vanya,* by Chekhov.

Maybe you know what the play is about. If not, I'm not
going to be much help to you. I paid two dollars for a
ticket and sat fairly close to the stage. (Actually, there were
only about fifty seats in the house, so it wouldn't have
been possible to sit very far from the stage.) Maybe thirty
of the fifty seats were empty. I sat and watched the play
without paying any attention to it. I don't know whether
it was good or not. I just couldn't concentrate. I would drift
off into thought chains and just let my mind wander all
over the place, and once in a while Kim Trelawney would
appear on stage and I would take some time out to look at
her, but she didn't have many lines and never hung around
long, and as soon as she went off I went off myself.

I guess the show must go on, although with this show I
couldn't quite see it. I mean, anybody could have played
Kim's part that night, for all she had to do up there. And
it wasn't as though an audience of thousands would have
killed themselves if they didn't see *Uncle Vanya* that night.
The way she had acted at the funeral, obviously taking it
all hard, I hadn't really expected her to show up for the
play.

There were two intermissions, and each of them drained
a little of the audience away, so by the time the final cur-

tain went down there were only about a dozen of us there
to applaud, and not all of us did it very enthusiastically.
The cast tried to take two bows, but by the time the cur-
tain came up a second time everybody had already stopped
applauding and people were on their way out of the theater.
It was sort of sad.

I managed to get backstage and meet Kim. She blinked
a little while I introduced myself, and when I said I was
a friend of Melanie's, she nodded in recognition. "I saw
you at the funeral," she said.

"I'd like to talk to you, if I could."

"About Melanie?"

"Sort of."

"I'll meet you out front," she said. "Just give me a few
minutes."

She took about four of them, and came out wearing
jeans and a peasant blouse and carrying a canvas shoulder
bag in red, white and blue. She suggested we have coffee
at O'John's, a little place on the corner of West 4th.

"Gordie's going to meet me there in a few minutes," she
said. "He doesn't like me walking home alone."

We got a window table and ordered two cups of coffee.
"Gordie's a little overprotective," she said. "Sometimes it
bothers me. But sometimes I like it."

"Was Gordie the fellow you were with this afternoon?"

"Yes." She smiled suddenly, and instantly reminded me
very much of Melanie, the way her entire face was so immediately transformed by her smile. "I haven't known him
very long," she said, "and I don't really know him very
well. In certain ways, that is. He's very different from the
type of boy I usually go out with."

"How?"

"Well, you know. He's not educated; he dropped out of
high school and went right to work on the docks. Sometimes I have the feeling that we don't really have very
much to talk about. And his ideas about women, I mean
they're very old-fashioned. He believes a woman's place is

in the home and everything, and he doesn't really think
very much of my being an actress. He's proud when I get
a part and like that, but he thinks it's just something for
me to amuse myself with until we get married and start
making babies."

"And you don't feel that way?"

She gnawed the tip of her index finger. "I don't know
exactly *how* I feel, Chip. From the time I was a little girl
I wanted to be an actress. It was what I always wanted.
After one semester of college I knew I had to get away
from classrooms and spend all my time around theaters.
But it's so hard. You can't imagine."

"I guess it's very hard to get started."

"It's almost impossible. You saw how many people we
had in the theater tonight. Maybe thirty."

"If that."

"I know. It was closer to twenty, and most of them were
friends who didn't pay for their tickets. And the actors
didn't get paid anything, we're all working for free in the
hope that somebody important will see us on stage and
have something else for us, and—"

She told me a lot more about what was wrong with
trying to act for a living. And then she said, "Sometimes I
think I should just forget the whole thing and marry
Gordie. That's what he wants me to do. It's a temptation,
you know. Just give it all up and have babies and enjoy
life. Except I worry that I would wake up some day years
from now and wonder what I had done with my life. It's
very confusing."

She looked straight into my eyes during this last speech
and I felt as though I could see clear through to the back
of her head. I found it easy to understand why Gordie was
overprotective. There was something about Kim that made
you want to put your arms around her and tell her everything was going to be all right. Even if it wasn't.

I was just about to reach across the table and take her
hand when something changed on her face. She raised her

eyes over my shoulder, then waved a hand. I turned, and of course it was good old Gordie.

He pulled a chair up and sat down. He did not seem overjoyed to see me there. (Which made it mutual, actually.) Kim introduced us, and I found out that he had a last name, McLeod. Then he found out that I was a friend of Melanie's and some of the suspicion left his face. Not all of it, but some.

"You see the play?" I admitted that I had. "Saw it myself a couple of times. Rather catch a movie myself. All these people just talking back and forth. What did you think of Kim?"

"I thought she was very good," I said.

"Yeah, only good thing about the play, far as I'm concerned. She's very talented."

I said she certainly was, or something equally significant.

"But I don't like the people she has to hang around with. It's a well-known fact they're all fairies in that business. A well-known fact. Still in all, as a way for her to pass the time until she settles herself down—"

He went off on a speech that Gloria Steinem would not have enjoyed. I have to admit that I didn't follow it too closely. It was already becoming clear to me that Gordie McLeod and I were never going to become best buddies. I was noting Kim's reactions to what he was saying and trying to figure out just what it was about this ape that attracted her. I had no trouble figuring out what it was about her that appealed to him.

"Well," he said, "it's gettin' to be about that time. Nice meetin' you, guy."

"There was something I wanted to discuss with Kim," I said.

"Oh, yeah?"

"About Melanie," Kim said.

He settled back in his chair. "Well, sure," he said.

"It's a little public here," I said. "Could we go somewhere more private?"

"What for?"

"So that we could talk in private."

"What's this all about, anyway?"

I wasn't making much headway. Kim came to the rescue and suggested we all go back to the apartment. She didn't say *her* apartment or *their* apartment, just *the* apartment. He didn't seem wild about the idea, but we went anyway. He insisted on paying for my coffee. I have to admit I didn't put up a fight.

The apartment, which did turn out to be their apartment, was on Bethune Street a few doors west of Hudson, which made it about equidistant from Kim's theater and the Hudson docks where Gordie did something muscular. It was on the second floor of a good old four-story building. There were three high-ceilinged rooms and a little balcony with a view of nothing spectacular.

There was a good feeling to the apartment, and it was hard to believe Kim had rented it less than a year ago. There were some nice Oriental rugs, a couple of floor-to-ceiling bookshelves, and furniture that was both attractive and comfortable. It was not hard to guess which of the two of them had done the decorating.

Gordie got himself a beer and asked me as an afterthought if I wanted one. I didn't disappoint him by accepting. He sprawled on the couch, took a gurgling swig of beer, and put his feet up. "Let's have it," he said.

I started my pitch. That I worked for Leo-Haig-the-Famous-Detective. That Haig and I had uncovered evidence that indicated a strong possibility that Melanie had been murdered. That there were grounds for speculation that Jessica, and perhaps Robin as well, had been similarly done in. That a client who I was not at liberty to name had hired Haig to nail the killer. That it was important to recognize that Caitlin and Kim might be in a certain amount of danger.

And so on.

I didn't get to deliver this entire rap all at once because

Gordie kept interrupting. He seemed to find it extremely difficult to follow a simple English sentence and even more difficult to put together one of his own, and he kept turning the conversation onto weird tangents. Earlier, I had found it disturbing that a girl like Kim was thinking about marrying an idiot like Gordie. Now I found it disturbing that she was living with him. What in hell did they talk about?

When I had been able to get it all out, and when Kim had a chance to ask a few questions of her own, Gordie took a last long drink of beer, crumpled the can impressively in one hand, and tossed it unsuccessfully at the wastebasket. "I'll tell you what I think," he said.

I was sure he would.

"What I think, I think it's a load of crap."

"I see," I lied.

"You know what your trouble is, Harrison? You're one of these college boys. You read all these books and listened to all these egghead professors and it scrambled your brains."

I didn't say anything.

"Me, I'm an ordinary Joe, you know what I mean? An ordinary man, your average human being. What I mean, I didn't have your advantages. I never even finished high school. I did my learning on the streets."

"So?"

"So I don't look for a complicated answer when there's a simple one staring me in the face. The whole trouble with this country is too many guys like you who went to Harvard and they couldn't recognize crap if they stepped in it."

"I didn't go to Harvard."

"Manner of speaking. Where'd you go? Yale? Princeton?"

"I didn't go to college. I didn't finish high school; I got thrown out in my last year."

"What are you trying to hand me?"

"Nothing in particular, I just—"

"Jesus Christ," he said. "I got no use for college boys, I'll tell you that straight out, but one thing I got less use for is a college boy pretends he's not a college boy. Who do you think you're kidding?"

Enough. "The point is," I said, "that if Kim is in any danger—"

"Kim's not in no danger. And if she is, that's what I'm here for. What are you saying, you're gonna protect her? I mean, I can't see you protecting a pigeon from a cat. No offense, but you get my meaning."

I got his meaning.

"Look," he said, "I'll be protecting Kim no matter what. This city's a fuckin' jungle; nothing but junkies and spades and fairies and weirdos. But all this murder shit, you're making a mountain out of a mole's hill. Robin, she's in a car and it cracks up. That sound like a murder? How many people go out like that every weekend?"

"Yes, but—"

"Then there's Jessica. She's a dyke and a whore and they're all crazy, so maybe she wasn't getting it regular enough or who knows why, but she goes out the window. Happens all the time. Then there's Melanie, who's some kind of a crazy hippie with drugs and shit and who knows what, and junkies are all the time shoving needles in their arm and winding up dead, you see it every night on television. I mean, let's face it, Kim's the only one in the goddamned family that has anything much on the ball. The older one, Caitlin, she just a nymphomaniac and a lush. Old man Trelawney must have been pretty sharp to make the score he made, I'll give him that, but he wasn't too good at having kids. Kim's okay but the other four were a batch of sickies."

"They had problems," Kim said. "Don't talk about them like that."

"Look, everybody has problems, kid, but those nuts—"

Kim's eyes flared. "I *loved* Melanie," she said. "And I

love Caitlin. I loved all my sisters, and I don't want to hear you *talk* like that about them!"

She stormed out of the room. Gordie's face darkened briefly, then relaxed. "Women," he said. "I'll tell you something, they're all of them a little nuts. They don't have thoughts the way men do. They have feelings. You got to know how to handle them."

After they were married, I knew how he would handle her. He would beat her up whenever he felt she needed it.

"Look," he said, "I want you to stay out of Kim's life. You get me?"

"Huh?"

"I know you got to work your angle like everybody else. You already got a client, you don't need to hang around Kim. I don't want her getting upset."

"I didn't know that I did anything to upset her."

"Seeing you upsets me. And when I get upset Kim gets upset, and I don't want that. You got an angle to work and I can respect that, but I don't want you getting in my way."

"I really want it to be him," I told Haig. "I want it to be him and I want them to bring back capital punishment. Someone has to throw the switch. I volunteer."

"Surely the fact he's living with Kim has nothing to do with your motivation."

"You mean am I interested myself? I don't honestly know. She reminds me of Melanie, and I can't make up my mind whether that turns me on or off. The thing is I *like* her, and I can't see her spending a lifetime with a clown like him. Hell, I can't see her spending a social evening with him."

"But he seems an unlikely suspect."

"I know. I can see him committing murder. I don't think he'd draw the line at something like that. But he wouldn't be so clever in choosing different murder methods. He'd probably just hit each of them over the head."

"I gather he's not enormously intelligent," Haig said dryly.

"He's about as dumb as you can get and still function."

"Is he crafty, though?"

I thought about that. I said, "Yes, I think he is. Animal cunning, that kind of thing."

"He assumed you were 'working an angle.' I submit he so assumed because he's working an angle of his own."

I nodded. "He was more or less telling me to stay off his turf. And he knows about the money. In fact he seems to know a lot about all the sisters. He hasn't been with Kim that long, and they weren't that close."

"That struck me," Haig said. His fingers went to his beard and his eyelids dropped shut. "He knows about the Trelawney money. He wants to marry Kim, to the point where she apparently feels pressured. She hasn't come into the principal of her inheritance yet, of course. And won't for three years." He remained silent for a few minutes. I knew his mind was working, but I had no idea what it was working on. Mine was just sort of treading water.

I got up and went over to watch the African gouramis. There were three half-grown guppies still swimming around. While I watched, the female gourami swam over to one of the guppies but didn't bother devouring it. I guess she wasn't hungry at the moment.

Haig raises several strains of fancy guppies. The species is a fascinating one, and the males of *Lebistes reticulata* are as individual as thumbprints. When they're about half-grown, you can tell (if you're Leo Haig) which ones are going to amount to something. Those you keep.

The others serve as food for other fish. Haig is fond of remarking that the best food for fish is fish, and some of ours require a certain proportion of live food in their diet. We have a pair of leaf fish, for example, who go through a dozen young guppies apiece every day. It used to bother me, the whole idea of purposely raising fish so that you can feed them to other fish, but that's the way Nature does it in the ocean. I used to know a guy who had a pet king snake and used to buy mice and feed them to it. That would bother me a lot more, I think.

"Chip." I turned. "There is a motive lurking here. I keep getting teasing glimpses of it but I don't have enough hard information to see it. We need to know more about wills and such. Tomorrow—"

But he didn't get to finish the sentence, because just then we heard glass shatter somewhere in the front of the house. We looked at each other, and I started to say something, and then the bomb went off and the whole house shook.

I stood there for a minute. Waiting for the next explosion, probably, but there wasn't one. I went into the front room and saw a crack in one of the front windows.

Then the girls downstairs started shrieking.

seven

It was a pipe bomb consisting
of a length of pipe filled with various goodies, but I'm not
going to go into detail. I mean, who knows what lunatic
out there might get inspired and follow my directions and
bomb a whorehouse on his own? Haig says that Alfred
Hitchcock once had a scene in which an assassin used a
gun built into a camera, and then a few months after the
picture was released someone assassinated somebody just
that way, in Portugal I think, and Hitchcock felt very
ginchy about it. I can understand that.

What happened was this: someone threw a pipe bomb
into the second floor front of our building. That was the
broken glass, the sound of the bomb going through the
window, which had not been open at the time. Then the
bomb went off, shaking the whole house and, more to
the point, giving Maria Tijerino and Able-Bodied Seaman
Elmer J. Seaton a greater thrill than they could possibly
have anticipated.

Shit. I don't want to be cute about this because it was
not at all nice. Maria and the sailor were in bed in the
front room at the time and the damned bomb blew them
to hell and gone. I went in there and looked, God knows
why, and then I went into the john and threw up. I mean,

72

I could make a few dozen jokes along the lines of If-you-gotta-go-etc. But the hell with it. I saw it, and it was ugly.

The explosion didn't hurt anybody but Maria and the sailor. It put some cracks in the plaster throughout the house without doing any real structural damage.

It also made some of our fish tanks leak.

Haig and Wong Fat and I missed a lot of the action because we were running around trying to make sure the fish were all right. That probably sounds very callous, but you have to realize that there was nothing we could possibly do for Maria or the sailor. And a leaking fish tank is something that requires attention. If a fish tank absolutely cracks to hell and gone, you can just go to church and light candles for the fish, but we didn't have any that got cracked. The thing is, shock waves will interfere with the structural soundness of an aquarium, which is basically a metal frame with a slate bottom and four glass sides, and quite a few of ours sprung slow leaks, and that meant we had to transfer the fish to sound tanks and empty the leakers before they leaked all over the place. Eventually we would have to repair all the leakers, a process which involves coating all the edges with rubber cement and cursing a lot when the tank leaks anyway.

So while we were scurrying around examining tanks on the third and fourth floor, I gather half the police in Manhattan were stumbling around on the first two floors. There were a couple of ambulances out front and a Fire Department rescue vehicle. There were beat patrolmen and Bomb Squad detectives and God knows who else, and, because it was established that Maria and her sailor were dead, which could not have been too difficult to establish, there were two cops from Homicide.

Yeah.

I suppose you already figured out that it would be the same two cops, Gregorio and Seidenwall. You must have.

Because you're reading this, and if I were reading it I would certainly expect to keep encountering the same two cops. (I gather this never happens in real life, but just the other day I read a mystery by Justin Scott called *Many Happy Returns* and the lead character kept cracking up oil trucks, of all things, and each time he turned a truck over the same two humorous cops turned up to glare at him. It didn't seem to matter what part of the city he was in, he always ran into the same goddam cops.)

The thing is, you're reading this in a book, so you know it's Gregorio and Seidenwall again. I wasn't reading it, I was living gamely through it, and they were the last thing I expected.

But there they were.

". . . check on the possibility of . . ." Gregorio said. I don't know how the sentence had started or how he was planning to end it. He had evidently begun it in the hall-way, undeterred by the lack of anyone to hear it, and he didn't end it, because he caught sight of me. "I'll be a ring-tailed son of a bitch," he said.

"Er," I said.

"You again," he said.

You again, I thought.

"I don't like this at all," he said. "A hippie girl OD's in a toilet on the Lower East Side and you're the one who discovers the body. A sailor and a spic hooker fuck themselves into an explosion and you're living upstairs. You know something, Harrison? I'm not crazy about any of this."

"We oughta take him in," Seidenwall said.

"I never believed in coincidence," Gregorio said. "It makes me nervous. I hate to be nervous. I got a stomach that when I get nervous my stomach gets nervous, and I can live without a nervous stomach. I can live better and longer without a nervous stomach."

"We oughta take him in," Seidenwall said.

"I don't like the sense of things fitting together like this,"

Gregorio said. "How long have you lived in New York, Harrison?"

"A couple of years," I said. "Off and on."

"We oughta take him in," Seidenwall said.

"Off and on," Gregorio said. "A couple of years off and on."

"We oughta take him in."

"A couple of years you were here, and a lot of years I was here, and all that time I never heard of you, Harrison. I never knew you existed. Now I see you twice in two days."

"Three days," I said.

"Shut up," Gregorio said.

"We oughta take him in," Seidenwall said.

Leo Haig said, "Sir!"

And everybody else shut up.

He said, "Sir. You are on my property without my invitation or enthusiastic approval. You have come, as well I can appreciate, to investigate a bombing. You wish to ascertain whether or not the bombing is impinging in any way upon myself and my associates. It is not. We are not involved. The building has been bombed. Living in a building which is sooner or later bombed is evidently a natural consequence of living in the city of New York. It is perhaps an even more natural consequence of living above a house of ill repute. I am not happy about this, sir, as no doubt neither are you. I am distressed, especially as this bombing causes me considerable inconvenience. I am increasingly displeased at your attitude toward my associate, and, by extension, toward myself."

Gregorio and Seidenwall looked down. Leo Haig looked up. Hard. Gregorio and Seidenwall looked away.

Haig said, "Sir. I assume you have no warrant. I further assume your contingency privileges obviate the necessity for a warrant to intrude upon my property. But, sir, I now ask you to leave. You cannot seriously entertain the notion that I or my associate did in fact bomb our own building.

We are not witlings. Each of us can vouch for the other's presence at the time of the bombing, as can my associate Mr. Wong Fat." Wong was at that moment cowering under his bed saying the rosary. "You can, sir, as your estimable colleague suggests, take Mr. Harrison into custody. It would be an unutterably stupid act. You could, on the other hand, quit these premises. It appears to me that these are your alternatives. You have only to choose."

I never heard the like. Neither, I guess, did Gregorio. They scooted.

I always wanted to call someone a witling," Haig said later. "Wolfe does it all the time. I always wanted to do that."

"You did it very well," I said.

"I have my uncle to thank for that," Leo Haig said. "I have my uncle to thank for many things, but one fact sums it all up. But for him, I would have gone through life without ever being able to call a policeman a witling."

We had a beer on the strength of that.

eight

I spent the night in Haig's house. It was late by the time we were done with the fish, even later before we finished talking about the bombing. We agreed that it was possible someone had bombed the whorehouse on purpose, and we also agreed that we didn't believe it had happened that way. That bomb had gone through the wrong window. It had been meant for us, and whoever threw it had his signals crossed.

Which was one of the reasons I spent the night on the couch. Somebody was trying to kill us, and I really didn't want to give him any encouragement.

"You ought to move in here," Haig said over breakfast. "It would expedite matters."

"Not if I have to spend any time on that couch."

"It was uncomfortable?"

"It was horrible," I said. "I kept waking up and wanting to stretch out on the floor, but moving was too painful."

"Of course you'd have a proper bed," Haig said stiffly. "And a proper room of your own, and the implicit right to entertain friends of your own choosing. In addition—"

He paraded the usual arguments. I paid a little attention to them and a lot of attention to breakfast. Corned beef hash, fried eggs, and the world's best coffee. I don't always

77

like coffee all that much, but Wong Fat makes the best I've
ever tasted. It's a Louisiana blend with chickory in it and
he uses this special porcelain drip pot and it really makes
a difference.

After breakfast Haig gave me a list of things to do regarding the fish. While I was upstairs attending to them he
was on the phone in his office. I finished up and was sitting
on my side of the partners' desk at a quarter after eleven.
Haig was reading one of Richard Stark's Parker novels. I
forget which one. He said, "Formidable," once or twice. I
spent ten minutes watching him read. Then he closed the
book and leaned back in his chair and played with his
beard. After a few minutes of that he took one of his pipes
apart. He put it back together again and started to take it
apart a second time, but stopped himself.

"Chip," he said.

I tried to look bright-eyed.

"I've made some calls. I spoke with Mr. Shivers and
Mrs. Vandiver. Also with several other lawyers. Also with
Mr. Bell and a man named LiCastro. Also—no matter.
There are several courses of inquiry you might pursue
today. You have your notebook?"

I had my notebook.

Indulgence was on the second floor of a renovated
brownstone on 53rd Street, between Lexington and Third.
The shop on the first floor sold gourmet cookware. I
walked up a flight of stairs and paused for a moment in
front of a Chinese red door with a brass nameplate on it.
There was a bell, and another brass plate instructed me to
ring it before opening the door. I followed orders.

The man behind the reception desk was small and precise and black. He had his hair in a tight Afro and wore
thick horn-rimmed glasses. His suit was black mohair and
he was wearing a red paisley vest with it. His tie was a
narrow black knit.

It was air-conditioned in there, but I couldn't imagine

how he could have come to work through all that heat in those clothes. And he looked as though he had never perspired in his life.

He asked if he could help me. I said that I wanted to see a girl named Andrea Sugar.

"Of course," he said, and smiled briefly. "Miss Sugar is one of our recreational therapists. Do you require a massage?"

"Uh, yeah."

"Very good. Are you a member?"

I wasn't, but it turned out that I could purchase a trial membership for ten dollars. This would entitle me to the services of a recreational therapist for thirty minutes. I handed over ten of Leo Haig's dollars and he filled out a little membership card for me. When he asked me my name I said "Norman Conquest." Don't ask me why.

"Miss Sugar is engaged at the moment," he said, after my ten dollar bill had disappeared. "She'll be available in approximately ten minutes. Or you may put yourself in the hands of one of our other therapists. Here are photographs of several of them."

He gave me a little leatherette photo album and I looked through it. There were a dozen photographs of recreational therapists, all of them naked and smiling. In the interests of therapy, I guess. I said I would prefer to wait for Miss Sugar and he nodded me to a couch and went back to his book. It was a collection of essays by Noam Chomsky, if you care.

I sat around for ten minutes during which the phone rang twice. The desk man answered, but didn't say much. I leafed through *Sports Illustrated* and read something very boring about sailboat racing. He went into another room and came back to report that Miss Sugar was waiting for me in the third cubicle on the right. I walked down a short hallway and into a room a little larger than a throw rug. The walls were painted the same Chinese red as the door.

The floor was cork tile. The only piece of furniture in the room was a massage table with a fresh white sheet on it.

Andrea Sugar was standing beside the table. She wasn't the girl I had seen at the funeral. She was wearing a white nurse's smock. (I think that's the right word for it.) She was tall, almost my height, and she looked a little like pictures of Susan Sontag. She said hello and wasn't it hot out and other conventional things, and I said hello and agreed that it was hot out there, all right, and she suggested I take off all my clothes and get on the table.

"I'm not really here for a massage," I said.

"You're not supposed to say that, honey."

"But the thing is—"

"You're here for a massage, sweetie. Your back hurts and you want a nice massage, you just paid ten dollars and for that you'll get a very nice massage, and if something else should happen to develop, that's between you and me, but I'm a recreational therapist and you're a young man who needs a massage, and that's how the rulebook reads. Okay?"

The thing is, I did sort of need a massage. My back still had kinks in it from Leo Haig's corrugated couch. I just felt a little weird about taking all my clothes off in front of a stranger. I don't think I have any particular hangups in that direction, actually, but the whole scene was somehow unreal. Anyway, I took off my clothes and hung them over a wooden thing designed for the purpose and got up on the table and onto my stomach.

"Now," she said. "What seems to be the trouble?"

I guess the question didn't need an answer, because she was already beginning to work on my back. She really knew how to give a back rub. Her hands were very strong and she had a nice sense of touch and knew what muscles to concentrate on. When she got to the small of my back I could feel all the pain of a bad night's sleep being sucked out of the base of my spine, like poison out of a snakebite.

"It's about Jessica Trelawney," I said.

The hands stopped abruptly. "Christ Almighty," she said softly. "Who *are* you?"

"Chip Harrison," I said. "I work for Leo Haig, the detective."

"You're not a cop."

"No. Haig is a private investigator. I was also a friend of Melanie Trelawney's."

"She OD'd the other day."

"That's right."

By now she had gone back to the massage. Her hands moved here and there as we talked, and when they strayed below the belt they began to have an effect that was interesting. I felt an urge to wriggle my toes a little.

"You really didn't come for a massage."

"No, but that doesn't mean you should stop. I came to ask you some questions. If you want me to get dressed—"

"No, that's no good. They look in from time to time and I should be doing what I'm supposed to be doing. You're a friend of Melanie's and you want to ask about Jess?"

"Yes."

"I hope you're trying to find out who murdered her. I just surprised you, didn't I? I never bought that suicide story. Not for a minute. I've never known anyone less suicidal than Jess. She was one of the strongest women I've ever known. How does this feel?"

"Great."

"You've got nice skin. And you're clean. You wouldn't believe some of the men who come in here. Have you ever had a massage before?"

"No."

"What were we talking about? Jess. No, I never believed she killed herself and I always believed she was murdered. It was a waste of time telling the police this. I was very close to Jess. As a matter of fact we were lovers. I met her in a Women's Lib group. Consciousness-raising. We responded to each other right away. She had made love with women before, but she had never had a real relationship.

We lived together; I moved into her apartment. We bought each other silly little presents. Roll over."

"Pardon?"

"You're done on this side. Roll over onto your back."

I did.

"I got her a job here," she went on. "She didn't have to work, of course. She was rich. But she wanted to work, she didn't like the idea of living off her inheritance and not establishing herself as a person responsible for her own existence. She was extremely tough-minded, Chip."

Her hands were working on my arms and shoulders and chest and stomach. She used a firm touch at first, but as she got further south she switched to a feathery stroking. My mind was not at all interested in sex, for a change, but my body was beginning to display a mind of its own.

I forced myself to talk about Melanie, and how Haig and I were convinced she had been murdered. I didn't go into details and I didn't mention the bombing the night before. I asked her if she had any ideas who might have wanted to kill Jessica.

"Some man," she said.

"I meant specifically."

She shook her head and ran her fingers over my thighs. "You meet strange people in this business," she said. "Some very unreal men. The names they'll call a woman when they get off. I don't think they're even conscious of it most of the time. It's automatic, some deep built-in hatred of the entire female sex, and their own sexuality is all mixed up with a desire to dominate and hurt. I had a theory about Jess."

"Tell me."

"Well, it doesn't point anywhere in particular. But I figured she had a client for a massage and he managed to get her home address. He went up there and fucked her and hurt her and then he killed her and threw her out the window. He could have beaten her up, you know. It wouldn't have showed because the fall would have hidden any injuries."

Haig and I had already discussed this. Anything less than a bullet hole would have been consistent with injuries suffered in that great a fall.

"But if Melanie was murdered, then probably it was the same person both times."

"Right," I said.

"Which makes my theory fall down. It's not just a man who hates women. It's a man with a particular hatred for women named Trelawney."

"Right."

"I can't think who it could be."

"Possibly someone who stands to gain by killing the five sisters."

"Who stands to gain?"

"It's hard to tell. The money wasn't entailed, it passed over completely to the girls under Cyrus Trelawney's will. Leo Haig is working on it."

"I wish I could help."

We chatted a little more, and then she drew her hands away and I thought the massage was over. I sort of hoped it was. I couldn't take very much more of this.

She said, "It's very warm in here, Chip. Would you mind if I removed my uniform?"

She had a fine body, long and lean and supple. Her breasts were very firm and her stomach perfectly flat. Her skin smelled spicy.

She put her hands right where I hoped she would put them. She pressed gently, then moved her fingers in that feathery stroke.

"There's one muscle group I haven't been able to relax," she said.

"Yeah. It's sort of embarrassing, if you want to know."

"I'd be embarrassed if you didn't react that way. Would you like me to do something about it?"

"I'd like that."

"You have to tell me what you want me to do."

"Uh."

She was not touching me now. "This isn't part of the standard massage," she explained. "You've had the standard treatment already." I had had the treatment, all right. "If there's anything else you would like, you have to tell me specifically what it is. And then you give me a present because you like me, and I do something very nice for you because I like you, and that's how it's done."

"I see."

"What would you like?"

"Uh. I don't know what the choices are."

"For a small present I could do something manual. For a large present I could do something oral."

"I see."

"You already know I have nice hands. I also have a very nice mouth."

"I'm sure you do."

"I've received lots of compliments on it."

"I'm sure you have."

"So if you'd like to ask me to do something—"

"How much is a small present?"

"Ten dollars would be a small present. Twenty dollars would be a large present. A lot of people give me larger presents than that, but I sort of like you. You're clean and you're not an unpleasant person."

I had about twenty-five dollars with me after paying my trial membership fee. But I was going to have to take cabs and be ready to spend money if the need arose. The twenty dollar present was out of the question and the ten dollar present seemed like a lot of money for a very second-best experience. And I really didn't like the idea of paying for sex. I could almost rationalize this on the grounds that it wouldn't be sex, exactly. I mean, there was nothing really sexual about it, for Pete's sake. It would just be a release from tension. Recreational therapy, you could call it.

What it comes to, really, is that if I had had a hundred

dollars in my pocket I would probably have given twenty of them to Andrea. Since I had twenty-five, I told her I was afraid I would have to pass.

"That's cool," she said, slipping back into her uniform. "Maybe you'll drop around again sometime."

"Maybe I will."

"And if there's any way I can help you find out who killed Jess—"

"Maybe there is," I said.

"How?"

"It might help if we knew the names of her customers for the week before she was killed. I don't suppose there would be any connection, but something might turn up."

She gave a low whistle. "That's a tough one. There's no record kept of what guy goes with what girl. They keep track of the number of massages everybody does because you get a percentage of that on top of the presents clients give you. And they keep the names from the membership forms, but you'd be surprised how many men are ashamed to give their right name."

"Not all that surprised, actually."

"I suppose I could find those records, though. For the week before Andrea died? I'll have to be sneaky. You're not supposed to have access to the records. I think they're afraid some of the girls might try a little blackmail. But I'm good at schemes and I shouldn't have much trouble getting around Rastus out there."

My face must have showed something. She laughed. "No, I'm not a racist," she said. "No more than the next bigot, anyway. That's his name."

"You're kidding."

"I don't think he was born with it. But it's his name now and he likes to watch people when he introduces himself. Don't forget your watch, Chip."

The watch I almost forgot told me that it was ten minutes after two when I left Indulgence. I went around the corner and had a cheeseburger and some iced tea. Walking was not a very pleasurable experience at the moment. Andrea Sugar had drained all the pain out of my backbone and rolled it up into a ball and stuffed it into my groin.

I'd given her Leo Haig's number and told her to call as soon as she had the records of clients for the week in question. I couldn't see how it would help, especially since anyone planning to kill Andrea would have likely used a name about as legitimate as old Norm Conquest himself, but it was something to do.

She had always been convinced that Jessica had been murdered. That was the sort of fact Leo Haig usually found interesting and suggestive, so I spent a dime telling him about it. By the time I left the restaurant I could almost walk without limping.

Almost.

nine

Ferdinand Bell's office was within limping distance on the ninth floor of a tall narrow building on 48th Street, just east of Fifth. The building directory in the lobby showed that most of the tenants dealt in stamps or coins. Or both.

In the elevator a man with a European accent said, "I can never recommend for appreciation any surcharges or overprints priced significantly higher than their regular issue counterparts. It is not merely that they may be counterfeited, but that the mere prospect of counterfeiting prevents their reaching their logical levels." I still do not have the slightest idea what he was talking about. I repeated the conversation to Haig, who understands everything, and of course he nodded wisely. He wouldn't tell me what it meant, though.

"If you want to learn about anything under the sun," he said, "you have only to read the right detective story. *The Nine Tailors* will tell you as much as you need to know about bell-ringing in English country churches, for example." (It told me more than I needed to know, to tell you the truth.) "For philately, MacDonald's *The Scarlet Ruse* is excellent. There are others that are less likely to be to your taste—"

"Philately? They were talking about stamps?"

"Of course."

"Well, I didn't know," I said. "How was I supposed to know?"

I haven't read *The Scarlet Ruse* yet. I suppose I'll get to it eventually. The thing is, Haig keeps giving me books to read, and it's impossible to keep up. I did read a couple of books with a coin-collecting background recently, one by Raymond Chandler and another by Michael Innes, so I now know a little more about numismatics than I did when I walked into Ferdinand Bell's office.

He was the man I'd picked out at the funeral as the most likely candidate for the Ferdinand Bell look-alike contest. Today he was wearing a short-sleeved white shirt, open at the throat, and a pair of gray pants that might have been from the suit he'd worn a day ago. They certainly looked as though he had been wearing them for a while.

I had established earlier that he was around forty-seven. He looked both older and younger, depending on how you looked at him. He was plump, with chipmunk cheeks and happy little eyes, and that made him appear younger than he was, but his hair (short and snow white, with a slightly receding hairline) added a few years to his appearance. He sat on a stool behind a row of glass showcases in which coins rested on top of two-by-two brown envelopes. There was a bookcase to his right, filled to capacity, and a desk to his left with a great many books and magazines piled sloppily on it.

He looked up when I entered, which I guess is not too surprising, and he blinked rapidly when I told him who I was.

"Yes, Mr. Haig called me. So I've been awaiting you. But somehow I expected an older man. Aren't you a little young to be a detective? And didn't I see you at the funeral?"

I gave him a qualified yes. Since I wasn't officially a detective the first question was hard to answer. And the second was impossible; I had been at the funeral, and I saw him there, but how did I know whether he saw me?

"Have a seat," he said. "Or should we go somewhere and have a cup of coffee? But I don't think we'll be disturbed here today. My Saturdays are usually quiet. I tend to mail orders and such matters. That's if I'm not out of town working a convention. The A.N.A. is coming up in two weeks. It's in Boston this year, you know."

I didn't. I also didn't know what the A.N.A. was, but I've since learned. It's the American Numismatic Association, and it's the most important coin convention of the year. He went on to tell me that he had a bourse table reserved and expected to be bidding on some choice lots in the auction. Large cents, I think he said.

"I understand you believe Melanie was murdered," he said. "I'm reading between the lines there. Your Mr. Haig was deliberately vague. Dear me, I've made an unintentional rhyme, haven't I? *Your Mr. Haig/Was deliberately vague.* And I gather you have a client in this matter?"

"Yes."

"I don't suppose you could tell me who it is?"

Haig had said I could, and so I did. I told him one of them, anyway.

"Caitlin! Extraordinary."

I wanted to ask him why it was extraordinary. Instead I started asking him some questions about his wife, Robin. Had she seemed at all nervous in the weeks immediately preceding her death? Had her behavior changed in any remarkable way?

He squinted in concentration and I swear his nose twitched like a bunny's. "As if she had some precognitive feelings about her fate? I never thought of that."

"Or as if she were afraid someone would murder her."

"Dear me. Now *that's* a speculation I've never entertained. Just let me think now. Do you know, I can't even concentrate on her attitude then because the whole idea of her having been murdered is so startling to me."

I nodded.

"Naturally I blamed myself for her death. After all, I was driving. I have a tendency to let my mind wander when I drive. Especially when tired, and I *was* tired that day; it had been a grueling weekend." He leaned forward and pressed his forehead with the fingertips of one hand. "I had never had an accident before. My woolgathering never seemed to interfere with my driving. Although I could never help thinking that if I had been paying a bit more attention to what I was doing I might have seen that patch of ice." He moved his hand to shade his eyes. "And Robin might be alive today."

I didn't say anything for a minute or two. He wiped his eyes with the back of his hand and straightened up on his stool. He forced his smile back in place.

A wistful look came into his eyes. "There's something I've always wondered about, Chip. May I call you that?"

"Sure."

"Something I've always wondered about. That skid I took. I grew up in an area where winter was long and severe. I learned to drive on snow and ice, how to react to sudden skids. Not to fight the wheel, to turn with the skid, all of those actions that are contrary to instinct and must consequently be learned and reinforced. And on the day of the accident I reacted as I had been trained to react."

"But it didn't work."

"No, it did not. And I've wondered if there couldn't have been a possibility of mechanical failure involved. I had the car looked at. It wasn't damaged all that severely, and if Robin had been sitting beside me and wearing a belt—" His face darkened. He bit his lip and went on. "They found that the steering column was damaged. I had never thought before that it might have been tampered with. Now I find myself wanting to seize on the possibility to white-wash my own role in the affair. If the car had been sabotaged, if some fiend intentionally caused that accident—"

He got to his feet. "You must excuse me," he said. "I have a nervous stomach. I'll be a few moments. You might like to have a look at the coins in that case. There are some nice Colonials."

I had a look at the Colonials. I couldn't really tell you if they were nice or not. I also had a look at the books on his desk and in the glass-fronted bookcase. They all seemed to be about coins, which probably stood to reason. Some of them looked very old.

I was thumbing through a book called *The United States Trade Dollar,* by John Willem, when Bell came back. "An illuminating book," he said over my shoulder. "The Trade dollar was coined purely to facilitate commerce in the Orient. The Chinese traders would put their personal chop marks on them to attest to their silver value. I've a few pieces in stock if you'd care for a look at the genuine article."

He showed me three or four coins, returned them to their little brown envelopes and put them away. "My library is my most important asset," he said. "There's a motto in professional numismatics—Buy the book before the coin. The wisest sort of advice and all too few people follow it. Numismatics is a science, not just a matter of sorting change and filling holes in a Whitman folder. Take those Trade dollars. The whole history of the China trade is waiting to be read there."

He went on like that for a while. I tend to look interested even when I'm not, which Haig tells me is an asset; people reveal more of themselves to people who appear interested. So I listened, and it really was pretty interesting, but it wasn't getting me any closer to the man who killed Melanie and tried to bomb Leo Haig's house.

I found an opportunity to get the conversation back on the rails and brought up the question of motive. "Suppose someone did sabotage your car. He couldn't have been certain of killing just Robin. He would have had a shot at killing you, too."

"That had occurred to me."

"Well, anyone who's busy killing off five sisters probably wouldn't draw the line at including someone else here and there. Who benefited by Robin's death?"

"Financially?" He shrugged his shoulders. "That's no secret, surely. Except for a few minor bequests, I inherited Robin's entire estate."

"But suppose you had both been killed in the accident."

"Dear me. I hadn't thought of that. I'd have to check that, but it seems to me that I recall a provision to cover my dying before Robin. It would also cover simultaneous death, I presume. It's my recollection that the estate would be divided among her surviving sisters."

"I see."

"I'd have to check, but that would present no difficulty. My lawyer has a copy of Robin's will. I could call him first thing Monday morning. Just let me make a note of that."

He made a note of it, then looked up suddenly. "I say, Chip. You don't think I ought to consider myself in danger now, do you?" He laughed nervously. "It's hard to take seriously, isn't it? But if it *ought* to be taken seriously—"

"Do you have a will?"

"Yes, of course. I drew up a new will shortly after Robin's death. A few thousand dollars to a couple of numismatic research foundations, some smaller charitable bequests, and the balance to my sister in Lyons Falls."

"And you inherited Robin's estate free and clear?"

"Yes. Shortly after we were married we drew wills leaving everything to one another absolutely without encumbrance." His eyes clouded. "I expected it would be my will which would be put to the test first. I was seventeen years Robin's senior. She preferred older men, you know. Her first husband was as old as I am now when she married him. There's a history of heart trouble in my family. I naturally expected to predecease Robin, and although I hadn't all that much to leave her I wanted my affairs to be in order."

I told him I didn't think he was in any danger. No one could now expect to profit from his death. The news didn't cheer him much. He was too caught up in thoughts of his dead wife.

I asked if he knew anything about Jessica's will. "I barely knew Jessica," he said. "The Trelawney sisters were not close, and Robin and I kept pretty much to ourselves. Most of our close friends were business associates of mine. Coin dealers are gregarious folk, you know. We hardly regard one another as competitors. Often we do more business buying from each other and selling to each other than we do with actual collectors. No, I don't know anything about Jessica's will. I did go to her funeral, just as I went to Melanie's. I don't honestly know why I attended either of them. I had little enough to say to anyone there. I suppose it was a way of preserving my ties to Robin." He lowered his eyes. "We had so little time together."

"How did you meet her? Was she interested in coins?"

"Oh, not at all. Although she did come to share some of my interest during our life together. She was growing interested in love money, those little pins and brooches made of three-cent pieces, a very popular jewelry form of the mid-ninteenth century. I would always pick up pieces for her when I saw them. No real value, of course, but she liked them." He smiled at some private memory. "How did I meet her? I was a friend of her first husband, Phil Flanner. I suppose I fell in love with Robin while she was married to him, although I honestly didn't realize it at the time. Phil died tragically; a stupid accident. I began seeing her not too long after the funeral. I was drawn to her and enjoyed her company, still not recognizing what I felt as love. Gradually we both came to realize that we were in love with one another. I wish we had realized this sooner, so that we might have been married sooner. We had so very little time."

ten

When I got back to the house

on 20th Street, Haig was on the top floor playing with his fish, repairing the leakers with rubber cement. When I asked if he wanted me to help, he grunted. I stopped in the kitchen where Wong was hacking a steak into bite-sized pieces with a cleaver. I left without a word. When he's chopping things he looks positively dangerous and I try to stay out of his way. I went downstairs and talked a little with some of the girls.

"Why they wanna blow up Maria?" Carmelita wanted to know. "She don' never hurt nobody. One guy, he say she give him a clop, but Maria never give nobody no clop. He get his clop somewhere else. Maria tell him, you get your clop from your mother, she say."

That was even more of a down than watching Haig swearing at his fish tanks, so I went over to Dominick's and had a beer and watched the Mets find a new way to lose. Matlack had a one-run lead going into the bottom of the ninth, struck out the first man, hit the second man on the arm, and got the third man to hit a double-play ball to short.

That was his mistake. They had Garrett playing short and he made the play without the ball. The ball went to left

field and the runners went to second and third, and somebody walked and Bobby Bonds hit a 2-2 pitch off the
fence and Dominick turned the set off.

"Shit," he said.

So I went back and read a couple chapters of an old
Fredric Brown mystery until Haig came down, and then I
gave him a full report. He made me go over everything a
few hundred times. Then he closed his eyes and fiddled
with his beard and put his head back and said "Indeed"
fifteen times and "Curious" eighteen times. He wouldn't
tell me what was curious.

I spent most of the night walking around the Village
looking for somebody to sleep with. It was hotter than hell
and there wasn't much air in the air. I didn't have any luck.
I have a feeling I wasn't trying very hard. I had a couple of
beers and a few cups of coffee and called Kim a couple of
times, but no one answered.

I went back to my room and played a Dylan record
over and over. I remember thinking that a little grass would
be nice and regretting having flushed it to oblivion. It was
a rotten night. I had run all over town and hadn't accom-
plished anything much. I was sorry I hadn't spent twenty of
Haig's dollars on a massage and realized I would have
been just as sorry if I had.

I thought about going downstairs to give Kim one more
call, and I decided the hell with it, and eventually I went
to sleep.

Nothing much happened Sunday. I slept late and had
breakfast around noon and walked over to Haig's house
because I couldn't think of anything else to do. I got there
in time to watch Wong devastate him at backgammon.
Wong beats hell out of me, but that was nothing compared
to the way he routed Haig. It was pathetic to watch.

"There's nothing for you to do," he said.

Which would have been all right except that I felt like
doing something. I hung around for a while and did some

routine maintenance on the fish, although Sunday was supposed to be a free day for me. Just before dinner I called Andrea Sugar at home to find out if she had managed to get the records. She wasn't in. I called her a couple of hours later and reached her and learned that she hadn't had a chance to do anything yet.

I read a couple of books at Haig's. After dinner I caught a movie. I don't remember which one.

On the way home I stopped at a pay phone and called Kim. I was a little worried about her, if you want to know. I also just found myself thinking about her a lot. I asked her if she had thought of anything significant, or if anybody had been following her or anything. She had nothing to report.

"The thing is," I said, "I'd like to go over things with you sometime. When Gordie's working or something, if you follow me."

"I think I follow you."

"Because he's not exactly crazy about me, and it's hard to get anyplace with him around. I mean as far as a conversation is concerned."

"He's here right now. He's in the other room. I don't think I'll tell him it's you on the phone."

"That sounds like a good idea."

"He'll be working tomorrow from noon to eight. I have a couple of classes during the afternoon, but the evening's clear."

"Don't you have a performance?"

"Monday's the dark night off-Broadway. Anyway, the play closed today."

"I'm sorry to hear that."

"Well, it wasn't very good. The critics hated it. Would you want to come over around six tomorrow?"

I said I would.

I went home and decided Gordie was the killer and that meant Kim was safe. He wouldn't kill her now. First he

would kill Caitlin, and possibly her husband as well, and
then he would marry Kim, and *then* he would kill her.

Monday there were things for me to do and places for
me to go, so of course it rained. Haig had made appoint-
ments for me all over the place. I had to see a couple of
lawyers, one on Fifth Avenue and one near City Hall just
a block from Addison Shivers. I decided to drop in on him
and let him know how we were doing, but he was in conference with a client when I got there. I went out and had
fish and chips for lunch and dropped in on him again, but
this time he was out having lunch, so I said the hell with it
and took the subway uptown as far as Canal Street, which
is not all that far. I walked up Mulberry to the address
Haig had given me.

It didn't look like a place where I was going to feel tre-
mendously welcome. It was the Palermo Social and Recreation Club, and there were a couple of old men playing
bocce over to the right, and two other men sitting over a
lackadaisical game of dominoes, and a fifth man watching
the curl of lemon peel swim around in his cup of espresso.
They all looked at me when I walked in. There was no
discernible gleam of welcome in their eyes.

I went to the man sitting alone and asked him if he was
John LiCastro. He asked who wanted to know, and I told
him who I was and who I worked for and he smiled with
the lower half of his face and pointed to a chair. I sat
down and he told me I was privileged to work for a great
man.

I agreed with him, but I wasn't too sure of this at the
moment, because it was beginning to seem to me that the
great man was not accomplishing a whole hell of a lot. The
great man had not left the house yet, which certainly gave
him a lot in common with Nero Wolfe, but neither had the
great man called any suspects together, or even established
that there *were* any suspects, for Pete's sake. The great
man was spending a lot of time on his fish while I was

keeping the New York Subway System out of the red, or trying to.

I didn't say any of this to Mr. LiCastro. I had a pretty good feeling that it was extremely unintelligent to say anything to Mr. LiCastro that Mr. LiCastro didn't want to hear. I told him what I had been instructed to tell him, and asked him what I had been instructed to ask him, and he took in my words with little darting affirmative movements of his head. At one point his eyes narrowed as he fixed on some private thought, and I realized that I was sitting across the table from a man who could kill a man at five o'clock and sit down to a huge dinner at five-thirty and not even worry about indigestion.

Then he ordered espresso for both of us and leaned back in his chair and asked some questions of his own, and there was a warm glow in his eyes and a look of complete relaxation on his face.

It was really something to see.

"So LiCastro is crazy about tropical fish," I said later. "I was wondering how on earth you would know somebody like him. His discus spawned, but a fungus got the eggs."

"That usually happens."

"He was tickled enough that he got them to spawn in the first place. He's trying a new fungicide and he wants your opinion of it. He didn't remember the name. He's going to call you later."

"And he'll make some inquiries about Gordon Mc-Leod?"

"That's what he said. I had a very eerie feeling about that. I wanted to make sure he just made inquiries. I thought he might think I was asking for something more serious than inquiries. Like he might have thought I was being subtle and indicating you wanted McLeod killed if I didn't spell things out."

"I doubt it."

"Well, I wasn't sure. Also I had the feeling that if you did want McLeod killed, and you said as much to LiCastro, then that would be the end of McLeod."

"That I do not doubt," Haig said. "Continue."

I continued. "Jessica Trelawney drew a will a couple of weeks after Robin died. I have the date written down if it matters."

"It may."

"Her lawyer says that's a common response to the death of someone close. He also says she left everything to a feminist group called Radicalesbians. I'm not making this up. He is sure the will is going to be challenged by attorneys for Caitlin Vandiver, and he told me off the record that he's just as sure it won't stand up. He more or less implied that he drew it in such a way as to make it easy to challenge. I'm pretty sure he's not a big fan of Radicalesbians."

"Indeed."

"So no one stood to gain a penny by Jessica's death, except for Radicalesbians, but that doesn't prove anything because no one necessarily knew about her will. Before that she had never drawn a will, and if she had died intestate, everything would have been divided among the surviving sisters. Which is what would have happened to Robin's money if she and Bell had died together in the car accident."

"Car wreck," Haig said.

"Indeed," I said.

"Precision is important. Language is a tool, its edge must be kept sharp."

"Indeed. Melanie did die intestate, which is a word I have now used twice in two minutes and can't remember ever using before. I suppose it's a part of keeping the edge of my tool sharp. So her money will be divided among Caitlin and Kim, and—"

"Between."

"Huh?"

"One divides among three persons and between two. I don't like to keep correcting you, Chip."

"I can tell you don't. I found out who Caitlin's lawyer is, but couldn't reach him."

"He wouldn't divulge information about her will anyway."

"He probably will, because it's Addison Shivers, but I couldn't get to see him. Anyway, I figured he would tell us or not tell us over the phone. I would guess that her money is scheduled to go to her husband, but you can't be sure, can you? I mean, she changes husbands pretty quickly, and if she's not morbid she might not want to have to change her will that frequently. The problem is that I keep going out after information and I keep getting it and it doesn't seem to get me anywhere."

"Sooner or later everything will fit into place."

"By that time everyone could be dead."

"In the long run everyone always is, Chip." He began filling a pipe, tamping down each pinch of tobacco very carefully. "We have to make haste slowly," he went on, while making haste slowly with the pipe. "We are making progress. We are in the possession of data we previously lacked. That is progress."

"I suppose."

"There are cases that lend themselves to Sherlockian methodology. Cases which are solved by the substance in a man's trouser turnups. Cases which hinge on a dog's silence in the night or the chemical analysis of coffee grounds." He closed his eyes and put the deliberately filled pipe back in the pipe rack. His hand went to his beard and he leaned back in his chair. "This, I think, is another sort of case entirely. There is someone somewhere with a logical reason to kill the five daughters of Cyrus Trelawney. He had a reason to sabotage Ferdinand Bell's car, a reason to pitch Jessica Trelawney out a window, a reason to inject Melanie Trelawney with a fatal overdose of heroin. If we determine the reason, we will have determined the killer."

He sat forward suddenly, and his eyes opened like those dolls that go sleepy-bye when you lay them down on their backs. "Do you know something, Chip? I think there's an element of Ross MacDonald in this. I can't avoid the feeling that the underlying motive is buried somewhere deep in the past. As though it all has its roots forty years ago, in Canada."

"Canada?"

"A figure of speech. So often Lew Archer uncovers something that started forty years ago in Canada, you know." He spun around in his chair and gazed at the rasboras. They didn't seem at all self-conscious. While he let them provide inspiration, I took out my nail file and cleaned out the dirt from under my fingernails. I only tell you this so you won't think I was just sitting there doing nothing.

He turned around again, eventually, and folded his hands on his round belly. He looked elfin but determined. "I shall call Addison Shivers," he said. "I have some questions to ask him."

He reached for the telephone, and it rang. So he picked it up, naturally enough. It doesn't seem to surprise him much when things like this happen. In fact he made it look as though he had been waiting for it to ring.

He talked briefly, mostly saying things like "Yes," and "Indeed." Then he hung up and raised his eyebrows at me.

"Our client," he said.

"Mr. Shivers?"

"Mrs. Vandiver. She's at her house on Long Island. She wants to see you immediately. She says it's rather urgent."

eleven

You get to Sands Point by tak-ing the Long Island Rail Road to the Port Washington stop. I understand that there are people who do this every day. What I don't understand is why.

I got on the train at Penn Station, and got off it at Port Washington. I stood there on the platform for a minute, and a very tall and very thin man came up to me. "You would be Mr. Harrison," he said.

"I would," I said. "I mean, uh, I am. Yes."

"I am Seamus," he said. "I've brought the car."

The car was a Mercedes, about the size of Chicago. I started to get in the front next to Seamus, but stopped when he gave me a very disappointed glance. I closed the door and got in back instead. He seemed happier about this.

There was a partition between the front and rear seats, which kept Seamus and me from having to make small talk to each other. I sat back and looked out the window at one expensive home after another. Finally, we turned onto what I thought was a side road but turned out to be the Vandiver driveway. It wandered through a stand of old trees and finally led to a house.

The house gave you an idea of what God could have

done if he'd had the money. That's not my line; I read it somewhere, but I can't think of a way to improve on it. There were these Grecian columns in front which you would think no house could live up to, and then the house went on to overpower the columns, and it was all about as impressive as anything I've ever seen. Caitlin and Melanie had each inherited the same amount of money, and Caitlin lived here, while Melanie had lived in Cockroach Heaven, and it wasn't hard to feel that Caitlin had a better appreciation of creature comfort.

She was waiting for me in a room carpeted in white shag and decorated in what I think they call French provincial. The furniture did not come from the Salvation Army. There were oil paintings on the walls, including one that I recognized as a portrait of Cyrus Trelawney.

"I'm so glad you're here," she said. "It's been such a bore of a day. Your drink is Irish whiskey, if I remember correctly. Straight, with a soda chaser?"

It was the last thing I wanted, but I evidently had an image to maintain. She made the drinks, fixing herself a massive Martini, and her eyes sparkled as we touched our glasses together. "To crime," she said.

I took a sip and avoided coughing. I'm sure it was excellent whiskey, but at that point it tasted a lot like shellac.

"I hope you didn't mind my sending Seamus for you," she said. "He's not really a chauffeur. He's more of a general houseman. I usually prefer to do my own driving, actually, but I hate waiting for anything. Especially trains, and the Long Island is hardly ever in on time. Did you have a dreadful ride?"

"It wasn't too bad."

"You were sweet to come. And your Mr. Haig does inspire confidence, doesn't he? It put my mind at rest just to talk to him for a few minutes."

"He's quite a man," I said.

She moved closer to me and put her hand on my arm. She was wearing the same perfume she had worn at the funeral. Her blouse was a black and white print and it was cut low in front. She was not wearing a bra.

"Let's step outside," she said. "Did it rain in the city? We had quite a storm out here this morning and it's actually cooled things off a bit. It's rather pleasant outside."

We took our drinks and walked through some paths in back of the house to a little garden walled in by oaks and beeches. Caitlin sat down on the grass and kicked her shoes off. I stood there for a moment, then sat down next to her.

"I gather there was something you wanted to tell me," I said.

"Oh?"

"Mr. Haig said you told him it was urgent."

She nodded solemnly. "I said it was rather urgent that I see you."

"That's what he said."

"Because I felt an urgent need to see you, Chip." She finished her drink and set the glass down on the lawn. She sat back, her arms out behind her to support her weight, and her breasts strained against the black and white blouse. "I felt quite bored," she said. "And quite lonely."

"I see."

"Do you? And of course I wanted a first-hand report on the case. Do you really think someone wants to murder me?"

"It looks that way."

"But why?"

"That's what we're trying to find out." It occurred to me that this would be a good time to find out about her will. "Haig says motive is the big question. He wants to know who would benefit from your death."

"Practically everyone, I imagine. I'm a very wicked woman, Chip."

"Uh."

"You have no idea just how wicked I can be. But of course, you're talking about my will. It's very straightforward, actually. Gregory and I made wills in each other's favor at the time of our marriage. Whichever of us goes first, the other picks up all the marbles."

"I see."

"But I really don't think Greg would murder me, do you? Or if he did, it wouldn't be for money or anything so vulgar. He might kill me out of justifiable rage. I do behave rather badly, you know." She ran her tongue over her lips. This is a very trite gesture, but she made it work anyway. "I suppose I could change my will and leave everything to Radicalesbians like my brilliant sister Jessica. Did you hear about that?"

"I just saw her lawyer today."

"What a dimwitted dyke she was. Not that I have anything against lesbians myself. I think they limit themselves, that's all. Like vegetarians."

"Vegetarians?"

"Vegetables are nice, but so is meat."

"Oh."

"And girls are nice, but so are men." She smiled softly. "I went through a gay period myself in my girlhood. I think I may have mentioned it to you the other day."

"Uh, sort of."

"I was in school at the time. There was this girl who was absolutely mad for me. She was a pretty thing, very small and dark, not like me physically at all. Her breasts just filled my hands. I liked that. She, on the other hand, was partial to large breasts. Do you like large breasts, Chip?"

"Uh, sure."

"I thought you probably did. She told me one day what she wanted to do to me. She wanted to lick me here." She indicated with her hand where the other girl had wanted to lick her. "So I let her. It was such heaven. She didn't insist that I do anything in return, but do you know something, Chip? I discovered that I wanted to. I suppose it was curiosity at first, but I found I enjoyed it very much. Going down on her, that is."

"Er."

"I liked the taste. I'll tell you something fascinating. At the time I only thought girls did it to each other. I didn't imagine that a man would want to do it. But I've since learned that some men enjoy it very much. Have you ever done it?"

"Yes."

"Do you enjoy doing it?"

"Yes."

"I rather thought you might." She opened the top buttons of her blouse. Her skin was creamy and flawless. "But to get back to what I was saying," she said. "About lesbians and how limited they are. Now I adored eating my little friend, you understand, but then I went to bed with an older man and he taught me ever so many things, and while I still found girls amusing, I certainly wasn't about to go without men for the rest of my life. Do you know what I particularly enjoyed?"

"What?"

"Fellatio."

"Oh."

"It's such a technical term for such an intimate act, isn't it?"

"I never thought about it."

"You never thought about fellatio?"

"I never thought about the, uh, term, uh."

"Such an intimate act," she said. Her hand was on my thigh now. "I'm mad for penises. Isn't that terrible of me? I like to feel them grow in my mouth. Oh, but yours has already grown, hasn't it? Oh, lovely. Lovely."

I took her by the shoulders and kissed her. Her mouth tasted of gin and tobacco and honey, and her perfume wrapped me up like a blanket. Her hand kept doing great things while we kissed.

She said, "This is a very private place, Chip. No one can see us here. We can take off all our clothes and roll around in the grass all we want."

We took off all our clothes and rolled around in the grass a lot. Her body was delicious, taut and sleek and smooth, and if there was any age worn into it, I couldn't tell you about it. We did a whole host of things I somehow don't feel compelled to tell you about, and then she decided that she wanted to conclude with the thing she particularly enjoyed.

"I can taste myself on you," she said. "I like that."

Then she didn't say anything any more, and neither did I, and it was a lot like going to heaven without the aggravation of dying first.

I'll tell you something. It was pretty embarrassing to write that last scene. According to Haig, the less sexual detail in these books, the better. "Archie Goodwin very obviously leads an active sex life," he says, "but he does no more than allude to it. He doesn't throw it in your face, doesn't drag you into various bedchambers with him."

But Mr. Elder says times have changed, and that if we expect him to publish these books, there better be a lot of screwing in them. "You've got to arouse the reader," he said. "The reports on the murders and what an interesting character Haig is, that's all fine, but you've got to turn the reader on in this day and age. And of course you've got to do it in good taste."

I don't know if I turned you on, and I don't know if it was in good taste or not. I have to admit I turned myself on just now, though. Just remembering how terrific it was.

A while later we were back in our clothes. We were also back in the room with the white shag carpet, and Caitlin was drinking another jumbo Martini. I had turned down the Irish whiskey in favor of a Dr. Pepper with a lot of ice.

"Oh, my," she said. "That was quite wonderful, wasn't it? I have a confession to make, Chip. I lured you out here for no other reason than to seduce you. Do you think you can possibly forgive me?"

I said I thought I probably could.

"You're such a charming boy, you know. And terribly attractive, and I've been wanting to take you to bed ever since our lunch together." She stretched like a waking cat. "And it's so deadly dull out here. There's Seamus, of course, but when one has sex with one's servants one is limited to the more conventional approaches. It is considered terribly declassé to perform fellatio upon the domestic help. Now if only I were Jewish, I could blow my chauffeur all I wanted."

That's a pun. Maybe you already knew that. I didn't, and so I didn't laugh, which must have annoyed Caitlin a little. The idea is that Jews have a trumpet made out of a ram's horn which they blow in synagogue on certain holy days, and it's called a *shofar*.

We talked about various things, most of them at least slightly sexual, and I had another Dr. Pepper while she had another Martini, and then I remembered that I had an appointment to see Kim around six. I mentioned this and Caitlin glanced at her watch.

"Hell," she said. "I'd planned on driving you back to the city myself."

"I can take a train."

"No, you wouldn't want to do that. One trip on the Long Island is as much as should be required of anyone. I wanted to drive you, but Gregory's due home soon and he likes me to be here when he arrives. I can't imagine why. I'll have Seamus drive you."

"You really don't have to bother."

"It's no bother," she said. "I've no use for him around here at the moment." She picked up the telephone and made a bell ring in another part of the house. When Seamus answered, she told him to bring the car around in a few minutes.

I kissed her a few times and told her not to worry about the murderer, which was silly in view of the fact that she could not have been worrying less about the murderer.

Then we went out and stood on the porch and watched Seamus drive the car almost fifteen feet before it exploded.

I was going to write that it was like nothing I had ever seen before, but of course I'd seen it a hundred times in a hundred movies. That's just what it looked like. All of a sudden the car went up into the air and came down in pieces. Most of the pieces were metal, but some of them were Seamus, and they were raining down all over the lawn. One hunk of metal actually landed within a few yards of us, and we were standing half a football field away from the car when it blew up.

"Oh Christ," Caitlin kept saying. "Oh Christ."

I didn't know what to do first. The police would have to be called, obviously, but the most immediate problem was Caitlin. She was shaking and all the color was gone from her face and she looked ready to pass out. I got her inside and tried to make her sit down, but her body went rigid.

"You have to fuck me," she said.

I stared at her, but she was already getting out of her clothes. "I have to have it right now, right now. I have to, you have to do it for me, that could have been me in that car, somebody planted a bomb to kill me, somebody wants to murder me. It's true, it's really true. Christ, you have to fuck me, you just have to."

I was positive I wouldn't be able to. I mean, watching a car blow up isn't normally my idea of a turn-on. But they say that a close escape from death makes you want to re-affirm the fact that you're alive in a sexual way, and it had crossed my mind that it could have been me in the car when it blew up, too, and I guess that made the difference. I got out of my clothes in a hurry, got down on the white shag rug with her, and we began screwing like minks, which is a vulgar way to put it, I guess, but that's what we were doing.

I never heard the door open. I may have left it open, as far as that goes. I don't think I would have heard an earthquake at that point. It was very basic and intense and without frills, and I don't suppose much time elapsed from start to finish, but the finish was a good one and I lay there on top of her wondering if my heart would ever go back to beating at its usual rate, and a man's voice said, "Caitlin, I believe I'm entitled to an explanation."

"He has always had an instinct for disastrous timing," she said in my ear. "Always."

"Caitlin—"

"At least he refrained from speaking until we finished," she went on. "Breeding tells, after all. That's something."

"I come home from work," Gregory Vandiver said reasonably. "I return to my house at my usual hour. I find my car blown to bits all over my lawn; I find my man-servant dead in the wreckage and I find my wife copulating with some strange young man on the middle of the drawing room floor. Now *wait* a minute. I've seen you before, haven't I? Yes, I daresay I have. Don't tell me, it'll come to me in a minute."

twelve

Between the Sands Point po-
lice and the Long Island Rail Road, it was almost ten
o'clock before I got back to the city. I did manage to call
Kim before that, from the station in Port Washington, but
it probably would have been better if I hadn't called her at
all. I didn't manage to say three sentences to her before
Gordie took the phone away from her.

"You take a lot of telling," he said. "I don't want you
coming here, I don't want you calling here, I don't want
you sticking your nose in where it ain't wanted." Then he
told me to do something I wouldn't have been able to do if
I had wanted to, which I didn't in the first place, and then
he slammed the phone down.

I walked from Penn Station to Haig's house. I had given
him a little of it earlier over the phone and now I gave him
the whole thing in detail. (I left out the sex part, at least
as far as going into details was concerned. I mean, I had to
let him know that Gregory Vandiver walked in and found
me screwing his wife. That was the kind of thing that might
turn out to be pertinent. So I told him what I had done,
you might say, without telling him how much I had enjoyed
it.)

"The timing," he said, "is very critical here."

112

"Right. The killer had about an hour and a half to plant the bomb. The car was all right when Seamus picked me up at the station."

"Indeed."

"She usually did her own driving. Anybody who knew her well would probably know that."

"Do the police know that?"

"No. The police think that the killer did what he was trying to do. It seems that Seamus was involved with some faction of the I.R.A. The police had a sheet on him because he was suspected of playing a role in a gun-running operation. So they think Seamus was the intended victim, and they also think they have several leads."

"I take it you and the Vandivers permitted them to continue thinking this."

"Yes."

"I'm not sure that was wise."

"Neither am I, but it seemed like a good idea at the time. I was passed off as a friend of Mrs. Vandiver's who happened to be visiting at the time. Her husband could have confirmed that we were friendly."

"Indeed."

"Gordie McLeod was back in the Village by eight-fifteen. Because I talked to him on the phone, and no, it wasn't my idea. I wanted to talk to Kim, but he included himself in. Of course he didn't have to stick around while a batch of Long Island public employees asked dumb questions and took pictures of everything, but I'm sure he was at work all day."

"He was not."

"Oh?"

"Mr. LiCastro called. The fungicide he wants to use will render the discus spawn infertile. I so informed him and gave him some suggestions. Gordon McLeod did not show up today for what I believe is called a shape-up. Mr. McLeod has been betting on quite a few horses lately. With little success."

"That's interesting."

"It is. Nor is he in debt to his bookmaker. His losses, however, have of late exceeded his wages, and yet he has been consistently able to settle his debts promptly, and in cash."

"He must be sponging off Kim."

"Perhaps. It would be useful to determine this."

I nodded. Haig put his feet up on the desk. He tries this every once in a while, but he's always uncomfortable because his legs are too short and his abdomen too large. He gave it up after a few seconds.

He said, "I had a visitor during your absence. Mr. Ferdinand Bell."

"What did he want?"

"To be helpful. A noble ambition, but I'm not sure he achieved its realization. He described the swerving of his automobile with an excess of detail. Listening to him, I very nearly felt that I was in it at the time. It was not a feeling I particularly enjoyed."

"Did he have anything else to say?"

"He had some things to say about Miss Andrea Sugar. He brought to my attention the possibility that a lesbian relationship might have existed between her and Jessica Trelawney."

"No kidding."

"He seemed shocked by this. I find his shock more interesting than the relationship itself, certainly. He also said that Mr. Vandiver is in serious financial difficulties."

"You couldn't prove it by the house."

"So I gather. Mr. Vandiver has apparently suffered some financial reverses."

"How would Bell know that?"

"I'm not sure he knew that he knew it. He was letting his mind wander in my presence, talking generally about the flightiness of the sisters Trelawney. Jessica's homosexuality, Melanie's hippie lifestyle, Kim's hour upon the stage—"

"Kim seems pretty straight-ahead to me."

"Your bias on the subject has already been noted. He also alluded to Caitlin's liberated sexuality, which he cloaked with the euphemism of nymphomania."

"I'm not positive it's a euphemism."

"Be that as it may. And that led him to Gregory Vandiver's infirmity of purpose. Vandiver made some substantial investments in rare coins about a year ago. He consulted Bell, and purchased the pieces through Bell and on Bell's recommendation. He specifically sought out items for long-term growth, the blue chips of the coin market. Barber proofs, Charlotte and Dahlonega gold, that sort of thing. Then a matter of months ago, Vandiver insisted that Bell unload everything and get him cash overnight. It seems Vandiver did realize a profit on his investment, if a tiny one, but that Bell would have advised him to hold indefinitely, and certainly to hold for several months, as an upturn could be expected in the market. But Vandiver insisted on selling immediately, even if he had to take a loss."

"Meaning that he needed cash, I guess."

"So it would seem. The money involved was considerable. I had to pry this from Bell, who evidently believes that matters communicated to a professional numismatist come under the category of privileged information. Gregory Vandiver liquidated his numismatic holdings for a net sum of $110,000."

"He had that much invested in coins?"

"I find that remarkable. I find it more remarkable that he had a sudden need for that much cash."

I nodded. "I wonder," I said.

"If he could have placed the bomb in the car?"

"Yeah. I suppose it's possible. Say he gets a train earlier than his usual one. He comes straight home and goes straight to the garage and wires the bomb to the Mercedes. He knows he's safe because he's not going to drive the car. He doesn't even think about Seamus because Caitlin usually drives herself." I stopped for a moment. "No, it doesn't add up. He wouldn't know she was going to use the car then. He didn't know I was there, so there was no way to know she would drive me home."

"He could assume she would use the car eventually, however."

"But why bother getting home earlier than usual? He could have planted the bomb some other time."

Haig leaned back and played with his beard. I asked a few more questions that he didn't respond to. I went over and watched the African gouramis while he did his genius-in-residence number. While I was watching them, I saw the female knock off a guppy. It didn't bother me a bit.

Haig said, "I would like to know at what time Gregory Vandiver left his office."

"So would I."

"I would also like to know where Gordon McLeod spent the afternoon. And his source of income."

"So would I."

"There are other things, too. Several extremely curious things. I am going to have to know considerably more about Cyrus Trelawney."

"I don't get it."

"Hmmmm," he said.

Wong brought us some beer and we sat opposite each other drinking it and arguing about where I was going to spend the night. "There is a pattern to all of this, Chip," he told me. "There are going to be more deaths. One develops the ability to sense this sort of thing. There have been four deaths already since the case engaged our interest. Melanie's was the first. The other three have been gratuitous. The prostitute, the sailor, the chauffeur."

"Manservant," I said.

"When a manservant dies at the wheel of his employer's car I have difficulty in not regarding him as a chauffeur. Three gratuitous deaths. There will be more deaths, and they will be more to the point. I sense this."

I went through my usual mental hassle as to whether he was a genius or a nut case.

"I would prefer that these deaths not occur. I will, in fact, endeavor to prevent them to the best of my ability. It is for this, after all, that I am employed. But, failing that, I would at least prefer that one of these deaths not be suffered by you."

"I'd prefer it, too." I said. "To tell you the truth."

"You expose yourself unnecessarily by returning to your rooming house."

"I expose myself to worse than that on the couch. I could die of a backache."

"You could have my bed," Haig said.

"Oh, don't be ridiculous."

"I would not mind the couch."

"Oh, come on. I'll walk a couple of blocks and I'll be home, for Pete's sake. It's nothing to worry about."

So I headed back to my rooming house.

That was my first mistake.

My second mistake happened as I was on my way up the steps to the front door. A guy came out of the doorway to the left of my building, and two other guys came out of the doorway to the right of my building, and one of them asked me if I was Harrison, and I made my second mistake. I said I was.

thirteen

They kicked the shit out of me.

fourteen

I'm going to leave it at that.

Haig doesn't think I ought to. He wants me to handle it like Dick Francis and describe the beating they gave me, a blow at a time. With the proper discipline, he maintains, I can run the scene to ten or twelve pages instead of getting it over and done with in seven words. The thing is, I don't want to spend that much time remembering it. They kicked the shit out of me, very coldly and systematically, doing everything to assure me that there was nothing personal in what they were doing. Then they walked off in different directions, and I crawled into my rooming house and upstairs and got into bed.

Everything was worse in the morning. Things really ached. I dragged myself over to Haig's office and he took one look at me and threw a fit. What infuriated him the most was that I hadn't called him immediately so that he could have had his doctor look at me. I said I was pretty sure nothing was broken. He called his doctor, who made a housecall, which I felt was completely unnecessary. I think he came over for an excuse to look at the fish. But while he was there he also looked at me and pronounced me physically fit. I had a lot of bruises, and they were going

119

to look increasingly ugly for the next week to ten days, but
I had no broken bones and there was no evidence of in-
ternal injuries.

"You should have stayed here last night," Haig said.

I suppose he couldn't resist saying that. I didn't bother
replying to it.

I had things to do, but they started with Kim and I
couldn't see her until after noon when the hulk would
either go to the docks or pretend to. I called Andrea Sugar,
but failed to reach her. So I helped Haig with the fish until
Wong brought us some lunch. I can't remember what it
was, only that it had slivers of almonds in it and it was delicious. Afterward Haig picked up the phone and called
Addison Shiver's office. The old lawyer was in conference,
but would return his call.

When Haig hung up I got through to Kim. "Gordie left
a few minutes ago," she said. "Chip, maybe you shouldn't
come over here. Gordie scares me a little."

He scared me more than a little, but I kept this fact to
myself. "There was another murder attempt yesterday," I
told her. "I'm on my way over."

This peeved Haig. "Mr. Shivers will be calling me
shortly," he said. "You ought to be here when he does."

"I thought you wanted to talk to him yourself."

He leaned back in his chair and folded his hands on his
stomach. "I do," he said. "But you should be present. I
have a strong feeling that he is going to provide me with
the solution to the case."

"Just like that?"

"Let us say he is going to give me evidence to support
the conclusion I have drawn already."

"Conclusion?"

"On the basis of evidence already available to us."

"Evidence?"

"You're beginning to sound like an echo, Chip. Try to
curb that tendency."

"I'll do my best. What evidence do we have already

available to us? We have to find where Gordie spent yesterday afternoon and where he's been getting his money;
we have to find out when Gregory Vandiver left his office
and how deep a financial hole he's in, we have to—"

He waved a small hand at me. The right one, probably.

"Superficial," he said.

"But we don't know anything. Unless you've found out
something and haven't told me."

"You have all the information I have."

"Do you want to tell me what I missed?"

"That would be premature," he said. He was disgustingly
pleased with himself. "If you'll wait for Mr. Shivers' call—"

I decided he was grandstanding and I also decided I had
better things to do than sit around waiting for the phone
to ring. I sprung for a cab and rode down to Kim's place
on Bethune Street. When she opened the door, the first
thing I did was give her hell for not making sure it was me
before unlocking the door.

"Then I'm in real danger," she said.

"You'd have to call it that. I was out on Long Island
yesterday. To see Caitlin. Somebody wired a bomb to her
car."

"Oh, God! She's not—"

"She's all right. But her chauffeur isn't. He was killed.
It's pretty unmistakable, Kim. Somebody wants to kill every
last one of you."

I got her to sit down and made her a cup of coffee. I
sat on the couch next to her and patted her hand a lot
and tried to be reassuring, which was tough because I had
started off trying to scare her silly. I went on patting her
hand, though, because I was beginning to enjoy it.

"I don't know what to do," she said.

Her eyes were wide with fear and innocence, and she
was just so damned beautiful I wanted to kiss her. Instead
I said, "Look, there are a lot of possibilities. One possibility is that you're not in any real danger at all. For the
time being."

"I don't understand."

"Depending on who the killer is."

She thought that over, and then her face tightened. "You mean if I'm the one. I suppose you have to suspect everyone—"

"That's not what I meant at all, for Pete's sake. Look, I have to ask you this. Where was Gordie yesterday afternoon?"

"He was at work."

"The hell he was. Mr. Haig knows somebody who can ask questions on the docks and get the right answers. Gordie didn't show up for the shape-up yesterday. He didn't work at all."

She looked at me.

"He told you he worked from noon to eight?"

"Yes. Where was he if he wasn't at work?"

"That's what I'd like to find out. It also seems he's been losing big sums of money betting on slow horses. He's been losing more than he's been earning and I'd like to know where he's been getting his money. Have you been giving him any?" I took her hand. "I know it's an embarrassing question, but I have to ask it."

"I don't mind. Because I've never given him anything. He's even tried to pay a share of the rent, but I haven't let him. He always takes the check when we go out together. He always seems to have plenty of money. A longshoreman can make a decent living and I thought—" She stopped suddenly.

"What's the matter?"

"I'm a slow study today, aren't I? You think he's been murdering my sisters."

"I think it's possible, yes. It's not the only possibility, but it's reasonably strong."

"It's so hard to believe."

"Could he have killed Melanie? That was Wednesday, sometime during the afternoon."

"He was working then. At least he told me so."

"And yesterday he had plenty of time to get out to Long Island and back. We'll have to find out if he has an alibi for Jessica's murder. I don't think he tracked Robin upstate and sabotaged her car. That sounds a little tricky. I think her death was accidental after all, but maybe it gave him the idea for the whole thing."

"How do you mean?"

"He must have figured that you would benefit financially by Robin's death. You don't, the money all goes to her husband, but he wouldn't necessarily know that. So he could have decided that if he killed off Jessica and Melanie and Caitlin you would have that much more money for him to marry."

She nodded with understanding. "So that's why I'm safe for the time being."

"Until you marry him and make out a will in his favor. That's if he's the killer. There are other possibilities."

"Who else do you suspect?"

"I don't want to mention any names yet. I wouldn't have said I suspected Gordie if there had been any other way to ask the questions I had to ask."

She went to make herself another cup of coffee and asked me if I wanted one. I said I wouldn't mind a beer. She brought one and poured it into a glass for me. She didn't crumple the can when it was empty.

"I don't know how I'm going to behave in front of him," she said thoughtfully. "Just being aware that he might be a murderer is going to make it difficult for me."

"You can't let him know that you suspect. He wouldn't want to murder you ahead of schedule, but if it's a choice of doing that or being caught for the murders he's already committed—"

"It's going to be hard not to let anything show."

"Well, you'll get a chance to find out how good an actress you are."

"I will, won't I?" She set her coffee cup down and folded her hands on her knee. "I could believe that he might become violent. He's that type of person, there's a real potential for violence there. But I can't see him doing it in a calculated manner, if you know what I mean."

"That's bothered me from the start."

"Well, I'll be very careful."

"You'd better. That means two things, you know. Being careful not to let Gordie know you suspect him, and being careful not to be alone with anybody else. Don't open your door when you're here alone."

"For strangers, you mean."

"Or for people you know."

"God," she said. "You mean I have to suspect everybody, is that it?"

"Just about."

"It's been hard enough living with Gordie lately. And now to have this on my mind—"

I said, "Look, it's not my place to say this, but I'll say it anyway. I agree it's hard to imagine Gordie involved in such a complicated series of murders. It's also hard to imagine him involved with you. I mean, I really can't figure out what you see in a baboon like him."

She picked up her coffee cup and looked into it for a long time. Then without raising her eyes she said, "Oh, I don't know exactly. I haven't had much experience with men. Before I met Gordie I fell in love with one of the boys in my acting class. He was a completely different type from Gordie. Very gentle and sensitive."

"I have a feeling I know how this ends."

"Of course. He turned out to be gay, which was something I probably should have recognized in the first place. The signs were all there. And it wasn't as though he did anything to encourage me to fall in love with him. He thought I knew what he was and just wanted to be friends." She looked up. "I took all of this terribly hard. And I decided that my next man was going to be as heterosexual as possible. Gordie was such a change, he had all this *macho* strength, and at the time I thought it was what I wanted."

"I gather you've changed your mind since."

"I know I couldn't marry him. Or even live with him much longer. Last night after your phone call I was furious with him. He had no right to act that way. I wanted to tell him to leave."

"What stopped you?"

"I think maybe I'm a little afraid of him. That he would take a punch at me or something." She managed a lopsided grin. "I'm a lot more afraid of him now than I was last night. After what you told me."

"Well, don't act any differently for the time being."

"I'll try not to. I can be a pretty good little actress when I have to."

"And an ornament to the stage. I think we'll crack the case in the next couple of days. And when all this is over—"

I left the sentence unfinished. I also left Kim's apartment after a few minutes because otherwise I might have found myself talking about what would happen when all this was over. I couldn't keep from having thoughts on the subject, but it was pretty silly to voice them at that stage. Premature, Haig would have called it.

I tried Andrea again. "I feel like a secret agent," she said. "I hoff zee documents."

"That's the worst Peter Lorre impression I ever heard, but it's good news. Can I come over?"

She gave me the address.

fifteen

She lived in the same building

she had occupied as Jessica's roommate. Not in the penthouse, however, but in a studio apartment on the third floor. She opened the door for me and motioned me inside. "Excuse the place," she said. "I haven't had time to buy any furniture that I like. That chair's not too bad."

As I was on my way to the chair that wasn't too bad she asked me if my leg was bothering me.

"Everything's bothering me," I said.

"I mean the way you walk. Did you hurt yourself?"

"I didn't have to. Someone did it for me."

"Huh?"

"I was beaten up last night. By professionals, I think. They didn't break any bones or anything like that. They just beat me to a pulp."

"Oh, God. Take your shirt off."

"Huh?"

"Take your shirt off and let me see. Christ, they really did a job on you. You're going to be stiff. Get undressed, Chip."

"Huh?"

"Take your clothes off and lie down on my bed. I'm serious, dumbbell. The only thing that's going to do you

126

any good at this point is a massage. You should get a daily massage for the next week, as a matter of fact. Well, you came to the right place. I happen to be a damned good masseuse."

"I remember."

"Most of the girls don't know anything about muscle groups. I took the trouble to take a decent course. Come on, lie down on your stomach. Oh, you poor baby. They really worked you over, didn't they?"

"Ouch."

"Your flesh is very tender and I'll have to hurt you a little, but you'll feel a lot better afterward. Just trust me and try to relax."

"Okay."

She really knew what she was doing. She hurt me a little from time to time, but I could feel a lot of soreness and tension draining away. I began to feel very drowsy, and she had stopped touching me for a while before I realized the absence of her hands.

I asked if we were finished.

"Nope," she said cheerfully. "I'm taking my clothes off. I work better in the nude. Okay, tiger. Roll over."

I rolled over and opened my eyes. That long lean body was even nicer than I remembered it.

I said, "I don't know about this."

"You don't have to," she said. "Just shut up and relax. Does this hurt?"

"Yes."

"Those rotten bastards. There, that's better, isn't it?"

I was beginning to feel a little stirring. You probably don't find that hard to believe. Her hands were very firm and very gentle, and her body was very beautiful, and she had that nice spicy smell to her skin. When she started touching my thighs with that feathery way she had, I started to sit up. She made me lie down again.

"Hey," I said.

"Feels nice, doesn't it?"

"Yeah, but I really don't want to wind up frustrated."

"That must have been awful the other day. I hated to see you leave like that."

"I didn't like it much myself, but I don't have any money now and I—"

"Who said anything about money, Chip?"

"Huh?"

She grinned wickedly. "Dumbbell. I'm not working now, you jerk. I'm on my own time, and I'm giving you a massage because you can use one. This is just therapy for you, baby. I'm not going to leave you tied up in knots. I'm going to untie knots you never knew you had."

"Oh."

"Now you lie still and just enjoy this. I'm going to take my time, and it may seem as though I'm teasing you, but it'll just make it that much better at the end. You're going to love this, baby."

She used her hands and her breasts and her lips and tongue. She found erogenous zones I hadn't known I had, and at times it did seem as though she was teasing me, and at times I thought I would die if it didn't end soon, and at times I wanted it to go on forever, and at the very end she turned her sweet mouth into a vacuum cleaner and turned me inside-out.

"Jesus," I said.

"I told you you were gonna love it."

"You're absolutely fantastic."

"Well, I do this for a living, honey. There's a lot to be said for professionalism."

"I guess there is."

"If I weren't reasonably competent by now, I'd go into some other line of work. But I don't get many complaints."

"You won't get one from me."

"Come on," she said, slapping me lightly on the thigh. "Put some clothes on and I'll show you what I stole for you. And where do you get off saying I do a lousy impression of Peter Lorre? That wasn't Peter Lorre. That was Akim Tamiroff, and I do a great Akim Tamiroff."

There was quite a stack of membership application forms from the two-week period preceding Jessica's death. Indulgence evidently did a hell of a business, and if all its recreational therapists were like Andrea, I could understand why.

What I couldn't understand at first was why I was bothering to go through this pile of paper, since every third person seemed to be named John Smith. And most of the others were pretty obvious aliases. I read in one of Haig's books that amateurs almost always use a first name, or a form of one, as the last name of their alias. So I ran into a high percentage of names like John Richards, Joe Andrews, Sam Joseph, and so on.

Then I hit a name I knew, and then I hit it again, and then I hit it a third time, and I cabbed to Haig's house with three pieces of paper in my pocket that would wrap up a murderer.

sixteen

He was at his desk. "**You left**
just before Mr. Shivers called me," he said. He looked intolerably smug. "You'll perhaps be pleased to know that
my instincts were quite on the mark. I thought I knew who
the killer was, and now all doubt has been removed."

"So has mine."

"Oh? That's interesting. I'd enjoy hearing the line of
reasoning you followed."

"I didn't follow any line of reasoning," I said. "My legwork evidently got to the same place as your brainwork,
and at about the same time. I reached Andrea Sugar and
checked the records of men who had been to Indulgence
shortly before Jessica was killed. I didn't expect anything
to come of it because I didn't figure he would use his right
name, but he probably had to because Jessica would recognize him."

"That's logical."

"Thank you. He didn't just go there once. He went there
three times within the week preceding her death. I was
thinking that you could call that a lot of nerve, but one
thing the guy has not lacked is nerve. He's about the
nerviest bastard I've ever heard of."

"That's well put."

"Thank you."

"You are welcome." His hand went to his beard. "I find it fascinating the way your legwork and my mental work found the same goal by opposite routes. Do you remember something I told you the other day? That there was a definite Ross MacDonald cast to this entire affair?"

"Something about forty years ago in Canada."

"That's correct. But it's closer to fifty years than forty, and the locale is somewhat south of the Canadian border." He closed his eyes and stroked his beard some more. "What an extraordinary amount of planning he devoted to all of this. The man has elements of genius. He's also quite mad, of course. The combination is by no means unheard of."

"Well, we've got him now. And these three slips of paper nail him to the wall."

And I passed them across to Haig.

"Gregory Vandiver," he read aloud.

"May he rot in hell."

"But this is very curious," he said.

"What's curious about it? I already explained why he must have figured he had to use his right name. Because Jessica would have known him already. You told me I was logical."

"I never said you were logical. I said that particular statement was logical."

"Well, what's the problem? Vandiver has had cash problems. Of all the people in the case, he's the only one with a real money motive. For most people the difference between two million dollars and ten million dollars doesn't matter much, but he got into investments over his head and needed the prospect of really big money. So he—"

"Be quiet, Chip."

"Oh, for Pete's sake—"

"Chip. Be quiet."

I became quiet. He turned around and watched the rasboras for awhile. They ignored him and I tried to. He turned to face me, but his eyes were closed and he was playing with his beard. Sometime I'm going to shave him in his sleep, and he'll never be able to think straight again.

He had been wearing his beard away for maybe five minutes when the doorbell rang. I stayed where I was and let Wong get it. A few seconds later he brought in a man who looked familiar. It took me a second or two to place him as one of the Sands Point police officers.

He said, "Mr. Harrison? I'm Luther Polk, we met yesterday afternoon."

"Yes," I said. I introduced him to Haig, who had by now opened his eyes. "I suppose you want a further statement, but I don't think—"

"No, it's not that," he said. "I will need a further statement from you eventually, but there's something else. Do you want to sit down?"

"No, but if you'd be more comfortable—"

He shook his head. "I have some bad news for you," he said slowly. "I felt I ought to bring it in person. Late last night or early this morning Mrs. Vandiver shot and killed her husband. She then took her own life. The bodies were discovered by servants at approximately ten this morning. Mrs. Vandiver left a sealed envelope addressed to you beside her typewriter. Under the circumstances it was necessary to open and read the letter. It's a suicide note, and explains the reasons for her actions. I thought you would like to have it. I'll need to retain it as evidence, but you may examine it now if you wish."

This is the note:

> Dear Chip,
>
> By the time you read this I will probably be dead by my own hand. Unless I lose my nerve, and I might. But I don't think so.
>
> It was Gregory who tried to kill me by planting a bomb in my car. It was also Gregory who killed Melanie and Jessica and Robin, and he would have killed Kim too in due time. I found

this out an hour ago when he tried a second time to kill me. He was attempting to strangle me in my sleep. I woke up in time to get loose. I've always kept a small pistol in my bedside table. I managed to get it in time. I shot him and killed him. In a few minutes I think I'll shoot myself.

I'm just so tired, Chip. Tired of everything. It's astonishing that I could have been married to this man for so long without sensing his evil nature. I merely took it for granted that he was a bore. I never had an inkling that he was a homicidal maniac into the bargain.

Maybe I'm in shock. Maybe suicide is an irrational act for me to perform. I certainly don't feel guilty for having killed Gregory. It was self-defense, certainly, and I would be let off for that reason. So maybe I'm just using this as an excuse for something I've wanted to do for a long time.

I don't know if you can understand this, since I scarcely understand it myself. But I somehow think you might be able to, Chip.

Please don't think too badly of me.

I read it through a couple of times. Then I gave it to Haig. "She was my client," he said, "and I failed to protect her."

Luther Polk said, "Sir, if she was determined to take her own life—"

"If I had had one more day," Haig said. "One more day."

"It was definitely self-defense, just as she wrote it," Polk went on. "There were abrasions on her throat from where her husband had tried to strangle her, and—"

"Pfui!" Haig said. "Caitlin Vandiver did not write this bit of fiction. Gregory Vandiver did not attempt to strangle her. She did not shoot him. She did not shoot herself."

Polk just stared down at him.

"A little over forty years ago," Haig said. "And a bit to the south of Canada."

I probably should have picked up on it by then, but I was only half hearing the words. I picked up one of the membership forms from the desk and looked at the signature, and then I got it.

"Oh," I said.

Haig looked at me.

"I just recognized the handwriting," I told him. "But what I can't figure out is why. I know, forty years ago in Canada. But why?"

"In a quick phrase?" He touched his beard. "Because he didn't have the guts to kill his father," he said.

I tried to make some sense out of that one while Haig began listing names on a memorandum slip. Polk was saying something in the background. He must have felt as though he had walked into a Pinter play after having missed the first act. We both ignored him. Haig finished making his list and handed it to me.

"I want these people in this room in an hour's time. Do what you have to do to arrange it."

I read half the list and looked at him. "Oh, for Pete's sake," I said. "You're not really going to do a whole production number, are you? Everybody in one room together while you show them what a genius you are. I mean, all you have to do is call the police."

"Chip." He folded his hands on his desk. "This is the most extraordinary case I have ever had. The criminal is an archfiend of terrifying proportions. I am going to play this one strictly according to the book."

seventeen

You wouldn't believe what I went through, getting them all there. And I couldn't possibly bring it off in an hour, even with Luther Polk on hand to expedite matters. Polk was helpful, especially once he came to the conclusion that he was not going to know anything about what was going on until Leo Haig was ready to tell him.

"He's a genius," I explained. "He was telling me just a few hours ago that there's a very thin line between genius and insanity. You can think of him as walking along that line, doing a high-wire act on it."

"But you say he's about to come up with a killer."

"He's going to come down on one," I said. "With both feet. And he's got enough weight to land hard."

"Not all that much weight," Polk said. "He'd be right trim if you was to stretch him out to a suitable length."

I pushed the image of Leo Haig being lengthened on a medieval rack as far out of mind as possible, and settled down to the serious business of setting the stage and assembling the audience. It took two hours and twelve minutes, and I think that was pretty good.

They arrived in stages, of course, but I won't burden you with the order of their coming, or the way I fielded their questions and settled them down. I'll just tell you what the room looked like when Haig condescended to enter it.

Wong Fat and I had set up a double row of chairs on my side of the partners' desk, facing Haig. My own chair was off to the side, between the audience and the door.

In the front row, farthest from me, sat Detective Vincent Gregorio. He was wearing a black silk suit with a subtle dark blue stripe and a pair of wing tip loafers you could see your face in if you were in a house where they covered the mirrors. I don't know where he bought his clothes, but between them and his twenty-dollar haircut he looked like a walking advertisement for police corruption. I was surprised that he had agreed to come so readily. Maybe he got a charge out of it when Haig called him a witling.

Andrea Sugar sat on Gregorio's right, which was an obvious source of pleasure to Kid Handsome, because he was doing a courtship dance that a male *Betta splendens* would have been proud of, preening and posing and not knowing how little good it was going to do him. Andrea was wearing a maroon dress with bright red cherries all over it, and if you can't think of the thoughts it inspired, that's too damned bad, because I am not going to spell them out for you.

I had put Addison Shivers, our sole surviving client, alongside Andrea. That also put him directly across the desk from Haig which seemed only proper. He was the angel for this theatrical production. His suit was probably as old as detective Gregorio, but it still looked good. He sat quite stiff in his chair, and when Haig came into the room he took off his glasses and cleaned them with his necktie.

Kim was seated next to Mr. Shivers, with Gordie McLeod on the other side of her, which put him in the chair closest to mine. This had not been my idea. I would have preferred to be able to look directly at Kim without having him around to play the role of an automobile graveyard at the foot of a beautiful mountain. That's a bad choice of words, actually, because Kim could not have looked less mountainous. She seemed to have grown smaller and more petite in the short time since I had seen her. She was wearing what she had worn earlier. I had seen nothing to object to then and I saw nothing to object to now, except for the hulking moron who was holding her hand in his paw.

McLeod was wearing something loutish. I think he'd put on a clean bowling shirt in honor of the occasion. His shoes needed a shine and probably weren't going to get one. They had thick soles, for stepping on people.

Detective Wallace Seidenwall was directly behind McLeod, which put him closer to me than I might have wanted him. He had not grown discernibly fonder of me since our last meeting. "This better be good," was a phrase which came trippingly to his lips during the waiting period. He didn't say it as though he thought it was going to, either. He was wearing a gray glen plaid suit that Robert Hall had marked down for good reason. Either his partner got all the graft, or Seidenwall was running a yacht, or something, because he was due for a bitter disappointment again this fall when the Best Dressed list came out.

Ferdinand Bell was next to Seidenwall, and he was the only one in the crowd who looked genuinely happy to be present. "This will be a treat," he said upon entering, and he enjoyed himself immensely making small talk with the others and asking the names of all of the fish. He had on the same suit he'd worn to Melanie's funeral. His short white hair set off his pink scalp, or maybe it was the other way around, and his plump cheeks reminded you more than ever of a chipmunk when he smiled, which was most of the time.

I had stuck Luther Polk next to Bell, which put him directly behind Addison Shivers. (I know I'm taking forever giving you the geography of all this, and I know you could probably care less about the whole thing, but Haig spent so much time charting it out that it is conceivably important. I know I'd catch hell if I didn't go through it all.) I don't think I described Polk before, but if you've seen Dennis Weaver in that television series where he plays an Arizona marshal attached to the New York Police Department, then I won't have to describe him for you. He had had relatively little to say to the two Homicide detectives, or they to him, and he sat there keeping his hand comfortingly close to the revolver on his hip.

Madam Juana was sitting on the far side of Polk. She was wearing her basic black dress and a string of pearls, and she looked like the stern-lipped administrator of a parochial school for girls. (I can't help it, that's what she looked like.)

Well, it wasn't what you would call perfect. I mean, there should have been three or four more obvious suspects present. John LiCastro would have been a nice addition to the group, but Haig had pointed out that it would have been an insensitive act to place him in the same room with policemen for no compelling reason. And it would have been even nicer if our other client had been present; if Haig had had just a few more hours to work with, Caitlin would have been alive.

So it wasn't perfect, but it was still a pretty decent showing, and I have to admit I got a kick out of it when Leo Haig marched into the room and every eye turned to take in the sight of him.

He seated himself very carefully behind his desk. I had a bad moment when I thought he was going to put his feet up, but he got control of himself. He took his time meeting the eyes of each person in the room, including me, and then he closed his eyes and touched his beard and went into a tiny huddle with himself. It didn't last as long as it might have.

He opened his eyes and said, "I want to thank you for

coming here. I am going to unmask a killer this afternoon, a killer who has in one way or another affected all our lives. Each of us has been thus affected, but not all of you are aware of the extent of this killer's activities. So you must permit me to rehash some recent events. Not all of them will be news to any of you, and one of you will know all of what I am about to say, and more. Because the murderer is in this room."

He was grandstanding, but of course it went over well. Everybody turned and looked at everybody else.

"This past Wednesday," Haig said, "my associate Mr. Harrison discovered the body of Miss Melanie Trelawney. She had died of an overdose of heroin. Previously she had told Mr. Harrison that she feared for her life. His observations of the scene at Miss Trelawney's apartment led Mr. Harrison to the certain conclusion that she had been murdered. When he confided his observations to me—"

"Wait a minute," Gregorio cut in. "Where do you get off concealing evidence from the police?"

"I concealed no evidence," Haig said. "Nor did Mr. Harrison. Nothing was suppressed, nothing distorted. It is not incumbent upon a citizen to apprise the police of his suspicions. Indeed, it is often unwise.

"To continue. When Mr. Harrison confided his observations to me, I concurred in his conclusion. Miss Trelawney's fears were predicated, it appeared, upon the fact that two of her sisters had recently suffered violent deaths, one the apparent victim of suicide, the other the apparent victim of an automobile accident. I determined at once to ferret out the killer and prevent him from doing further damage. I have at least succeeded in the first attempt, if not in the second."

Gregorio broke in again. "I'd like to know what made you think that OD was murder," he said. "If we missed something, I'd like to know what it was."

"In due time, sir. In due time. Permit me, if you will, to explore events chronologically. The day after Miss Trelawney's death, Mr. Harrison and I began a series of inquiries. In the course of so doing, we were engaged by Mr. Addison Shivers to look after the best interests of Cyrus Trelawney, deceased. It is perhaps unusual for an attorney to engage detectives for the benefit of a client who is no longer living. In my eyes, Mr. Shivers' act stands greatly to his credit."

The hand went to the beard again. I looked around the room and watched everybody watching Haig. Gordie McLeod looked as though he was trying to understand the big words. Juana looked as though she was trying to understand the English words. Kim looked as though she was trying to figure out how Haig could hold an audience in the palm of his hand, just by sitting there with his eyes closed while he played with his facial hair.

"On the following day Mr. Harrison attended Miss Trelawney's funeral, both to pay his respects to the deceased and to press our investigation. There he met Mrs. Gregory Vandiver, the former Caitlin Trelawney, who also engaged us to look into the matter of her sister's death. I accepted a retainer from her, feeling no conflict of interest was likely to be involved."

He paused to glance directly at Addison Shivers, who gave a barely perceptible nod.

"Mr. Harrison returned to this office. We were seated in this very room when a pipe bomb was thrown into the front room a floor below. Several of my aquaria suffered minor damage. This was galling, but of little actual importance. Of major importance was the fact that the bombing caused two deaths. Maria Tijerino, an associate of Miss Juana Dominguez, and Elmer J. Seaton, a seaman on shore leave, were in the room into which the bomb was hurled. Both were killed instantly."

A couple of heads turned to look at Madame Juana, who crossed herself several times.

"Detectives Gregorio and Seidenwall, who investigated the bombing, assumed that the premises below were the bomber's target. The nature of the business carried on downstairs would tend to further such a suspicion. The world overflows with maniacs who feel they are doing the Creator's work by blowing brothels to smithereens. Mr. Harrison and I interpreted the bombing in a different fashion."

"I told you we oughta take him in," Seidenwall said. "What did I tell you? I told you we oughta take him in."

Haig ignored this. "My immediate thought was that the bomber had chosen the wrong window. It did not take me long to realize that I was in error. A person anxious to kill me would do a better job of it, especially in view of his skill in arranging other murders. No, the bombing had been meant either to discourage me from further investigations, or to pique my interest in the case. I could not, at that stage, determine which.

"But the bombing did tell me certain things about the killer. It told me, first of all, that he knew I was on his trail. This did little to narrow the field of suspects. It told me, too, that the man I was dealing with was quite ruthless, willing to liquidate innocent strangers in order to advance his machinations. I was on the trail of a dangerous, desperate and wholly immoral human being."

Haig picked up a pipe, took it deliberately apart, ran a pipe cleaner unnecessarily through it and put it back together again.

"My investigations continued. Yesterday my associate visited Mrs. Vandiver at her home on Long Island. While he was there, a bomb wired to the automobile of Mrs. Vandiver was detonated, killing her chauffeur, one Seamus Fogarty. The local police officers assumed Mr. Fogarty was the intended victim because of his political activities. I assumed otherwise. An attempt had been made on my client's life.

"Last night my associate, Mr. Harrison, left this house against my advice—" He had to rub it in, damn it. "—and returned to his own lodgings. He was set upon and badly beaten by three strangers, evidently professionals at that sort of thing." Eyes swung around to look at me. There was concern in Kim's, surprise in Ferdinand Bell's, and what looked annoyingly like satisfaction in Seidenwall's.

"And later last night," Haig went on, "or perhaps early this morning, the killer struck again. He murdered Mr. and Mrs. Gregory Vandiver and arranged things to suggest that Mrs. Vandiver shot her husband and then took her own life."

Kim let out a shriek, and the whole room began mumbling to itself. McLeod reached for her. She drew away. Haig tapped on the desk top with a pipe.

"I learned of this last act just a few hours ago. My first reaction was to feel personally responsible for the deaths of Mr. and Mrs. Vandiver. By the time I learned of their fate, I already knew the identity of their killer. I did not know, however, at the time they were killed. Perhaps I could still have done something, taken some action, to prevent what happened to them. I had held strong suspicions of the murderer's identity for some time."

He closed his eyes for a moment. I took a good long look at the killer, and did not obtain the slightest idea of what was going through his mind.

"Officer Polk brought me the news of what happened to my client and her husband. He also brought a typed and unsigned suicide note which the murderer had had the temerity to write. The note was designed to wrap up all of the crimes to date and pin them upon Gregory Vandiver, who was supposed to have attempted to kill his wife, was then killed by her, after which my client is supposed to have suffered an uncharacteristic fit of remorse at the conclusion of which she killed herself.

"There was no reason for Officer Polk to doubt this charade. I suspect his department might have doubted it ultimately. But Mr. Harrison and myself immediately recognized it as illusion, and read in the purported suicide note additional confirmation of the identity of the actual killer."

Polk said, "How did you know so quickly the note was a fake?"

I fielded that one. "I knew it on the first line," I said. "The murderer spelled my first name right. C-h-i-p. Caitlin thought I spelled it with two p's; she made out a check that way. I never corrected her." I didn't add that I had suspected Greg Vandiver all along and it just about took the note to change my mind. Let them think I was as brilliant as Leo Haig.

"The concept of leaving a typewritten suicide note was a bad one," Haig added. "But the murderer had developed an extraordinary degree of gall. Success engenders confidence. Mr. Harrison has described the killer as the nerviest bastard he ever heard of. I told him that was exceedingly well put, as you will come to realize."

I watched the killer's face on that line. I think it got to him a little bit.

"The killer wanted to round things off neatly," Haig went on. "He knew better than to leave a note when he pushed Jessica Trelawney out of her window. Now, though, he wanted to establish Gregory Vandiver as the villain of the piece, and award him a posthumous citation for multiple homicide. At this very moment he may be cursing himself for his stupidity. He might better save himself the effort. I already knew him as the killer. This was by no means his first witless act. But it is to be his last."

Haig closed his eyes again. I can't speak for the rest of the company, but for me the tension was getting unbearable. I knew something the rest of them didn't know, and I wished he would hurry up and get to the end.

"This morning I called Mr. Shivers. In addition to being my client, he was for a great many years both attorney and friend to the late Cyrus Trelawney. He was able to supply me with the last piece of my jigsaw puzzle, the question of motive.

"I had realized almost from the beginning that motive

was the key element of these murders. The most immediately obvious motive was money. The case is awash with money. Cyrus Trelawney left a fortune in excess of ten million dollars. But the more I examined the facts, the less likely it seemed that money could constitute a motive.

"Why, then, would someone want to murder five women who had virtually nothing in common but their kinship? Several possibilities presented themselves. The first was that, having determined to murder one of them for a logical reason, he might have wished to disguise his act by making it one link in a chain of homicides. Gregory Vandiver, for example, could have had reason to do away with his wife. If he first killed some of her sisters, he would be a less obvious suspect for the single murder for which he had a visible motive.

"The fault in this line of reasoning is not difficult to pinpoint. If a person wished to create the appearance of a chain of murders, he would make the facade an unmistakable one. He would not disguise his handiwork as accidental death or suicide. He would make each act an obvious murder, and would probably use the same murder method in each instance. So this was not a *faked* chain of murders, but a very *real* chain of murders.

"And then I saw that the answer had to lie in the past. These girls were being killed because they were the daughters of Cyrus Trelawney. The man had died three years ago, and after his death his daughters began dying. First Robin, then Jessica, then Melanie. And now Caitlin."

He did start to put his feet up then, I'm positive of it, but he caught himself in time.

"I've told Mr. Harrison that this case reminded me of the work of a certain author of detective stories. Our New York has little of the texture of Lew Archer's California, but in much the same way the sins of the past work upon those of us trapped in the present. If I were to find the killer, I had to consider Cyrus Trelawney.

"Cyrus Trelawney." He folded his hands on the desk top. "An interesting man, I should say. Fathered his first child at the age of forty-eight, having beforehand amassed a fortune. Continued fathering them every three years, spawning as regularly as a guppy. Brought five girls into the world. And one son who died in his cradle. I began to wonder about Cyrus Trelawney's life before he married. I speculated, and I constructed an hypothesis."

He paused and looked across his desk at Addison Shivers. "This morning I asked Mr. Shivers a question. Do you recall the question, sir?"

"I do."

"Indeed. Would you repeat it?"

"You asked if Cyrus Trelawney had been a man of celibate habits before his marriage."

"And your reply?"

"That he had not."

(This was paraphrase. What Mr. Shivers had actually said, Haig told me later, was that Cyrus Trelawney would fuck a coral snake if somebody would hold its head.)

"I then asked Mr. Shivers several other questions which elicited responses I had expected to elicit. I learned, in brief, that Mr. Trelawney's business interests forty-five to fifty years ago included substantial holdings in timberlands and paper mills in upstate New York. That he spent considerable time in that area during those years. That one of those mills was located in the town of Lyons Falls, New York."

"That's very interesting," the killer said.

"Indeed. But the others do not understand what makes it interesting, Mr. Bell. Would you care to tell them?"

"I was born in Lyons Falls," Bell said.

"Indeed. You were born in Lyons Falls, New York, forty-seven years ago last April 18th. Your mother was a woman named Barbara Hohlbein who was the wife of a man named James Bell. James Bell was not your father. Cyrus Trelawney was your father. Cyrus Trelawney's

daughters were your half-sisters and you have killed four
of the five, Mr. Bell, and you will not kill any more of
them. You will not, Mr. Bell. No, sir. You will not."

eighteen

Of course everybody stared at
the son of a bitch. He didn't seem to notice. His eyes were
on Leo Haig and he was as cool as a gherkin. His forehead
looked a little pinker, but that may have been my imagination. I couldn't really tell you.

"This is quite fascinating," Bell said. "I asked around
when I heard you were investigating Melanie's death. I
was told that you were quite insane. I wondered what this
elaborate charade would lead to."

"I would prefer that it lead to the gas chamber, sir. I
fear it will lead only to permanent incarceration in a hos-
pital for the criminally insane."

"Fascinating."

"Indeed. I shouldn't attempt to leave if I were you, Mr.
Bell. There are police officers seated on either side of you.
They would take umbrage."

"Oh, I wouldn't miss this for the world," Bell said. His
cheeks puffed out as he grinned. "Why, if this were a
movie I'd *pay* to see it. It's *far* more thrilling in real life."

Haig closed his eyes. Without opening them he said, "I
have no way of knowing whether or not Cyrus Trelawney
was your father. You do not resemble him, nor do I perceive any resemblance between yourself and his legitimate

offspring. Very strong men tend to be prepotent, which is to say that their genes are dominant. Much the same is true of fishes, you might be interested to know. I would guess that you resemble your mother. I suspect you inherited your madness from her."

A muscle worked in Bell's temple. He didn't say anything.

"I don't doubt that she told you Trelawney was your father. I don't doubt that you believe it, that you grew up hearing little from her than that a rich man had fathered you. It certainly made an impression upon you. You grew up loving and hating this man you had never met. You were obsessed by the idea that he had sired you. Had he acknowledged you, you would have been rich. Money became an obsession.

"One learns much about a man from his hobbies. You collect money, Mr. Bell. Not in an attempt to amass wealth, but as a way of playing with the symbols of wealth. Little pieces of stamped metal moving from hand to hand at exorbitant prices. Pfui!"

"Numismatics is a science."

"Anything may be taken for a science when enough of its devotees attempt to codify their madness. There is a young man in this city, I understand, who spends his spare time, of which I trust he has an abundance, analyzing the garbage of persons understandably more prominent than himself. For the time being he is acknowledged to be a lunatic. If, heaven forfend, his pastime amasses a following, garbage analysis will be esteemed a science. Learned books will be published on the subject. Fools will write them. Greater fools will purchase and read them. Pfui!"

"You know nothing about numismatics," Bell said.

Haig grunted. "I could dispute that. I shall not take the trouble. I am not concerned with numismatics, sir. I am concerned with murder."

"And you're calling me a murderer."

"I have done so already." He stroked his beard briefly.

"I've no idea just when you planned to become a murderer. At your mother's knee, I would suppose. You came to New York. You established yourself in your profession. You kept tabs on your father. And, because of your infirmity of purpose, you bided your time.

"Because you could not kill this man, nor could you think of relinquishing the dream of killing him. You waited until time achieved what you could not: the death of Cyrus Trelawney."

"And then I married Robin."

"Then you married Robin Trelawney," Haig agreed with him.

"And then I crashed up the car and killed her, I suppose. The only person I ever loved and I crashed up my car on the chance that I would live through the wreck and she would not."

"No, sir. No in every respect. But I'll back up a bit. Before you married Robin, indeed before Cyrus Trelawney died, you had all of your plan worked out. The first step called for you to murder Philip Flanner."

"Now I *know* you're insane," Bell said.

"You told Mr. Harrison that you were a friend of Flanner's, that he was a fellow numismatist. He was not. You did become a friend of his, but not until after he and Robin were married. You ingratiated yourself with him because he had recently taken her as a wife."

"He fell in front of a subway car."

"You threw him in front of a subway car."

"You couldn't prove that in a million years."

"I haven't the slightest need to prove it. You are a very curious man, Mr. Bell. You took your time ingratiating yourself with Robin. You waited until her father was at last in his grave before you persuaded her to marry you. Then you waited a couple of years before you killed her. You must have thought about the murder method for all of that time and more."

"I loved Robin."

"No, sir. You have never loved anyone, except insofar as you loved Cyrus Trelawney. I leave that to the psychiatrists, who will have ample opportunity to inquire. You drove with Robin to a coin convention. At some time in the course of the ride back, you broke her neck. That would not have been terribly difficult to manage. Then you put her in the back of the car and found a place where an icy road surface could explain an accident. You then effected that accident, sir, which no doubt took a certain amount of insane courage on your part."

"No one will believe this."

"I suspect everyone in the room already believes it, sir. But they will not have to, nor will anyone else." Haig turned around and looked at the rasboras. I was astonished, and I was used to him, so you can imagine what it did to everybody else. But I'll be damned if anyone said a word. I was wondering how long he was going to milk it, when he turned around again and got to his feet.

"The order of the murders," he said. "Robin, Jessica, Melanie, Caitlin. I was shocked when I learned that Caitlin was dead. Doubly shocked, because I thought you would save her for last. You were trying so hard to throw suspicion upon Gregory Vandiver. Inventing some nonsense about financial insolvency, some prattle about his having invested large sums in rare coins and being forced to liquidate them. One would have thought you would wait until Kim was safely dead before disposing of him. He, surely, would have done so before killing his wife, had he the financial motive you suggested.

"But that becomes clear when one devotes some thought to it. You did not merely want to murder your half-sisters. You wanted to have sexual relations with them as well.

"First Robin. You married her in order to have sex with her. Then Jessica. You went at least three times to her place of employment in the week preceding her death.

You signed Gregory Vandiver's name to the membership application, having already planned to use him as a scapegoat should there be need for one. Through this contact with Jessica, you were able to arrange to see her privately at her apartment. You did so, sir, and you pitched her out of her window."

"You can't prove that," Bell said.

"But I can. Miss Sugar no doubt recognizes you. If not, her colleagues very possibly will. In any event, I have here three pieces of paper confirming the dates of your visit. They identify you as Gregory Vandiver, sir, but they are in your handwriting."

Which is how I had tipped to the whole thing. I remembered where I had seen that precise penmanship. It was on a 2 x 2 coin envelope.

"You had an affair with Caitlin. I have had it established that this was not terribly difficult for one to achieve. I knew at an early date that you were probably in touch with her. I learned that when Mr. Harrison reported on his conversation with you Saturday."

I said, "How?"

Haig glared at me.

"I'm serious. How did you know that?"

"Because you've learned to report conversations verbatim. I spoke to Mr. Bell over the telephone to prepare him for your visit. I identified you as my associate, Mr. Harrison. I did not mention your first name. Nor did you mention it when introducing yourself. Mr. Bell asked if it was all right for him to call you Chip. The only person likely to have told him your name was Caitlin, yet he gave the impression that everything you were saying to him was coming as a great surprise. This made me instantly suspicious of Mr. Bell, a suspicion I never had cause to relinquish."

"I was not having an affair with Caitlin," Bell said stiffly. "As a matter of fact, she did ask my advice after

Harrison talked to her. She had second thoughts about hiring him, and wanted my opinion."

"Indeed."

"I never had sexual relations with her. Or with Jessica. Perhaps it's true that I visited her at that massage parlor. If I signed Gregory's name, it was on a whim. I only visited her to have a half hour of her time, so that we could talk about Robin. It was a way of bringing Robin back to life for me."

Haig closed his eyes. He opened them and sighed and sat down behind his desk again. "I won't comment on that," he said. "Nor shall I attempt to determine what sexual act you performed with Melanie Trelawney. I suspect it might have been you who put the thought in her mind that her two sisters had been killed. Or you might have become aware of her suspicions by virtue of her having called you to inquire if there was any possibility that Robin's death was not wholly accidental. At any rate, it should have posed no problem for you to gain access to her apartment. Once there, you could have had little difficulty in rendering her unconscious. She was completely nude when Mr. Harrison discovered the body. It has not been my observation that people habitually disrobe before injecting themselves with heroin."

"Happens some of the time," Gregorio said.

"Sometimes yes, sometimes no. You wouldn't get suspicious either way," Seidenwall said.

Haig nodded. "So you would not have disrobed her to make her the more obvious victim of death from a drug overdose. I'm sure you did something with her. I do not care to know what it was, nor do I care to know whether it took place before or after you injected a fatal overdose of the drug into her bloodstream."

I don't care to know that either, to tell you the truth.

"You can't prove any of this," Bell said. Not for the first time.

Haig stared at him. He was on his feet again. "I can

prove almost all of it," he said. "Once the facts are known and established, the proof is rarely hard to come by. Had you taken your time, you might have managed to bring it off. You did come very close at that. You killed four out of five. Had sex with four of your sisters, killed four of your sisters.

"And you were very patient at the onset. You waited to kill Philip Flanner, waited to marry his widow, waited to kill her. But then you got a taste of it and you liked it, didn't you? *You loved it.*"

Bell didn't say anything. The muscle was really having a workout in his temple, and he didn't look his usual happy self.

"You incestuous murdering bastard," Haig said. "You never did what you wanted to do. You never killed your father and you never slept with your mother, and you used your sisters as surrogates for both, one after another. But you'll never get the last one, Bell, you'll never put a hand on her!"

The son of a bitch moved fast. He had the knife out of his pocket and the blade open before I could even blink.

A fat lot of good it did him. He wasn't even out of his chair before Seidenwall had an arm wrapped around his throat and Luther Polk's long-barreled automatic was jabbed into the side of his head.

They took turns advising him of his rights. He went limp, but that didn't make Seidenwall let go of his throat or Polk stop jabbing him in the head with the gun barrel.

On the way out, his hands cuffed behind his back, he turned and smiled at me. It was a smile I will never forget as long as I live. I can close my eyes and see it now. I wish I couldn't.

"You know," he said, "I had absolutely nothing to do with having you beaten up. I hope you can believe that."

nineteen

After the three cops had es-
corted Ferdinand Bell out of there, I figured everybody
would start talking at once. I guess nobody wanted to make
the first move. They all just sat there staring at each other.

Finally Addison Shivers said, "The vagaries and inconsistencies of human nature. How many persons did that
man kill?"

"I know of nine," Haig said. "The four sisters; Philip
Flanner; Maria Tijerina; Elmer Seaton, the sailor; Seamus
Fogarty; Gregory Vandiver. Nine. There may have been
others, but I doubt it."

"And yet the one crime he was anxious to deny was the
administration of a beating to young Chip."

"Indeed," Haig said. "He was not responsible for it,
as it happens."

Kim said, to me, "You never told me you were beaten
up."

I agreed that I never did.

"If he didn't do it, then who did?"

I got to my feet. It was doomed to be anticlimactic, but
it was my part of the show. "That's easy to answer," I
said. "Gordie McLeod set me up. Didn't you, old buddy?"

Everybody stared at him. He didn't return the favor. He

154

stared at his hands, mostly. Kim got up and drew away
from him as if he was a leper. Which, come to think of it,
he more or less was.

I said, "Well?"

He stood up. "I made a mistake," he said.

I just looked at him.

"Well, I'll tell you, man. All I could see is you're
nosin' around my girl. And then I find out you've got some
people down to the docks askin' questions about me. What
do I need with people askin' questions, and I don't know
about any murders, and I figure maybe you're doin' a
number, and if you're doin' a number I figure maybe I
can cool things out is all. I told 'em to take it easy with
you."

The look on Kim's face was worth the price of admission.

"So I made a mistake," he went on. "You know, the
way I feel about Kim and all, and so I got carried away. I
never had your advantages, I never went to college, never
joined a fraternity, I'm just your ordinary guy, works hard
all his life and tries to make a go of it."

"You were also born stupid. Don't forget that."

"Well, I never said I was the brightest guy in the world.
Just your average Joe." He gave his shoulders a shrug. He
had a lot of shoulders and they moved impressively.
"Look," he said, "I'm the kind of guy gives credit where
credit's due. I had you wrong. You're okay. I made a
mistake." He extended a paw like an overtrained retriever.
"No hard feelings, huh?"

"None at all," I said, and I extended my hand and
moved toward him, and for some odd reason or other my
hand kept going right on past his hand, fingers bunched
and rigid, and the fingers jabbed him almost exactly three
inches north of his navel, assuming he was born once and
had one, and that's where the solar plexus is supposed to
be, and that's where his was, and I'll be damned if it didn't
work like a charm.

He doubled up and turned sort of orange, and he started folding inward like a dying accordion, and I interlaced my fingers and cupped the back of his head with both hands and helped him fold up, and at the same time I raised my right knee as high as it would go, and it couldn't go all the way up because it met his face coming down.

You wouldn't believe the sound it made.

After Wong sponged the blood off him, we put him in a chair, and I stood in front of him trying not to look at his nose. It was a pleasure not to look at it.

"No hard feelings," I said, "but I've had a yen to do that since I first saw you. It was the sort of yen that kept getting stronger until there was just no restraining myself. Do you understand what I'm saying, or should I use smaller words?"

He tried to glare at me.

"Here's the point," I said. "I have a feeling I'm going to get that yen over and over. It's not the sort of thing you do once and get bored with. So it would probably be a good idea if you arranged your life so that you and I were not in the same place at the same time, because kicking the shit out of you could get to be a habit with me.

"I'll tell you something else. You don't give a shit about Kim, beyond the fact that she's easy to look at and worth a couple of million dollars. She's far too good for you, and even you must be bright enough to realize that. She would have written you off a long time ago, but she was afraid of you. I think she can see that you're nothing much to be afraid of. You're not going to see Kim any more."

He tried a little harder to glare at me.

"You didn't beat me up to keep me away from Kim. You had your buddies work me over to keep me off your back, because you've got a nice little hustle going and you figured I might turn it up. I did. We got a call just before you got here today. It was from—never mind who it was from. You take days off from the docks now and then.

You have one talent on God's earth: you can start a car without the key, and that's what you've been doing for a living. I could tell you just where you drive them, and just how much you get for them, but you already know. Or maybe you write the address on your shirt cuff so you won't forget it."

"Who told you?"

"Mr. Haig has some very good friends. Mr. Haig's friend asked that his name not be mentioned so I'm not going to mention it. Mr. Haig's friend asked if he could take care of this for us. He said a good friend of his has a paving contract up in Rockland County. He wanted to know if we wanted him to arrange to tuck you under a section of four-lane divided highway."

His face got very white. Except for around the nose, where it was still doing a little low-grade bleeding.

"We told him you weren't worth the trouble. If you start being worth the trouble, meaning if you turn up on Kim's doorstep again, Mr. Haig will call him and say he changed his mind. A lot of this man's friends are in the highway construction business. I guess it's profitable."

"You son of a bitch," he said.

"I'm not finished. I'm also supposed to tell you that the auto theft people don't want to work with you any more. And that you may have a certain amount of trouble getting picked in the dock shape-up. People may tend to overlook you. You think I'm bluffing, don't you? Mr. Haig's friend didn't want his name mentioned, but there was another name he told me to mention to you."

I did so, and I never thought four syllables could have such an effect. He did everything but die on the spot.

I said, "I think you should go away now."

He went away.

So did the rest of them, ultimately. They had questions, most of them, and Haig answered them. He got into a long psychoanalytical rap with Andrea Sugar, who turned out to be very knowledgeable on Jungian psychology.

Madam Juana took him aside and told him something, and kissed his cheek, and Haig went beet-red. He had never done this before in my presence. I can't swear to what she said to him, but I can make a guess based on my instincts and my experience, because before his blush had a chance to fade she came over to me and gave me a kiss on the cheek and whispered in my ear, and what she whispered was, "You a wonnerful boy and you get the bom who kill my Maria, and anytime you wanna girl you come down and I give you best inna house, no charge, anytime you wanna fock."

Eventually Kim was the only one left. I took her upstairs and showed her the fish. She was very interested. She was also still a little nervous, so I waved at Haig and took her back to her apartment.

"I never thought you were violent, Chip. I thought of you as, you know, gentle and sensitive and aware."

Like the actor who turned out to be a faggot, I thought.

"And Gordie is so big and strong—"

"Well, Wong Fat showed me how to do a few things. I'm basically a very non-violent person. The only time I ever had to hit anybody was when I was a deputy sheriff in South Carolina."

"A what?"

"It was an honorary position, basically. What it came down to was that I was a bouncer in a, well, in a whorehouse, if you want to know. Sometimes guys would get drunk and pull knives, and I would have to hit 'em upside the head with this club they gave me."

"Upside the head?"

"The local expression."

"You really didn't go to college, did you?"

"I told you. I had to drop out of high school. My parents were sort of high-class con men, although I didn't know it at the time, and they got caught, and they killed themselves, and Upper Valley threw me out a few months before graduation. They were all heart."

She looked at me with those wide eyes. "You've really lived," she said.

"Well, I tend to keep moving."

"I've never met anyone like you before, Chip."

So that's about it. Ferdinand Bell is wearing a strait-jacket, and will spend what's left of his life in a cell with spongy walls. This infuriates Haig, who would like to see the return of public hanging. We still haven't spawned the African gouramis, but John LiCastro finally got the results he wanted, and has a whole twenty-nine-gallon tank full of baby discus fish. Haig went over to see them the other day and says they're doing fine, and that you would have thought LiCastro had fathered them himself, the way he was carrying on.

Gordie McLeod hasn't been heard from. He never turned up to take his stuff out of Kim's apartment, and a couple of days ago I got all his things together and tucked them neatly into the incinerator. Kim said that wasn't very nice, and I said it was too bad.

I ran into Andrea Sugar at the funeral for the Vandivers. She volunteered to teach Kim the art of massage. I sort of sidestepped that one. It was probably just a nice gesture on her part, but she may have had an ulterior motive. I have nothing against lesbians, but I wouldn't want my girl to marry one.

What else? Addison Shivers called the other day. He sent a check around, and Haig returned it, and the old gentleman was displeased.

"I have not earned it, sir," Haig told him. "You hired me to look out for the interests of the late Cyrus Trelawney. I exerted myself enough to justify retaining the advances I received from yourself and Mrs. Vandiver, but I cannot say that I did much for Cyrus Trelawney, certainly not enough to warrant my accepting additional payment."

They talked some more, and an hour later the check arrived again. A messenger brought it and he tried to deliver it downstairs, which confused the girls. No one had ever tried to pay by check before. This particular check was for five thousand dollars, and it was no longer payment for work performed. Instead it was an advance against work to be performed. Because Haig had been rehired to look out for the interests of Cyrus Trelawney. Specifically, he's going to prove that Ferdinand Bell's mother was nutty as a Mars bar, and the killer wasn't Trelawney's son in the first place.

Which means I'll be making a trip to Lyons Falls before very long. I can't say I'm looking forward to it, if you want to know. The heat wave just broke and New York is not a bad place to be.

Haig has been driving me crazy lately. He keeps handing me furniture catalogues and asking me to pick out the kind of bed I like best. He won't give up, he's as single-minded as Cato on the subject of Carthage. So far I've been stubborn and have gone on paying the rent on my furnished room.

Which is probably silly. I've been spending most of my nights on Bethune Street lately, anyway.

One

As I STARTED through the door a man stepped in front of me and stood there like the front four of the Miami Dolphins. I was about six inches taller than him, and he was about forty pounds heavier than I was, and I figured that gave him quite an edge. He was wearing plaid pants and a striped jacket over a sky-blue silk shirt. He had the face of an ex-boxer who had put on a lot of weight without going to fat. His nose had been broken more than once, and his eyes said he was just waiting for someone to try breaking it again. Someone very well might, sooner or later, because people usually get what they want, but I wasn't going to oblige him.

He said, "Read the sign, kid."

There were a lot of signs, so I started reading them aloud. " 'Treasure Chest,' " I said. " 'Girls! Girls! Girls!' 'Topless Stopless Dancing!' 'Come in and see what Fun City is all about!' "

"You read nice," he said.

"Thanks."

"What you call reading with expression," he said. He took a step closer to me. "That particular sign," he said, pointing. "Let's see you read that one."

" 'You must be twenty-one and prove it,' " I intoned.

"Beautiful," he said. "Nice phrasing," he said. "Now get the fuck out of here," he said.

"I'm twenty-one," I lied.

"Sure you are, kid."

"Twenty-two, actually," I embroidered.

"Sure. You wanna try proving it?"

I took my wallet from the inside breast pocket of the sport jacket it was too damned hot to be wearing, and from the wallet I took a green rectangle with Alexander Hamilton's picture on it. I folded the piece of paper in half and put it carefully into his paw.

"My I.D.," I said.

His eyes grew very thoughtful. Actually, you don't have to be twenty-one to drink in New York. You have to be eighteen, which is something I can be with no problem whatsoever. But you have to be twenty-one to go into a place where ladies flash various portions of their anatomy at you. This is rarely a problem for me since I don't generally bother with that kind of place. Not because it does nothing for me to look at ladies with no clothes on, but because it does. I mean, I also don't go browsing in French restaurants when I don't have the price of a meal in my pocket. Why torture yourself, for Pete's sake?

But this was business. Leo Haig had a case and a client, and his client was performing at the Treasure Chest, and since Leo Haig was no more likely to hie himself off to a topless club than I was to enter a monastery, I, Chip Harrison, was elected to serve as Haig's eyes, ears, nose, and throat.

Which explains why I had just tucked a ten-dollar bill into a very large and callused hand.

"Ten bucks?" said the owner of the hand. "For ten

bucks you could go to a massage parlor and get a fancy hand job."

"I'm allergic to hand lotion."

"Huh?"

"I get this horrible rash."

He frowned at me, evidently suspecting I was joking with him. He had a ready wit, all right. "Yeah," he said. "Well, I guess you just proved your age to the satisfaction of the management. One-drink minimum at the bar. Enjoy yourself, tell your friends what a good time you had."

He stepped aside and I moved past him. At least it was cooler inside. The Treasure Chest was located on Seventh Avenue between Forty-Eighth and Forty-Ninth, a block which is basically devoted to porno movies and dirty bookstores and peep shows, but they didn't account for the temperature outside all by themselves. What accounted for it was that it was August and it hadn't rained in weeks and some perverse deity had taken a huge vacuum cleaner and sucked all the air out of Manhattan, leaving nothing behind but soot and sulphur dioxide and carbon monoxide and all the other goodies that only rats and pigeons and cockroaches can breathe with impunity. The sun was out there every day, having a fine old time, and when night finally came it didn't do much good because the buildings just grabbed onto the heat and held it in place until the sun could come up again and start the whole process over. It had been a sensational couple of weeks, let me tell you. Haig's place was air-conditioned, which was nice during the day, but my furnished room two blocks away was not. This made the nights terrible, and it also made it increasingly difficult for me to resist Haig's suggestion that I give up my room and move into his quarters.

"Archie Goodwin lives with Nero Wolfe," Haig said, more than once. "He is a ladies' man in every sense of the word. His cohabitation with Wolfe does not seem to inhibit his pursuit of the fair sex."

There were a lot of answers to this one. Such as mentioning that Wolfe had a brownstone to himself, while Haig had the top two floors of a carriage house in Chelsea, and you can't very well bring home an innocent young thing to the top two floors of a place the bottom two floors of which are occupied by Madam Juana's Puerto Rican cathouse. But what it came down to was that I liked having my own room in my own building, and that I could be very stubborn on the subject, almost as stubborn as Leo Haig himself.

But this is all beside the point, the point being that it was cooler inside the Treasure Chest. There wasn't much more to be said for the place, however. It was dimly lit, which worked to its advantage; what I could see of the furnishings suggested that they were better off the less you could make them out. There was a long bar on the left side as you entered, and behind the bar there was a stage, and on the stage, dancing in the glare of a baby spotlight, was our client, the one and probably only Tulip Willing.

She didn't have any clothes on.

I wasn't prepared for this. I mean, I should have been, and everything, but I somehow wasn't. I had seen Tulip that afternoon and what she'd been wearing then had made her figure overwhelmingly obvious to me. Tight jeans and a tight tee-shirt, both worn over nothing but skin, don't leave you very much up in the air as to what's going on underneath them. And also when you go into a topless-bottomless place you ought to be prepared to be confronted by some skin. That's what people go there for, for Pete's sake. Not because the drinks are terrific.

If it had been somebody else up there I think I could have handled it better. But I'd spent a few hours with Tulip, first at Haig's place and then at her apartment, and I had gotten to know her as a human being, and at the same time I had become enormously turned on by her

personally, and there she was up there, twisting her unbe-
lievable body around to a barrage of loud recorded hard
rock, swinging her breasts and bumping her behind and
strutting around on those long legs that seemed to go all
the way up to her neck, and—

Well, you get the picture.

I took a deep breath of air that was probably just as
polluted as all the other air but seemed better because it
was several degrees cooler. I held the breath for a while,
looking at Tulip, surveying the club, then looking at Tulip
again. She looked a lot better than the club. I let the
breath out and walked over to the bar. There were two
empty stools and I took the closest one. I had the other
empty stool on my right, and on my left I had a man
wearing a dark three-button suit and an expression of
rapt adoration. I wouldn't say that his eyes were on stems
exactly, but they weren't as far back in his head as most
people's are, either. He looked as though he'd leaped out
of a fairy tale, trapped forever halfway between prince
and frog.

"Jesus Christ," he said. He may or may not have
been talking to me. He wasn't looking at me, but I don't
think he'd have bothered looking at me if I had had a live
chicken perched on my shoulder. Nothing was going to
make him take his eyes off Tulip.

"Jesus," he said again, reverently. "Never saw anything
like that. Longest legs I ever seen in my life. Biggest tits I
ever seen in my life. Jesus Christ on wheels."

The barmaid came over. A record ended and another
began without interruption and Tulip went on doing crea-
tive things with her body. The barmaid wasn't a beast
herself, a slim redhead wearing black fishnet tights and a
black body stocking. She had a heart-shaped face and al-
mond eyes, and I got the feeling that she'd spent her last
incarnation as a cat. I started to think of all the different
ways I could rub her to make her purr, but she was shift-
ing her feet impatiently, and I decided that my heart

(among other parts of me) already belonged to Tulip. I didn't want to spread myself too thin.

"Bottle of beer," I said.

I probably would have preferred something like whiskey and water but Tulip had warned me against it. "They make all the whiskey in New Jersey," she had said, "and it all comes out tasting like something you use to take the old finish off furniture, and then they water it, and then they serve it in shot glasses with false bottoms, and then they charge two dollars a drink for it." So I ordered beer, which came straight from the brewery in a nice hygienic bottle. It also cost two dollars a copy, which is a little high for beer, but it was a business expense if there ever was one so I didn't mind.

"Just look at that bush," my companion said. "Soft and blond and gorgeous. I wonder is she gonna do a spread."

I was rather hoping she wasn't. I was feeling rather weird, if you want to know. On the one hand Tulip was turning me on with her dancing and all, and on the other hand I was a little upset about the fact that this was someone whom I knew personally and professionally, and whom I sort of wanted to know a lot better in the future, and here she was not only turning me on but also turning on a whole roomful of creeps, including this particular creep next to me.

"Some clubs they come right up on the bar," the creep said. He must have been about forty-five, and he had a pencil-line moustache that was really pretty offensive. I noticed he was wearing a wedding ring. "Right up on the bar," he went on, and I still didn't know if he was talking to himself or to me or to the man on the other side of him. "Right up on the bar," he said again, "and you give 'em a tip, you slip 'em a buck, and they squat down so you can eat 'em. Go right down the line and everybody who wants to slip 'em a buck and goes ahead and has theirselves a taste."

I thought seriously about hitting him. Half-seriously,

anyway. I'm not particularly good at hitting people, and also he couldn't possibly know that he was talking about the girl I fully intended to be in love with.

"Love to eat this one," he said. "Start at her toes and go clear to her nose. Then go back down again."

He went on like this. He got into some rather clinical anatomical detail and I gave some further thought to hitting him. Or I could do something less extreme. I could tip my beer into his lap, for example.

It was about that time that Tulip noticed I was there. You might have thought she would have spotted me right off, but you have to remember that she was up on an elevated platform with a bright spotlight in her eyes, and that the rest of the room was dark. Also she was off to the side so that I was not standing directly in front of her. But she did notice me now, and for a second I thought she was going to blush a little, but I guess when you do this sort of thing five nights out of seven you lose the capacity to blush, because instead she just flashed me a little half-smile and tipped me a wink and went on dancing.

This time the creep did turn to me. "See that?" he said. "I'll be a son of a bitch. The cunt is crazy about me."

"Huh?"

"She winked at me," he said. "She smiled at me. Some of these broads, they wink at everybody, but that's the first since she came on and she was smiling straight at me. What do you bet she comes over here after her number's done? Man, I'm gonna get lucky tonight. I can feel it."

The thing is, I happened to know that she *would* come over after her number. This wasn't standard; one of the good things about the Treasure Chest, from the dancers' point of view, was that you didn't have to work the bar hustling drinks between numbers. A lot of the clubs worked that way but not Treasure Chest, which was one of the reasons Tulip and her roommate Cherry were willing to work there. But Tulip would come over to meet me because we had arranged it that way, and the last thing I wanted was for her to be confronted by this idiot who was convinced she was crazy about him.

I said, "It was me she smiled at."

His mouth spread in an unpleasant grin. "You? You gotta be kidding."

"She was smiling at me."

"A young punk like you? Don't make me laugh."

"She's my sister," I said.

The grin went away, reversing itself in slow motion.

"My sister," I said again, "and I don't much care for the way you were talking about her."

"Listen," he said, "don't get me wrong. A person, you know, a person'll make remarks—"

"What I was thinking," I said, "is this. I was thinking about taking my knife out of my pocket and cutting you a little. Just a little bit."

"Listen," he said. He got off his stool and edged away from the bar. "Listen," he said, "the last thing I want is trouble."

"Maybe you ought to go home," I said.

"Jesus," he said. He headed for the door but he went most of the way walking backward so that he could keep his eyes on me and make sure my hand didn't come out of my pocket. It's awkward walking like that, and he kept stumbling but not quite falling down, and at the door he turned and fled.

I let out my breath and took my hand out of my pocket. I *had* been holding a knife in it, as a matter of fact. The knife is attached to my key chain. It's an inch long, and it has a half-inch blade. It takes about a minute to get the thing open, and I usually break my fingernails in the attempt. Haig gave it to me once. I've never figured out a use for it, but you never know when something will come in handy. I doubt that it would be the greatest thing in the world for cutting someone open with. You'd be better stabbing him with one of the keys on the chain.

A few seconds later the barmaid turned up. She pointed

to the creep's half-finished drink and the pile of bills next to it. There was a ten in the pile and five or six singles.

"He coming back?"

"Not without a gun."

"Pardon me?"

"He had to leave in a hurry," I said. "He remembered a previous engagement."

"He forgot his change."

"It's for you," I said.

"It is now," she said, scooping up the bills and change. "What do you know."

"No, he meant it for you," I said.

"Oh, yeah?"

"That's what he said."

"What do you know," she said. "I pegged him for El Cheapo. You never know, do you?"

"I guess not," I said.

I sipped at my beer and turned my eyes to Tulip again. Or they turned that way of their own accord, without my having much to do with it. The music was moving toward a climax, and so was half the audience. There was a little rumble of encouragement from my fellow patrons at the bar. You could make out little encouraging show biz phrases like "Show me that pretty pussy, baby," and other tasteful bons mots. Tulip had her head back, her long blond hair swaying from side to side behind her, her large breasts pointing at the ceiling in a way that would have forced Newton to reappraise the Law of Gravity. Her whole body shuddered, and the record hit its final grooves, and she put her hands on her thighs and opened herself to the band of dirty old men, and I told myself to close my eyes, and didn't, and I'm sure it was my imagination but I thought I could see all the way to her throat.

Then the lights went out.

There was quite a bit of applause. Not a roar or anything, but more than a polite ovation. A few of my fellow voyeurs scooped change from the bar and headed for the exit. Most of us stayed where we were. The lights had only stayed off for a second, and another record had already been cued and started up, more of the same monotonous rock. If that's the music of my generation, then I guess I'm a throwback or something.

There was no emcee. I had been sort of afraid of some Neanderthal in a checkered sport coat coming up and telling dirty jokes, but Treasure Chest stuck with the basics; when one girl went off, another one came on. A male voice came over the loudspeaker and said, "That was Miss Tulip Willing, ladies and gentlemen. Let's have a big hand for her now. Tulip Willing." I looked around the club for the ladies he'd been talking about and didn't see a one. I suppose there might have been some at the tables but there certainly weren't any at the bar. Nor, for that matter, did I see anybody I would be inclined to label a gentleman. The audience gave Tulip another weaker round of applause in response to his request, and as it died out he said, "And now, ladies and gentlemen, for your viewing pleasure here at the one and only Treasure Chest, a girl with a chestful of pleasure, a pint-sized lady with queen-sized attributes, the one and only Cherry Bounce."

A pair of curtains parted and Tulip's roommate stepped into the spotlight. I knew she was Tulip's roommate because Tulip had told me so. I was seeing her for the first time and my immediate reaction was to wish that she was *my* roommate.

She was a tremendous contrast to Tulip. Tulip was about six feet tall, give or take an inch, and Cherry was maybe five-two in platform shoes. Tulip's hair was long and blond, Cherry's short and jet black. Tulip was built on a grand scale, reminding you that you can't have too much of a good thing, and Cherry was slim, pointing out that good things come in small packages. The one thing that both of them made you dramatically aware of was that human beings are mammals.

She started to dance. She was naked, incidentally. I guess I didn't mention that. I understand that some of the topless-bottomless clubs start out with the girls wearing something, but Treasure Chest kept it simple. She was naked, and she started dancing, and as grubby as the club was and as much as I disliked the music and atmosphere, I decided there were places I would be less happy to be.

The thing is, she was a pretty good dancer. Tulip had moved around nicely and all, but what she was there for was to show you her body and the dancing was more or less incidental. With Cherry, the whole performance was enhanced by the fact that she could really dance. I don't know if this made any difference to the rest of the crowd but I noticed it and I suppose in some way it heightened my reaction to her.

"That's my roommate," a voice said.

A hand touched my arm. I turned to see Tulip standing beside me. She was wearing clothes, but not the jeans and Beethoven tee-shirt I had seen her in earlier. Now she wore a loose-fitting navy dress. You still got a fair idea of what was lurking beneath the dress, but it was a good deal less obvious.

"Oh, hi," I said.

"Hi yourself. I gather you like my roommate."

"Uh."

"She's pretty, isn't she?"

"Uh, yeah. She's, uh, pretty."

I had been wondering what it would be like when Tulip joined me at the bar. I more or less expected some aggravation from the other males, which was why I had been moved to do the number on the creep with the thin moustache. But evidently men who get off on staring at naked girls are unsettled to be in the company of those very girls, naked or otherwise, and nobody tried to sit in on our conversation. As a matter of fact, the fat man on Tulip's right actually moved a stool away.

"Cherry dances better than I do," she said.

"I thought you danced very well."

"Oh, come on, Chip. You're sweet, but I'm not a dancer. I'm just up there to wiggle my tits and ass at the customers. That's really all it is."

"Well, uh—"

"Cherry's a real dancer. Look how graceful she is." I looked. "The trouble with Cherry is she thinks this is going to lead her to a career in dance. At least I have a realistic attitude. This is an easy way to make a dollar and not much more. Cherry thinks she can make the easy dollar and still use the place as a stepping stone. But she's generally naïve, you know. I take a harder line on reality."

I didn't take any kind of line on reality at that point. What I took was a sip of beer. I did this carefully. I don't know if I'm Mr. Ultra Cool generally, but we had established earlier that whatever cool I normally possessed tended to get lost when Tulip was in the immediate vicinity. So I sipped the beer carefully to avoid gagging on it if she said something disarming.

"Did you like my act, Chip?"

"Yes. Very much."

"Did it turn you on?"

When I didn't answer she said, "I'm not asking because I'm trying to embarrass you. It's just that I'm trying to understand the particular head of the men who come here. You know, like I don't think I would get off watching a man dance around naked. I can't say for certain because I never watched that, although I was reading where a bar at one of the big midwestern colleges has one night a week with male nude dancers, and the college girls go there and really get off on the whole thing. So maybe it would get me excited, but I don't think so. In fact I don't think those college girls would get off after the first few times. Like they would be getting off on the *idea* of it, you know, but after it became a frequent thing it would be boring for them."

"I see what you mean."

"But men really get off looking at naked women, don't they?"

I glanced briefly at the absorbed men on either side of us. "Evidently," I said.

"So I wasn't asking to put you on the spot. But you seem like a sane, healthy guy, and I was wondering how you reacted, because sometimes I'm inclined to think of the general audience here as a batch of perverts, which may or may not be fair of me, and I was wondering how someone like you would react."

I didn't know exactly what to say, because I didn't know what my reaction was, exactly. It had been a turn-on watching her on stage, but then it had been at least as exciting in many ways being with her that afternoon, and it was hard to decide whether I would have reacted to her the same way on stage if she had been a total stranger instead of someone who had already Put Ideas In My Head. In some ways it might have been more of a turn-on if I hadn't known her, especially at the end when she did the spread number. That might have been a turn-off in any context—it was sort of humiliating and demeaning and like that—but how could I tell? If it was a total stranger up there I might have gone ape like all the other card-carrying sex maniacs in the audience.

I tried to judge some of this on the basis of my reaction to Cherry, but that didn't really work either. Because even though I hadn't met her she was already someone I knew by proxy. I had stood in her messy bedroom, I had pictured her in my mind, so it wasn't the same thing.

I was trying to decide how all this worked, and how much of it I wanted to mention to Tulip, when the barmaid turned up and asked if I was ready for another beer. I still had a half-filled glass and there was some left in the

bottle, so what she meant was that I was drinking too
slowly and the joint wasn't in business for its health.

"Chip's with me," Tulip said. "You can let up on the
salesmanship number, Jan."

"Sorry about that," Jan said, and winked. "Didn't
know."

I smiled back, and we sort of carried on a conversation
without getting back to the subject Tulip had raised. She
said that Cherry would join us after the show. It was her
last number, and we could all get the hell out and go
someplace quiet for coffee, and I could ask Cherry
various questions and we could see if we learned anything.

"It should be fascinating," she said. "I've always wanted to see how a detective works."

"Well, you know the questions Haig and I asked you
this afternoon."

"Oh, this is different. I mean, I was the one you were
asking questions. I'll be watching you ask questions of
somebody else and that should make a big difference."

"Maybe."

"Do you know what questions you're going to ask
her?" I was looking for an answer to that one when Cherry's first number ended. There was a round of applause
approximately equal in volume to what Tulip got, and
then another record was cued and Cherry went into her
second and last number.

"Do you know what questions you're going to ask her,
Chip?"

I knew what questions I wanted to ask her. I wanted to
ask her where she'd been all my life. She was putting a
little more sex into her routine on this number, letting her
hands glide upward from the sides of her thighs to her
genuinely impressive breasts, and giving little ooohs and
ahhhs to indicate that she was turning herself on. I don't
know if she was really turning herself on, but I can swear

to you that she was turning me on, and I don't think I was the only person in the audience who was having that reaction.

"Chip?"

"Er," I said. "Uh, with questions and all that. You sort of have to play it by ear."

"I see."

"It's best not to have everything all scheduled in advance like a presidential press conference or something. You sort of see how one question leads to another."

"It sounds fascinating."

I was glad she thought it was fascinating, because what I thought it was was bullshit. The fact of the matter was that I didn't have the foggiest idea what I was going to ask Cherry, or even why. The more I thought about this case of ours, the more I found myself leaning toward the conclusion that Leo Haig had finally done it. He'd finally slipped over that thin line between genius and insanity, because we never should have taken this absurd case in the first place, because—no matter who Tulip Willing happened to be in her spare time—there was absolutely no excuse for investigating a case involving—

"Chip?"

I broke off my reverie and looked at her. "What?"

"Is Cherry a suspect?"

"Everybody's a suspect."

"Because it's hard to believe she could commit murder."

I looked at her, and I decided it wasn't at all hard to believe that she could commit murder. Not directly, but I could see where she could hand out coronaries to half her audience every night just by doing what she was doing.

I said, "There's one thing you have to realize. Everybody's a suspect until proven otherwise."

"I thought everyone's innocent until proved guilty."

"Absolutely. And everybody's suspicious until proved

innocent. That's how it works. Cherry's a suspect, Glenn
Flatt's a suspect. Haskell Henderson's a suspect. So's
his wife. That Danzig is a suspect. Simon What's-his-
name—"

"Barckover."

"Barckover, right." I was supposed to remember things
like Barckover's last name, Haig had told me, just as I
was supposed to be able to repeat all conversations verbatim. If Archie Goodwin can do something, I'm supposed to train myself to do it, too. (Sometimes, let me tell
you, Archie Goodwin gives me a stiff pain.) "Barckover,"
I said again, carefully training my memory. "And Andrew
Merganser—"

"You mean Mallard."

"Well, I knew it was some kind of a duck. The hell
with Archie Goodwin."

"Pardon me?"

"Forget it," I said, a little more savagely than I'd intended. "Mallard and Helen Tattersall and Gus Leemy
and whoever the hell else you mentioned. Everybody—"

"Don't say Gus's name so loud. He's probably in the
club tonight."

"Well, they're all suspects," I said, not so loud this
time around. "And so are other people we haven't even
thought of yet, and one of them's a killer."

"It's still hard to believe."

I let the conversation die there. If she thought that was
hard to believe, she didn't know the half of it. What I
found hard to believe was that Haig and I were involved.
True, Haig was only really happy when he had a murder
case to bother his brain with. And true, this case involved
murder, and not just one murder, not just another
murder, but—

Tulip's fingers closed on my elbow. "Watch now, Chip.
She's coming to the end and she really makes a production out of it. She shows a lot more than I do. Watch!"

So I watched. I mean, maybe you would have looked

up at the ceiling or something. Anything's possible. But what I did, see, is I watched.

Watched as she lowered herself first to her knees, then lay almost full-length, her perfect breasts suspended over the apron of the stage. Watched her straighten up and swing that body around, shaking those breasts from side to side, always perfectly in time to that awful music. Watched as she displayed herself, giving everybody a much longer look than everybody needed. Watched as she put one little hand to her mouth, miming shock at what she had done, straightening up now, drawing herself primly together, her shoulders held back to bring her breasts into the sharpest possible relief.

And heard her sudden gasp.

And saw the bead of blood on her left breast just an inch above the nipple. And watched her hands, moving in awful slow motion, struggling to touch the bead of blood.

And watched her fall, still in slow motion, falling backwards and to her left, falling as only dead things fall, landing at last on the floorboards of the stage with the impact of a gunshot.

I guess my reaction time was pretty good. It didn't seem to be at the time, but the fact remains that I was the first person to vault the bar and leap onto the stage and have a look at Cherry Bounce.

On the other hand, fast or slow, my reaction was wrong. What I should have done was forget the stage entirely and go straight to the door to keep anybody else from going through it. Because I had seen the way Cherry tried to reach her breast and couldn't, and I had seen her fall, and I really didn't have to go up onto the stage to examine her in order to know there was nothing I could do for her.

Haig has always said it's nothing to berate myself for. He says anybody's natural and proper reaction is to establish first of all that the victim is beyond assistance.

Well, that was my reaction, all right, and that was what I established.

Our murderer had just claimed his one hundred twenty-fourth victim, and he had done it right in front of my eyes.

Two

WHEN THE DOORBELL rang that afternoon I was spooning brine shrimp into a tank of *Labeo chrysophekadion.* They were cute little rascals, about half an inch long, and most people who keep tropical fish call them black sharks. Which is sort of weird, because they are not sharks at all and in no sense sharklike, being peaceful types who function as scavengers in an aquarium, picking up on food that other fish have missed. Ours weren't black, either, but white and pink-eyed like Easter bunnies. Leo Haig had come up with a couple of albinos in an earlier spawning, and now he had bred them to each other, and the two hundred or so fish I was presently feeding were the result.

Haig couldn't have been prouder if he had sired them himself. I was kind of pleased with them too, but I couldn't see what they had to do with Being a Resourceful Private Detective, which was what I was supposed to be. When I would bring up the subject Haig would tell me that the aquarium was the universe in microcosm, and the lessons it taught me would ultimately find application in life itself. He says things like that a lot.

Anyway, the doorbell rang. I gave the unblack un-sharks a last spoonful of brine shrimp and went to the door and opened it, and it was good I had left the spoon and the saucer of shrimp in the other room, because otherwise I would have dropped them.

Instead I dropped my jaw. I stood there with my mouth open and stared at her.

There was a whole lot of her to stare at. I'm reasonably tall, although no one would mistake me for a professional basketball player, and she was just about my height. There the resemblance ended. She had long golden hair framing a face with absolutely nothing wrong with it. High cheekbones, wide-set blue eyes the color of a New York sky at sunset, a complexion out of an advertisement for sun-tan lotion, a mouth out of an advertisement for fellatio.

The part below the face was no disappointment, either. She was wearing jeans and a Beethoven-for-President tee-shirt, and she wasn't wearing anything under the tee-shirt, and I really couldn't find anything about her body to object to. I suppose a purist might argue that her legs were a little too long and her breasts were a little too large. Somehow this didn't bother me a bit.

For a while she watched me stare at her. She gave a sort of half-smile, which suggested that she was used to this reaction but liked it all the same, and then she said, "Mr. Haig?"

"No."

"Pardon me?"

"I'm not him. I mean, I'm me. Uh."

"Perhaps I came at a bad time."

"Oh, no," I said. "You came at a wonderful time. I mean you can come anytime you want to. I mean. Uh."

"Is this Leo Haig's residence?"

"Yes."

"Leo Haig the detective?"

He's Leo Haig the detective all right, but that's not a phrase that rolls off most people's tongues. As a matter of fact he's pretty close to being an unknown, which is not the way he wants it, and one of the main reasons he hired me as his assistant. A chief function of mine is to write up his cases—at least the ones that turn out triumphant—so that the world will know about him. If it weren't for Dr. Watson, he says, who would have heard of Sherlock Holmes? If Archie Goodwin never sat down at a typewriter, who would be aware of Nero Wolfe? Anyway, that's why he hired me, to make Leo Haig The Detective a household phrase, and that's how come you get to read all this.

"Leo Haig the detective," I agreed.

"Then I came to the right place," she said.

"Oh, definitely. No question about it. You came to the right place."

"Are you all right?"

"Oh, sure. I'm terrific."

"May I come in?"

"Oh, sure. Right. Great idea."

She gave me an odd look, which I certainly deserved, and I stood aside and she came in and I closed the door. I led her into the office which Haig and I share. There's a huge old partner's desk, which we also share, although I don't really have much use for my side of it. I pointed to a chair for her, and when she sat down I swiveled my desk chair around and sat in it and looked at her some more. She was a little less intimidating when she was sitting down. There was still just as much of her but the overall effect was not quite so awesome.

"Is Mr. Haig in?"

"He's upstairs," I said. "He's playing with his fish."

"Playing with them?"

"Sort of. I'm his assistant. My name is Harrison. Chip Harrison."

"Mine is Tulip."

"Oh."

"Tulip Willing."

"It certainly is," I said.

"Pardon me?"

I was really having a difficult time getting my brain in gear. I took a deep breath and tried again. I said, "You wanted to see Mr. Haig?"

"That's right. I want to hire him."

"I see."

"There's a matter that I want him to investigate."

"I see," I said again. "Could you tell me something about the matter?"

"Well—"

"I'm his assistant," I said. "His confidential assistant."

"Aren't you young to be a detective?"

I'm not exactly a detective. I mean I don't have a license or anything. But I didn't see any point in telling her that. What I wanted to say was that you don't have to be all that old to spoon brine shrimp into a fish tank, but I didn't say that either. I said, "If you could give me some idea—"

"Of course." She leaned forward and I took another quick look at Beethoven's eyebrows. Her breasts had fantastic stage presence. It was hard not to stare at them, and you sort of got the feeling they were staring back.

"It's a murder case," she said.

I don't know if my heartbeat actually quickened, because it had been operating faster than normal ever since I opened the door and took my first look at her. But I certainly did get excited. I mean, people don't generally turn up on our doorstep wanting us to investigate a murder. But it happens all the time in books, and that's the kind of detective Haig wants to be, the kind you read about in mystery novels.

I said, "A homicide."

"Not exactly."

"I thought you said a murder."

She nodded. "But homicide means that a person has been killed, doesn't it?"

"I think so."

"Well, this is murder. But it's not homicide."

"I don't think I understand."

She put her hand to her mouth and nibbled thoughtfully at a cuticle. If she ever ran out of cuticles to nibble I decided I'd gladly lend her one of mine. Or any other part of me that interested her. "It's hard to say this," she said.

I waited her out.

"I had to come to Leo Haig," she said eventually. "I couldn't go to the police. I never even considered going to the police. Even if they didn't actually laugh at me there's no way they would bother investigating. So I had to go to a private detective, and I couldn't go to an ordinary private detective. It has to be Leo Haig."

That's the kind of thing you want every client to say, but Tulip Willing was the first one ever to say it.

"I guess the only way to say it is to come right out with it," she said. "Someone murdered my tropical fish. I want Leo Haig to catch the killer."

I climbed a flight of stairs to the fourth floor, where Haig was playing with his fish. There are tanks in all the rooms on the third floor, but on the fourth floor there are nothing but tanks, rows and rows of them. I found Haig glowering at a school of cichlids from Lake Tanganyika. They had set him back about fifty bucks a fish, which is a lot, and no one had yet induced them to spawn in captivity. Haig intended to be the first, and thus far the fish had shown no sign of preparing to cooperate.

"There's an element missing," he said. "Maybe the rockwork should be extended. Maybe they're accustomed to spawning in caves. Maybe they want less light."

"Maybe they're all boys," I suggested.

"Phooey. There are eight of them. With six fish one is

mathematically certain of having a pair. That is to say that the certainty is in excess of ninety-five percent. With eight the certainty is that much greater."

"Unless the cunning Africans only ship one sex."

He looked at me. "You have a devious mind," he said. "It will be an asset professionally."

"I have a devious mind," I agreed. "You have a client."

"Oh?"

"A beautiful young woman," I said.

"Trust you to notice that."

"I wouldn't trust anyone who didn't notice it. Her name is Tulip Willing."

"Indeed."

"She wants you to investigate a murder and trap a killer."

He bounced to his feet, and the African cichlids no longer meant a thing to him. He's about five feet tall and built like a beachball, with a neatly trimmed little black goatee and head of wiry black hair. He likes to touch the beard, and he started doing it now.

"A homicide," he said.

I didn't make the distinction between murder and homicide. "She says only Leo Haig can help her," I went on. "She hasn't been to the police. She needs a private detective, and you're the only man on earth who can possibly do the job for her."

"She honestly said that?"

"Her very words."

"Remarkable."

"She's in the office. I told her I was sure you would want to talk to her yourself."

"Of course I want to talk to her." He was on his way to the stairs and even though his legs are about half the length of mine I had to hustle to catch up with him.

"One thing you ought to know before you talk to her," I said.

"Oh?"

"About the victims."

He was positively beaming. "Victims? Plural? More than one victim?"

"Over a hundred of them."

He stared, and his face showed a struggle between delight and disbelief. He really wanted it to be a murder case with a hundred victims, and at the same time he was beginning to read the whole number as a put-on.

"One thing you ought to know," I said. "The victims aren't people. They're fish."

He said, "Miss Willing? I'm Leo Haig. I believe you've already met my assistant, Mr. Harrison."

"Yes, I have."

"I understand some fishes of yours were murdered. Could you give me some specific information on the crime?"

I had to hand it to him. I don't know what kind of reaction I'd been hoping for but it wasn't what I got. I had sent him up in a pretty rotten way, when you stop to think of it, and he was returning the favor by treating Tulip Willing and her massacred fish like the crime of the century. Instead of telling me to get rid of her, either by showing her the door or calling the men in the white coats, he was going to take his time getting her whole story, and I was going to have to write it all down in my notebook. I made it game, set and match to him.

So I sat there with my notebook on my side of the desk, and Haig sat on his side of the desk and played with a pipe, and Tulip Willing sat in the chair I'd put her in originally. I sensed that the three of us were going to waste an hour or so of each other's time. I didn't really mind. I hadn't been doing anything that sensational with my time in the first place, and I couldn't think of anyone I'd rather waste it with. (Than Tulip, I mean. Wasting time with Haig is something I do almost every day of my life. It's enjoyable, but there's nothing all that exotic about it.)

"There are many ways an entire tank of fishes can be destroyed at once," he was saying. He has this professorial air that he likes to use. "Certain diseases strike with the rapidity and force of the Black Death, wiping out a whole fish population overnight. Air pollution, paint fumes, these can cause annihilation on an extraordinary scale."

"Mr. Haig—"

"Occasionally equipment malfunctions. A thermostat may go haywire, boiling the inhabitants of an aquarium. On the other hand, a heater may burn out and the resulting drop in temperature may prove fatal, although this is more likely to be a gradual matter. In other situations—"

"Mr. Haig, I'm not an idiot."

"I didn't mean to imply that you were."

"I'm familiar with the ways fishes can die. Naturally you would assume that the death was accidental. I made the same assumption myself. I ruled out the possibilities of natural and accidental death."

"Indeed."

"The fish were poisoned."

He took his pipe apart. He's given up smoking them because they burn his tongue, but he likes to fiddle with them. He bought the pipes originally because he thought they might be a good character tag and he knows that great detectives have to have charming idiosyncracies. He keeps trying on idiosyncracies looking for one that will fit. I've wanted to tell him that he's odd enough all by himself, but I can't think of an acceptable way to phrase it.

I waited for him to ask how she knew the fish were poisoned. Instead he said, "What sort of fish? A community tank, I suppose? Mollies and swordtails and the like?"

"No. I don't have a community tank. These were Scats."

"Ah. *Scatophagus argus.*"

"These were *Scatophagus tetracanthus,* actually."

"Indeed." He seemed impressed. He thinks everybody should know the Latin name of everything, and I get a lecture to that effect on the average of once every three days. "The *tetracanthus* are imported less often. And most retailers sell them as *argus* because few hobbyists know the difference. These were definitely *tetracanthus,* you say?"

"Yes."

"How many did you have?"

"One hundred twenty-three."

"Indeed. You must be rather fond of the species. You must also have had an extremely large tank."

"It's a twenty-nine gallon tank."

He frowned. "Good heavens," he said. "You must have stacked them like cordwood."

"All but two were fry. They had plenty of room."

"Fry?" His eyebrows went up, first at the word she used, then at the implications. Most people who keep fish, and certainly most people who look anything like Tulip Willing, call baby fish baby fish. She called them fry. Then, when the whole idea sank in, he leaned forward and waggled a finger at her. "Impossible," he said.

"What's impossible?"

"Neither of the *Scatophagus* species has ever spawned in captivity."

"I spawned them. And it's been done before."

"By Rachow, yes. But he had an accident and lost the lot, and he was never able to repeat the procedure. Nor has anyone else had any success."

"I had success," she said.

"Impossible," he said again. "No one but Rachow ever induced the little devils to spawn. And he was working with *argus,* not *tetracanthus.*" He paused abruptly and his eyes crawled upward and examined the ceiling. "Wait just one moment," he said. "Just one moment."

I looked at Tulip and watched her wait one moment. There was the hint of a private smile on her lips.

"There *was* a spawning," he said finally. "Not of *argus*. Of *tetracanthus*. It was reported in *Copeia* a year ago. The fish spawned but a fungus destroyed the spawn before they hatched. The author was—let me think. Wolinski. T. J. Wolinski. He's done other articles for aquarist publications."

"Not he," Tulip said.

"Pardon me?"

She was really smiling now. "Not *he*," she repeated. "She. Me, actually. They spawned a second time and I used a fungicide and it worked. I got a seventy percent hatch. One hundred twenty-one fry, and they were doing beautifully. I left the parent fish with them."

"Your name is Willing. Tulip Willing."

"That's a stage name."

"And your real name is—"

"Thelma Wolinski."

Haig was on his feet, his jaw set firmly beneath the neat little beard. "T. J. Wolinski," he said, with something verging on reverence. "T. J. Wolinski. Extraordinary. And some creature poisoned your scats? Good heavens. You'll pardon me, I hope, for treating you like a witling. I never would have guessed—well, that's by the way. Some villain poisoned your fishes, did he? Well, we shall get to the bottom of this. And I shall have his head, madam. Rest assured of that. I shall have his head."

So the whole thing was out of control. It was my fault, and although there was a certain amount of thrill in the idea of being on a case, I can't say I was anywhere near as thrilled as Haig was.

Well, I'd asked for it. I'd been baiting him, never figuring he'd bite, and now he was hooked right through the gills.

Three

IT MUST HAVE been around three in the afternoon when
Tulip Willing rang the doorbell. It was close to five when
Haig was finished asking questions. He went over everything and enabled me to fill a great many pages in my notebook with facts that would probably turn out to be unimportant. It's his theory that there is no such thing as an
absolutely inconsequential fact. (The first time he told me
this I replied that in 1938 the state of Wyoming produced
one-third of a pound of dry edible beans for every man,
woman, and child in the nation. He agreed that it was
certainly hard to see how that could turn out to be consequential, but he wasn't going to rule out the possibility
entirely.)

I'm taking matters into my own hands and leaving out
some items that never did seem to have any more bearing
on the case than the fascinating fact about dry edible
beans. That still leaves plenty of bits and pieces to report
from Haig's questioning of Tulip.

Item: The fish had died four days ago, on a Saturday.

Tulip had come home at four Saturday morning after a
long night at the Treasure Chest, where she had been
working for five months, having been previously employed in a similar capacity at similar nightspots, among
them Tippler's Cove and Shake It Or Leave It. (I am not
making any of this up.) She came home, exhausted and
ready for bed, and she went over to say goodnight to the
fish, and they were all floating on the top, which is never
a sign of radiant good health. When she was done being
hysterical she did something intelligent. She removed the
two parent fish and preserved them in jars of rubbing alcohol in case an autopsy should ultimately be indicated,
and she took a sample of the water in the tank and another sample of water from another aquarium as a control. These she took to a chemical laboratory on Varick
Street for scientific analysis, and Monday the laboratory
called her and informed her that the sample from the tank
of scats contained strychnine, which is no better for fish
than it is for people. There was enough strychnine present
to kill any human being who drank a glass of the water,
but then not that many people go around drinking out of
aquariums, and I'd venture to say that those who do are
asking for it.

Item: She assumed that the murder of the scats was
motivated not by a specific hatred of the fish themselves
but by hatred of their owner. Someone was trying to upset
her or punish her or terrify her by killing her pets. This
was, as far as she could determine, the first instance of
hostile behavior to be directed at her, aside from the
usual obscene telephone calls she received intermittently.
The phone calls had not increased in frequency lately,
and in fact she hadn't heard from one of the callers in a
long time and was a little concerned that something might
have happened to him. She said that he had a very unusual approach, but she didn't go into detail.

Item: The scats had been in fine fettle when she left the
apartment Friday afternoon at two o'clock. The strych-

nine would presumably have worked instantly upon its introduction into the aquarium, but she had been unable to determine just how long the fish had been dead. So somewhere between two Friday afternoon and four Saturday morning the villain had entered her apartment and had done the dirty deed.

Item: While I don't guess there was anybody who could properly be labeled a suspect at this stage of the game, the following people were sufficiently a part of Tulip's life to find their way into my notebook:

Cherry Bounce. I know, I know, but if you can accept a name like Tulip Willing, why be put off by Cherry Bounce? Cherry and Tulip had been roommates for just about five months. They met when Tulip went to work at Treasure Chest, where Cherry had already been employed. Tulip had recently broken up with her boyfriend and needed a place to live, and Cherry had recently broken up with a boyfriend of her own and needed someone to share her rent. The two of them had been getting along well enough, although they didn't have much in common outside of their profession. Tulip characterized her as flighty, flitting from one pursuit to another, health foods to astrology to bio-feedback. As far as the fish were concerned, Cherry thought they were cute. Cherry's name off-stage was Mabel Abramowicz, so I guess she would have had to change it to something.

Glenn Flatt. Tulip's ex-husband, whom she had met and married four years ago when she was picking up a doctorate in marine biology at the University of Miami, and whom she had divorced two years later. I could understand why she had divorced him—she wanted her own name back. No one built like Tulip could be happy with Flatt for a surname. (According to her, she left her husband because he was a compulsive gambler. If you said *Good Morning* to him he'd lay odds that it wasn't. This would have been all right if he won, but he evidently didn't.) Flatt lived on Long Island where he was employed as a research biochemist by a pharmaceutical manufacturer. This fact prompted Haig and me to glance meaningfully at each other—Flatt's job would undoubtedly give him access to strychnine. On the other hand, it would probably give him just as good access to any number of nondetectable vehicles for ichthyicide. Flatt and Tulip were "very good friends now," she said, and they occasionally had dinner or drinks together, and now and then he turned up at the club to catch her act. Flatt had never remarried.

Haskell Henderson. Tulip's current boyfriend and the owner of a half-dozen local health food stores. They had been seeing each other for almost three months. Henderson would spend two or three afternoons a week at Tulip's apartment. I don't guess he devoted much of this time to staring at the fish. When he wasn't keeping company with Tulip or minding the stores he was in Closter, New Jersey, where he shared a cozy little house with . . .

Mrs. Haskell Henderson. Tulip had never met Mrs. H. H., and had no way of knowing whether or not the woman even knew of her existence, but anyone with that sound a reason for wanting unpleasant things to happen to Tulip certainly deserved an entry in my notebook. The entry was pretty much limited to her name because Henderson evidently didn't talk about his wife very much.

Simon Barckover. Tulip's agent, and Cherry's agent too, for that matter. His relationship with both clients was strictly professional, but he got in the notebook because he was the only person around who might have a specific grudge against the fish. He thought Tulip was genuinely talented and that she had a future in show business if she applied herself. Tulip admitted that he might be right but she wasn't interested. The topless dancing paid well and was generally undemanding, leaving her free to concentrate on her chief interest, which was ichthyology. Barckover had told her on several occasions that the damn fish were standing in the way of her career and that he would like to flush the lot of them down the toilet. She couldn't believe he would actually do it, but then she couldn't believe anybody would want to poison the scats, so he got in the notebook.

Leonard Danzig. Cherry's boyfriend. She had been dating him for a month or so, although she continued to see other men as well. He got on the list because Tulip couldn't stand him, describing him charitably as "a kind of a slimy character." I gather she disliked him because he kept trying to get her into bed, either just with him or with Cherry along for threesies. Tulip was spectacularly uninterested in either prospect. No one seemed to know what Danzig did for a living, but Tulip guessed it was at least somewhat criminal. Cherry had met him at the club. He always seemed to have a lot of money, and if he worked at all he didn't seem to have any set hours. His feelings toward the fish were unknown, except that he had once remarked that it would "take a hell of a lot of the bastards to make a decent meal."

Helen Tattersall. All that Tulip knew about Mrs. Tattersall was that she lived in the apartment immediately below hers and was a pain in the ass, constantly complaining about noise, even when no noise whatsoever was emanating from the apartment. She had on one occasion reported Tulip and Cherry to the police, alleging that the two were running a bordello in their apartment. Tulip wasn't sure whether the woman actually believed this or was just making a nuisance of herself. "She's the sort of frustrated old bitch who might poison somebody's pets just out of meanness," Tulip said.

Andrew Mallard. Tulip's former boyfriend, the one she was living with before she got together with Cherry. He was an advertising account executive, recently divorced, and evidently rather strange. He had moved in with Tulip; then, when they broke up, she had moved out and let him keep the apartment because the idea of actually going out and finding a place of his own gave him anxiety attacks. He still called her occasionally when he was drunk, generally at an hour when he should have known she was sleeping. Now and then he caught her act at Treasure Chest, always tipping heavily in order to get a ringside table, always attending by himself, always staring at her breasts as if hypnotized, and never speaking a word to her. Every once in a while she got flowers delivered backstage with no note enclosed—though never on nights when he was in the audience—and she sort of assumed he was the source. He had liked the fish very much while they lived together, but she figured he was a possible suspect because murdering fish was clearly an insane act, and Andrew Mallard was hardly playing with a full deck himself.

Gus Leemy. He owned the Treasure Chest. At least he was the owner of record, but Tulip had the impression that the club was a Mafia joint of one sort or another and that Leemy was fronting for the real owners. She wasn't even sure he knew she had fish and couldn't imagine why he would have anything against her or them. I think she brought his name up because she didn't like him.

So I had those nine names in my notebook, and there was a fourteen-hour period of time during which any of them could have gone to Tulip's apartment and done something fishy to her fish. Possibly any or all of them could account for their time, but Tulip didn't know about it. And possibly one of the fourteen million other residents of the New York metropolitan area was the killer. I mean, if you're going to do something as fundamentally insane as feeding strychnine to tropical fish, they wouldn't have to be the fish of someone you know, would they? If you're going to be a lunatic about it, one fish tank is as good as another.

A little before five Haig leaned back in his chair and put his feet on top of his desk. I've tried to break him of this habit but it's impossible. Tulip and I sat there respectfully and studied the soles of his shoes while the great man searched for meaning in the ceiling.

Without opening his eyes he said, "Chip."

"Sir."

"I need your eyes and ears and legs. The scene of the crime must be examined. You will go with Miss Wolinski to her apartment. Miss Wolinski? I assume that will be convenient?"

Tulip agreed that it would be. She had a dinner date at eight-thirty and a performance at ten o'clock but she was free until then.

"Satisfactory," Haig said. He swung his feet down from the desk. "You will visit Miss Wolinski's apartment. You will be guided by your intelligence and intuition and experience. You will then return here to report."

"If that's all—" Tulip said.

Haig had turned to look at the Rasboras. They're little pinkish fish with dark triangles on their sides, and Haig has a ten-gallon tank of them directly behind his desk chair at eye level. He's apt to turn around and study them in the middle of a conversation. This time, though, his attention to the Rasboras was a sign that the conversation was over.

The hell it was. I said, "I'll make out a receipt for Miss Wolinski for her retainer."

Haig said, "Retainer?"

Tulip said, "Oh, of course. You'll be wanting a retainer, won't you?"

I don't know what he'd do without me. I swear I don't. The trouble is, Haig keeps forgetting that if you're going to be a detective for a living you ought to do your best to make a living out of it. For most of his life he lived in two ratty rooms in the Bronx, breeding tropical fish and trucking plastic bags around to pet shops, peddling his little babies for a nickel here and a dime there. All the while he read every mystery and detective story ever published, and then his uncle died and left him a fortune, and he bought this house and let Madam Juana keep the lower two floors and set up shop as a detective, which is terrific, no question about it. But his capital isn't really enough to keep us together, so when we get a case it's a good idea for us to get money out of it, and here he was going to let Tulip hire us without paying anything.

"Of course," Tulip said again, digging in her bag for a checkbook. When she came up with it I uncapped a pen and handed it to her. She started to make out the check, then looked up to ask the amount.

"Five hundred is standard," I said.

Haig almost fainted. I think he would have asked her for fifty bucks and let her talk him down. But the five hundred didn't phase our client for a second. I guess all she had to be told was that it was standard. She finished making out the check and passed it to me, and I wrote out a receipt on a sheet from my notebook and gave it to Haig for him to sign. He wrote his name with a flourish, as usual. Imagine what he could do if he had more than seven letters to work with.

"I intend to earn this," he said, holding the check in his pudgy little hand. "You'll receive full value for your money, Miss Wolinski. In a sense, you might say your troubles are over."

And ours are just beginning, I thought. But then Tulip got to her feet, sort of uncoiling from her chair like a trained cobra responding to a flute, and I decided that any case that forced me to go to her apartment with her couldn't possibly be all bad.

"He's quite a man," Tulip said. "It must be very inspiring to work for someone like Leo Haig."

"It's all of that," I agreed. "And do I call you Miss Wolinski or Miss Willing?"

"Call me Tulip. And may I call you Chip?"

Call me darling, I thought. "Sure," I said. "Call me Chip."

"What's that a nickname for?"

"It's the only name I've got," I said, which is certainly true now. I had started life as Leigh Harvey Harrison, both Leigh and Harvey being proper names in my less-than-proper family, but in the fall of '63 my parents decided that wouldn't do at all, and I've been Chip ever since. I understand there are a lot of Jews named Arthur who were known to the world as Adolph until sometime in the '30s.

We talked a little more about Haig, and then the cab dropped us at her building, a high-rise on the corner of 54th and Eighth. The lobby reminded you a little of an airline terminal. "It's not exactly overflowing with warmth and charm," Tulip said. "It's sort of sterile, isn't it? Before I moved here I lived in a brownstone in the Village. I really liked that apartment and I would have kept it except it would have meant keeping Andrew, too. This place has all the character of an office building, but on the other hand the elevators are fast and there's plenty of closet space and there aren't any cockroaches. My other place was crawling with them, and of course I couldn't spray because of the fish."

"Couldn't you try trapping them and feeding them to the fish?"

"Is that what Leo Haig does?"

"No, it just occurred to me. What we do, Wong Fat puts some kind of crystals in the corners of the kitchen, and the roaches eat it and die. They come from miles around to do themselves in. I don't know what Wong does with them. I suppose he throws them out." I thought for a moment. "I *hope* he throws them out."

On the elevator she told me another bad feature of the building. "There are prostitutes living here," she said. "I wouldn't mind if they just lived here. They also work here, and you can't imagine what that's like."

I could imagine.

"There are these men coming and going all the time,"

she said, which was probably true in more ways than she meant. "And they see a girl in the building, any girl, and they take it for granted that you're in the business yourself. It's very unpleasant."

"I'm sure it is."

"As if I didn't get enough of that aggravation at the club. Just because a girl displays her body men tend to assume that it's for sale. I mean, I don't kid myself, Chip. Cherry thinks she's an artist, she takes singing lessons and dancing lessons, the whole bit. She's waiting to be discovered. I think she's a little bit whacky. Men don't come to watch me because I'm such a sensational dancer. I'm a pretty rotten dancer, as a matter of fact. They come to see me and they pay two dollars a drink for watered rotgut because they enjoy looking at my tits."

"Oh."

"That's all it is, really. Tits."

"Uh."

"If it weren't for my tits," she said, "I'd be teaching high school biology."

I couldn't think of anything to say to that one, but as it turned out I didn't have to because we had reached her door and she was fishing in her purse for the key. She got it out, then rang the bell. "In case Cherry's home," she explained. We stood around for a while, long enough for her to conclude that Cherry wasn't home, and then she opened the door and walked inside. I didn't follow her, and she asked me what I was waiting out in the hall for.

"Just a minute," I said. I dropped to one knee and examined the lock. There were two cylinders but one was just a blind to confuse burglars. The other was a Rabson, a good one, and I couldn't find any scratches on the cylinder or on the bolt. That didn't necessarily mean the killer had had a key; if he had a good set of picks and knew how to use them he could open the lock without leaving evidence behind. "Of the nine people you mentioned before," I said, "how many have keys?"

"Oh. He got in with a key?"

"It's possible."

"So you want to know who has keys?"

I got out my notebook and went through the nine of them. Cherry had a key, of course, it being her apartment. Glenn Flatt, the ex-husband, had been to the apartment a few times but had never been given a key. Haskell Henderson, the current boyfriend, had a key. Mrs. Haskell Henderson hadn't been given one, but she could have swiped or duplicated her husband's, assuming she knew anything about it. Leonard Danzig had a key, as did any number of past and present boyfriends of Cherry's. Helen Tattersall, the neighbor, didn't, but there was always the possibility that she had access to the building's master key. There was a chainbolt on the inside of the door, but when nobody was home it wasn't locked and the master key would open the other lock.

Andrew Mallard did not have a key and had never been to the apartment. Maybe Tulip was afraid that if she ever let him in she would have to move again. Simon Barckover might well have a key, since Cherry gave them out rather indiscriminately, but Tulip wasn't sure one way or the other. And Gus Leemy probably didn't have a key.

"But anybody *could* have one easily enough," Tulip said. "The thing about Cherry, she tends to misplace things. Especially keys. I think she's borrowed my key four times in the past five months to have duplicates made, and she always has several made at a time. Anyone could have borrowed her key to have a duplicate made, and if he didn't put it back when he was done she would just assume she lost it again. It's sort of a nuisance."

"It must be."

"And then sometimes she sets the latch and doesn't bother taking a key, and it's even possible that she came back here Friday night to change or something and left the door unlocked, and then came back again and locked it. So anybody at all could have walked in. Just some or-

dinary prowler, trying doors and finding this one unlocked."

"Just some ordinary prowler looking to find an open
apartment with a fish tank he could pour strychnine
into?"

"Oh."

"I think we can rule out the Ordinary Prowler theory."

"I guess you're right. I'm not thinking very clearly."
She dropped into a chair, then bounced back up again.
And *bounced* is precisely the word to fit the act. She
bounced, and her breasts bounced, and I'd just about
reached the point where I was able to look at her without
being very close to drooling, and that little bounce she did
put me right back at square one again.

"I'm a terrible hostess," she said. "I didn't offer you a
drink. You'll have a drink, won't you?"

"If you're having one."

"I am, but what does that have to do with it? What
would you like?"

I tried not to look at the front of her tee-shirt. "I'll
have a glass of milk," I said.

"Gee, I don't think we've got any."

"That's all right," I said. "I don't even like milk."

"Then why did you ask for it?"

"I don't know," I said. "The words just came out that
way. I'll have whatever you're having."

"Great. I'm having bourbon and yogurt. Do you want
yours on the rocks or straight up?"

"I guess on the rocks. What's so funny?"

But she didn't answer. She was too busy laughing. Most
women tend to giggle, which can be pleasant enough, but
Tulip put her head back and gave out with a full-scale
belly laugh, and it really sounded great. While she stood
there laughing her head off I rewound some mental recording tape and played back the conversation, and I
said, "Oh."

"Bourbon and yogurt!"

"Very funny," I said.

"On the *rocks!*"

She actually slapped her thigh. You hear about people doing that but I didn't think anybody really did. She laughed her head off and slapped her thigh.

"I guess I got distracted," I said.

"A glass of *milk!*"

"Look, Miss Wolinski—"

"Oh, Chip, I'm sorry." She came to me and put her hand on my arm. I didn't want to react because I wasn't feeling sexy, I was feeling mad, but what I wanted didn't have very much to do with it. She put her hand on my arm, and it was as if I'd stuck my big toe into an electrical outlet.

"I was just teasing you a little," she said.

"I hope you never tease me a lot. I don't think I could handle it."

"How about a beer?"

"Great."

I told her I'd like to look around the apartment while she poured the beer. She said that was fine. There was the living room, fairly good sized, and there were two small bedrooms, each furnished with a platform bed and a night table and a chest of drawers. The first bedroom I entered looked like an ad for disaster insurance. The bed was unmade, assuming it had ever been made to begin with, and there was so much underwear scattered around that it was hard to find the floor. I sort of hoped that was Cherry's bedroom because I didn't want to learn that our client was that much of a slob. When I looked in the other bedroom I established that it was Tulip's. It was immaculate, and there was a fish tank in it.

I sat on the edge of the bed and looked in the tank. There was a glass divider in the middle and an African Gourami on each side of it.

"Here's your beer," she said from the doorway. "Hey, did anything happen to those guys?"

There was real alarm in her voice. "They're fine," I said. "What species are they? I mean I know they're *Ctenapoma* but I don't recognize the species."

"*Ctenapoma fasciolatum.* I don't suppose he's started building a bubble nest, has he?" She came over and looked over my shoulder. "He hasn't, darn it. That's the third female I've had in there with him. He killed the other two. I used the divider when I put the second female in, and I waited until he had a nest built, and I figured that was a clear signal that he was madly and passionately in love, so I lifted out the divider and the little bastard charged right at her and killed her." She sat down on the bed next to me and gave me a glass of beer. I took a long drink of it. "So I don't really know what to do," she went on. "This time he's not even building a nest. He just ignores the poor old girl completely. And you can see she's ready to spawn. She's positively bursting with eggs, the little angel. I must be doing something wrong."

"Mr. Haig might be able to tell you."

"Has he bred *fasciolatum*?"

"No, but he's had results with some of the other *Ctenapoma* species. He has some secrets."

"Do you think he'd tell me?"

"If you told him how you managed the scats."

She grinned, then suddenly lost the grin when she remembered what had happened to the scats. "I didn't even show you that tank," she said. "Or did you find it yourself? It's in the living room."

I hadn't noticed it on my way through, so the two of us went back to look at it. There wasn't really a hell of a lot to look at. When you've seen one aquarium you've seen them all, when all they contain is water. This particular water may have had enough strychnine in it to kill a lot of people, but it certainly looked innocuous enough.

"I siphoned out the dead fry," she said. "Then I was going to get rid of the rest of the water, but is it safe to pour it down the sink? There's poison in it, after all, and I don't want to wipe out half of Manhattan."

"It would just go in the sewers," I said. "It would probably get completely diluted. But if you don't want to risk it I guess you can let the water evaporate and then throw out the tank."

"Throw out the tank?"

"Well, I don't know much about strychnine. Would it evaporate along with the water? And meanwhile there's the chance someone would drink out of the aquarium. I admit it's not much of a chance, but why take it?"

"Maybe we'd better flush it down the toilet," she said. "I can find out later how to clean the tank so that it's usable again. It won't be destroying evidence, will it? I have the lab report and everything."

I assured her that it wouldn't be destroying evidence, and the two of us lugged the tank into the bathroom and emptied it down the toilet. And yes, it did take two of us, and if she hadn't been a big strong lady it would have taken three of us, because water is a lot heavier than you might think. After it was empty Tulip sloshed water into it from a bucket and rinsed it out a few times, and then she put it in a closet where it could rest until she found out how to cleanse it thoroughly.

I couldn't see how we had destroyed any evidence, but what I didn't bother to tell her was that evidence didn't make much difference. Granted that she wanted to know who had killed her fish, but with all the evidence in the world we weren't going to take whoever it was to court and prosecute him. I didn't mention this because it might lead her to wonder why she was spending good money to track the villain down, and I didn't want this thought to cross her mind until her check cleared.

When the tank was tucked away in the closet, Tulip heaved a sigh. "That's a lot of exercise," she said. "Not like dancing all night, but all that lifting and toting. I used muscles I don't normally have any call for. Look, I'm all sweated up."

She didn't have to tell me to look. I was already looking. Her tee-shirt was damp now and Beethoven was plastered all over her. I've been apt to envy a lot of people in the course of my young life, but this was the first time I had ever been jealous of a dead composer.

"Just look at me," she said, lifting her arms to show the circles of perspiration beneath them, and then she saw that I was indeed looking at her, and she managed to read the expression on my face, which I guess you didn't have to be a genius to read anyhow, and then she laughed again. "Bourbon and yogurt! On the *rocks!*"

I told her to stop it.

And that was about that. She had a dinner date, and she was going to have to shower and change, but we had time to sit around and talk for a while. She told me a little about some of the names in my notebook but nothing worth recording, or even worth training my memory to retain. She also told me a great deal about herself—how someone had given her a couple of baby guppies when she was eleven years old, and how she had really gotten into fish in a big way until her parents' house was hip-deep in fish tanks, and how in high school she had grown profoundly interested in biology and genetics, and how someday she hoped to make an important contribution to ichthyological knowledge. In the meantime she was dancing naked, making decent money, saving as much of it as she could, and not at all certain where her career should go from here.

"I suppose I could get some sort of institutional job," she said. "At a public aquarium, or preparing specimens for museum collections. I have good qualifications. But I haven't found an opening that turns me on at all, and I'd rather prefer to live in New York, and I can't see myself clerking in some place like Aquarium Stock Company for two-fifty an hour."

There was a lot of conversation which I didn't bother reporting to Haig and won't bother reporting to you because it was trivial. But trivial or not, it was also pleasant, and I was sorry when it got to be time to go.

"Come to the club tonight," she said. "Come around one and you can catch my last set, and you'll get to see Cherry too. You'll want to talk to her, won't you?"

"Sure," I said. "But she might have plans, and—"

"So at least you'll get to see my number, Chip." She grinned hugely. "You wouldn't mind watching me do my dance, would you?"

I took the subway to 23rd and Eighth and walked the few blocks to Leo Haig's house. Wong had waited dinner until my return. He doesn't say much, but he cooks really fantastic Chinese things, and he never seems to dish up the same thing twice. Which is a shame, because there are plenty of dishes I'd like to return to.

I *hope* he throws out the roaches—

We talked business throughout our dinner. Haig has this tendency to imitate Nero Wolfe, and he attempts to avoid it by not making Wolfean rules for himself, like no business at meals and set hours with the orchids—which is to say fish in his case. So we talked, or rather I talked and he gave the appearance of listening, pausing periodically in his eating to ask a question or wipe some hoi-sin sauce from his beard. When the meal was finished we went back into the office and Wong brought the coffee. There was no dessert. There never is at Haig's house. He thinks if he never has dessert he will get thin. So we skipped dessert, as usual, and he opened his desk drawer, the second from the top on the left, and took out a Mars bar and two Mallo Cups. I passed, and he ate all three of them. If he keeps up like this he'll be nothing but skin and bones before you know it.

"Five hundred dollars," he said at one point, between bites, "is a rather large retainer for a case involving the murder of fish."

"It's standard," I said.

"Phooey."

"All right, it's large. It works out to almost five dollars a fish, which is about the going rate for scats, although I don't suppose fry would bring that much, would they? On the other hand she lost a breeding pair, and since they're the only known breeding pair of *Scatophagus Tetracanthus* they might be worth the full five hundred all by themselves. On the other hand—"

"You already said that."

"On the third hand, if you prefer, we're not going to bring the fish back to life even if you *are* a genius, so maybe that's the wrong way to approach it. Look at it this way—"

"Chip."

"Yes, sir."

"I assume you had a reason for setting so high a price."

"Yes. A few of them. First of all, the rent Madam Juana pays you isn't enough to cover our overhead, and I have a vested interest in that overhead since I'm a part of it. We can use the money. That's one. Two is I wanted to see if she could write a check for five hundred dollars without batting an eyelash. I watched her closely and she didn't bat a single one of them."

"You were not looking at her eyelashes."

"I'll let that go. The third reason is I thought that a high retainer might shame you into telling her to go swim upstream and spawn. How the hell are we going to find out who wiped out her scats? And where's the glory in it for you if we do? I know you didn't take the case for the money or you would have remembered to *ask* for the money, so you've got to be doing it for the glory, and if you think this is going to make your name a household word like stove and refrigerator and carpet—"

"Chip."

I stopped in midsentence. When he uses that particular tone of voice I stop. I stopped, and he spun around and regarded the Rasboras, and I waited for something to happen.

He spoke without turning from his fish. "I suppose it must be as it is," he said. "The Watson character is expected to lack subtlety. Thus the detective sparkles in comparison to his less nimble-witted assistant."

"You always pick the nicest ways to tell me how stupid I am."

"Indeed. You're quite useful to me, you know, and yet it's remarkable how you can simultaneously ignore subtleties while overlooking the obvious."

"I can also walk down the street while chewing gum."

"I'll accept your word on that." He turned around again and put his feet up, dammit. "Of course you'll go see our client perform tonight."

"All right. If you're determined that she's still our client—"

"I am."

"Then I'll go."

"And you'll interview Miss Bounce after the performance."

"If you say so."

"I do. With whom is Miss Wolinski dining tonight?"

"I don't know. Someone who's luckier than I am. Why?"

"You didn't ask?"

"Sure I asked. She said it wasn't one of the names in the notebook, so I—"

"But she didn't give the name."

"No."

He closed his eyes. I was still there when he opened them, and I don't think the fact delighted him. "You may leave," he said. "I want to read. Could you get me that new Bill Pronzini mystery?" He pointed and I fetched. I asked politely if the book was part of Pronzini's series in which the detective does not have a name.

"He has a name," Haig said. "The name is not revealed to the reader, but clearly the man has a name."

"Well, you know what I mean."

"What Pronzini's detective does not have," he said, "is an assistant." He glared at me, then lowered his eyes to the book. I thought about wishing him a goodnight and decided against it.

I went out and killed time. I had a beer at Dominick's and watched the Mets. They were playing the Padres and they lost anyhow. It took some doing. They went into the ninth two runs ahead. Then Sadecki struck out the first two batters and it looked hard to lose. He hit the next batter, and this rattled him so that he walked the next two, at which point Berra yanked him and sent in Harry Parker, who got the batter to hit a slow grounder to Garrett. Garrett fielded it cleanly but didn't throw to first because he couldn't find the ball. It was lost somewhere in his glove. That loaded the bases and upset Parker, who threw the next pitch six feet over Grote's head, cutting the lead to one. That was it for Parker. Berra brought in somebody just up from Tidewater, who made his major league debut by promptly hanging a curve for Nate Colbert. I think the ball's still in the air somewhere over Queens. That made it 5 to 3, and we went down in order in our half of the ninth, and that, to coin a phrase, was the ballgame.

"Jeez, they stink," Dominick said.

I couldn't argue with that. I walked around for a while, and then I went to Treasure Chest, and I guess that brings you up to date, because there I was on the stage and there was a beautiful girl named Cherry Bounce on the stage next to me and she was a hundred percent dead and, this was something my ingenuity and intelligence and experience had not prepared me for.

Four

I JUMPED DOWN from the stage, and then I vaulted up onto the bar and slid on the residue of someone's drink. I landed somewhat imperfectly on the customers' side of the bar. A lot of people were moving toward the stage, curious to know what was happening, and a lot of other people were moving toward the door, and the second group were the ones I was concerned with. I did some fancy broken-field running and got to the door ahead of most of them. I planted myself in the doorway with my arms and legs wide and tried to look as substantial as possible.

"Nobody leaves," I said. "A girl has been killed. Nobody leaves until the cops get here."

A couple of men took my word and turned away. I was on the point of congratulating myself on my menacing snarl when a few other guys headed toward me and looked prepared to walk right through me. "Nobody leaves," I said again, terrified that my voice would crack. They kept right on walking.

Then someone moved up against me from my right, and I turned my head, and it was my friend the door-tender, plaid pants and striped jacket and sky blue shirt and all. He moved into the doorway and I moved over to give him room, and he planted himself there in the identical stance I had taken, but he looked as though he meant it.

"Everybody stay where you are," he said. He didn't speak as loudly as I had. Then again, he didn't have to. The people milled a little, but then they turned back and resigned themselves to the fact that they weren't going anywhere.

"I gotta hand it to you, kid," the doorstop grunted. "You got moxie."

I beamed idiotically for a moment, then ducked back into the club myself. A lot of people were behaving pretty hysterically at this point and I can't say I blamed them much. I hadn't noticed any women in the club—except for Tulip and Cherry and the barmaid, obviously—but evidently there had been women at some of the back tables, or else someone had hired a batch of women to run into the club and scream when Cherry's body hit the stage. There was plenty of screaming, that's for sure.

I managed to find Tulip, who was not contributing to the screaming one bit. At first she looked oddly calm, but then I took a second look and recognized her expression as the kind of calm you get when someone has recently hit you over the head with a mallet.

She said, "She's—"

I was going to let her finish the sentence herself but she just plain stopped. So I finished it for her. "Dead," I said.

"What was it? A heart attack?"

"It was murder."

"But—"

"There's no time," I said. "This must be tied in with the scats and it proves Leo Haig is a lot smarter than I'll ever be but I already knew that. Listen to me. Are you listening?"

She nodded.

"All right. You and I don't know each other. No, the barmaid knows we do. Shit. All right."

"Chip?"

"You don't know anything about Haig. You don't mention anything about fish. You don't even know Cherry was murdered except that's what people have been saying. Are you a good liar?"

"I don't know. I guess so."

"Well, do the best you can. Now all I have to do is figure out a way to get the hell out of here." I looked at the door, and my friend the gorilla was still in place; now that I had taught him not to let anybody out, it was a cinch he wasn't going to let *me* out. I tried to figure out something, and while I was standing there like an idiot a man in a tuxedo came along and supplied the one powerful argument that would have whisked me past the gorilla in nothing flat.

"You!"

He was looking at me, and he was pointing at me, but the expression of absolute fury and indignation on the face of a man I had never seen before in my life convinced me that he had someone else in mind. I figured maybe he was a little cockeyed, and I looked over my shoulder to see who it was that he was furious with, but there was nobody there. Then he was standing right in front of me and his finger would have been touching my nose if either the finger or the nose had been half an inch longer.

"You!"

Tulip said, "Mr. Leemy—"

"Shut up," Leemy said, and my trained memory remembered that one Gus Leemy was the owner of record of Treasure Chest, and it stood to reason, Leemy being in another class entirely from Smith and Jones, that the Leemy with his finger in my face was Gus himself. Tulip said his name again, and he told her brusquely to shut up again, and that inspired exchange gave me a couple of seconds to look him over.

I decided that what he looked like was a bald penguin. The tuxedo, of course, and an absolutely hairless dome atop a long narrow head. He moved like a penguin, too; little jerky motions like old silent movies before they learned how to get the timing right.

"You're not twenty-one," Leemy said.

I opened my mouth and closed it again. Somehow I didn't think another portrait of Alexander Hamilton was going to cut much ice with the man.

"My fucking dancer drops dead on the fucking stage and the place is going to crawl with fucking cops and I need you like a fucking hole in my head. Out!"

"But—"

"Out!" He grabbed me by the arm, tugged me toward the door. He wasn't all that big or strong and at first I stood my ground, and then I remembered that he and I agreed that I should get out of there. At which point I stopped resisting.

He said, "Joint crawling with cops and all I need is trouble with the fucking S.L.A. about my fucking liquor license, all I fucking need, out, you little prick, and don't come back, and—"

I couldn't have agreed with him more, and I could have walked faster if he'd just let go of my arm. But he didn't, and I couldn't have walked fast enough anyway, because we were still maybe a dozen steps from the door when three or four gentlemen in blue uniforms filled the doorway.

"Oh, shit," Gus Leemy said.

The patrolmen mostly stood around and made sure that nobody entered or left the premises. One of them went up on the stage to confirm that Cherry was dead. When he came back down somebody asked if the girl was dead and he refused to commit himself. "We'll let the medical examiner settle that question," he said. I guess Dylan was wrong; some people really do need a weatherman to know which way the wind is blowing.

I did manage one feat while the patrolmen stood around waiting for the heavyweights to reach the scene. I found the phone booth and looked in my pocket for a dime. I only had a quarter, and my ingenuity and experience told me not to waste time getting change. I dropped the quarter and dialed my favorite telephone number, and when Wong Fat answered I told him to wake Haig, and he said he couldn't because Haig hadn't gone to sleep yet. He put the great man on the phone and I talked a little and listened a little and was off the phone by the time the detectives from Homicide, flanked by a couple of other detectives from Midtown West, came plainclothesing their way through the door.

The phone booth was not far from the door they entered. I saw them before they saw me, but not very much before. Just long enough for my heart to sink a little. I recognized them right away, but they needed two looks at me to make the connection. They worked in perfect unison, those two homicide cops in the middle, looking simultaneously at me, looking away, then doing a beautifully synchronized double-take.

"You!" they said. Much as Gus Leemy had said it. And I figured if we were going to stand their trading Gus Leemy lines, I had mine all picked out.

"Oh, shit," I said.

The one on the left was Detective Vincent Gregorio, a tall and dark and handsome number with one of those twenty-dollar haircuts and a suit you'd never find at Robert Hall. The one on the right was Detective Wallace Seidenwall, and I'd decided some time ago that Gregorio liked having him for a partner for the same reason pretty girls like having ugly girlfriends. Seidenwall's suits always looked as though someone else had bought them at Robert Hall, then wore them day and night for a year before passing them on to Seidenwall. I never had trouble remembering his name because he was built like the side of a wall.

The first time I met the two of them was when I discovered the body of a girl named Melanie Trevelyan. The second time I met them was when somebody bombed Madam Juana's whorehouse. That was the memorable day when Haig called them witlings, which was accurate if not diplomatic. The third meeting was in Haig's office, when he unmasked a murderer and presented him to them on a Sheffield platter. You'd think they might be grateful, but you'd be wrong.

If there were two things Seidenwall and Gregorio hated, I was one of them. Haig was the other.

Five

"IT WAS A Mexican standoff," I told Leo Haig. "Gregorio wanted to arrest me and Seidenwall wanted to arrest your client. I was hoping they would arrest us both and lock us up in the same cell, but then I figured you'd have Addison Shivers down there with a writ just when Tulip began to realize that it's hip to be involved with younger men."

Haig grunted. "There are other things in life beside sex," he said.

"I know," I said. "That's the whole trouble. One of the things there is beside sex is coffee. At the moment I'll settle for second best. Is there any?"

Haig picked up a little bell and rang it, and before the vibrations quit Wong entered with a couple of mugs full of hot black coffee. He's extraordinary that way. You hardly ever have to tell him what it is that you want.

In this case maybe it wasn't all that extraordinary. It was six-thirty in the morning and I had been up all night, and while Haig had dozed on the couch waiting for me to turn up he hadn't had anything you'd be likely to call real sleep. Of course we wanted coffee.

By the time I had finished my cup and rung for a refill, I had brought Haig up to date to the point where the cops walked in. I gave him everything reasonably verbatim and he took me back over various points until he was satisfied.

Then I went through my own interrogation. I had gotten off some good lines and I was careful to repeat them all, but since then I've reevaluated them, and while they were nice enough at the time, I don't think I'm going to inflict them on you. I'm not really all that inclined to play smartass with New York's Finest, but those two bring out the wiseacre in me and I have trouble controlling myself. To give you an example of the level of repartee, at one point Gregorio tried a trap question, asking me why I'd been jealous of the girl in the first place, and I said Haig had selected her to crossbreed with one of his fish in the hope that half the offspring would be mermaids and the other half would be Esther Williams. And that was one of my better lines, so now you know why you'll never hear the others.

Haig perked up at that particular line, as a matter of fact. "Then they know about Miss Wolinski's fish?"

"Yes, sir. They were going to find out she had fish, and even the police can add two and two. I told them I was at the club because I was friendly with Tulip, and I said the friendship had happened because Tulip had consulted you as a fellow aquarist about a problem connected with her hobby."

"Which is not untrue," Haig murmured.

"I know that. I don't lie to the police unless I have to. Tulip overheard me say this, and she picked up the ball neatly enough. She said she doesn't know how good a liar she is. If they grill her I guess she'll find out."

"And will they grill her?"

"Over and over again. She was Cherry's roommate, she

was a few yards away from her when she was murdered. They'd have to be crazy not to grill her."

"There's no doubt that Miss Bounce was poisoned?"

"None. I saw the blood on her breast. So did someone else, so the M.E. knew where to look for a wound. Just a pinpoint puncture."

"And the cause of the puncture was not found."

"No. I looked. The first thing that I thought of was poison. I thought of it before she hit the ground. God damn it, I was looking right at her and I never saw anything hit her. I just saw the blood and then she reached for herself and started to fall. Christ."

"Chip?"

"I'm all right. When I got up on the stage I was looking for the weapon at the same time that I was determining that she was dead. Not that it was hard to determine. She was all blue in the face. I forget what that's called. Cyanitis?"

"Cyanosis. And you weren't looking for the weapon. You were looking for the projectile. A gun is a weapon and a bullet is a projectile."

"Well, you knew what I meant."

"My cryptographic ability does not justify your abandoning the English language. You found nothing?"

"Nothing. I didn't know what I was looking for. Something sharp, but that was as far as I got. A dart or a needle or, hell, anything at all. I didn't have much time and of course the lighting was terrible, and if it was something like a needle it could have rolled between the floorboards and disappeared."

"If it's there, the police will find it. Whatever it may be."

"Maybe."

"Absolutely." He took a pipe from the rack and began twisting it apart. The end of the stem broke off inside the shank and he stared at it, sighed, and dropped both pieces into his wastebasket. He looked at me to see if I was going to smirk, and when I didn't he went on. "That is their strength. Scientific methodology, exhaustive investigation. If pressed they could find a needle in a haystack. Certainly they can locate one in a nightclub. Unless the murderer has already removed it."

I thought about that. "He could have," I said. "It must have hit her and bounced off after puncturing her skin, and if he saw it land he'd have had plenty of time to pick it up. I didn't make the world's greatest search for it. I felt it was important to keep as many people inside the place as possible until the police got there."

"You were probably right," he said. He cupped his beard, making sure that all the hairs were the right length. "I gather the murderer could have left before you barred the door."

"Easily. He could have been out the door before Cherry hit the stage, and then he would have had another minute or two while I was checking out the body. A lot of people did leave, I know that much."

"Hardly an admission of guilt on their part. One can readily appreciate the concern of any number of innocent citizens not to have their presence in such an establishment a matter of public record. All those gentlemen who habitually assure their wives that they are working late at the office."

"There were enough of those who didn't get out. When the cops went around taking names, you wouldn't believe the number of John Smiths who turned up. Of course the cops insisted on seeing identification and took down everybody's name and address."

"And you recognized some of the names."

I stared at him, which of course pleased him no end. "How did you know that?"

He waggled a finger at me. "You're still a boy who eats the cake and then the frosting, Chip. You save the best for last. If none of our suspects had been present you would have said so earlier. Who was there?"

I got out my notebook and flipped it open. "I can't say who might have left beforehand. And I can't be sure that I got the names of all the suspects who *were* there, because Seidenwall and Gregorio didn't take me into their confidence. I overheard a few names and I got together with Tulip and she pointed out a couple of people. She didn't know any of them were there until she happened to see them. Incidentally, her dinner date tonight was with a cousin from Chillicothe, Ohio. He came into town on business yesterday morning and flew home after they had dinner at the Autopub. I didn't find out what they had for dinner but I could probably check it out for you."

"Chip."

"Yes, sir. Gus Leemy was there, obviously. I told you how he did his impression of a bald penguin. That's not suspicious because he's always there. Andrew Mallard was there. That's the ex-boyfriend, the one who kept Tulip's apartment so she had to find another one."

"Indeed. And Tulip did not know of his presence beforehand?"

"No. He never talks to her. He usually gets a good table, but what I found out is that there's no such thing as a good table as far as being up close is concerned. The bar is between the tables and the stage. He came alone, of course. Tulip said he always does."

"Did you speak to him?"

"I didn't have a chance. I got a good look at him, though, and I got the impression of a man who goes through life in a fog. He's tall and thin and he'd be taller if he straightened out his spine a little. He walks with a stoop. Oh, and he wears very thick glasses. From where he was sitting, if he shot a dart or something into Cherry, he was probably aiming at Tulip."

"Continue."

"Simon Barckover was there. Tulip didn't know about this, either, but that wasn't unusual either. He drops in occasionally with someone he's trying to convince to book one of his clients. And he usually doesn't give advance warning that he's coming to keep his clients from getting uptight. He was there with a man who books acts for a nightclub in West Orange. I didn't get the name."

"I doubt that it matters."

"Well, I tried, all the same. Barckover's a forty-five-year-old hippie. Embroidered pre-faded jeans, the kind of counterculture clothing you can buy for about two hundred dollars a pair in the East Sixties. A buckskin jacket with fringe that probably cost him double that. Aviator glasses, wears his hair in a Hebro."

"I beg your pardon?"

"It's Tulip's word but I think I like it and I'm going to make it mine. A Hebro. Sort of a Jewish Afro."

"Indeed."

I closed the notebook. "That's it. Just those three, and it wasn't unusual for any of them to be there. Leemy owns the place, or pretends to. Mallard comes in a lot because he likes to look at Tulip's breasts while he drinks. Barckover had a professional reason for being there. It's possible that there were other suspects there. I don't mean of the ones who ducked out when they had the chance, but besides that. For instance, Mrs. Haskell Henderson might have been there and how would we know it? Tulip's never met her."

Haig sighed. Then he folded his hands, and then he extended his index fingers and played here's-the-church-here's-the-steeple. I got up and looked at some fish.

He said, "The poison. Strychnine?"

"I don't know. They'll have to do an autopsy. What do people look like when they die of strychnine poisoning? Besides dead, I mean."

"The symptoms you described are not incompatible with a diagnosis of strychnine poisoning. It works on the nervous system, the effects are rapid, there's spasmodic paralysis. But it's almost invariably given orally. I suppose it could be used to tip a dart or arrow or whatever projectile was employed." He furrowed his eyebrows. "If it was a poison other that strychnine—"

"Then what?"

He grunted, shook off the question.

"If it was strychnine, then it ties in with the fish. Is that what you mean?"

"No," he said.

"Well—"

"It's tied to the fish in any case," Haig said impatiently. "A young woman comes to see us. Her fish have been deliberately poisoned. Less than twelve hours after she sets foot in this office, her roommate and co-worker is also deliberately poisoned, and under our eyes. Your eyes, at any rate, and you in turn function as my eyes. The connection is undeniable. Anyone who would raise the gray banner of coincidence would—how did that congressman put it? If a mouse walked into the room, he would say that one could not be certain that it was a mouse, that it might well be an elephant with a glandular condition."

It was the other way around; if an elephant walks into the room one says it might be a mouse with a glandular condition. But as much as I like to nitpick with Haig, if only to give him some of his own back, this didn't seem to be the time to pick that particular nit.

Instead I said, "Well, I took it for granted the two things were connected. Obviously. But what difference does it make if it was strychnine both times?"

"Perhaps none. Who else was in the club?"

"The names of all the people whose names didn't ring a bell? God, I don't know. I couldn't run around writing everything down, for Pete's sake. I think most of the men I overheard were from out of town. There could have been a boyfriend or two of Cherry's there. She evidently had a lot of them, former and current. Tulip wouldn't recognize them either by name or face, so I couldn't say. I know Leonard Danzig wasn't there because Tulip would have spotted him."

"You mentioned a short heavy man who tended the door. A bouncer, I presume."

"Well, he tried to bounce me. And if I hadn't slipped him a ten he would have done it with no trouble. His name is Buddy Lippa. I assume he has an official first name, but all I heard was Buddy."

"Waitresses? Or waiters?"

"Definitely waitresses. Two of them working the tables, and I didn't bother to get their names, but not because I was being stupid. I figured I could get them later from Tulip. Or from Leemy or anywhere else."

"And behind the bar?"

"Her name is Jan and I could probably fall in love with her if I wasn't already committed to Tulip. I understand Tulip doesn't like to play threesies. Leonard Danzig tried to arrange that once and she didn't go for it. But maybe she was just saying that because she was shy, meeting me for the first time and all. After this is over Tulip and Jan and I can get together and work it all out. As a matter of fact—"

"Chip."

I finished my coffee. It was cold, but that was all right. We sat around for a while, and then Haig turned on the news and we had the story, and there wasn't much to it that we didn't already know. They gave Cherry's real name but they got it wrong, and they said that the police expected to make an arrest very shortly."

Haig grunted and shut off the radio.

"Well, we're out of it," I said. "The police expect to make an arrest at any moment. Of course whoever killed Cherry also killed the fish, so they'll be solving your case for you. Do we give Tulip her check back or not? I'm not sure of the ethics involved."

Haig didn't answer me. After a moment he said,

"You'll want to sleep, I suppose. There's a convertible sofa in your room. I've had Wong—"

"There's nothing but a bed and chest of drawers in my room and you know it. If you mean the guest room, that is not my room, and we've been through this enough so that you should have figured it out by now."

He held up a hand. "Please," he said. "The police are not going to apprehend the murderer. Either they will not make an arrest at all or they will arrest the wrong person. That was the seven o'clock news. Sometime between now and noon the police will come here. I want you here when they arrive."

"You're sure they'll come?"

"It's beyond doubt. Wong has made up the bed for you. This does not commit you to living here. You know as much. Get what sleep you can."

"All right."

I got to my feet. He said, "Chip? I'd like to amend a comment I made earlier. Your talents are a very important part of this operation of ours. You performed satisfactorily tonight."

"I was slow getting onto the stage and slow getting to the door."

"Immaterial. You think well on your feet while I think well seated. We work well together. Don't doubt that you're appreciated."

"For Pete's sake," I said. "I'm not used to that kind of talk." He averted his eyes. "I mean, I'll be up for hours wondering what you meant by that. How am I going to get any sleep now?"

As a matter of fact, I did have a tough time getting to sleep. I went so far as to take off my clothes and get under the covers. Then I closed my eyes.

And that was all it took. The next thing I knew Wong Fat was shaking me awake. I made a few horrible noises and buried my face in the pillow but this didn't seem to faze him.

"Police gentlemen here," he said. "Mistuh Haig want you downstairs chop-chop."

I sat up and rubbed my eyes. "What time is it?"

"Is ten-thirty. He want you velly soon, chop-chop."

"Oh, come off it, Wong," I said. "Nobody talks like that. Not even you."

"Is to make innasting character for book you lite," Wong insisted. "Mistuh Haig, he want it just so."

I got out of bed. "Tell him I'll be down in a minute, will you?"

"Ah, so."

"And Wong?"

"Mistuh Chip?"

"Tell him he's a plick."

Six

As I APPROACHED the door I heard Haig telling them that it was no use, that he wasn't going to tell them anything until I was present. Seidenwall sputtered a little at that, and I was tempted to wait out in the hall and let him sputter, but instead I went in and nodded at them and sat down in my chair at the desk. Haig was in his chair across the desk from me and Seidenwall was slumped in the floral wing chair and Gregorio was on his feet. He had changed his suit since I saw him. His partner hadn't.

Haig said good morning, which it clearly wasn't, and I backed him up and wished him a good morning right back. He said he hoped I slept well, and I said it was long on quality if short on quantity, and Seidenwall mentioned a popular organic fertilizer often to be found in stables.

"Now then," Haig said. "What seems to be the matter, gentlemen?"

Seidenwall went purple in the face and squeezed the arms of his chair. Gregorio said, "Look, you silly little butterball, I want some cooperation from you. When I saw this punk who works for you last night I figured you were all wrapped up in this one. I never yet ran into Harrison here without somebody being dead. And what do I get from him? I get a fish story."

"Precisely," Haig said.

"A whole load of crap about how this Tulip broad is just a good friend of his, and he's friends with her because she raises fish and you raise fish and you had a cute little conference about your goddamned fish, and on the strength of that he went to see her dance."

"But that's quite true," Haig said. "Miss Wolinski lost a valuable batch of fish. She wanted me to determine how the fish had perished."

"Yeah, fish." Gregorio looked disgusted. "She even gave me their goddamned names. *Scatophagus tetracanthus.* For the hell of it I looked it up. You know what *Scatophagus* means?"

"Certainly."

"It means eater of excrement. In other words they eat shit, and so does your story."

"It's a misappellation," Haig said dreamily. "The species lives in foul water and subsists on detritus, but I don't believe they actually consume excrement."

"Well, your story does. The fish didn't just die. They were poisoned."

"So it would appear."

"Strychnine," Seidenwall said.

"Strychnine," Gregorio said. "Now who in the hell would dump strychnine into a tankful of fish?"

"An excellent question, Mr. Gregorio. And it was precisely Miss Wolinski's question, which prompted her to consult me. I have as yet been unable to hit on the answer."

Gregorio stared at him. Staring at Leo Haig does you no good whatsoever, but I didn't point this out to Gregorio. There's no point in volunteering information to the police. They never really know what to do with it, anyway.

"Awright," Seidenwall said. "Where does your little pal Harrison get off keeping this all to himself last night?"

"I'm sure I don't know," Haig said. "Chip? Did the police ask you if Miss Wolinski's fish were poisoned?"

"The subject never came up," I said.

"Now wait a minute—"

"Did they mention strychnine? Did they inquire as to whether any professional relationship existed between ourselves and Miss Wolinski?"

"Nope."

"Well then," Haig said. "Gentlemen, I don't understand. You accuse my associate of failing to cooperate. Of prevaricating. Yet he has neither lied nor withheld information. Why should he assume that the death of a group of fish bore any relationship to the death of a topless dancer? Had he even suggested this line of inquiry, no doubt you would have accused him of wasting your time."

They both started calling Haig names. Seidenwall called him a lump of shit while Gregorio called him a fat dwarf. Haig did not seemed ruffled. He took a pipe apart and put it back together again. This time he didn't break it.

Seidenwall said. "The hell, Vinnie. Let's get to the point."

"Right." Gregorio walked over to the desk. He planted himself next to me so that he could glower down at Haig. I was tempted to check out the material of his suit but I restrained myself. "All right," he said. "We could go round and round with this but it's a waste of time. You're too damn cute. You sit on your fat ass and play with your pipes and your fish and talk your way out of everything. But you're covering for a client, dammit, and you're withholding evidence and I want it."

Haig looked at him.

"You know what I'm talking about. Or didn't your little chum tell you? He was sitting right next to the Wolinski broad when she put the dart in her roommate. I'd make it twenty-to-one he saw her do it, but I don't suppose we could ever prove it."

"Indeed."

"Then he was on the stage before the body stopped twitching. That's when he picked up the murder weapon." Haig didn't tell him he meant projectile. "And you can't deny he was on the stage, damn it. A dozen people saw him hop over the bar and onto the stage."

"Why deny it?" I put in. "I told you all that last night. I might have looked around for a murder weapon if I knew she'd been murdered, but how was I supposed to know that? I didn't even know she was dead. That's what I went up onto the stage to find out, and she was. What does that prove?"

"It proves you're a fucking liar," Seidenwall said.

"Harrison has the murder weapon," Gregorio went on. "He's got it and I know he's got it and, damn it, you know he's got it. Some dumb broad raises tropical fish and that makes her okay in your book and you're covering for her. Well, I've got her locked up and I'm going to nail her on Murder One, and if you don't come up with the dart or whatever it was I'll have you and Harrison in the dock on an accessory charge."

"Indeed," Haig said. He heaved a sigh. "Your thesis seems to be that Miss Wolinski murdered Miss Abramowicz."

"You know damned well she did."

"It's curious. First Miss Wolinski poisoned her own fish with strychnine for reasons we cannot begin to explain. Then, no doubt wracked by guilt over what she had done, she hired me to find her out. And, unbalanced at the thought of discovery, she pumped more strychnine into her roommate while my associate sat beside her. Ingenious reasoning, Mr. Gregorio. I applaud you."

"It wasn't strychnine."

"Pardon me?"

"It was curare. The stuff South American Indians put on their arrows."

"I know what curare is," Haig said.

"So she didn't poison her own fish. The two girls hated each other. One of them took a boyfriend away from the other one, so the Abramowicz one got hold of some strychnine—"

"How?" Haig demanded. "Where?"

Gregorio ignored the demands. "—and poisoned Wolinski's fish. Wolinski hired you and you found out Abramowicz did the job. So Wolinski got ahold of some curare and gave Abramowicz the needle, and now you're trying to cover for her."

Haig stood up. This didn't increase his height all that much, but he has a way of getting to his feet that is pretty theatrical. Maybe it's because he stands as infrequently as possible, so that when he finally gets around to it you're really ready for something spectacular.

"Mr. Gregorio. Mr. Seidenwall. I have intimated in the past that I regard you as witlings. I cannot imagine that you are sufficiently mindless to believe the story you have just propounded. It is enough of a mark of your lack of intellect to recognize that you expect me to believe you believe it."

(I don't think they got the gist of that. If you have to read it over a few times yourself, don't feel like an idiot. It's a complicated paragraph. Haig might think you're a witling if you don't get it first time out of the box, but I won't hold it against you.)

"I will not dignify your conjecture with rebuttal," he went on. "Why refute something you already know to be absurd? We have already wasted enough time. Have you taken my client into custody?"

"You're damn right."

"Have you indeed. Mr. Gregorio, there is a blind man

who operates a newsstand at the corner of Sixth Avenue and 42nd Street. Perhaps you know him."

"So?"

"Simply this. Were that blind man my client of the moment instead of Miss Wolinski, and had Mr. Harrison been present last night when Miss Abramowicz was murdered, you would have arrested the newsdealer and let Miss Wolinski go. You are trying to put pressure upon me, sir. You are trying to coax me to solve a case which baffles you, and you are trying to force me to do so on your own terms instead of my own. Have you formally charged my client?"

"Not yet."

"Not yet and not ever, as you well know. You have put her through a profound indignity in order to obtain from me information which I do not have and would not be obliged to give you if I did. You do not know by whom Miss Abramowicz was killed. You do not know the motive. Do you at least know what weapon was employed?"

"Something small and sharp with curare on the tip."

"So you do not know that either. You do not know anything except, I am sorry to say, my address. My inclination is to close up like a clam. First I will volunteer certain information to you. Negative information. Neither I nor Mr. Harrison knows who poisoned Miss Wolinski's fish. Neither of us knows who murdered Miss Abramowicz. Neither of us possesses any factual knowledge not in your own possession. And, finally, neither of us intends to respond further to accusations, charges, questions, or such other irritation as you might be inclined to visit upon us. I have previously merely intimated that you are witlings. I now state it categorically. You are witlings, gentlemen. Your behavior defines the term to perfection. I would urge you to leave my house."

"Now wait a minute—"

"I will wait for eternity if I must. Having admitted you, I cannot legally order you to leave. In the future you shall not be admitted without a warrant. Since you are inside, you may wait here until hell freezes. Such a course of action would be futile for you, but not inconsistent with your character and mental agility. You will excuse me if I do not offer you refreshment."

He rang the bell. Wong came in with his tray. There were two cups of coffee on it. Not four. Just two. Wong gave one to Haig and one to me. He always knows.

They didn't wait for hell to freeze. They tried a couple of questions and bright lines, concentrating on me. "I don't like it," Seidenwall said. "Whenever there's drugs in the picture, this punk turns up."

Gregorio told me to roll up my sleeves.

"Oh, for Pete's sake," I said. "Drugs? Because somebody put strychnine in a fish tank? And what do you mean I turn up when there's drugs involved? What drugs?"

"That hippie chick who took an overdose a while back."

I stared at him, and I started to say something, and Haig said, "Chip. I don't think it's incumbent upon you to play a role in this farce. You need not reply to questions."

"I think you're right," I said. "Do I have to roll up my sleeves?"

"Yes," Seidenwall said.

"No," Leo Haig said.

I took Haig's word for it and sat there sipping coffee. They asked some more questions and got no replies from either of us, so they made some threats and left. I bolted the door after them, and when I got back into the office Haig was already on the phone to Addison Shivers, making arrangements for Tulip's release from custody. Since Addison Shivers is around a hundred and ten years old, I didn't figure he would run around from precinct to precinct himself. But he would make sure someone did it and did it right.

When the phone was cradled again Haig leaned back in his chair. I said, "They're terrific, those two."

"Mmmmm," he said. "I wonder what they meant about drugs."

"Oh, it's just their way of being playful. The first time I met them they asked me to roll up my sleeves and I was wearing a short-sleeved shirt, for Pete's sake."

"I wonder."

"It doesn't mean anything."

"Everything means something," Haig said sleepily. He leaned back and put his feet up and closed his eyes. I didn't object to the gesture now because he was thinking, and a genius is fully entitled to think in whatever position suits him best. He thought for a long time, and when it was questionable whether he was thinking or sleeping I gave up and got some brine shrimp and wheat germ and Tetramin and went around feeding the downstairs fish. I did the other rooms first, then came back to the office. Haig was still leaning back with his feet up and his eyes closed, but at my approach he opened his eyes and fixed them on me.

"The unadulterated nerve," he said. "As if we would willingly shield a murderer. Chip."

"Sir?"

"Could she have done it?"

"Yes, sir. Easily. She made a point of urging me to watch Cherry go into the finale of her act. She could have had a little blowpipe palmed out of sight, and she could have plinked Cherry's tit while I wasn't looking, and Bob's your uncle. There's not a chance in hell that that's what happened, but she could have done it. It would have been a cinch."

"But then why would she have come here?" He sighed.

"No. Impossible. Our client is innocent. Someone else committed the murder."

"The same person who dosed the fish with strychnine."

"No. I believe I know who killed the fish. And someone else killed Miss Abramowicz."

"What? You *know* who killed the fish?"

"I believe so. It would be premature to offer conjecture at this point in time. Chip."

"Sir?"

"I never said 'At this point in time' before Watergate. It is a cumbersome cliché. I don't like it. Should I use it in the future, please call it to my attention."

"Sure thing. All part of my job. Feed the fish, clean out the filter traps, change the glass wool and charcoal, chase the murderers, and correct your English. Who killed the fish and how does it tie in with everything?"

He shook his head. "Not now. It would be premature. And we have more pressing concerns. You are going to have to see a great many people and learn as much as you possibly can. Your notebook, please."

Seven

HASKELL HENDERSON OWNED six health food stores, all
of them in Manhattan, all located between 72nd Street
and Eighth Street. I called one of them and established
that he wasn't there, but that he was most likely at the
store on Lexington and 38th. I called that one, and they
said he was there, and I hung up before he could come to
the phone and went out and got a cab.

The store was called Doctor Ecology, and it was a lot
larger than the usual watering holes for health nuts. It was
the size of a small supermarket, with about half a dozen
aisles and shopping cars that you could wheel up and
down them while stocking up on gluten bread and soy
flour and raw sugar and jerusalem artichokes and tiger's
milk and other gourmet treats. At the back there was a
lunch counter for people who probably weren't all that
hungry in the first place. I hadn't really eaten anything yet
that day, and it was close to noon, so I took a stool at the
counter and looked at a menu. If only I'd been a rabbit I
could have had a hell of a time. I decided that I didn't

want anything they had, so I settled for a cup of coffee. Only it wasn't coffee. It was a coffee substitute made by grinding up dandelion roots. The idea was that it wouldn't keep you awake, and it's always seemed to me that the only thing coffee really has going for it is that it *will* keep you awake.

You probably think you can imagine what that dandelion coffee tasted like. Don't bet on it.

I sipped enough of it to know that it was never going to be one of my all-time favorites. I paid for it and left the waiter a large tip because I felt sorry for him. Then I looked around to see if I could pick Haskell Henderson out of the crowd. When that didn't work I asked a cashier if he was around, and she told me he was in his office and pointed out the door that led to it. I knocked on the door and a voice told me to come in.

I walked into a tiny office. Haskell Henderson was standing behind a desk piled so full of invoices and pamphlets and correspondence that the desk top didn't show through anywhere. He was talking on the phone, and the conversation seemed to involve just which brand of brown rice was the most yang, which has something important to do with the macrobiotic diet. I was sort of familiar with the macrobiotic diet because there was a time when I lived with some people in the East Village who were very into it. They ate nothing but brown rice. They also did a lot of speed, which I don't believe is a standard part of the macrobiotic diet, and they talked about all the sensational things they were going to accomplish once they got their heads together. Sure.

While he talked I looked at him. I didn't see anything marvelous, but the fact that he was Tulip's current boyfriend probably prejudiced me against him. He was maybe thirty-five, and he had his hair combed to hide the fact that his hairline was ebbing, and he had a scraggly little goatee to hide the fact that he didn't have much of a chin. He was wearing white jeans and a tee-shirt with "Doctor

Ecology" in white letters on a blue background. All the employees wore tee-shirts like that.

He finished his conversation, told the person at the other end of the line to stay healthy, and scuttled out from behind the desk. He thrust out his hand, which I shook, and he gave me a smile designed to show me what great shape his teeth were in.

"Well now," he said. "Haskell Henderson. What can I do for you?"

"My name is Harrison," I said, "and I work for Leo Haig."

"Leo Haig. Leo Haig. Let me see. Dew-Bright Farms? Over in Jersey? I've heard good things about your vegetables."

"Leo Haig the detective," I said.

"Detective?"

I nodded. "Mr. Haig is working for Tulip Willing. Or Thelma Wolinski."

He looked at me suspiciously. "Why would Tulip need a detective? She's not jealous. Wait a minute. Just *wait* a minute now. You're not working for Tulip."

"Mr. Henderson—"

"You're working for my wife," he said, pointing his finger at me. At least it didn't come as close to my nose as Gus Leemy's finger. "You're working for my wife," he said again. "Well, get this straight, fella. I don't know any Tulip Willing, or whatever you said her name was, whoever she may be, and—"

"Shut up."

I don't know why I said that. As far as that goes, I don't know why it worked. Maybe nobody had ever told Haskell Henderson to shut up before, and maybe he didn't know how to relate to it. He opened his mouth, and he closed it, and he stared at me.

I said, "Cherry Bounce was murdered last night."

"Oh, Christ. Yeah, I heard about that. Somebody killed her in the middle of her act. They get the guy yet?"

"They made an arrest. But they didn't get the killer, and the person they got isn't a guy. It's Tulip."

"They arrested Tulip? Jesus, that's ridiculous. I don't get it."

"Well, that's why Tulip hired a detective," I said. "She doesn't get it either, and she's not crazy about it. I want to ask you some questions."

"Why me?"

"Because you're Tulip's boyfriend, and because—"

"Whoa!" He displayed his teeth again and the light glinted on them. "Tulip's boyfriend? You gotta be kidding, fella. I'm a happily married man. Oh, I see Tulip from time to time. no question about that. When a man keeps himself in good physical shape he's got all this energy, he has to find an outlet for it. But Tulip's just one of the girls I see from time to time. It's nothing heavy, you understand? Just a friend, that's all. A casual friend with whom I have an enjoyable physical relationship. You don't want to make a whole big deal out of it."

What I wanted to do was play a tape of this speech for Tulip. Why was she wasting her time on this playboy when I was available? I said, "Look, your wife didn't send me. Honest."

"So?"

"So don't make speeches about how you relate to Tulip like a sister. That's not the point. You're her friend, and you were at the Treasure Chest last night, and—"

"The hell I was!"

I did my best to look confused. I even scratched my head, mainly because I've seen so many people do it when they're confused, especially in movies. The only time I normally scratch my head is when it itches. "That's funny," I said. "According to the information we have, you were at Treasure Chest until just before the time of the murder."

"Well, that's bullshit," he said. He reached into a jar on his desk and stuffed a handful of things into his mouth.

They looked like newly hatched fish, little spherical bodies and long stringy tails. (I found out later that they were alfalfa sprouts.) He munched them and said, "I don't know where the hell you heard that. Where did you hear it, anyway?"

"You got me. Mr. Haig said that was his information, but I don't know who told him. Where were you last night, then? Because when I tell Mr. Haig his information was wrong, he'll want to know where you were."

He told me what I could tell Haig to do. It was something I've often wanted to tell Haig to do, as a matter of fact. "I don't have to account for my movements to Leo Haig," he said. "That's for damn sure."

"You don't have to," I agreed. "But, see, the police don't really know anything about you, and if Mr. Haig doesn't have any other way of finding out where you were, he'll let them know about you and let them ask you the same question. If Haig is satisfied, he wouldn't have any reason to mention your name to the police. After all, they're not his clients. Tulip is his client."

I watched his eyes while I delivered this little set piece. There was a moment when he contemplated a show of righteous indignation, but then his eyes shifted and I could tell he knew it wouldn't wash. "Oh, the hell with it," he said. "I have nothing to hide. As a matter of fact, I was home last night. I was watching television. Do you want to know what programs I saw?"

"Not particularly, but maybe the Neilson people would be interested. Well, that's no problem, then. You were home watching television so that lets you off the hook."

"What hook? You don't suspect me of killing Cherry, do you?"

"Of course not," I said. "How could you? You were home watching television."

"Right."

I started toward the door, then turned around. "While I'm here," I said, "could you tell me a little about Tulip and Cherry? There's a lot I don't know, and since I know you're not a suspect I would be able to rely on what you tell me. It won't take too much of your time."

He wasn't tickled with the idea but he liked the notion of not being a suspect. I asked him a lot of questions and he answered them and I made some notes in my notebook. His chief slant on both of the girls was nutritional. Tulip ate a lot of garbage, he said. Nature had given her a spectacular physique and she was taking a chance of ruining it because she actually ate meat and fruit that had been sprayed and a lot of other no-nos. He had tried to interest her in nutrition but so far it hadn't taken. Cherry, on the other hand, was far more open to new ideas. The impression I got was that he liked Cherry more than he liked Tulip, probably because she was dumb enough to pay attention to him, but he didn't like having Cherry around that much because when he stole over there for an afternoon all he really wanted to do was crawl into the feathers with Tulip, who turned him on something wonderful.

No, he didn't know anyone who would want to kill Cherry. No, he didn't know anyone who had anything against Tulip, either. I slipped in an oblique reference to Tulip's fish and he didn't seem to have strong feelings about them one way or the other. Instead he turned them into nutritional propaganda.

"She knows nutrition is the secret of conditioning," he said. "That's how she gets the breeding results she does. Plenty of live foods. Everything raw. Nothing cooked. She even knows to mix kelp and wheat germ into their formula. My God, they eat a better diet than she does! If she ate what she gives the fish, she'd be in fantastic shape."

If she were in any better shape, I thought, she'd be capable of turning on statues. I was beginning to understand why Tulip had offered me a bourbon and yogurt. It was probably Haskell Henderson's favorite cocktail.

"I guess that's it," I said finally. "Thanks very much for

·your cooperation, and I'm glad to know you were home watching television last night. That's one name off the list."

"Well, it's not the kind of list I'd want to be on."

"I don't blame you." I gave him my no. 3 warm smile. "Mr. Haig will just ring up your wife and confirm your story, and then we'll be all set."

I would probably respect myself a lot more if I didn't get such a kick out of doing things like that. I mean, I couldn't feature old Haskell as the killer. If he wanted to do somebody in he'd probably poison them with refined sugar and synthetic vitamins, not strychnine or curare. But we still had to know what he was doing last night, and anybody who'd believe the television story has probably already bought the Brooklyn Bridge several times over.

It was fun to watch him. He made the kind of noise in his throat that you make when you get a shirt back from the laundry and button the collar and find out it wasn't Sanforized. Then he took six deep breaths and said, very very quietly, "You can't call my wife."

"Why not?" I grinned. "Oh, sure. You don't want her to know anything about Tulip, right?"

"That's right. She probably suspects I . . . uh . . . see other women. But to have it thrown in her face, and the fact that a girl I know is peripherally involved in a murder case—"

"You don't have a thing to worry about."

"I don't?"

"Not a thing. Mr. Haig is very discreet. The way we'll do it, see, is we'll call up and pretend we're a television survey. Ask her what programs she was watching last night. Then we'll ask if anyone else in her family was also watching television, and she'll say you were, and—"

"She won't say that."

"Oh?"

"I wasn't actually *watching* television. I was in the other room, you see, so she'll say she was the only one *watching* the set, and—"

"We'll ask if other family members were home but weren't watching. Mr. Haig knows all the angles, Mr. Henderson."

"Uh."

I put a little steel into my voice. Or maybe it was brass. "*All* the angles," I said.

"Uh—"

"Where does your wife think you were last night?"

He went for the alfalfa sprouts like a drunk for a drink. He munched and shuddered. "Meeting with the owner of a rival store to discuss a possible merger."

"That's a pretty good line. I don't suppose you can use it too often but it has a nice ring to it. What time did you get to Treasure Chest and what time did you leave?"

"I wasn't there!"

"Where were you? And don't tell me you were with one of the other girls with whom you have a warm physical relationship and you can't drag her name into it because she's respectable. Don't even try that one on."

He met my eyes. "Jesus," he said. "You're just a kid."

"I've had a hard life. What did you do last night?"

"I went to a movie."

"All by yourself, of course."

"As a matter of fact, yes."

I had the notebook open. "What movie?"

"I don't know."

"Oh, come on."

"I don't know the name of it. It was a pornographic movie, one of those, you know, one of those X-rated pictures. I don't remember the title and I can't tell you the plot because it didn't have one. They never have a plot. And of course I went to it alone because who goes to those things *with* somebody? Shit. I thought you believed me about watching television." He got another hit from the jar of sprouts. "I guess I don't have much of an alibi," he said miserably. "Do I?"

Now the next thing that happened is something I never bothered to recount to Haig. I hadn't planned to recount it to you, either, and if you want to skip right on ahead to the beginning of the next chapter, I wouldn't blame you a bit. The following sequence has nothing whatsoever to do with the annihilation of Tulip's fish or the murder of Tulip's roommate, not so far as I can see. Of course if you're into cosmic tides and karmic things and like that, and if you can grok the concept that all things are intimately bound up in one another, then maybe you can justify including the following in this book. I can't, but I don't have much choice in the matter.

What happened was this: I left Haskell Henderson at Doctor Ecology at Lexington and 38th, and I decided to head over to Simon Barckover's office in the Brill Building. But in the meantime I remembered that a friend of mine lived on 37th Street between Third and Second, which wasn't all that far out of my way, and I remembered that I hadn't seen her in a long time, and I remembered what it had been like the last time I had seen her.

So I went over there.

On the way I stopped at a florist's and bought a dollar's worth of flowers. I don't know what kind of flowers they were. (I don't think it matters.) I carried them for a block and remembered that I was going to see Ruthellen, and there was just no way I could walk in there carrying flowers. I didn't really know what to do with them. I mean, you have to be pretty much of a callous clod to stuff a fresh bouquet of flowers into a trash can. I stood there feeling slightly stupid, and then I saw one of the oldest ladies in the world walking one of the oldest dachshunds in the world, and I gave her the flowers. (The lady, not the dachshund.) I walked quickly on while she was still instructing God to bless me.

I couldn't take flowers to Ruthellen because that wasn't the kind of relationship we had. Her problem, which she had laid out for me early on, is that she can't respond at all to people who are nice to her. She's not into whips and chains or anything, but she suffers from what her shrink calls "low estimate of self," and thus she's only turned on by people who despise her. I don't despise her, but I'm willing to pretend to, and it's not hard for me to be aloof and never call her and just drop in on her now and then because, to tell you the truth, she doesn't do all that terribly much for me and I really don't want to get very heavily involved with anybody quite as sick as she is. So maybe I *do* despise her, come to think of it, and maybe that's why she enjoys seeing me.

(Not that it matters. None of this matters at all. That's the whole point.)

I rang her bell. Her voice over the intercom asked who it was. "Chip," I snapped. She asked again. "Chip Harrison," I snarled. She buzzed and I opened the door and climbed two flights of stairs.

She was waiting in the doorway of her apartment. She's about twenty-five, maybe a little older, with a surprisingly good complexion considering that she hardly ever leaves her apartment during daylight hours except for her weekly visit to the shrink. She keeps her shades drawn day and night. She has this thing about daylight. She and the shrink are working on it, she's told me. I don't think they're making much progress, either of them.

"Haven't seen you in ages," she said.

I shrugged. "Been busy."

"Come on in. Can I get you something? A drink?"

"Haven't got time," I said. I sort of swaggered into her apartment and sat down in the comfortable chair. (There's only one.) Ruthellen sat on the couch in a nest of pillows and lit a cigarette.

"Put it out," I said.

"The cigarette?"

"I don't like the smell."

"All right," she said, and put it out. One of the reasons I see her as infrequently as I do is that I don't really like to be a total bastard with a woman. And what I especially don't like is that I can occasionally get into it, and that's a little scary, if you stop to think about it.

(Not that any of this has anything to do with Tulip and her fish and her roommate.)

"Well," she said. "So what's new?"

"Nothing much."

"You don't feel like talking?"

"No."

"That's cool. We'll just sort of sit around and relax. Sure I can't get you anything?"

I grunted. It was a grunt Haig would have been proud of. I sat back and looked at Ruthellen, who, while not the best-looking woman in the world, was by no means the worst. She's tall, about five-eight or so, and very thin, but not so much so that you'd mistake her for Twiggy. Her hair is a dirty blond. Literally, I'm afraid; she doesn't wash it too often. She doesn't do much of anything, really, which is another of the things she and the shrink are supposed to be working on. What she does is sit in her apartment, live on things like Rice Krispies and candy bars—you wouldn't believe how little she and Haskell Henderson would have in common—and cash the monthly check from her father in Grosse Pointe. The check pays for the rent and the Rice Krispies and the candy bars and the shrink, and since that's about all she has to do in life, that's about all she does.

"Chip?"

I looked at her.

"Would you like me to do anything?"

"Take your clothes off."

"Okay," she said.

I could have said *Take your robe off* because a robe was all she was wearing. She took it off and put it on the couch. Then she turned to face me, her hands at her sides, and stood still as if offering her body to me for inspection. Her small breasts were flushed, the nipples erect. She was excited already. So was I, in an undemanding sort of a way, but I didn't let it show. I had to go on being Mr. Casual because that was what was turning her on.

"Chip—"

"You could go down on me," I suggested.

"Okay. Do you want to come to bed?"

"Right here's good. You could like kneel on the floor."

"Okay."

And she did. I sat there, Mr. Cool, while she knelt in front of me and unzipped my zipper and, like Jack Horner, put in her hand and pulled out a gland. "Oh, he's so strong and beautiful," she said, talking to it. "Oh, I love him so. Oh, I want to eat him up."

And she did.

It's all we ever do. And it's all according to the same ritual—she always invites me to bed and I always tell her to kneel in front of me like a servant girl, and she always does, and I'll tell you something. Maybe the repertoire is limited, but she certainly plays that one piece perfectly. She doesn't do all that much, Ruthellen, but what she does she does just fine.

Afterward she sat back on her haunches, grinned, wiped one elusive drop from the tip of her chin with the tip of her forefinger, and told me she was glad I had come. She wasn't the only one. "I like it when you drop by," she said. "It gets lonely here."

"You should get out more."

"I guess. The shrink says we're making progress."

"Well, that's good, I guess."

"I guess."

"Well, I'll, uh, see you."

"Take care, Chip."

"Yeah, you too."

Okay.

I feel I owe you an explanation. You're probably wondering why the hell that episode was dragged in out of the blue and thrust in front of your eyes. Of course it took place during the time we were working on this case, but lots of things take place that I don't plague you with. I don't mention every time I go to the toilet for instance. Which is not to say that seeing Ruthellen is like going to the toilet. Except, come to think of it, it is, sort of.

Okay.

When I wrote this book, the Ruthellen bit wasn't in it. And then I got a call from Joe Elder, who is my editor at Gold Medal.

"Like the book," he said. "But there's a problem."

"Oh."

"Not enough sex."

"Oh."

"I'm sure you can think of something."

I argued a lot, but I didn't get anyplace. "We're not in business to sell books," he said. "We're selling hard-ons. Hard-ons sell books. You need a sex scene fairly early on in the book to hook the reader's attention and rivet his eye to the page."

Well, that's why the Ruthellen bit is in. I mean, it did happen, so I suppose it's legitimate. But I'm not really happy with it, and I'd be much happier if Mr. Elder would change his mind and cut it out after all, and—

Oh, the hell with it. Let's get back to the story.

Eight

SIMON BARCKOVER'S OFFICE was in the Brill Building at 1619 Broadway. I went into the lobby and found his name on the board while half the musicians and performers in America walked past me. I rode up to the seventh floor in an elevator I shared with two men carrying saxophones and one swarthy woman toting a caged parrot. I got off and found a door with a frosted glass window labeled *Simon Barckover—Artists' Representative.* There was a buzzer. I pressed it, and a female voice told me to come in.

A girl with red hair and freckles smiled at me from behind a green metal desk that almost matched her eyes. She asked if she could help me. "My name is Harrison," I said, "and I work for Leo Haig. I believe Mr. Barckover is expecting me."

"Oh, yes. You called earlier."

"That's right."

She glanced at the phone on her desk. One of its four

buttons was glowing. "He's on a call right now. Won't you have a seat?"

"Thanks but I'll stand."

She took a cigarette from a pack on her desk. "I guess you want to see him about Cherry," she said. "That was a shock. It was really terrible."

"Did you know her? I guess you must have, working in this office."

"I've only been here a couple months."

I looked at her for a moment. "I've seen you before," I said. "You were there last night."

"I was working there. Sometimes if I have a free night I do substitute waitress work in some of the clubs that book a lot of acts through Mr. Barckover. Mostly as a favor, but the extra money helps. Some places you get really decent tips."

"Do they tip well at Treasure Chest?"

"They didn't last night. I've only worked there a couple times and actually they never tip well there. They figure they're being taken, you know, paying such high prices for such rotten drinks, and then there's a cover charge at the tables, so they take it out on the poor waitress by leaving her next to nothing. Last night most of the people didn't even pay their checks in the confusion and everything. But I don't like clubs like Treasure Chest. I just did it last night as a favor to Mr. Barckover."

"Is he a good man to work for?"

Her hesitation answered the question for me. "Well, the pay isn't great," she said. "He's a nice man. He loses his temper a lot but that's because he's in such a high-pressure business. And he's very tolerant. He doesn't get uptight if I smoke dope or like that, and we have an agreement that I can take off whenever there's an audition I want to check out."

"You're in show business?"

"Let's say I'm going to be in show business. I'm a singer. So far nobody's in a rush to pay me money to sing, but I'll make it. Someday you can hear me at the Persian Room of the Plaza."

"I'll take a ringside table."

"You'd better make your reservations now. My opening's going to be sold out months in advance." The green eyes twinkled. "That's why I'm working for Mr. Barckover. He may not be the best agent in the business, but you get a real inside view of things working in an office like this. It's not just making contacts, although that doesn't hurt. It's learning how the business works and how to make your own openings."

I considered telling her that if her voice was as pretty as the rest of her she had nothing to worry about. But in a job like that she'd probably heard every line in the world, and mine was neither all that original nor all that terrific. While I hunted for a way to revise it, the little light on the phone went off.

"I'll tell him you're here," she said, and did. "He'll see you now," she said. "Right through that door."

I went right through that door. Barckover took a bite out of a sandwich and motioned me toward a seat, chewing furiously. He washed it down with a swig of coffee from a styrofoam container, bit a chunk out of a jelly doughnut, swallowed some more coffee, then lit a half-smoked cigar and leaned back in his chair. It was one hell of a change from Haskell Henderson and the alfalfa sprouts.

So was the conversation. Barckover didn't have to try hiding his presence at Treasure Chest from me because the police already knew about it, and he had a bonafide business reason for being there. The police had already pumped him dry. He'd agreed to see me because he couldn't very well refuse to, since Tulip was his client, but this didn't make him enthusiastic about it. He figured it was a waste of time. Actually more of my time than his got wasted, because he went ahead taking calls during the course of our interview, telling clients that he didn't have anything for them, telling club owners how sensational his clients were. The interruptions were a nuisance but there wasn't much I could do about it.

"I been over this with the police five or six times already," he said. "I was off in the back with this spastic prick from New Jersey. Like I only looked at the stage every ten minutes or so to make sure somebody was on it. You don't know what this business is like, man. After a few years you get so sick of tits and asses that the only way you can get a hard-on is if your woman wears clothes to bed. I never even saw Cherry take her fall. I heard the commotion and I looked up and I couldn't see anything by then because she was lying down and out of sight. I didn't see anybody do anything suspicious. I didn't even think to look for anything suspicious. I figure she fainted from popping too many pills or else she had a bad heart or something. What was it, something pygmies put on darts?"

"Something like that," I said. "Did Cherry take a lot of drugs?"

"For all I know she never even dropped an aspirin. Just going on generalities. Most of the go-go dancers and the topless-bottomless chicks do uppers. All that moving around and all those geeks gaping at them and it gets to them, and a little dexie straightens everything out and they can prevail, they can maintain, if you dig it. Like Lennie Bruce, baby, you got to be on top of it in order to get it out."

I had already been thinking of Lennie Bruce. One line of his in particular. He said there's nothing sadder than an old hipster.

I asked what Cherry was like.

"A comer," he said. "That kid started with nothing. She showed me some pictures of herself taken four, five years ago. Nothing. Big nose, flat in the chest. Not a pig but you'd never look at her twice."

"Cherry?"

He flicked the ash from his cigar. "Plastic surgery," he said. "Her old lady died and left her a couple of K's, no fortune, just a couple of K's, and she went and spent the whole bundle putting herself together. New nose, a trim job for the ears, silicone for the tits, a little of this, a little of that. Changed her name from something nobody can pronounce to Cherry Bounce. Great little name. Usually I pick names for them because most of these girls, they aren't too long in the imagination line. Cherry already had her name picked out when I got ahold of her."

"Did you pick out Tulip's name?"

He shook his head. "Nobody picks out anything for that one. She's smart, you got to hand it to her. Smart, well-educated, the whole bit. I'll tell you something, I think she's too fucking smart for her own good. With the face and body she's got she could have a future in this business. But she won't put out."

"I thought you didn't really have to do that anymore."

"Huh?"

"Put out."

He waved the cigar impatiently. "I don't mean sexual. I mean give out with everything you've got. Take the singing lessons, take the dancing lessons, make all the auditions, cultivate the right people. Cherry took the trouble. She put out. Tulip, she's got so much going for her, and all she wants to do is coast on what she's got. Pick up the easy bread showing her tits to the visiting firemen and waste all her time with those fucking fish."

"Well, that's her career."

"Career?" He looked at me as though I was an ambulatory psychotic. "You call that a career? Siphoning shit out of fish tanks? What's she gonna make, fifteen K a year running some fucking museum? You call that a career? There's chicks clearing that much a week in Vegas that haven't got half the equipment that girl has."

"But that's not what she wants."

"This year it's not what she wants. Five years from

now she'll be Assistant Fish Librarian in East Jesus, Kansas, and that's when she'll realize what she wanted all along was a career in show buisness. And by then it'll be too late."

I turned the conversation back to Cherry and tried to learn more about her personal life. Barckover turned out to be a less than perfect source. At one point he said that an agent was always in the middle, he was the one with the shoulders that everybody cried on, but Cherry evidently either didn't cry or found other shoulders. He didn't know much of anything about the men in her life, and in his opinion she had been murdered by some sort of weird pervert who got a thrill out of killing strange girls. "You watch it," he said. "There's gonna be a string of hits like this, a Jack the Ripper type killing topless dancers. Probably a religious fanatic." Evidently he didn't know that Tulip's fish had been poisoned, which poked a few holes in the Ripper theory.

An admirable thing about Cherry, according to Barckover, was that she never got seriously involved with any individual male. "Her career always came first," he said. "You get chicks who get hung up on one guy, and I get 'em a week in the mountains and they don't want to leave the guy, so either they pass up the gig or they take it and then they're lousy because they spend all their time pissing and moaning about being lonely. Not Cherry. She knows the priorities. If she's playing house and I get her two weeks in Monticello she goes without a second thought. There's always some dude around to go to bed with, but there aren't always jobs growing on trees."

(He would have been proud of a girl I know named Kim Trelawney. For a while we were almost living together, and she got signed for the ingenue part in a road company version of *The Estimable Sailor,* and although she may have shed a tear or two, off she went. That had been three months ago, and she was still treading the boards in places like Memphis, and we didn't bother

writing to each other, and by the time she came back I
had the feeling we wouldn't have much to say to each
other. It had been a long three months, let me tell you,
and maybe that was a contributing factor to the way I
reacted to Tulip, but I have to say I'd have probably gone
just as bananas over her anyway, to be perfectly honest.)

I asked him about some of the people on our suspects
list, and others who had been around Treasure Chest
when Cherry was murdered. He had never heard of Haskell Henderson. He'd met Andrew Mallard while Mallard
and Tulip were living together, and he said that in his
book Mallard was a total feeb. His word, not mine. He'd
been delighted when Tulip and Mallard split up.

He knew Leonard Danzig by sight and reputation and
could not recall having seen him at the club. And he was
surprised to know that Danzig had been keeping company
with Cherry. "He's no good," he said. "He's trouble."

"What does he do for a living?"

"You hear lots of things," he said.

"Would you happen to remember any of them?"

"A little of this, a little of that. He plays angles, he
hangs with some heavies. I don't know what he does but
if it's honest I'll spread it on toast and eat it." He hesitat-
ed for a moment. "If he had a beef with a chick, he
wouldn't get fancy with poison darts. I don't even think
he'd kill her. Maybe he'd beat her up. Or with a beautiful
girl like Cherry he'd do something like throw acid on her
or cut her so it would leave a scar. That's more his style."

I didn't get a whole lot more than that. If Cherry was
having trouble with Helen Tattersall, the downstairs
neighbor, Barckover didn't know about it. He had never
met Glenn Flatt, Tulip's ex-husband, and didn't know
anything about him. He was on nodding terms with
Buddy Lippa, Leemy's bouncer and gate-tender, and said
only that Lippa was a former boxer, a good club fighter
who did a decent job of keeping order in the joint. He got
evasive when I asked about Leemy, and when I probed to

find out who really owned the nightclub he made it obvious that he didn't want to carry that particular ball any further. I asked if either Leemy or Lippa made a practice of making passes at the hired help. He assured me they were both happily married men, which didn't strike me as an answer to the question I had asked, but I let it go.

He didn't know the other waitress or the barmaid, and I didn't ask him about his own secretary because I figured it would be more fun to ask her myself. I wound up the session with Barckover and went into the outer office and perched on the corner of her desk, notebook in hand. "I'm playing detective," I said. "Mind if I ask a couple of questions?"

She grinned. "You mean you're going to grill me? I already told you everything I know."

I told her we'd just go over a couple of things, and we did. I didn't learn much. I found out that the other waitress was named Rita and that was all she knew about her. Jan the barmaid was a regular at Treasure Chest, but my green-eyed friend hadn't had much contact with her except to order drinks and get change. She hadn't seen anything suspicious, hadn't recognized anybody except for Barckover and the people who worked at the club, and she knew nothing about Cherry's private life.

"There's something else," I said. "How am I going to catch you at the Persian Room if I don't know your name?"

She smiled. She didn't show me as many teeth as Haskell Henderson, but they looked better on her. "It's Maeve O'Connor," she said. I made her spell her first name and she did. She also told me it was Irish, but I could have figured that part out by myself. Then she pointed out that she didn't know my first name, so I supplied it, and then I told her I'd better take down her phone number.

"Is that what detectives always do?"

"Not always," I said.

"You could reach me through the office."

"But what if a case starts to break in the middle of the night and I need to check something with you? Mr. Haig would give me hell if I didn't have your number."

She gave it to me and I wrote it down. Then we looked at each other for a minute or two, and I could feel myself beginning to fall in love, which is something I probably do more readily than I should. I would have enjoyed perching on her desk for the rest of the afternoon, but Haig had given me a million things to do and there wasn't all that much time to do them in. I said I guessed I'd better be going, and she said "Goodbye, Chip," and I said, "I'll see you, Maeve," and that was that.

I called the advertising agency where Andrew Mallard worked and got a secretary who said that he was away from his desk. I asked when he would be likely to return to his desk and she said she didn't know. I pressed a little, and it turned out that he hadn't been at his desk all day, that he in fact had evidently taken the day off. I don't know why she couldn't come right out and tell me this straight out, but I guess when you work in advertising you get in the habit of doing things obliquely.

I tried Mallard at his home number and the line was busy. I looked at my watch and saw that it was almost three and remembered that I hadn't had anything to eat all day except for a sip of dandelion coffee substitute. I realized that I had to be hungry. I don't know if this would have occurred to me if I hadn't happened to look at my watch, but once I did I was starving. I found a luncheonette down the block and had a hamburger and three glasses of milk and a cup of coffee. I decided not to look at my watch again because it might remind me how little sleep I had had and I wanted to be awake when I talked to Mallard. Except that I wasn't destined to talk to Mallard. I called him after I'd finished my meal and the line was busy again, and I decided it wasn't the usual sort of busy signal, and I called the operator and asked her to check the line for me. She went into a huddle and came back with the news that the phone was off the hook. (What she actually said was that the instrument's receiver was disengaged, and it took me a second or two to translate it.) That had been my guess, and I decided Mallard had been up half the night with the police and the other half brooding, and now he was taking the day off and having himself a nap.

There's a way the operator can make the phone ring even when it's off the hook, and I considered telling her something about it being a matter of life and death, but they probably hear that line all the time and I didn't think I was likely to get the right note of conviction into my voice. Then too, if Mallard was sleeping it off he probably wouldn't welcome my making a bell ring in his apartment.

The next name on my list was Glenn Flatt, Tulip's ex-husband and current friend. He worked at Barger and Wright Pharmaceuticals in Huntington, Long Island. I got the number from Information and placed the call. The switchboard at Barger and Wright put me through to a man who told me that Flatt was in some laboratory or other and couldn't be disturbed. He asked me if I wanted to leave a number, so I left Haig's.

I didn't have a number for Leonard Danzig, and from what I'd heard about him I decided I wanted to take my time approaching him. Mrs. Haskell Henderson—I still didn't know her first name—lived on the other side of the Hudson. I would eventually want to see her in person, and I'd have to do that during the day when there would be no chance of running into Mr. Wheat Germ himself.

Helen Tattersall was on my list. I had no idea what questions to ask her, but sooner or later I would have to get a look at her, if only to see whether I had spotted her at the club. Tulip's building was in the neighborhood; I could just walk over there and invent a story.

Except that I didn't really want to. Treasure Chest was

also in the neighborhood, and Tulip had said that they were open afternoons so that businessmen could stop and goggle at some breasts before heading home to their wives. I wasn't sure that I wanted to look at breasts, but I had to talk to Gus Leemy and he could give me a line on the other waitress and supply Jan's last name and address. He could also pin my arms behind my back while Buddy Lippa beat me to a pulp.

I decided to chance it.

Nine

"THEY DIDN'T BEAT me up," I said. "What they basically did was ignore me. I had a lot of trouble making them believe I was a detective. They thought I wanted the girls' names because I was trying to make out with them, for Pete's sake."

"They seem good judges of character," Haig murmured.

I ignored that. "The barmaid is Jan Remo. She's been working there for almost a year. She's divorced and has a two-year-old kid. The other waitress—not Maeve—is named Rita Cubbage. She just started there about a week ago. I can see them both late tonight if I'm awake because they'll be working their usual shifts."

"The club will be open, then? In spite of the tragedy?"

"Leemy doesn't think it's a tragedy. He thinks it's a bonanza. He's got a sign in the window that you'd love. *'See the stage where Cherry Bounce was murdered! See the show so hot it might kill you!'* "

"You're making this up."

"I am not."

"Heavens," Haig said.

We were in his office. It was almost five-thirty and I had just finished summing up my day in my inimitable fashion. I had wanted to rush my report so that I could see Tulip, who had finally been sprung from jail by one of Addison Shiver's underlings and had been conveyed directly to Haig's house after a quick stop at her apartment to shower and change her clothes and feed her fish. Haig had spent about an hour grilling her, and then when I got back I hardly had time to say hello before he'd banished her to the fourth floor so that he could hear my report privately.

She hadn't seemed to mind the banishment—she'd been itching to study Haig's operation up there—but I minded. So I tried to hurry my report but Haig wasn't having any. He made me go over everything in detail and then he sat there with his feet up and I wanted to yell at him.

I said, "So far I'm putting my money on Haskell Henderson. His motives aren't entirely rational, but no one who eats like that is going to behave rationally. You wind up with alfalfa on the brain. Here's what happened. He resented the fact that Tulip's fish ate a better diet than she did. He kept giving her wheat germ and she kept feeding it to the fish and this infuriated him. He figured if he poisoned her fish she'd have to eat the wheat germ herself because there wouldn't be any fish to feed it to and she wouldn't want to let it go to waste. So he made himself some strychnine. I looked up poisons in the encyclopedia, incidentally. Strychnine and curare are both neurotics, which would give them something in common with old Haskell."

"That means they act on the nervous system."

"I know what it means. I was making a funny. I learned that strychnine is extracted from the seeds and bark of various plants. Henderson's got seeds and bark of everything else at Doctor Ecology, so why not *Strychnos Nux-Vomica*? I've been training my memory, that's how come I remember the name of the plant. I hope you're proud of me. He extracted the strychnine and poisoned the fish."

"Phooey."

"Is that all you're going to say? I thought it was a brilliant theory."

He raised his eyebrows. "And Miss Abramowicz? Why did he murder her, pray tell?"

"Give me a minute. I'll come up with something."

"Bah. This is childish. Call Miss Wolinski and—"

"Wait, I just figured it out. Tulip was his girl because he was crazy about her and enjoyed having a warm physical relationship with her, but Cherry was more experimental about nutrition. So he kept bringing health food to Tulip and what the fish didn't eat Cherry ate. So he killed Cherry for the same reason he killed the fish. All in the interest of getting Tulip to stop eating cooked meat and other poisonous things. What's the matter? I think it's neat the way I tied it all together. Why don't you call Gregorio and tell him to pick up Henderson? I won't let on that it was all my idea. When I write up the case I'll give you all the credit."

"Fetch Miss Wolinski," he said. "Perhaps she'd like a cocktail before dinner."

"Maybe some carrot juice," I suggested. "Alcohol's bad for the vital bodily fluids."

He gave me a look and I went upstairs to fetch Tulip.

I don't know exactly what dinner consisted of but I'm sure Haskell Henderson would have turned green at the thought of it. Wong had marinated squares of beef in something or other, then sprinkled them with toasted sesame seeds and mixed in some stir-fried vegetables, and the whole thing came together beautifully as always. During the meal Haig talked with Tulip about the problems

of breeding the *Ctenapoma* species. I didn't get the hang
of more than a third of their conversation, and I won't
plague you with any of it.

Afterward the three of us sat in the office. Tulip and I
had coffee. So did Haig, who also had two Mounds bars
in lieu of dessert. I picked up the phone and dialed Andrew Mallard's number again, and I got the same odd
busy signal as before.

"Sometimes he just leaves it off the hook for long
stretches of time," Tulip said. "He gets into these de-
pressed states where he decides that there's no one on
earth he could possibly want to talk to. It was really aggravating when I was living with him. I'd get calls for jobs
and I would never know about it."

"What does he do if somebody rings his doorbell when
he's in a state like that?"

"He generally answers it. But not always."

"That's great."

Haig said, "Miss Wolinski, you formerly shared that
apartment. Do you still possess a key?"

"I think so. Yes, I'm sure I do. I think it's still on my
key ring." She fumbled in her purse and detached a key
from the ring. "This is it," she said.

"Might he have changed the locks? You moved out
some time ago, I believe."

"It was five months ago." She thought for a moment.
"No, he wouldn't change the locks. He'd think of it but he
would never get around to it."

I wondered why she had ever set up housekeeping
with Mallard in the first place. He wasn't all that much to
look at, and the more I heard about him the less enthusiastic I got about seeing him.

"You had better take that key," Haig said. "You
needn't see Miss Remo or Miss Cubbage until late tonight. Mrs. Henderson can keep until tomorrow. Miss
Tattersall can probably keep throughout eternity as far as
we are concerned. A cranky old woman might be capable

of harassment. Such persons frequently poison other people's dogs and cats. It's a form of paranoia, I believe. I cannot imagine her flipping curare-tipped darts at a topless dancer."

"She wouldn't even walk into Treasure Chest," Tulip said. "Not a chance."

I felt like a character in a comic strip with a little light bulb forming over my head. "Just a minute," I said. "Earlier today you said the person who poisoned the fish was someone different from the person who poisoned Cherry." Tulip gaped and started to say something but I pressed on. "Does that mean the Tattersall woman poisoned the fish? And how do you know that, and why don't I talk to her and find out why? Because we already decided the two things tied in, they had to tie in, and—"

Haig showed me the palm of his right hand. "Stop," he said. "Helen Tattersall did not poison the fish. Let us for the moment forget Helen Tattertsall entirely."

"Then who did poison the fish? And how—"

"In due course," Haig said. "There is a distinction between a surmise and conclusion. There is no need to air one's surmises. It's odd that Mr. Flatt hasn't called. When did you see him last, Miss Wolinski?"

She thought it over, trying to frown her memory into supplying the answer, and the phone picked that minute to ring. I reached for it but Haig waved me off and snatched it himself.

He said, "Hello? Ah, Mr. Flatt. I was expecting your call. Yes. Let me make this short and to the point. I am representing your ex-wife, Miss Thelma Wolinski, in an investigation of the murder of her roommate. . . . If you'll permit me to continue, Mr. Flatt. Thank you. I have only one question to ask you. Why did you quit the premises of Treasure Chest so abruptly last night when Miss Bounce was murdered? No, sir, the identification was positive. No, I have not informed them. The police and I do not pool our information, sir. Indeed." There was a

pause, and Tulip and I spent it looking at each other. "I
want you in my office tomorrow afternoon, Mr. Flatt. At
three o'clock. No, make that three-thirty. I don't care
what you tell your employers. Three-thirty. 311½ West
20th Street, third floor. I look forward to it."

He hung up the phone and tried not to look smug. It
was a nice try but he didn't quite make it.

Tulip said, "How did you know he was there? I didn't
see him. Who told you?"

"Mr. Flatt told me. Just now."

"But you said—"

He shrugged. "Chip left a message for Mr. Flatt almost
five hours ago. He might have called back immediately,
routinely returning a call. He did not. He took time to establish that I am a detective and to stew a bit in his own
juices. Then, knowing that I am a detective and guessing
what I wanted of him, he ultimately returned my call. If
he had called back immediately or not at all he might well
have had nothing to hide. By taking the middle course, so
to speak, he established to my satisfaction that he was at
Treasure Chest last night."

This absolutely impressed the daylights out of Tulip.
She couldn't get over how brilliant he was, and he was so
delighted with her admiration that he celebrated with a
Clark bar and rang Wong for more coffee.

Wong brought two cups. He must have sensed that I
wasn't having any. I would have liked another cup but I
would have had to stay in that room to drink it and that
was out of the question. And he'd had the nerve to say
phooey to my theory about Haskell Henderson and the
health food conspiracy! I'd been babbling, for Pete's
sake, but I'd come as close to reality as that load of crap
about he-didn't-call-early-and-he-didn't-not-call.

It had been a bluff, pure and simple. If Flatt just told
him he was crazy he could roll with the punch, and if
Flatt bought the whole pitch then he was home free. It
was a bluff, and a fairly standard bluff, and not too far

removed from what I'd pulled on Henderson. I had to give him credit, he'd read his lines beautifully, but all it was was a bluff and the explanation he thought up later was just that, something he thought up afterward to fit the facts and make him look like the genius he wanted to be.

Of all the goddamned cheap grandstand plays, and of course Tulip bought it all across the board. And I'd had to sit there and watch. Well, I didn't have to put up with any more of it. I dialed Mallard's number once more, just as a matter of form, and then I scooped the key off the desk and got away from Miss Willing and Mr. Wonderful.

Andrew Mallard's apartment—by virtue of squatter's rights it was his, anyway—was on Arbor Street near the corner of Bank. I had more time than I needed to get his story before I was due at Treasure Chest, and I wanted to walk off some of the irritation I felt toward Haig, so I hiked down Eighth until it turned into Hudson Sreet, and then I groped around until I found Bank, made a lucky guess, and located Arbor Street. I usually get lost in the West Village, and the farther west I go the loster I get. I can find almost any place, but only if I start out in the right place. (I'm not the only one who has that trouble. When you've got a geometrically sensible city with streets running east and west and avenues running north and south, and then you rig up a neighborhood in which everything goes in curves and diagonals and Fourth Street intersects with Eleventh Street, you're just begging for trouble.).

I looked for a bell with Mallard on it and couldn't find one. Then I went through the listings carefully and found one that said Wolinski. He really was an inert type, no question about it. I mean, he'd been there five months by himself, and for a certain amount of time before that he'd shared the place with her, and her name was still on the bell and his wasn't.

I rang his bell and nothing happened. I rang it again

and some more nothing happened, and I tried Tulip's key in the downstairs door and of course it didn't fit, it was the key to the apartment. I wondered why she hadn't given me both keys and then I wondered why this hadn't occurred to me earlier. I said a twelve-letter word that I don't usually say aloud, and then I rang a couple of other bells, and somebody pushed a buzzer and I opened the door.

Mallard's apartment was on the third floor. I knocked on his door for a while and nothing happened. I decided he was either out or asleep or catatonic and there was no point in persisting, but it had been a long walk and I had the damned key in my hand so I persisted.

At 8:37 I let myself into his apartment.

Ten

AT 8:51 I LET myself out.

Eleven

I WALKED INTO the first bar I saw, went straight up to the bar and ordered a double Irish whiskey. The bartender poured it and I drank it right down. Then I paid for it, and I scooped up a dime from my change and headed for the phone booth in the rear. I invested the dime and dialed seven numbers and Leo Haig answered on the fourth ring.

I said, "How clean is our phone? Do you suppose we're all alone or do we have company?"

"Let us act as though we have company."

"Probably a good idea. I'm at a pay phone and I understand they're all tapped. But who has the time to monitor all of them? Of course if somebody was listening in I'd be a dead duck and that would make two tonight."

"I see."

"I was hoping you would."

"You're certain of the fact?"

"Positive."

"Do you know how the condition was induced?"

I shook my head, then realized that wouldn't work over the telephone. "No," I said. "He could have done it himself, he could have had help, or it might be God's will. No way I could tell."

"Hmmmm." I waited, and turned to glance through the fly-specked glass door of the phone booth. Several heads were turned in my direction. I turned away from them and Haig said, "I trust you have covered your traces."

"No. I took my lipstick and wrote *Catch me before I kill more* on the bathroom mirror."

"There is no need for sarcasm."

"I'm sorry," I said. "It shook me, I'll admit it. Do I report this?"

"Yes, and right away. Use a different phone."

"I know that."

"You said you were shaken."

"Not *that* shaken," I said. "Hell."

"Report the discovery and return here directly."

"Is our friend still with you? Because she's—"

"Yes," he cut in. "Don't waste time." And he hung up on me, which was probably all to the good because I really *was* a little rattled and I might have found ways to prolong the conversation indefinitely.

I went back to the bar and ordered another shot, a single this time, and a man came over to me and said, "Oh, let me buy you this one, why don't you. You seem terribly agitated. Nothing too alarming, I hope?"

I looked at him, and at some of the other customers, and I realized I was in a gay bar. "Oh," I said.

"I beg your pardon?"

I couldn't really resent it. You go drinking in a gay bar and people have the right to jump to conclusions. "Never mind," I said. "I don't want the drink anyway." I pocketed my change and left, feeling very foolish.

Two blocks over I found a booth on the street. I dialed 911 and changed my voice and told whoever it was that answered that there was a dead man at 134 Arbor Street and gave the apartment number and hung up before any questions could be asked of me. I walked another block and got in a cab.

I had found Andrew Mallard in the bedroom. The whole apartment had reeked of whiskey and vomit, and I figured he'd passed out. He was lying on his bed with his shoes off but the rest of his clothes on, laying on his back, a trickle of puke running from the corner of his mouth down his cheek.

I very nearly turned around and left at that point, and if I'd done that I'd have been in trouble, because I wouldn't have bothered wiping my fingerprints off the doorknob and a few other surfaces I'd touched. But something made me put my hand to his forehead. Maybe I sensed unconsciously that he wasn't breathing. Maybe I was toying with the idea of shaking him awake, though why would I have wanted a wide-awake drunk on my hands? For whatever reason, I did touch him, and he was cold, the kind of cold that you're not if you're alive. Then I reached for his hand and it was also cold, and his fingers were stiff, and at that point there was no getting around the fact that Andrew Mallard was a dead duck.

"But I can't tell you what killed him," I told Haig. "I counted five empty scotch bottles around the apartment, and that was without a particularly intensive search. If he emptied them all since the police let him go this morning then I know what killed him. Alcohol poisoning."

"He tended to leave garbage around," Tulip said. "I went back once for some stuff and there were newspapers three weeks old, and lots of empty bottles."

"Well, he emptied one of them today. The whole place smelled of booze and he reeked of it. I don't know if he drank enough to kill him."

Haig frowned. "You said he had been sick."

"You mean he threw up? Yes. Not a lot, though. Just a trickle."

"Hmmmm."

"He could have been poisoned. He could have had a heart attack or a stroke. I couldn't tell anything from what I saw, but then I'm not a medical examiner, I don't know what to look for. If his throat had been cut or if there was a bullet hole in his head I probably would have noticed. Then again, somebody could have strangled him or shot him in the chest and I probably *wouldn't* have noticed. I didn't want to disturb the body or anything."

"That was wise," Haig said. "The police will determine cause of death and time of death. They are sound enough in that area. Any efforts you might have made would only have served to render their work more difficult."

"That's what I figured."

"Did anyone see you enter the building?"

"I don't know. I wasn't trying to avoid being seen. I made sure nobody saw me leave. Anyway it doesn't really matter if they can prove I was there around 8:30. I don't know how long he was dead, I don't know how long it takes a body to lose body heat, but it was awhile."

Haig nodded absently, then leaned back in his chair. This time he kept his feet on the floor. His hand went to his beard and petted it affectionately.

I turned to Tulip. The expression on her face was like the one I had seen last night when Cherry was killed, a sort of numb look.

"It's so hard to believe," she said. "I slept with him, I lived with him. I was in love with him." She stopped to consider, then amended this. "At least I *thought* I was in love with him. For a while. And then he got to be a kind of a habit, you know. He was there and he needed me, and it took awhile to break the habit. But it's horrible that he's dead. He was a very nice man. He was a loser, you know, but he was a decent sort of a guy. If he could ever have gotten ahold of himself he would have been all right, but he never quite managed to, and now he never will, will he?"

I moved my chair away from the desk and closer to hers. She reached out a hand and I took it. Her hands were large—everything about her was large, for Pete's sake—but her fingers were very long and thin, and the touch of her hand was cool. She got her hand around mine and squeezed. There was a sad half-smile on her face and her eyes looked to be backed up with tears she had no intention of shedding.

"We shall have to play something of a waiting game," Haig said thoughtfully. "Three possibilities exist. No, four. Mallard could have been murdered. He could have committed suicide. He could have had a heart attack or something of the sort. Finally, he could have committed a sort of involuntary suicide due to overindulgence in alcohol. I don't suppose there was an empty bottle of sleeping tablets beside the bed?"

"It's the sort of thing I probably would have mentioned."

"Quite." Haig heaved a sigh. I'd say he heaved it just about halfway across the room. "We'll act on the supposition that the man was murdered. All deaths in the course of a homicide investigation ought to be regarded as homicides themselves until proven otherwise. It's by far the best working hypothesis. Miss Wolinski."

"Yes?"

"You will remain here this evening. There is a reasonably comfortable bed in the guest room. Wong Fat will change the linen for you. There is a murderer on the loose and he has already demonstrated that he can gain access to your apartment. I would be remiss in my duties if I permitted you to spend the night alone. I will brook no argument."

"I wasn't going to argue," Tulip said.

"Oh? Then you are a rational woman, and I am delighted. Mr. Harrison always resists my urgings to spend the night. But he too will stay here."

"No argument," I said.

"Oh? Extraordinary."

I didn't see what was so extraordinary about it. Any-body who wouldn't welcome the chance to spend the night under the same roof as Tulip needed hormone shots.

"Wong will make up the couch for you," he went on. "But first you have some places to go and some people to see."

Buddy Lippa was wearing a sport jacket that would have kept him safe in the hunting season. It had inch-square checks of bright orange and black, and I had the feeling that it glowed in the dark. He was also wearing blue-and-white striped slacks, a canary silk shirt, and a troubled frown. "You're gettin' to be a regular," he said. "I don't know if it's such a good idea. Bein' as you're un-derage and all."

"I showed proof of age last night," I reminded him. "I can't afford another ten."

"Oh, I wasn't lookin' for that. All it is, the boss might get tired of seein' you. Say, you happen to know when Tulip's gonna be workin' again? The two bimbos we got on tonight are strictly from Doggie Heaven."

I told him Tulip wasn't sure when she'd be returning to work. He let me through and I went up to the bar and or-dered a bottle of beer. Jan uncapped it and poured it into a glass for me. "How's Tulip?" she wanted to know. "Is it true she was arrested? Are you really a detective? Do they know who murdered Cherry?"

I said, "She's fine. Yes, I am. No, they don't, but Leo Haig is working on it."

She squinted for a moment and assigned the three an-swers to the three questions. She started to say something else but some clown from Iowa was tapping his glass im-patiently on the bar to indicate that it was empty. She moved off to take care of him. I looked up at the stage and watched a rather skinny blonde move around. She had a vacant expression on her face and whatever music she was dancing to was not the music they were playing. I guessed that she was tripping on something, either mescaline or speed. Whichever it was she probably did a lot of it, which would help to explain why she looked like she was suffering from terminal starvation. Her ribcage was more prominent than her breasts.

"Jesus, you again." I turned around and it was Gus Leemy and he still looked like a bald penguin, except now he looked like a constipated bald penguin. "Finish the beer and move on," he said. "Guys like you could cost me my license. No hard feelings, but I want to stay in business." He accompanied this last sentence with the most unconvincing smile anyone has ever flashed at me.

"I could cost you your license anyway," I said. "How long do you think you'd stay open if Leo Haig decided to go after you? There's a racket going on in your own club and you don't even know about it. You should be more worried about that than about me drinking a beer."

His eyes widened. "I don't know what you're talking about," he said.

"Of course you don't. That's the whole point. I think you'd better show up at Leo Haig's office tomorrow at three-thirty in the afternoon."

"What's it all about?"

"Three-thirty tomorrow," I said. "That's when you'll find out."

He started to say something else but changed his mind. He gave me a long look. I held his eyes for a few seconds, then turned back to my beer. If he'd kept up a barrage of questions I don't know exactly where I would have gone with them. It's easy to say *no comment* to a reporter, but reporters don't have Buddy Lippa around to hit you if you give them a hard time. I think this may have been running through his mind. Anyway, he decided against it and left me to drink my beer in peace.

I moved down the bar to where the waitresses came to

pick up their drinks. I sat there nursing my beer. Maeve
O'Connor came over after a few minutes to order three
whiskey sours and a pousee-café. Jan said she didn't
know how to make a pousse-café and it was no time for
her to experiment. Maeve said she'd see what else they'd
settle for and went away. She hadn't noticed me, which
was sad. She came back and said to change the pousse-
café to a stinger, and I said hello, and she smiled as if
genuinely pleased to see me. Which was nice.

I asked if her boss was around. She said he'd dropped
in earlier but had left about an hour and a half ago.

"The other waitress," I said. "Is that Rita Cubbage?
The girl who was working last night?" Maeve nodded.
"I'd like to talk with her," I said. "Ask her to stop by for
a minute."

Rita Cubbage turned out to be a black girl wearing a
blond wig. I hoped she took it off when she left the club;
most of the Times Square hookers wear wigs like that,
and if Rita walked down the street with it on she probably got a lot of offers.

I said, "Hello. My name's Chip Harrison and I work
for Leo Haig."

"The detective," she said. "Maeve told me. You were
here last night, weren't you?"

"Yes, but were you? Not with that wig."

"No, I left it off last night. Do you like it?"

"It's striking," I said.

"You don't like it." She grinned. "That's all right. Neither do I. But it boosts the tips, if you can dig it. My
hair's normally in an Afro and it puts the dudes uptight
because they figure I must be terribly militant. This way
they figure I put out."

I asked her about what she had seen last night, and
what she knew about Cherry and Tulip and the other
people involved in the case. She didn't seem to know very

much. There wasn't much point to it, as far as I could see, but I invited her to come to Haig's house at three-thirty. If he wanted a party, the least I could do was provide a full list of guests. She copied down the street address and put the tip of the pencil between her lips, a sudden frown of concentration on her face.

"Something," she said.

"You can't make it?"

"Oh, I guess I can. Something just on the tip of my tongue and now I can't get hold of it. You know how that'll happen?"

"Something about last night?"

"No, goes back a few days. Damn."

"Maybe it'll come to you."

"I just know it will," she said. "What I'll do, I'll sleep on it. Then in the middle of the night it'll come to me."

"Keep paper and pencil on the table next to your bed so you can write it down."

"Oh, that's what I always do. I'll be sleeping, and all of a sudden something'll pop into my head, and I'll write it down. Only thing is half the time the next morning I won't know what it means. Like one time I woke up and there was the pad of paper on the bedside table, and what it said on it was, 'Every silver lining has a cloud.' "

"That's really far out."

"Yeah, but what did I have in mind? Never did figure that one out." She winked. "See you tomorrow, Chip."

I went back to my beer. When Maeve came to pick up an order of drinks I gave her the same invitation. "And tell your boss it would be a good idea for him to show up, too. Three-thirty at Haig's place."

A few minutes later I got to extend the invitation to Jan Remo. I waited until she was pouring me a second beer and then I told her the time and the place. If her hand shook any, I didn't notice it.

"Three-thirty," she said. "I suppose I can make it. I'm having my hair done earlier but I should be through in plenty of time. But what's it all about?"

"Mr. Haig doesn't tell me everything," I said. "If I had to guess, I'd say he intends to trap a murderer."

"I thought the police solve murders."

"They do, occasionally. So does Leo Haig."

"And you're his assistant."

"That's right."

"Does Mr. Haig know who killed Cherry?"

"I told you he doesn't tell me everything. That's one of the things he hasn't told me."

She broke off the conversation to fill a drink order, then got Maeve's attention and asked her to handle the bar while she took a break. "You won't have to do much," she said. "If you don't push drinks at them they don't order much. Just cover for me while I go to the head."

I chatted with Maeve for a few minutes. Not about murder or other nasty things but about her career in show business and how she had a driving need to make a success of herself. I was pleased to hear this. It's a theory of mine that women with one driving need have other driving needs as well, which tends to make them more interesting company than other women. I don't know how valid this is, but I guess it'll do until a better theory comes along.

We didn't have all that much time to talk before Jan was back. They stood side by side for a moment, both of them rather spectacular to look at and both of them redheads, and a part of my mind started thinking idly in troilistic terms, which I gather is a fairly standard male fantasy. I suppose it's something I'll have to try sooner or later, but I have the feeling it wouldn't be as terrific in actuality as it is in fantasy, because it would be hard to concentrate and you wouldn't know which way to turn. At any rate, I was fairly certain I wouldn't get to try it with

Maeve and Jan. I had the feeling they were less than crazy about one another.

Then Maeve went back to her tables and Jan said, "I guess I'll be there tomorrow, Chip. But there's really nothing I know. Nothing that would help."

"You were right here when she got killed," I said. "Didn't you see anything at all?"

"The police asked me all that."

"Well, maybe you saw something and didn't know you saw it. I mean, you know, it didn't seem important at the time."

"I didn't even see it," she said. "I was pouring a drink. The first I knew something was wrong was when everybody took a deep breath all at once. Then I turned around and Cherry was lying on the stage and that was the first I saw of it."

"Well, I think you should come tomorrow anyway."

"I will."

I finished most of my beer and decided I could live without the rest of it. I left some change on the bar for Jan, decided it was a puny tip and added a dollar bill. I nodded a sort of collective goodnight on the chance that someone was looking my way and I walked to the door and out onto Seventh Avenue.

I thought about a cab and decided I would take the subway instead. The AA train stops at Eighth Avenue and Fiftieth, so I started uptown, and I walked about ten steps and felt a pair of hands take hold of my right arm. I was just getting ready to find out who owned them when two more hands took hold of my left arm and a voice said, "Easy does it, kid."

I said, "Oh, come on. It's the middle of Times Square and there are cops all over the place."

"Oh, yeah? I don't see no cops around, kid. Where are all the cops?"

Collecting graft, I decided. Sleeping in their cars. Be-

cause I couldn't see a single cop anywhere. I heard a ca-
lypso verse once that maintained that policemen, women,
and taxi cabs are never there when you want them. It's
the God's honest truth.

"We're just gonna take a nice ride," the voice said.
They were walking me along and they had my arms in a
disturbingly effective grip.

"Suppose I don't want to go?"

"That would be silly."

"Getting in a car would be sillier."

"Now what you got to do is use your head," said another voice, the one on my left. "A man wants to talk to
you. That's all there is to it. He says not to hurt you long
as you cooperate. What the hell, you're cooperating,
aren't you? There's the car, right around the corner, and
you're walking to it like a nice reasonable kid. So what's
the problem?"

"Who's the boss?"

"The guy we're going to see."

"Yeah, right," I said. We walked up to the car, a long
low Lincoln with a black man behind the wheel. He was
wearing sunglasses, his head was shaved, there was a gold
earring in his ear, and he had a little gold spoon on a
gold chain around his neck. That's either a sign that you
use cocaine or that you want people to think you do.

I said, "Look, tell me who the boss is or I don't get in
the car."

"If we want you to get in the car, kid, there's not a hell
of a lot you can do about it."

"I can make it easier," I said. "Just tell me who we're
going to see."

One of them let go of my arms and stepped around to
where I could see him. He wasn't much to look at, but he
didn't have to be to do his job. He looked like a hood,
which stood to reason, because that was evidently what he
was.

He said, "What the hell, you'll know in ten minutes

anyway. The boss is Mr. Danzig. You gonna get in the car now?"

"Oh, sure," I said. "I mean, why not? I was supposed to see him anyway."

Twelve

I DON'T KNOW what I expected exactly. He had already surprised me. I'd had the impression that he was very small-time, not important enough to have a couple of musclemen and a driver working for him. Of course he could have hired them for the occasion from Hertz Rent-a-Hood, but somehow I doubted this.

But whatever I had expected, he wasn't it. He was waiting for me in a penthouse apartment on top of a high-rise on York Avenue in the Eighties. One whole wall of the living room was glass, and you could look out across the East River and gaze at more of the Borough of Queens than anyone in his right mind would want to see. He was doing just that when we walked in, all dolled up in a black mohair suit and holding a glass of something-on-the-rocks in his hand. When he turned to look at me I got the feeling he was disappointed that it was only me and not the photographer from *Playgirl* magazine.

But he wasn't disappointed at all. He flashed me a smile that showed almost as many teeth as Haskell Henderson's without looking half as phony. "You must be Mr. Harrison," he said. "I'm so glad to see you."

He crossed the room. This wasn't as easy as it sounds because there was a lot of room to cross and all of it was covered by a light blue carpet deep enough to make walking a tricky proposition. He transferred his drink to his left hand and held out his right hand. I took it, and we shook hands briskly, and he let me have the smile again.

"I hope these gentlemen behaved properly," he said, indicating the two muscle types. The driver had stayed with the car. "And let me apologize for the manner in which I had you brought here. In my field, the direct approach is often the only possible approach. You weren't abused, I hope?"

"No."

"That's good to know," he said. He smiled past me at the two heavies. "That's all for tonight," he said. "And thanks very much."

There was something about the way he talked that made his sentences go on ringing in my head after he was done saying them. You just knew that he hadn't talked like this years ago, and that he wouldn't speak the same words or use the same accent if, say, you woke him up suddenly in the middle of the night. He was all dressed up in a suit as good as one of Gregorio's, and he had at least as good a barber, and his teeth were capped by the world's greatest dentist, and underneath it all you had a hard tough monkey who could beat a man to death with a baseball bat and then go home and tuck himself in for a good eight hours' sleep.

I had met the type before. Haig has a good friend named John LiCastro who spends a lot of his time sipping espresso in a neighborhood social club on Mulberry Street, making little executive decisions, such as who lives and who dies. LiCastro raises tropical fish, mostly cichlids, and when his fish die he practically puts on a black arm band. Leonard Danzig was an up-to-date version of the same type.

"You'll want something to drink," he said to me now. "I believe you generally drink beer. I have Heineken's and Lowenbrau."

There's nothing wrong with either, but I'd had enough beer. I asked if he happened to have Irish whiskey. He didn't, and he seemed genuinely apologetic. He gave me my choice of three different brands of expensive scotch. I took Dewar's Ancestor, which turned out to be what he was drinking, too. He made a drink for me and freshened his own and motioned me to a pair of chairs near the wall of glass. He took one and I took the other and we both sipped whiskey.

He said, "I have a problem. It started last night when Cherry was murdered. It's not getting simpler. It's getting more difficult."

I didn't say anything.

"You're with Leo Haig. He's a private detective. I also understand he's something of an oddball."

I admitted that some people probably thought so. I didn't bother to add that I was one of them.

"But I also understand he gets results."

"Well, he's a genius," I said. "And the only way to prove he's a genius is by solving impossible crimes, so that's what he does. He gets results."

"So I've heard." Danzig leaned forward, set his glass down on top of a small marble-topped table. He didn't use a coaster. Either glasses don't leave rings on marble or he didn't care. He could always throw the table away. I kept my drink in my hand. He said, "Cherry was a friend of mine, you know."

"I know."

"I had been seeing her for about a month, maybe a little longer than that. I probably would have gone on seeing her for another month. No more than that." He smiled disarmingly. "I don't seem to be very good at sticking to a woman. I find that any reasonably good-looking woman can be exciting company for perhaps two months. Then they become boring."

I didn't have an answer for that one.

"Unfortunately," he went on, "Cherry was murdered. I'm sorry about that if only because I genuinely liked her. She was a warm, sweet person." The smile went away. "I'm particularly sorry that she happened to be killed while I was involved with her. It's awkward for me. As long as the case remains unsolved, the police have an excuse to intrude in my affairs. They might even keep the case open on purpose in order to provide themselves with an excuse to harass me. In my business, that's a liability."

I didn't ask him what his business was.

"It's unfortunate that I have to be exposed to this simply because of my friendship for Cherry. I've been friendly with quite a few of the young ladies who've worked at Treasure Chest. I go there frequently, I get acquainted with the people who work there. The dancers, the barmaids, the waitresses. I'm in a position to be of assistance to them in their careers, you understand. And they like a taste of the high life. They work hard, they don't earn all that much money, they appreciate a decent dinner and civilized company."

"I see," I said. I didn't, if you want to know, but it was something to say.

"You familiar with a fellow named Andrew Mallard?"

"I never met him."

"Neither did I," Danzig said. He smiled again. "That's not what I asked."

"I know who he is." (I'm very proud of that sentence, let me tell you. Is. Not was. That's thinking on your feet, if I say so myself.)

"Was," Danzig said. "Not is. He died tonight."

"Oh?" (I'm less proud of that sentence, but they can't all be zingers.)

He nodded. "It was just on the radio. They identified him as a former close associate of Tulip Willing, roommate of murdered dancer Cherry Bounce. Somebody tipped the police and they found him dead in bed. His bed.

"How did he die?"

"Choked to death on his own vomit," Danzig said. He picked up his scotch and took a dainty sip. "Got drunk, passed out, then threw up in his sleep and sucked it into his lungs or something. You all right?"

"Just a little nauseous."

"Yeah, well, it's only dangerous if you happen to be unconscious at the time. Freshen that drink for you?"

"No thanks."

He crossed to the bar and put another ounce or so of scotch in his own glass. "Now here's my line of thought," he went on, returning to his chair. "I think it would be very convenient if it happened to turn out that Andrew Mallard murdered Cherry. He was there. He could have done it. Any list of suspects would have to have him on it, wouldn't you say?"

"I suppose so."

"There it is," he said. "All Leo Haig has to do is prove Mallard killed Cherry. Then he got full of remorse over what he'd done and did some heavy drinking. And so on How do you like it?"

"Well, it's certainly possible."

"That's the ticket." He drew an alligator wallet from his jacket pocket and pulled out a sheaf of bills. They were hundreds, and he counted out ten of them, paused, studied me for a moment, and counted out ten more. I don't know what he saw in my face that doubled the ante. Maybe the whole thing was just theatrics. "Two thousand dollars," he said.

"Uh."

Then he did something incredible. He took the twenty bills and tore them in half. I guess I wasn't perfect at keeping a straight face, because he grinned at my expression.

"For Haig," he said, offering me what managed to be half of two thousand dollars without being one thousand dollars. "Here, take it. He gets the other half when he proves that Andrew Mallard murdered Cherry Bounce. That's if he brings it off within three days. Take it."

I took it because it was impossible not to, but instead of holding onto it I set it down on the table next to Leonard Danzig's glass of scotch. "There's one problem," I said.

"Let's hear it. I'm usually fairly good at straightening out problems."

I could believe it. I said, "The thing is, you don't know Mr. Haig. I'm not saying he wouldn't work for you, but suppose Andrew Mallard didn't murder Cherry Bounce? Suppose someone else did?"

Danzig thought this over. I'd hate to play poker with him. Nothing at all showed in his face. At length he shrugged and said, "All right, I just thought it was easier that way. No loose ends. What I'm concerned with is the time element. If Haig gets the murderer in three days he gets the other half of the two thousand. How's that?"

"Whoever the murderer is?"

"Whoever."

I asked if I could use the phone. He pointed at one halfway across the room. I don't suppose it was more than forty yards from me. "It might be tapped," he said. "I pay a guy to check them out periodically, but he hasn't been around for a few days."

I told him it didn't matter. I didn't dial Haig's number because the phone had buttons instead of a dial. I *pushed* Haig's number and got him. I said, "I'm at Mr. Leonard Danzig's apartment. I just learned that Andrew Mallard died earlier today. It was on the radio." I went on to tell him the cause of death, then brought him up to date on Danzig's proposal and my counterproposal. He said "Satisfactory" a couple of times, which made me very proud of myself, and then he talked some more and I listened. Finally he said, "I am going to sleep now, Chip. Don't disturb me when you return. Your report can wait until morning. You made all the necessary arrangements?"

"Yes."

"Goodnight, then. And come directly home when you leave Mr. Danzig's apartment."

I said I would and hung up. To Danzig I said, "Mr. Haig says I should take your money."

Danzig smiled and pointed to the little pile of bills.

"There are a couple of qualifiers first. You mentioned a three-day limit."

"If it went a few hours over—"

"That's not the point. Would it be worth a bonus if Haig wrapped it up within twenty-four hours. Say to-morrow afternoon?"

"It wouldn't hurt any. What kind of a bonus?"

I was supposed to use my judgment on this one, so I judged quickly. "Double," I said. "Four thousand if it's wrapped up tomorrow. Two thousand if we make the three-day limit. Beyond that you don't owe us anything and you get the stack of homemade fifties back."

"Done."

"All right. The second point is that I'm supposed to ask you some questions now. Mr. Haig said he's assuming that you did not kill Cherry and don't know who did. He says only a rank fool would hire him under those circum-stances, and I've used my intelligence guided by my ex-perience to decide that you're not a fool."

"I'm honored."

"Were you at Treasure Chest the night Cherry was murdered?"

"Yes."

The admission was so direct that it stopped me mo-mentarily. I got back into gear and said, "Were you there when it happened?"

"I was on the premises."

"You missed the police dragnet."

"I went out the back. I didn't know it was murder but I gathered she was dead and I didn't want to be found on the premises in an official investigation."

"Are you the owner of Treasure Chest?"

"Let's say I'm a good friend of Gus Leemy's. Will that do for the moment?"

"Sure. Do you have any idea who might want to kill Cherry?"

"No one now. She's already dead."

"I mean—"

He crossed one leg over the other. "Just a small joke," he said. "No, frankly, I have no suspects. I rather like the idea of Andrew Mallard, but that's simply because it would be so convenient that way. And he seemed to be a disturbed person. Would a sane man choose that way to kill a woman?"

I wanted to say that a sane man wouldn't kill anybody for any reason but I didn't know how well this would go down, because I had the feeling that Danzig had killed people now and then, or had had them killed, and this would mean calling him a lunatic by implication.

"And you saw nothing suspicious?"

"Nothing. I was in no position to see anything at the time the incident occurred. I was in the office in the rear with Gus."

"Was anyone else with you at the time? I don't mean that you and Gus can't alibi each other, that's all right. But if other people were with you we could also rule them out."

"I'm afraid we were alone together."

I drank the last of my scotch. It was really great scotch. I said I guessed that was about it. "Mr. Haig wants you at his office at three-thirty tomorrow afternoon," I said. "You might as well bring the other half of the two thousand. Plus another two thousand."

He got to his feet and we began the long walk to the door. "Three-thirty," he said. "I'll be there. I wouldn't want to miss it. He really thinks he can come through in that short a time?"

"Evidently. He wants to earn the bonus."

But the bonus wasn't the big consideration, I knew. What Haig really wanted was the applause.

Thirteen

THE CAB DROPPED me at West 20th Street around two-thirty. I used one key to let myself into the courtyard, climbed two flights of stairs, and used another key to let me into Haig's half of the house. There was a light on in the office and I guessed that he hadn't been to sleep after all, but when I went in ready to hit him with some smartass remark or other his chair was empty and Tulip was sitting on the couch reading a Fredric Brown novel. *Mrs. Murphy's Underpants,* one of the late ones.

"This is pretty good," she said. "Have you read it?"

"Sure. Mr. Haig made me read everything of Fredric Brown's. That's not supposed to be one of his best."

"I'm enjoying it anyway. I like the way the two detectives play against each other. An uncle and a nephew."

"Ed and Am Hunter, right."

"Do you and Mr. Haig interact the same way?"

"Not exactly. Of course we're not related, which helps. Or hinders. I'm never entirely sure which. Also Ambrose Hunter is supposed to be reasonably sane."

"Well, Mr. Haig—"

"Is crazy," I said.

"But—"

"That doesn't mean he isn't a genius. Maybe all geniuses are crazy. I couldn't honestly say. For instance, thirteen hours from now he's going to trap a murderer. Don't ask me how because I don't know. Don't ask him, either, because I'm not convined he knows, and even if he does he's not telling. But he's going to have the whole crowd here, all sitting on chairs with their hands folded, and if he doesn't deliver he's going to look like Babe Ruth would have looked if he pointed to the fence and then struck out. The one thing he doesn't want is to look ridiculous, and with his shape and mannerisms he has a good head start in that direction, so he really has to deliver. And he probably will, but don't ask me how."

"It's kind of exciting," she said.

I agreed that it was. I said I thought I'd have a beer and asked her if she wanted anything. She didn't. I uncapped the beer in the kitchen and brought the bottle into the office with me. I asked her when Haig had gone to sleep.

"Right after he got your call. He said he was very tired. I guess he didn't get much sleep last night."

"Nobody did," I said, and yawned. "I'm completely shot myself. As soon as I finish this beer and unwind a little I'm going to stretch out on the couch and make Z's."

"Oh! I'm sorry, this is where you're going to be sleeping, isn't it? I'll go upstairs now."

I waved her back to the couch. "I have to unwind first," I said. "And you're the one who ought to be exhausted. Did you get any sleep last night?"

"Not really. They kept moving me around from one stationhouse to another."

"Yeah, the old cop shuffle. The hell of it is that they knew damned well you didn't kill Cherry. They just wanted to give you a hard time because you were Haig's client." I yawned. "Ed and Am Hunter. That's funny. Am Hunter was in a carnival for years. Can you see Leo Haig as a pitchman? I can't."

"Oh, I don't know." She considered, then giggled. I liked her wide-open laugh better.

"What's so funny?"

"Well, Ed Hunter certainly goes over well with the girls in this book."

"Thanks," I said.

"No, I meant it as a compliment."

"You did?"

"Well, yeah. You probably do pretty well yourself. And the two of you do play off each other the same way, even if you're not related."

"We were almost related," I said. "A couple of months ago the cops picked me up and held me for seventy-two hours. They were just making a nuisance of themselves. As usual."

(It was an interesting case, incidentally. I never wrote it up because there wasn't enough to it to make a book out of it, and there was no sex in it, and Joe Elder at Gold Medal insists it's impossible to sell a book without sex in it. Maybe I'll try to write it up as a magazine story one of these days.)

Tulip frowned. "I don't get it," she said. "I mean, it's terrible that they locked you up and all, but how does that make you and Haig almost related?"

"It doesn't *make* us almost related. What it did was *almost* make us related. See, they wouldn't let him visit me in jail because he was neither a relative nor an attorney. He decided this might come up in the future so what he wanted to do was adopt me. He said it made perfect sense considering that my parents are dead. I told him it was ridiculous because I might someday become a partner in the firm."

"So?"

"So Haig & Harrison is possible," I said. "But Haig &

Haig is ridiculous, unless you happen to be producing scotch whiskey. That wasn't the reason I wanted to avoid being adopted but it was a reason that made perfect sense to him, and—"

She began to laugh, and I joined in, and we really did quite a bit of hard-core laughing. Then we stopped as suddenly as we started and Tulip looked at me with her upper lip trembling slightly and I thought she was going to cry. I sat on the couch next to her and took hold of her hand.

"Everything's so funny," she said, "and then I re-member that Cherry's dead and Andy's dead and I don't know how I can laugh at anything. And the murderer must be someone I know. That's the most frightening thing in the world. Somebody I know committed murder."

I put an arm around her and she sort of settled in against my shoulder. I gave her shoulder a squeeze and took her hand with my other hand.

"Who do you think did it, Chip?"

"I don't know."

"Could it have been Andy?"

"I suppose it could have been anybody. How did he get on with Cherry?"

"I'm not even sure they met. Where would he get hold of poison? Where would he get a key to my apart-ment? I don't understand."

"Neither do I." ·

"I'm just so confused."

She snuggled closer and I got a healthy lungful of her perfume. It was all I needed. I mean, the whole scene was beginning to get a little strange. I was playing a kind of comforting Big Brother role, which was weird in that she was not only older than me but bigger. And at the same time she was turning me on something terrible, and it shouldn't have been that way because the scene itself wasn't fundamentally sexual, but go tell yourself that when you're turned on. I looked down at her body and remembered what it looked like with no clothes on it, dancing merrily away on the stage at Treasure Chest, and then I closed my eyes because the sight of her was doing things to me, and having my eyes shut didn't really help at all because I could see her just as well with them shut.

"It's all so rotten," she said.

I took a breath. "Look," I said, "I think you'd better go to sleep, Tulip. It's late and you're exhausted, we're both exhausted. Things will look better in the morning."

"That's what people always say, isn't it?"

"Well, I didn't claim to originate the line."

"Maybe things *will* look better in the morning. But will they *be* any better?"

"Uh."

"I guess you're right," she said. She got to her feet. "Could you show me where my room is?"

I walked her to her room. "Come in for a minute," she said. "You don't mind, do you?"

We went into the room. She flicked on a light. The bed had been opened and Wong had changed the sheets. I hadn't really had enough time to dirty them.

"It looks comfortable," she said.

"I'm not sure whether it is or not. I spent a couple hours on it this morning, but I was too tired to notice whether the bed was any good. It probably beats the couch. I slept on that one night before Haig bought the bed and it was like spending a night on the rack. I woke up with my spine in the shape of the letter S."

"Oh, and now you have to sleep on it again because of me! I'm sorry, Chip."

I used both hands to get my foot out of my mouth. It was a struggle. "Oh, I was exaggerating," I said, not too convincingly, I think. "It's not really all that bad. Anyway as tired as I am it won't make any difference." I made myself yawn. "See? Can't keep my eyes open. Well, goodnight, Tulip. Guess I'll see you in the morning, and in the meantime—"

"Chip?"

"What?"

"Look, we don't really know each other, and maybe this is silly, and of course I'm probably too old for you and you couldn't possibly be interested, but—"

"Tulip?"

"Don't go, Chip."

It started off being basically closeness and warmth and comfort, and we were both deliciously exhausted, and we drifted gradually into a beautiful lazy kind of lovemaking. Then it stopped being lazy and we stopped being aware that we were all that exhausted, and then we stopped being aware of much of anything, actually, and then, well, it became too good to talk about.

And a while later she said, "I thought it might turn you off. Me being older than you."

"Oh, sure. You really turned me off, Tulip. That's what you did, all right. Like a bucket of cold water."

She giggled. It was a pretty sexy giggle, actually. "Well, I thought it might turn *me* off, then. I was attracted to you, you know, but I'm used to older men. And we were both so tired but I wanted to do it anyway." She put her hand on my stomach and moved it gradually lower. "You must be really exhausted now," she said, holding on to me. "Oh."

"Uh-huh."

"How did you get so wide-awake so fast?"

"It's one of the advantages of younger men," I said. "We have these incredible recuperative powers. Especially when we're in bed with somebody like you."

"How nice," she said. "But you must be tired."

"I'm not *that* tired," I said.

The last conscious thought I had was that I'd damn well better get from her bed to the couch before I fell asleep. Because Haig would either say something or maintain a diplomatic silence, and one would be as infuriating as the other. I had that thought, all right, but that was as far as it went. The next thing I knew it was morning.

Fourteen

I WAS THE last one awake. I yawned and stretched and reached for Tulip and encountered nothing but air and linen. I yawned some more and got up and put clothes on. They were having breakfast. I slipped out without saying hello, walked the few blocks to my own rooming house, showered and changed clothes and went back to Haig's. By then they were in the office and the great man was on the telephone. I couldn't tell who was on the other end of the line or what they were talking about, because all Haig said was "Yes" and "No" and "Indeed" and, at last, "Satisfactory." For all I could tell he had called the weather bureau and was talking back to the recording.

"There you are," he said to me. "I thought you'd gone off without instructions. You'll want to see Mrs. Henderson without further delay. And there are other errands for you as well."

I got out my notebook.

"I also want your report. Last night, from the time you

307

left for Treasure Chest until your return. Verbatim, please."

I came as close to verbatim as possible and he listened to it with his feet on the desk. When I'd brought it to the point where I left Danzig at his apartment and hopped a cab home, he took his feet off the desk and leaned forward and frowned at me. "How did Mr. Danzig know where to find you?" he demanded.

"I thought about that. Jan Remo."

"The barmaid."

I nodded. "She excused herself to go to the bathroom. I don't think she went to the bathroom. I think she went to the telephone."

"And called Mr. Danzig."

"Right. I think she fingered me. That's the right term, isn't it?"

"I believe so."

"Well, I believe she fingered me." I pictured Jan, the red hair, the feline face, the fishnet stockings, the body stocking filled with just what I'd always wanted for Christmas. "She fingered me," I said. "I'd like to return the favor."

"I beg your pardon?"

"Just thinking out loud," I said.

Haig grunted—his way of thinking out loud—and spun around to consider the Rasboras. I looked over at Tulip and she gave me the world's most solemn wink. I don't know if I blushed or not. I probably did.

Haig turned around again. "There's another variable. Rather surprising. You had a telephone call this morning during your absence."

"Oh?"

"From another topless dancer, I assume. One of those inane stage names." He turned to Tulip. "Your pardon, Miss Wolinski. No criticism is intended."

She assured him none was inferred.

"I don't recall that you've mentioned this one," he went on. "You know your reports must be as comprehensive as possible. The slightest detail—"

"There was no other dancer. Oh, there were a couple new ones last night, but I didn't talk to them. I didn't even get their names, and if that was an oversight I'm sorry. Who was it that called?"

He consulted a slip of paper. "She gave her name as Clover Swann," he said. "I've no idea what her real name might chance to be. She left a number."

"Oh, for Pete's sake," I said. "She's not a topless dancer."

"Indeed?"

"She's an editor," I said. "At Gold Medal." The image of Clover Swann, Gold Medal's resident hippie, dancing nude on the stage of Treasure Chest, suddenly flashed somewhere in my mind. It was by no means an unappealing image, but I had the feeling she was happier editing books.

"It was not an illogical assumption," Haig said. "Clover Swann indeed."

"Well, she's an editor. She probably wants to know when I'm going to do another book for them. I'll call her tomorrow or the next day."

"You'll call her now."

I just looked at him.

"Now," he repeated. "Bear in mind, Chip, that I hired you as much for your journalistic ability as anything else. It is not enough to be a brilliant detective. The world must know that one is a brilliant detective. Call Miss Swann. I have the number right here."

"I know the number," I said. I picked up the phone and dialed it, and after I'd given the operator everything but my Social Security number I got through to Clover.

"I've been reading the papers," she said. "It sounds as though you're right in the middle of an exciting case. Topless dancers and everything."

"And everything," I agreed.

"It ought to be perfect for your next book. Are you going to write it up?"

"That depends," I said. "A few hours from now Mr. Haig is going to reach into a hat. If he pulls out a rabbit I'll have something to write about. If he comes up empty it's not going to make much of a book."

Haig scribbled furiously, passed me a note. I read it quickly. It said: *"Show more enthusiasm."*

Clover must have read the note because she showed plenty of enthusiasm. She went on telling me what a great book it would make, that it had all the ingredients. "And it should be a cinch to have a lot of sex in this one," she said. "You know what Joe always says."

I knew what he said, all right. *"People like to read about what a character Haig is and all that, Chip, but if you want to sell books to them you have to give them a hard-on."* That's what he always said.

"I'm not sure there's too much sex in it," I said.

"Oh, who do you think you're kidding?" She laughed heartily. "Topless dancers? Chip Harrison cavorting with a batch of topless dancers? If I know you, you're bouncing around like a satyr in a harem."

"Er," I said.

"Just let me know how it goes today, Chip, and we'll draw up a contract. You could even start thinking about a title."

"Uh," I said.

I wrapped up the conversation and then I had to give Haig a *Reader's Digest* version of it. Then he told me what I had to do next, and I made some notes in my notebook and headed for the door.

Tulip walked me to the door. When we were out of Haig's hearing range she slipped an arm around my waist.

She turned her body so that her breasts rubbed companionably against my chest.

"Not enough sex," she purred. "Ho, boy! How about a fast bourbon and yogurt?"

I'm sure I blushed that time. Damn it.

I got the Cadillac from the garage. It's my car, but if it weren't for Haig I wouldn't be able to go on owning it. He pays fifty dollars a month so that it can live in a garage on Tenth Avenue. Maybe twice a year I have occasion to use it, and yes, it would be a lot cheaper to rent a car, but I like this one and Haig doesn't seem to mind the expense. The car was given to me by Geraldine, who runs a whorehouse in Bordentown, South Carolina, where I worked for a while as a deputy sheriff.

(You could read about it if you want. It's in a book called *Chip Harrison Scores Again*. I want you to know that the title was not my idea.)

Anyway, the car's a Cadillac, which sounds impressive, but it's also more than twenty years old, and I guess it's the last stick-shift automobile that Cadillac ever made. It's in beautiful shape, though. Geraldine only drove it on Sundays. To church and back.

I picked it up at the garage, crossed over to Jersey and managed to find the Palisades Parkway. I got off at the Alpine exit and found the town of Closter, and I only had to ask directions four times before I found Haskell Henderson's house. It was a colonial, painted yellow with forest green trim, set fairly far back on a lot shaded by a great many large trees. A huge dog in a fenced yard next door barked at me. I waved at him and walked up a flagstone path to the front door and poked the bell. An elaborate series of chimes sounded within the house. I waited for a while and was about to hit the bell again when the door opened. A woman stood in the doorway with a cigarette in one hand and a glass of colorless liquid in the other. She said, "If you're from the Boy Scouts, the newspapers are stacked in the garage. If you're from the ecology drive the bottles and cans are in a bin next to the newspapers. If you're selling something I've probably already got it and it doesn't work and the last thing I want is to buy another one."

I was standing close enough during her little speech to identify the colorless liquid in her glass. It was gin. Mrs. Haskell Henderson was in her early thirties, built like the Maginot Line, and already sloshed to the gills at ten twenty-five in the morning.

"I'm not," I said.

"You're not which?"

"Any of them," I said. "My name is Chip Harrison and I work for Leo Haig."

"I don't."

"I beg your pardon?"

"I don't work for Leo Haig. I don't work for anybody. My name is Althea Henderson and I drink a lot. And why shouldn't I, huh? That's what I want to know."

"Well. May I come in?"

"What the hell, why not." She stood aside and I entered the house. "Why shouldn't I drink?" she demanded. "Kids are at camp, husband's at the office, why shouldn't I drink?" She gestured vaguely and some of the gin moved abruptly from the glass to the oriental rug. She didn't appear to notice. "Bad for the liver," she said. "Well, what the hell do I care, huh? Who wants to drop dead and leave a perfectly good liver behind? What you got to do in this world is wear out all at once. It's a question of timing."

"Oh."

"Wanna drink?"

"It's a little early for me, thanks."

"Then how 'bout some carrot juice? Carrot juice, papaya juice, dandelion coffee—that's the kind of crap my husband drinks. How 'bout a nice bowlful of sprouted alfalfa, huh? Just the thing to set you up for a hard day's work, right?"

"Speaking of your husband, Mrs. Henderson—"

"Call me Althea."

"Speaking of your husband, Althea—"

"What about him?" Her eyes narrowed, and I got the impression she wasn't quite as drunk as she made out. She'd been drinking, certainly, and it was getting to her, but she had been riding it a little, either for my benefit or because it felt good. "What about him? Is he in some kind of trouble?"

"It's possible."

"It's that girl who was murdered, isn't it? The one with the big tits."

"Cherry Bounce, yes."

"Cherry Bounce my ass," she said. "That little bitch must have given her cherry the bounce when she was eleven years old. Was he fucking her?"

"No."

"That's a surprise. Maybe her tits weren't big enough. Were they big ones?"

"Well. Uh. Yes, uh, they were."

"Then I'm surprised he could keep his hands off them," she said. She took another swig of gin and asked if I was sure I didn't want to drink. I was sure, and said so. "He's a tit man, Haskell is. Always has been. A health freak and a tit freak. That's why he runs around the way he does. Oh, hell, if you were thinking about keeping his secret, he hasn't got any secret to keep. The two of us play a game. He pretends I don't know he runs around and I pretend the same, but all it is is a game."

She flopped into a chair. "He can't fool me. All the health crap he eats, all the vitamins he takes, the man's got more energy than Con Edison. He used to make it with me twice a night and once every morning. Rain or shine, three times a day. He was wearing me out. And now he hasn't made it with me in almost three years."

I didn't say anything.

"Because of these," she said, cupping her enormous breasts in her hands.

"I don't get it."

"Neither do I," she said. "Used to get it three times a day and now I don't get it at all. Because of these. They used to be the reason he married me, and now—"

"Uh—"

"The hell of it is that I love the bastard. And he loves me. But I don't turn him on anymore. Because he's a tit man and that's all there is to it."

"You lost me," I said.

She stood up. "C'mere," she said. I stepped closer to her. She put the index finger of her right hand to the tip of her left breast. "Feel," she said. "Christ sake, don't just stand there. Grab yourself a handful. Go on, dammit!"

I cupped her breast with my hand.

"Don't be shy. Give it a little squeeze."

I gave it a little squeeze.

"Feel good?"

"Uh, yes."

"Now the other one."

"Look, Mrs. Henderson—"

"Althea, dammit."

"Look, Althea—"

"Shut up. Feel the other one, will you?"

I followed orders.

"Well?"

"Well what?"

"Uh—"

"Both feel the same?"

"Sure."

"Not from this end they don't. Wait right here. Don't go away." I waited right there and didn't go away and she came back with a hat pin about four inches long. "Stick it in my tit," she said. "The left one."

"Don't be ridiculous. Look, Mrs. Henderson, Althea, maybe I should come back some other time. I—"

"Oh, hell," she said, and plunged the hatpin into her left breast. My stomach flipped a little but she didn't seem to feel a thing. She drew out the pin. There was no blood on it. Her eyes challenged me and I began to get the picture.

"Foam rubber," she said. "The other one's real. Until a couple of years ago they were both real and Haskell was crazy about them. Then I had to have a mastectomy because some knife-happy surgeon decided I had the big C. Turned out it was benign but by that time he'd already done his cutting. Only half a woman now. Used to turn Haskell on. Now all I turn him is off. Still loves me, I still love him, but he takes all his vitamins and drinks his carrot juice and eats his alfalfa and walks around horny as a toad and I don't do him any good. That's why he needs his topless dancers."

I stood there wondering why floors never open up and swallow you when you want them to. She went out to the kitchen for more gin. I thought she was lucky she wasn't too drunk when she did her trick with the hatpin or she might get the wrong breast by mistake and it would probably hurt. When she came back I managed to steer the conversation back in its original direction. I asked her what she had been doing the night before last, and what her husband had been doing.

"He was working late at the store," she said. "Do you believe that?"

"Well—"

"And I was drinking carrot juice and counting my nipples. Do you believe that?"

"Althea—"

"He was chasing women in New York. And I was here, sitting in front of the television set and drinking scotch. Not gin. I never drink gin after four in the afternoon.

Only a pansy would drink gin after four in the afternoon."

"I see. Can you prove it?"

"Prove it? Hell, everybody knows only a pansy would drink gin in the nighttime. What's there to prove?"

"Can you prove you were home watching television?"

"Oh," she said. She thought it over. "You think I went into New York and stuck a pin in that girl's tit. What was her name again?"

"Cherry Bounce."

"Why the hell would I do a thing like that? I don't go around sticking pins in tits all the time like some kind of a nut. I just did it now to prove a point. Lessee. Kids are at camp so they can't gimme an alibi. Oh, sure. My neighbor from down the street was over here. Got here about nine o'clock, left when Johnny Carson went off the air. Marge Whitman, lives just down the street. She's in the same boat as me. Well, not exactly. She's got two tits but she's got a pansy for a husband. Leaves her out here and spends his night picking up sailors on Times Square, the fucking pansy. Drinks gin all night long, the goddamn fruit."

I got the Whitman woman's address and started backing toward the door. She asked me where I was going. "I have some other calls to make," I said.

"I turn you off too, don't I?"

"No, not at all, but—"

"You're a tit man like my husband."

"Not exactly."

"You don't like tits?"

"I like them fine, but—"

"You're not a pansy, are you?" I shook my head. "What do you drink in the evening?"

"Whiskey, usually. Sometimes a beer. Why?"

"Not a pansy," she said. And then she took her blouse off, and then she took her bra off, and I just stood there. She had one absolutely perfect breast, and where the other had been there was smooth skin with an almost imperceptible scar from the incision.

"Sickening, isn't it?"

"No, not at all."

"Deformed."

"No."

"Turns you off, doesn't it?"

The weird thing is that it was turning me on. I don't know how to account for it and I'd rather not stop and figure it out. It probably just proves I'm kinkier than I realized, but why go into it too closely?

"C'mere," she said. I did, and she opened my zipper and groped around. "I'll be a sonofabitch," she said. "Well, you're not a faggot, are you?"

"No, and—"

"And I don't turn you off, do I? Maybe you're a sensible tit man, that's what it must be. You figure half a loaf is better than none. Right?"

"Uh."

Her hand clutched me possessively. She turned and began leading me toward the staircase. I had the choice of following her or leaving part of my anatomy behind, and I've always been attached to it. I followed.

If Althea had had her way she would have kept me there for hours. And I'll tell you something. If we weren't in the middle of a case I would have stayed. She evidently had an enormous complex about her absent breast, which old Haskell must have done a good job of reinforcing, and as a result she did everything she could to compensate for what she regarded as a terrible deficiency. As far as I was concerned, passing her up because she only had one breast was like refusing to listen to Schubert's Eighth Symphony because he never got around to finishing it.

I finally managed to get out of there after promising to return when I got the chance. Then I stopped at the Whitman house to confirm Althea's alibi, although I

didn't really need confirmation. But Haig would be sure
to ask and I would have to have the answers.

Mrs. Whitman was quick to recall watching television
with Althea on the night in question. She was also quick
to offer me a cup of coffee, which I declined because I
was really in a hurry. And I got the impression that she
would have gladly offered me a lot more than coffee. She
was a good-looking woman, a little older than Althea,
but certainly nothing to complain about.

Back in the car, I wondered if Mr. Whitman was really
homosexual. The fact that he drank gin in the evening
didn't strike me as sufficient evidence in and of itself. I
know a lot of perfectly straight people who drink gin in
the evening. I think they're crazy, but it doesn't make
them gay.

Then I began thinking about the conversation with
Clover, and how I'd told her there probably wouldn't be
much sex in the book. I wondered if our talk had had
anything to do with the fact that Althea and I wound up
in bed. I suppose it could have operated on a sort of sub-
liminal level. Maybe it was my aspirations as an author
that goaded me to respond to Althea's advances.

Somehow I doubt it.

I drove back over the George Washington Bridge and
down the West Side Drive. I got off at 72nd Street and
drove down to Tulip's building. Of course there was no
place to park. I circled a few blocks a few times and then
stuck it in a lot. The attendant was very impressed by the
car and flipped completely when he saw he was going to
have to shift it. "A Cad with a stick shift," he said.
"Where'd you ever find it?"

"South Carolina."

"There a lot of 'em down there?"

"Thousands," I said.

On the way to Tulip's building I spent a dime on a telephone and made my report. It took some time and I had

to feed the phone extra change. I left out the part about going to bed with Althea. Verbatim only goes so far is the way I figure it.

Haig told me it was satisfactory. I was glad to hear it. He said, "After you see Miss Tattersall, you'll go to Tulip's apartment and feed her fish. You have the key?"

"Yes, sir. She gave it to me a couple of hours ago. You told her to, remember?"

"The *Ctenapoma* receive brine shrimp. There's some in the freezer compartment of the refrigerator. I believe that's all they receive. One moment."

He asked Tulip if this was so, and she said there were also some bloodworms and mealworms in jars in the refrigerator, and I should give them that if it was no trouble. "They're strictly carnivores," I heard her say. "Unless —I wonder if that's what's keeping them from spawning! I used to give the scats a lot of wheat germ and it put them in great breeding condition."

Haig said, "Chip."

"Yes."

He covered the mouth piece with his hand and I couldn't make out what he and Tulip were saying to each other. Then he said, "There is a jar of Kretchmer wheat germ in the cupboard to the right of the sink. On the second or third shelf, Miss Wolinski doesn't recall precisely where."

"I'll manage to find it. You want me to give some to the *Ctenapoma*?"

"No! Absolutely not."

"Fine. Hold your horses. Then what difference does it make what shelf it's on?"

"Bring the wheat germ back here with you. Do not open the jar. Be very careful of the jar. Wrap it so that it won't break should you happen to drop it. Do you understand?"

"Oh."

"Do you understand, Chip?"

"I think so," I said. "I think I do."

Fifteen

HAIG MAKES ME read a lot of mysteries. Since we don't get all that many cases, and since you can only spend so much time feeding fish and cleaning out filters, that leaves me with plenty of time to humor him. It's his theory that you can learn anything and solve any puzzle if you just read enough mystery novels. Maybe he's right. It certainly seems to work for him, but he's a genius and I feel that constitutes special circumstances.

Well, if you've read as many of them as I have—not even as many as Haig has, because nobody has read that many—then you know what happened when I finally got around to seeing Helen Tattersall. I mean, her name came up early on, and I kept ducking opportunities to see her, so naturally one of two things had to happen. Either she turned out to be the killer or she supplied the one missing piece of information that tied the whole mess together. Right?

Wrong. Absolutely wrong.

I got in to see her by posing as someone investigating

her complaint about her neighbors. Even then I had a
hard time because she really didn't like the idea of opening her door, but I explained that I couldn't act on the
complaint unless I interviewed her face-to-face. Much as
she didn't want to open her door, she decided to risk it if
it would facilitate her making trouble for somebody.

When she opened the door I decided on my own that
she hadn't gone to Treasure Chest and planted a poisoned
dart in Cherry Bounce's breast. Because Helen Tattersall
was in a wheelchair with her leg in a cast, and the first
thing she did was inform me that she'd been in the cast
for two months and expected to be in it for another four
months, and she didn't sound very happy about it.

The next thing she said was, "Now which complaint
have you come about? The upstairs neighbors? Those
prostitutes? Or the man next door who plays the flute all
day and all night? Or the married couple on the other side
of me with that dreadful squalling baby? Or the man across
the hall who gives me dirty looks? Or the evil man down by
the elevator who puts poison gas in everybody's air-condi-
tioners? Or could it be my complaints about the building
employees? The superintendent is a Soviet agent, you
know—"

So she didn't even have a personal vendetta against
Tulip and Cherry. Instead she had just one enemy: man-
kind. And she complained about and tried to make trouble for every member of the human race who called himself to her attention.

Well, I couldn't get out of there fast enough. I began
wishing I were Richard Widmark in *Kiss of Death* so that
I could push the old bitch down a staircase, wheelchair
and all. I'm not saying I would have done it, but I might
have given it serious consideration.

I suppose there should have been one little thing she
said that got my mind working in the right direction, one
little thread she might unwittingly supply, but I'm sorry,
there just wasn't anything like that. It was a waste of

time. I had sort of thought it would be a waste of time, and that's why I'd postponed seeing Helen Tattersall as long as I did, in addition to having suspected that meeting her wouldn't be one of my all-time favorite experiences. I was right on all counts, and it was a pleasure to get out of her apartment, believe me.

I found a staircase and climbed a flight to Tulip's apartment and used her key to open her door. I got a rush when I walked in, remembering how I had let myself into Andrew Mallard's apartment the previous evening, and half-expecting to find another corpse or two now. I don't guess I really thought that would happen, but I have to admit I went around touching things with the heel of my hand to avoid leaving fingerprints.

No corpses, thank God. Not in the fish tank, either. The two *Ctenapoma fasciolatum* swam around on either side of their glass divider. They were doing a great job of ignoring each other, and the male had done absolutely nothing about building a bubble nest.

I sat on the edge of the bed and watched them for a while. "C'mon," I said at one point. "Clover Swann wants plenty of sex in this book, gang. You can't expect me to supply all of it myself, can you?"

I don't think they cared.

So I gave up on them and went into the kitchen. I found brine shrimp in the freezer and broke off a chunk, and I found containers of bloodworms and mealworms in the fridge. I went back to the bedroom and fed them until they wouldn't eat any more, then returned the food to the kitchen. I opened a couple of cupboards until I spotted the jar of wheat germ. I reached for it, and then I stopped with my hand halfway to it, and I told myself not to be silly, fingerprints never solved anything anyway and all that, and then I got a paper towel and used it to take the jar from the shelf and set it on the counter top. There wouldn't be any useful prints and I knew it, but if Haig did check the jar for prints and found mine all over it I would never hear the end of it.

I wrapped the jar in several thicknesses of paper towels and found a paper bag in another cupboard and put the jar in that. Then I left it in the kitchen and took a careful look around the apartment without knowing what I was looking for.

I suppose the police must have tossed the place fairly thoroughly the night of the murder, but I had to credit them with doing a neat job of it. As far as I could tell nothing was out of place.

I went into Cherry's room, and of course it was impossible to tell whether anything was out of place there or not, because nothing had been in place to begin with. I remembered standing there just two days ago when the only victims had been scats, remembered thinking that Cherry was evidently something of a slob, and now I found myself muttering an apology to her. I guess a girl can throw her underwear around the room if she wants to. I guess it's her own business.

We'll get him, I promised her. I don't know who he is, and I don't know if Haig knows who he is, but we'll get the bastard.

I tucked the jar of wheat germ under my arm and got out of there. The guy at the parking lot ground the Caddy's gears a little but it didn't sound as though he'd done any permanent damage. I gave him a quarter and drove back to our garage and turned the car over to Emilio, who never grinds the gears, and who occasionally polishes it when he has nothing else to do. We don't pay him to polish the Cadillac. He does it because he likes to.

Then I tucked the jar of wheat germ under my arm again and walked back to Haig's house.

Sixteen

I WANTED TO get up a pool on who would be the first to arrive. But Haig wouldn't play. At a quarter to three he sent Tulip to the guest room and ordered her to stay there until he called for her. After she was tucked away he and I discussed the seating arrangements. I hate having to tell people where to sit, although I have to admit it usually works out fairly well. You can take a person into a room with twenty chairs in it, tell him he's expected to sit in one specific one, and it's a rare case when he gives you an argument. I suppose that proves we're a nation of sheep just looking to be led, but I'm not sure about that. I figure people are just relieved to be saved the aggravation of making an unimportant decision.

At twenty minutes to three Haig went upstairs to ask the fish who killed Cherry Bounce. I hoped they would tell him because it was going to be awfully embarrassing if he ran the whole number and nothing happened. I don't know whether he had it all worked out at that point or not. I figured the reason he went upstairs was so that he

325

would be able to make a grand entrance after they were all seated and waiting for him.

Anyway, I would have been glad to get up a pool, and I would have lost. My pick was Haskell Henderson, and I had a reason for picking him, but since I was wrong there's no point in going into the reason. The first person to show rang the doorbell at four minutes of three. I passed the kitchen on my way to the door and exchanged glances with Wong. "Here we go," I said, and he said something in his native tongue, and I opened the door. There was a man standing on the welcome mat whom I had never seen before in my life.

He had a very youthful face if you didn't spot the pouches under the eyes or the lines at their corners. His hair was the color of sand, neither long nor short, and his eyes were as clear a blue as I have ever seen. He had an open friendly Van Johnson kind of face. He was wearing a gray plaid suit and his tie, loose around his neck, was a striped job.

He said, "I have an appointment with a Mr. Haig."

"You're in luck," I said. "We have a Mr. Haig who will probably fit the bill very nicely. Your name is Glenn Flatt and you're early."

He stared at me. He looked as though he had had his next line of dialogue prepared days in advance and I had blown his timing with an ad lib. I told him to come in, closed the door, and led him to the office. Wong and I had set up a double row of chairs on my side of the partner's desk, facing Haig's chair. I showed Flatt which chair was his and he sat, then popped up again as if there had been a tack on the seat.

"Just a minute," he said. "I don't understand any of this. I came here because I wanted to help Mr. Haig. He said he was working on my ex-wife's behalf and I wanted to help him. Where is he?"

"He's busy," I said. "He'll be along in a while. That's

your chair but you don't have to sit in it if you don't want to. You can look at the fish if you'd rather."

"Fish," he said.

I was waiting for him to ask me who I was, but he didn't. I guess he didn't care. Nor did he look at the fish. He sat down again, opened his briefcase, and took out a copy of the *Post*. He opened it to Jack Anderson's column and checked out the current entry in the corruption sweepstakes. I sat in my chair for a minute or two but it got to be sort of heavy, just the two of us in a roomful of empty chairs, so I went into the kitchen and watched Wong sharpen his cleaver.

The next two customers showed up together, and neither of them was Haskell Henderson, so I lost the place and show money too. They were Simon Barckover and Maeve O'Connor. Maeve looked bubbly and radiant and beautiful and Barckover looked pissed off.

"What's this all about?" he demanded. "I'm a busy man. I've got things to do. Who does this Leo Haig think he is? Where does he get off ordering me to come here?"

There were just too many questions so I didn't answer any of them. I told him he was absolutely right, which gave him pause, and I led the two of them into the office and showed them to their seats. They looked at Glenn Flatt and he looked at them, and then he went back to his newspaper and Barckover sat staring straight ahead while Maeve went and looked at some fish.

After that they all started to show up, and I kept scurrying back and forth from the door to the office, ignoring questions and mumbling inane replies and getting everybody in the right seats. First Haskell Henderson showed up, looking about the same as yesterday but twice as nervous. He'd changed from white jeans to dove-gray jeans, but the goatee was still scraggly and he was wearing either the same Doctor Ecology tee-shirt or one just like it. I no sooner got him parked than Gus Leemy came along with

Buddy Lippa in tow. Neither of them said a word, and when I brought them into the office they acted as if they were entering an empty room. They took their seats without acknowledging the presence of any of the others in any way whatsoever.

As far as that goes, there was a lot of mutual ignoring going on in the office. A lot of these people had met before, but evidently they had managed to piece out the fact that Haig intended to expose a murderer, which meant that one of them was due to be the exposee, and I guess they didn't quite know how to relate to that. It was fine with me, just so they stayed in their chairs and didn't make waves.

Jan Remo came next, asking if she was late. I told her she was right on time, and as I was leading her to the office the bell rang again. I hurried her in and came back to admit Rita Cubbage. She wasn't wearing the wig this time and her tight Afro cap was a significant improvement. "Much better," I told her, taking a long look. "You ought to give that wig to the boss. Your boss, not mine. He's bald as an egg and it might be an improvement. Did you remember what it was that you couldn't quite remember last night?"

"I dreamed something," she said. She opened her purse and took out a slip of paper. "And when I woke up this was on the bedside table, but I don't recall writing it down."

I took the slip of paper from her. On it, in a very precise handwriting that no one would be capable of managing in the middle of the night, she had written: *"Some white boys can be fun to sleep with."*

"I do wish I recalled that dream," she said. "It must have been a good one."

"I wish I'd been there."

"Just might be that you were," she said.

I opened my mouth, and then I closed my mouth, and then I seated her and came back in time to open the door for Leonard Danzig. There was a man on either side of him, and they were the very same men who had taken hold of my arms the night before. I was trying to decide how to tell them they couldn't come in when he turned to them and told them to wait outside, which made things a whole lot simpler for me.

"Well," he said. "Everything proceeding on schedule?"

"So far."

"And your boss is going to make it all come together, is that right?"

"That's the plan."

"Well, if he makes it work, I'll pay off on the spot." He tapped the breast pocket of his suit, indicating that he'd brought the money along. "If I owe somebody something, I see to it that the debt is paid."

A sort of chill grabbed me when he said that. He was talking about money, about paying money if he owed it, but I had the feeling that I never wanted him to owe me something else. Like a bullet in the head, for example. Because I was sure he'd pay that debt just as promptly, and with the same kind of satisfaction.

I took him into the office and parked him, and there were two seats left, one on either side of the second row. I went into the kitchen, picked up the phone and buzzed the fourth floor.

"All but two," I said.

"Who hasn't arrived?"

"The twins. New York's Finest."

"They'll be here within five minutes. Buzz me when they arrive."

They were on hand within three minutes, and they were not happy to see me. "I don't like any of this," Gregorio informed me. "If Haig has something he should tell us. If he's got nothing he should stop wasting our time. If he wants to put on a performance let him hire a hall."

"Sure," I said. "That's his plan, actually. He's going to play the title role in *Tiny Alice*. Let's face it, you're here because this case has you up a tree and you figure Haig's going to hold the ladder for you. Either he'll get your murderer or he won't, and either way is fine with you. You wind up with a case solved or you get to see Haig fall on his face."

"I'd like that," Seidenwall said.

"You probably would but I don't think he's going to oblige you. Now you know the rules. You take your seats and you let Leo Haig run the show. This is his house and you're here by invitation. Understood?"

I swear the best part of my job is getting to talk to cops that way now and then. It makes it all worthwhile. They didn't like to put up with it, but they knew they didn't have any choice. I showed them their chairs, putting Gregorio on the far side of the room and Seidenwall nearest to the door. That way anyone who tried to leave in a hurry would have to go through Seidenwall, and I wouldn't want to try that myself unless I was driving a tank.

Let me go over the seating for you, in case you care. *I* don't, but it's one of the things Haig insists on.

The desk was where it always was, with Haig's chair behind it and mine in front of it and an armchair alongside of it, presently empty.

Then two rows of chairs facing the desk. In the first row, from the far side, were Leonard Danzig, Rita Cubbage, Glenn Flatt, Maeve O'Connor, and Simon Barckover. In the back row we had Detective Vincent Gregorio, Haskell Henderson, Gus Leemy, Buddy Lippa, Jan Remo, and Detective Wallace Seidenwall. I looked at them and decided they were a reasonably attractive group, well-mannered and neatly groomed. Leemy was wearing a business suit instead of a tuxedo so he didn't look like a penguin today, and Buddy wasn't wearing a sport jacket at all so he had nothing to clash with his slacks and shirt, but otherwise they looked about the same as always. I wished they would fold their hands on the tops of their desks and wait for the teacher to come and write something adorable on the blackboard.

I buzzed Haig from the kitchen. Then I went back to the office and sat down in my chair, and a minute or so later our client entered the room. Our original client, that is. Tulip. She took the armchair alongside the desk without being told.

Then Haig walked in and sat behind his desk and every eye in the room was drawn to him.

Including mine.

Seventeen

FOR A LONG moment he just sat there looking at them. His eyes scanned the room carefully. I thought I saw the hint of a smile for a second, but then it was gone and his round face maintained a properly stern and serious look. He put his hands on top of the desk, selected a pipe, put it back in the rack, and drew a breath.

"Good afternoon," he said. "I want to thank you all for coming. All but one of you are welcome in this house. That one is not welcome, but his presence is essential. One of you is a murderer. One of you is responsible for one hundred twenty-five deaths."

There was a collective gasp at that figure but he went on without appearing to notice. "All but two of those deaths were the deaths of fish. The penalty which society attaches to ichthyicide is minimal. Malicious mischief, perhaps. Certainly a misdemeanor. The other two victims were human, however. One would be difficult to substantiate as homicide. While I am mortally certain that Andrew Mallard was murdered—"

"Hey, wait a minute," Gregorio cut in. "If you've got any information on that you've been holding it out, and—"

"Mr. Gregorio." Gregorio stopped in midsentence. "I have withheld nothing, sir. I remind you again that you are here by invitation." He scanned the room again, then went on. "To continue. While I may be certain that Mr. Mallard was murdered, and while I could explain how the murder was committed, no jury would convict anyone for that murder. Indeed, no district attorney in his right mind would presume to bring charges. But the other murder, that of Miss Abramowicz, was unquestionably a case of premeditated homicide. The killer is in this room, and I intend to see him hang for it."

He'd have a long wait. While Haig longs for a return of capital punishment, and thinks public hanging was a hell of a fine way to run a society, the bulk of contemporary opinion seems to be flowing in the other direction.

"The day before yesterday," he said, "Miss Thelma Wolinski sought my assistance. An entire tank of young *Scatophagus tetracanthus* plus her breeder fish had died suddenly and of no apparent cause. Miss Wolinski is possessed of a scientific temperament. She had a chemical analysis of the aquarium water performed, and the laboratory certified that the water had been poisoned with strychnine. Miss Wolinski could not imagine why anyone would want to kill her generally inoffensive fish. She concluded that the crime was the work of a madman, that an attack upon her fish represented hostility toward her own person, and that she herself might consequently be in danger."

"She should have called the police," Seidenwall said.

Haig glared at him. "Indeed," he said. "No doubt you would have rushed to investigate the poisoning of a tankful of fish. Miss Wolinski is no witling." Seidenwall winced at the word. "She came to me. She could scarcely have made a wiser decision."

That sounded a little pompous to me, but nobody's hackles rose as far as I could tell. I looked at Tulip. I couldn't tell what she was thinking. She looked beautiful, and quite spectacular, but then she always did.

"Of course I agreed to investigate. That was quite proper on my part, but it also precipitated a murder. That very evening Miss Mabel Abramowicz was murdered. Some of you may know her as Cherry Bounce. She was killed while performing at a nightclub. Your nightclub, Mr. Leemy."

"Not my fault. I run a decent place."

"That is moot, and a non sequitur in the bargain. Miss Abramowicz was also poisoned, but not with stychnine. She was killed with curare, a lethal paralytic poison with which certain South American savages tip their arrows."

Haig picked up his pipe again and took it apart. He looked at the two pieces, and for a moment I thought that was all he had and he was waiting for a miracle. We'd be out four grand and I wouldn't get to write a book.

"It was instantly evident that the deaths of the fish and the death of Miss Abramowicz were related. It was furthermore a working hypothesis that the same person was responsible for both outrages. Finally, it seemed more than coincidence that Miss Abramowicz's death followed so speedily upon Miss Wolinski's engaging me to represent her interests. Once I was working on the case, Miss Abramowicz had to be disposed of as rapidly as possible. Had the time element not been of paramount importance, the murderer would not have had to take the great risk of committing his crime in full view of perhaps a hundred people.

"And it was an enormous risk, to be sure. But our murderer was very fortunate. While I have never met her, my associate Mr. Harrison assures me that Miss Abramowicz's endowments were such as to make her the center of attention during her performance. Everyone watched her as her act neared its climax. No one saw—or, more accurately, no one paid attention to—her murderer.

"With one exception, I would submit. Andrew Mallard saw something. He may not have known what he saw. He was clearly not certain enough or self-assured enough to make any mention of his observations to the police. Whether this testifies to Mr. Mallard's lethargy and reticence or to the inefficiency of police interrogation is beside the point. In any event—"

"I'll pretend I didn't hear that," Gregorio said.

"An excellent policy," Haig murmured. "In any event, the murderer struck, the murder weapon was not recovered, and the murderer seemed to be in the clear."

The projectile, I thought. Not the weapon.

"A surface examination would suggest that the murderer was irrational. Item: He poisons Miss Wolinski's fish with strychnine. Item: He poisons Miss Abramowicz with curare. The two incidents cannot fail to be related, yet how are they linked in the mind of the murderer? I must admit that, after I learned of Mr. Mallard's death, there was a moment when I entertained the hypothesis that the murderer was attempting to strike at Miss Wolinski by destroying everything associated with her—first her pets, then her roommate, finally a former lover. I dismissed this possibility almost at once. I returned to the fish. I decided to assume the killer was rational, and I asked myself why a rational killer would poison fish with strychnine.

"The answer was that he would not. If he wished to kill the fish and make it obvious that he had done so, he might have tipped over their aquarium and let them perish gasping upon the floor. If he wished to make the death look accidental he could have caused their demise in any of a dozen ways which would not have aroused any suspicion. Instead he chose a readily detectable poison without having any grounds for assuming that Miss Wolinski would bother to detect it via chemical analysis.

"The conclusion was obvious. The fish had been killed by mistake. The murderer did not put the strychnine into the aquarium."

Tulip frowned. "Then who did?"

"Ah," Haig said. He turned to her, a gentle smile on his round face. "I'm afraid you did, Miss Wolinski. Unwittingly, you poisoned your own fish."

Tulip gaped at him. I looked around the room to check out the reactions of the audience. They ran the gamut from puzzlement to disinterest. Seidenwall looked as though he might drop off to sleep any minute now. Gregorio seemed to be enduring all of this, waiting for Haig either to make his point or wind up with egg on his face. I tried to find a suspect who indicated that he or she already knew how the strychnine got in the tank. I didn't have a clue.

Haig opened a desk drawer and took out a paper bag that looked familiar. Gingerly he extracted the jar of wheat germ from it and peeled away the protective layers of paper toweling. He wrapped a towel around his hand and pushed the jar toward my side of the desk.

"This is a jar of wheat germ," he said. "I have found it to be an excellent dietary supplement for fishes. I am told it is similarly useful for human beings. I have no grounds for confirming or disputing the latter. Mr. Henderson. Do you recognize this jar? You may examine it closely, but I urge you not to touch it."

Henderson shrugged. "I don't need a close look," he said. "It's Kretchmer, one of the standard brands. They sell it all over the place, supermarkets, everywhere. What about it?"

"Do they also sell it in health food emporia?"

"Sometimes."

"I understand you run a chain of such establishments. Do your stores carry Kretchmer wheat germ?"

"I think so."

"You don't know for certain, Mr. Henderson?"

"As a matter of fact we do carry it. Why not? It's a good brand, we move a lot of cases of it."

"Do you recognize this particular jar, Mr. Henderson?"

"They're all the same. If you're asking did it come from my place, I couldn't tell you one way or the other."

"I could," Haig said. "On the reverse of this jar there is a label. It says 'Doctor Ecology' and there is an address beneath the store name. That label would tend to suggest that this jar of wheat germ came from one of your stores."

"Well, then it must have. What's the point?"

Haig ignored the question. He picked up the bell and rang it, and Wong Fat came in carrying a two-quart goldfish bowl. There were a pair of inch-and-a-half common goldfish in the bowl. Haig buys them from Aquarium Stock Company for $4.75 a hundred and feeds them to larger fish that have to have live fish as food. Wong put the bowl on the desk. I wondered if it was going to leave a ring.

His hand covered with a paper towel, Haig screwed the top off the jar. He reached into the jar with a little spoon he used to use to clean the crud out of his pipes back in the days when he was trying to smoke them. He spooned up a few grains of wheat germ and sprinkled them into the goldfish bowl.

The fish swam around for a few seconds, not knowing they'd been fed. They weren't enormously bright. Then they surfaced and began scoffing down the wheat germ.

"Now watch," Haig said.

We all watched, and we didn't have to watch for very long before both fish were floating belly-up on the surface. They did not look to be in perfect health.

"They are dead," Haig said. "As dead as the *Scatophagus tetracanthus*. As dead as Miss Mabel Abramowicz. I have not had a chemical analysis run on the contents of this jar of wheat germ. It does seem reasonable to assume that the wheat germ is laced with strychnine. Miss Wolinski."

"Yes?"

"How did this jar of wheat germ come into your possession?"

"Haskell gave it to me."

Henderson's eyes were halfway out of his head. Alfalfa sprouts or no, he looked as though a coronary occlusion was just around the corner. "Now wait a minute," he said. "You just wait a goddamned minute now."

"You deny having given this jar to Miss Wolinski?"

"I sure as hell deny putting strychnine in it. Maybe that's the jar I gave her and maybe it isn't. How the hell do I know?"

"You did give her a jar, however?"

"I gave her lots of things."

"Indeed. You gave her a jar of wheat germ?"

"Yeah, I guess so."

"Have you any reason to assume this is other than the jar you gave her?"

"How the hell do I know?" Haig glared at him. "Okay," he said. "It's probably the same jar."

Haig nodded, satisfied. "Miss Wolinski. Was Mr. Henderson in the habit of gifting you with health foods?"

"Yes."

"And what did you do with them?"

Tulip lowered her eyes. "I didn't do anything with them," she said.

"You didn't eat them?"

"No." She shrugged, and when you're built like Tulip a shrug is a hell of a gesture. "I know that kind of food is supposed to be good for you," she said, "but I just don't *like* it. I like things like hamburgers and french fries and beer, things like that."

"If you would just *try* them—" Henderson began.

"Mr. Henderson. Had Miss Wolinski tried the wheat

germ she would be dead." Henderson shut up. "Miss
Wolinski," Haig went on pleasantly. "You did nothing
with the health foods? You merely put them aside?"

"Well, I used to feed the wheat germ to the fish some
of the time. It's a good conditioner for breeding."

"It is indeed. I employ it myself. What else became of
the health foods Mr. Henderson was considerate enough
to give to you?"

"Sometimes Cherry ate them."

"Indeed," Haig said. He got to his feet. "At this point
things begin to clarify themselves. The strychnine was introduced into the aquarium not by the murderer but by
Miss Wolinski herself. And it was added to the wheat
germ not in an attempt to kill fish but in an attempt to kill
Miss Abramowicz. Oh, sit down, Mr. Henderson. Do sit
down. I am not accusing you of presenting Miss Wolinski
with poisoned wheat germ. You are neither that stupid
nor that clever. The strychnine was added to the wheat
germ after it had come into Miss Wolinski's possession,
added by someone who knew that Miss Abramowicz
rather that Miss Wolinski was likely to ingest it. Sit
down!"

Haskell Henderson sat down. I decided Haig was
wrong on one point. Old Haskell was stupid enough to do
almost anything. Anybody who would discontinue making
love to Althea simply because she had less than the usual
number of breasts didn't have all that much going for him
in the brains department.

Haig turned to Tulip once more. "Miss Wolinski," he
said. "I first made your acquaintance approximately
forty-eight hours ago. They have been eventful hours, to
be sure. When did you decide to consult me?"

"Tuesday. The day after I got the lab report. That was
when I decided, and then I thought it over for a while,
and then I came here."

"Who knew of your decision?"

"Nobody."

"No one at all?"

"I didn't tell anyone after I saw you. You told me not to. Oh, wait a minute. I said something to Cherry that morning, that I was going to see you and you would find out how it happened."

"So you told Miss Abramowicz. And she might have told anyone."

"Cherry wasn't very good at keeping things to herself."

"She may have told anyone at all," Haig went on. "What we do know for certain is that she told her murderer. He realized that I would rapidly determine that the poisoning of the scats constituted a misdirected attempt at Miss Abramowicz's life. He had to act quickly."

Haig cleared his throat and let his eyes take a tour of the audience. I don't know what he was looking for so I don't know whether or not he found it. What I saw was Rita Cubbage picking at a cuticle, Buddy Lippa scratching his head, Gus Leemy frowning, Vincent Gregorio picking lint off his lapel, Simon Barckover glancing at his watch, Maeve O'Connor licking her lower lip, Glenn Flatt cracking his knuckles, Jan Remo rubbing her temples with her fingertips, Wallace Seidenwall yawning, and Leonard Danzig sitting in perfect repose, giving Leo Haig every bit of his attention.

Whatever Haig was looking for and whether he found it or not, he evidently decided that the Rasboras were more interesting to look at than the eleven of them. He swung his chair around and stared into the fish tank, presenting his audience with a great view of the back of his head.

That's it, I thought. That's all he's got. I decided it was still pretty good, better than the police had managed to come up with, but why blow it by putting the show together prematurely? Unless he expected one of them to crack, but could you count on that happening? I decided you couldn't.

Haig swiveled his chair around again. "Mr. Flatt," he said. "Mr. Glenn Flatt."

There was a lot of head-turning as our customers tried to figure out which of them was Glenn Flatt. They finally took a cue from Haig and looked where he was looking, and the boyish Ivy Leaguer frowned back at Haig.

"Yes, I was hoping you'd get around to me," Flatt said. "I came here to help Tulip. I used to be married to her and we're still good friends and you said you were working for her. I didn't know I was going to be part of a carnival." He stood up. "I told you I had work to do. I came here as a favor to Tulip but this is ridiculous. I'm leaving."

"You are not. You will stay where you are. If you attempt to leave Mr. Harrison will knock you down and return you to your chair. Sit down, Mr. Flatt."

Flatt sat down, which took a load off my mind, believe me. If you think I was all that confident of my ability to knock him down you don't know me very well.

"Mr. Flatt. You came here because last evening I told you that I knew you were at Treasure Chest on the evening when Miss Abramowicz was murdered. That is why you are present this afternoon. When I told you I had a witness placing you at the scene you elected to cooperate."

"Where'd you get a witness?" Gregorio wanted to know. "And why did you hold that out?"

Haig made a face. "I had no witness," he said. "I merely said I had one."

"You were lying," Flatt said. It was a pretty dumb thing to say, and he sounded pretty dumb saying it.

"You might put it that way," Haig allowed. "Or you might say that I was bluffing. I trust you're conversant with the term, Mr. Flatt. You gamble quite a great deal, do you not?"

"Sometimes I'll make a bet on a horse."

"Indeed. Or on an athletic event, or on an election, or on the turn of a card. Would you say you are a compulsive gambler, Mr. Flatt?"

"Not in a million years," Flatt said. He looked somewhat less boyish now. "I like a little action, that's all. So I gamble. There's no law against it."

"Tommyrot. There are innumerable laws against various forms of gambling. The fact that such statutes are absurd does not wipe them from the criminal code. But we are not assembled here to convict you of gambling, Mr. Flatt. Rest assured of that."

"Look, I don't—"

Haig put his pipe back together again and tapped the bowl on the top of the desk. "I would be inclined to label you a compulsive gambler," he said. "The evidence seems clear enough. Your marriage to my client dissolved largely because you kept going into debt as a result of your gambling. Your debts have increased considerably over the years. A friend of mine was in a position to make inquiries among various bookmakers on Long Island. You are well known to several of them. You gamble heavily. You almost invariably lose."

"I don't do so badly."

"You do pay your debts," Haig said. "According to my information, in the past four months you paid an amount to bookmakers slightly in excess of your salary during the same period."

"That's ridiculous. And you couldn't possibly prove it."

"I don't have to. I told you I don't intend to convict you of gambling. And your gambling doesn't interfere with your ability to earn a livelihood, does it? You continue to be gainfully employed in a responsible position."

Flatt eyed him warily. "So?"

"As a pharmaceutical chemist, I understand."

"That's right."

"A position which would give you ready access to any number of interesting compounds. Such as strychnine and curare, to cite two examples."

"Now wait a goddamned minute—"

"Mr. Flatt, you're much better off if you keep your mouth shut. Take my word for it. You have access to such compounds and it would be puerile of you to deny it. That crossed my mind when first I learned of your occupation. Various poisons are readily obtainable. Strychnine is not. Neither is curare. You and I have not met before, Mr. Flatt, and we did not speak to one another until last evening, but you have been an important suspect since I first learned how the fish had died." He said all this in a calm conversational tone. Then abruptly he raised his voice to as close as he could come to a bellow. *"Why were you at Treasure Chest the night before last?"*

"You can't prove I was there."

"Phooey. You've already admitted you were there. Have the courage of your errors, Mr. Flatt. Why were you there?"

Flatt bought himself a couple of seconds by glancing to either side of himself. If he was looking for support he picked the wrong place to look for it. Everybody seemed to want to hear the answer to the question.

"I wasn't there when Cherry was killed," he said. "I left before her act started, I was miles away when she was killed. And I can prove it."

"That won't be necessary," Haig said. "You did not kill Miss Abramowicz."

"But—"

"Nor have you answered the question. Why did you go to that night club that evening?"

He shrugged. "No particular reason. I'm sorry if I was out of line but I thought you were accusing me of murder." He managed a boyish grin. "It certainly sounded that way for a while. For a little guy, you certainly know how to boss people around."

"You still haven't answered my question, Mr. Flatt."

"Oh, hell. Look, I wanted a couple of drinks. Why did I pick a topless club? Jesus, you know the answer to that one. Or maybe you don't, who knows with you? I like to look at girls. That's all there is to it. I used to be married to Tulip and we're still friends so I picked that club rather than one of the others. My luck I had to be there on that particular night. But, you know, I go there a lot. Maybe not a lot but I'll drop in now and then."

"Interesting," Haig said. "Mr. Lippa? Can you confirm that?"

Buddy Lippa nodded. "I seen him before," he said. "I dint make him at first but I seen him. Comes in once, twice a week, sits at the bar. Never stays any length of time. And he's right about leaving before Cherry got the needle. I can't swear to the time but I'd guess he came in like nine-thirty and left by ten o'clock. That's not on the dot but it's close."

"Absolutely right," Flatt said. "I was out of there by ten. And I was in a bar on Long Island by midnight, and I can prove that with no trouble whatsoever."

"You needn't," Haig said. "So you've been in the habit of patronizing Treasure Chest once or twice a week. That's interesting."

Flatt didn't say anything.

"There are topless clubs on Long Island, are there not? And are they not more conveniently located, since you both live and work there?"

"Sometimes I'm in New York on business."

"Precisely my point. I submit that your visits to Treasure Chest are a business matter."

"I don't know what you're talking about."

"Nonsense," Haig said. "You know precisely what I am talking about. Five months ago Miss Wolinski went to work at Treasure Chest. You have kept in contact with her and visited the club, perhaps out of curiosity. You needed money, you have always needed money, your gambling habit is such that you shall always need money. And you met someone at Treasure Chest who showed you a way to make all the money that you needed."

"You're out of your mind."

"That's not inconceivable. It is, however, irrelevant to the present discussion. You met someone at Treasure Chest, someone who was regularly present there during the ensuing months. You got into conversation. You mentioned your occupation, and your new acquaintance saw possibilities for profit. You had access, I have mentioned earlier, to poisonous compounds. There is, thanks be to God, no enormous profit at present in such compounds. But you also had access to quantities of a subtler, slower form of poison. As a pharmaceutical chemist, Mr. Flatt, you had access to drugs."

I looked at Flatt. He was keeping a stiff upper lip but the effort was showing. I glanced at Gregorio and saw him nodding thoughtfully. Leonard Danzig had a wary look in his eyes. Gus Leemy was frowning.

"You stole drugs from your employers," Haig was saying. "Perhaps you produced others. I understand lysergic acid can be readily synthesized by anyone with a middling knowledge of chemistry. With your background and your laboratory facilities it would be child's play. You brought consignments of drugs to New York, once or twice a week, and you delivered them to your associate at Treasure Chest—"

"That's horseshit." Gus Leemy was leaning forward, the light glinting off the top of his head. "I run that place clean. It's not a front for nothing at all. It's a decent operation."

Gregorio said, "There's drugs coming out of there, Gus. Been going on for months, the rumbles we get."

"You're crazy." He glanced at Danzig, then averted his eyes quickly as if remembering that he and Danzig were supposed to be pretending they didn't know each other. Since the two of them gave each other an alibi for Cherry's murder I didn't quite grasp the logic of this, but they could play it whatever way they wanted. "I run that place clean," Leemy said. "I don't fuck with drugs, I never did and I never will."

"I never accused you, sir." Haig tapped his pipe on the desk again, then frowned suddenly at the bowl with the two dead goldfish in it. He rang the bell. I thought that would probably throw Wong, who wouldn't know what to come in with, but instead Wong came in emptyhanded. Haig nodded at the bowl and Wong removed it. "I never accused you, Mr. Leemy," Haig went on. "If you stand accused of anything it is incompetence. Your nightclub served as a focal point for the dissemination of drugs, but this occurred without your knowledge. While that does not make you a particularly efficient manager, neither does it make you a criminal. It certainly does not make you a murderer." Haig stroked his beard. "Or you, Mr. Danzig. You or Mr. Leemy might well have killed the person selling drugs out of the Treasure Chest, or issued an order that the person be killed, but neither of you would have had any reason to do away with Miss Abramowicz."

Danzig didn't exactly glower but his face hardened a little. "Your reasoning is interesting," he said. "But I'm not sure how my name got in that last sentence. I was going out with Cherry, that's all. That's the only reason I'm here."

"Oh, come off it, Danzig," Gregorio said. He leaned forward and put a hand on Danzig's shoulder. "Everybody knows Leemy just fronts for you. And nobody much gives a shit. The boys from the State Liquor Authority might be unhappy but they can't prove anything, and as far as we're concerned we don't care."

Danzig smiled. "I have no connection with Treasure Chest. Mr. Leemy is a friend."

"Sure, if that's the way you want it."

"That's what the record should show," Danzig said.

All of this was fascinating, but none of it had much to do with who killed Cherry and I was getting impatient. The suspense was fairly thick in the room. I looked at all of them, and the most agitated one was Glenn Flatt, although he wasn't approaching hysteria yet. He should have been the coolest; I mean, he presumably knew who his contact was, and thus he knew who committed the murder.

"I could sue you," Flatt said.

"Oh, come now," Haig said. "You're going to go to jail at the very least for selling illegal drugs and as accessory to the fact of murder in the first degree. Do you really think you could find a lawyer to represent you in a libel action? I somehow doubt it."

"You can't prove any of this."

Haig grunted. "I will tell you something," he said. "There is nothing much simpler than proving something one already knows to be true. The proof generally makes itself available in relatively short order. No, Mr. Flatt, your position is hopeless. You have been selling drugs through a confederate. And what do we know about this accomplice of yours?" He ticked off the points on his fingers. "Your accomplice is regularly to be found at Treasure Chest, either as an employee or an habitual hanger-on. There are several here in this room who fit that description. Miss Wolinski, for one. Mr. Danzig. Mr. Leemy. Mr. Barckover. Miss Remo. Miss Cubbage. Mr. Henderson frequents Treasure Chest often, but if he were selling drugs he would no doubt do so through the medium of one or another of his stores, and—"

"Drugs!" Haskell was outraged. "Me sell drugs? You have to be out of your mind. Drugs are a death trip."

"Indeed. We have already excluded you, Mr. Henderson, so you've no need to offer comments. To continue. Miss O'Connor has not been regularly employed at Treasure Chest, so she too may be ruled out. Mr. Leemy and Mr. Danzig may also be excused; they quite clearly did not know what was going on in the establishment. I would further exclude Mr. Lippa because I find the whole nature of this operation incompatible with my impressions of the man."

"Does that mean I'm in or out?" Buddy wanted to know, and Haig nodded and said that was exactly his point, and that Buddy was in the clear.

"Now let us reconstruct the day of the crime. Mr. Flatt's accomplice in the drug operation—let us call him X, as a sop to tradition—has learned directly or indirectly from Miss Abramowicz that I have been hired to investigate the death of the fish. X realizes that my participation will quickly establish that an attempt has been made on Miss Abramowicz's life and that the fish were unintentional victims. When this became known, Miss Abramowicz would realize that she possesses some information which makes her dangerous to X, and this information would at once be brought to my attention. That, to be sure, was the original motive for disposing of Miss Abramowicz. She somehow learned enough about the drug operation to make her dangerous, especially in view of the fact that she seems to have been rather scatter-brained and loose-tongued. One hesitates to speak thus of the dead, but the fact appears to be beyond dispute.

"Thus X must act, and act quickly. So X contacts Mr. Flatt—yes, sir, it happened just that way, and you needn't attempt to deny it by shaking your head. X contacted you, Mr. Flatt, and demanded a contact poison. Whether curare was specified or not I have no idea. It hardly matters. You had already supplied strychnine to X, although I cannot state with certainty that you knew how it was to be employed. It is often used as an adulterant in drugs to boost their potency and you might well have furnished it without knowing you were to be the instrument in a homicide. But if there is any other use for curare I am unaware of it. You knew Miss Abramowicz was to be killed, sir. You brought the curare that night with that specific purpose in mind. That was why you took pains to leave the club early, why you established an alibi in Long Island. You are a knowing accessory to murder, sir."

Flatt stared at him, and Haig stared back, and Flatt couldn't take it. He looked down at his hands.

"You brought the curare," Haig went on. "You delivered it to X. You left. And X waited, because the last thing X wanted was to murder Miss Abramowicz on the premises of the nightclub. Ideally X would have waited until the evening had come to a close. X and Miss Abramowicz would have left together, and X would have managed to perform the deed in private. This plan was spiked when Mr. Harrison made an appearance at the club. X learned his identity, realized he was my associate, and recognized that there would be no opportunity to go off with Miss Abramowicz and deal with her as planned. Mr. Harrison would instead be interrogating Miss Abramowicz immediately after she finished her performance, at which time her knowledge might well be passed on to him. And this was something X was wholly unprepared to leave to chance.

"And so X waited, waited until the last minute. Waited until Miss Abramowicz was at the very conclusion of her act, and then injected curare into her bloodstream and killed her."

I saw it all again in slow motion. The finale of the act, Cherry shaking her breasts over the edge of the stage, straightening up, doing her spread, going coyly prim, then trying so desperately to reach her breast—

"When we think of curare," Haig said, "we think of savages in the jungles. We think of blow darts, we think of arrows tipped with the deadly elixir. And when we consider this crime, we assume that X must have employed such a device, that some projectile served to carry curare from X's hand to Miss Abramowicz's breast. No projectile remained stuck in the breast in question; hence we assume that the dart or arrow or whatever struck the breast, pierced the skin, and then fell away. Mr. Harrison was the first person to leap onto the stage after Miss Abramowicz fell. He had the presence of mind, after determining there was no office he could perform for the victim, to make a quick search for the projectile. And he—"

"And he put it in his pocket." This from my old friend Wallace Seidenwall. "I knew Harrison had it. I been saying so all along, and I been saying—"

"You have been saying far too much, sir. Mr. Harrison did not find the projectile. Neither did the police, who may be presumed to have subjected the premises to an exhaustive search. Dismissing such preposterous theories as an arrow with an elastic band tied to it—and I trust we can dismiss such rot out of hand—it is quite inconceivable that X could have retrieved the projectile. Sherlock Holmes established the principle beyond doubt, and I reiterate it here and now: When all impossibilities have been eliminated, that which remains is all that is possible. There was no projectile."

I suppose everybody was supposed to gasp when he said this. That's not what happened. Instead everybody just sat there staring. Maybe they had trouble following what he'd just said. Maybe they were confused about the difference between a weapon and a projectile. I'd already had a lesson in that department so I managed to stay on top of things, and at that moment I finally figured out who X was. Instead of feeling brilliant I sat there wondering how it had taken me so long.

"There was no projectile," Haig said again. "Miss Abramowicz was stabbed with some sort of pin. A hair pin, a hat pin, it scarcely matters. The pin was pressed into her breast and withdrawn. Then—"

"Wait." It was Gregorio. "Unless I'm off-base, she was all alone on that stage. How did someone stick a pin in her breast without anyone seeing it?"

"Because she was bending over the edge of the stage. She did this at the conclusion of every performance, leaning forward almost parallel to the floor with her breasts suspended over the stage apron. This was X's genius—it would have been simpler by far to inflict a wound in her foot, for example, but by waiting for the one perfect moment X could guarantee that everyone would assume that a nonexistent projectile had been employed."

I said, "How come she didn't feel anything? She went right ahead and got up and danced around for a minute, and then there was suddenly blood on her breast and she started to crumble."

"Curare is not instantaneous. Poisons borne by the bloodstream need time to reach the heart. And small puncture wounds rarely begin bleeding immediately. Indeed they often fail to bleed at all. As for her failure to react, she was caught up in an intense dance routine. She might have been too involved to feel a pinprick. She might have assumed it was an insect bite and ignored it. For that matter, she might not have felt it at all. She had had silicone implants. The skin of her breasts was thus stretched to accommodate their enlargement, the nerve endings consequently far apart. Some nerves may even have been severed when the silicone was implanted."

Haig shrugged. "But it hardly matters. Once one knows how the murder was committed, the identity of X is instantly obvious. Indeed it has been obvious to me for some time that only one person was ideally situated to commit the murder. That same person was also ideally situated to receive consignments of drugs from Mr. Flatt and dispense them in the normal course of occupational routine.

"Miss Remo. I suggest you keep your hands in plain sight and avoid sudden movements. Mr. Wong Fat has you within line of sight. He could plant his cleaver in your head before you could get your purse open. Yes, keep your hands right where they are, Miss Remo. Mr. Seiden- wall, I trust you thought to bring a pair of handcuffs? I suggest you put them on Miss Remo. She is rather more dangerous than she looks."

Eighteen

SEIDENWALL PUT THE cuffs on her. He may have been a witling but he knew how to follow orders. I didn't take my eyes off her until the bracelets snapped shut. Then I let out a breath I hadn't remembered taking and glanced at the doorway. Wong was standing there and he still had the cleaver raised. He wasn't taking any chances.

Gregorio lit a cigarette and blew out a lot of smoke. He said, "You don't really have anything, do you? Just a theory. I'm not arguing with your theory. I have to hand it to you, you tied all the ends together and made it work. And if we put the jury in this room and let you put on a show for them they might bring in a conviction, but that's not how the system works. Maybe it should be but it isn't."

"You need proof."

"Right."

"And I told you earlier that proof is the world's cheapest commodity. The contents of Miss Remo's purse might prove interesting. Even if she has been bright

355

enough to avoid bringing anything incriminating with her,
you should have little trouble tying her to Flatt and to the
drug operation. Once you know what to look for it's a
simple matter to find it. You might start by establishing a
link between Mr. Flatt and the strychnine in this jar." He
tapped the jar of wheat germ. "Odd that this would be
left accessible, but perhaps neither of them had an opportunity to retrieve it."

That was all Glenn Flatt needed. He whirled around
and glared at Jan Remo. "You stupid ass-faced little
bitch! You said you switched jars yesterday afternoon.
What in the hell is the matter with you?"

Jan Remo didn't turn a hair. She just closed her eyes
for a moment, and when she opened them she spoke in a
calm and level voice.

She said, "Now I know why you're such a terrible
gambler, Glenn. How many times do you let the same
man bluff you out of a pot? There was nothing in that jar
of wheat germ. He doctored it with something that would
kill the fish." She sighed. "I think it's about time somebody advised me of my rights. I have the right to remain
silent. I intend to remain silent. Glenn, I think you should
remain silent, too. I really do."

Gregorio advised them both of their rights and put
cuffs on Flatt, and he and Seidenwall led the two of them
away. Wong closed the door after them and returned to
the kitchen to hang up his cleaver. In the office everybody
seemed to be waiting for somebody else to say something.
When the silence got unbearable I broke it by asking how
he knew Mallard had been killed.

"I don't," he said. "I *believe* he was killed. A police
investigation might establish that either Mr. Flatt or Miss
Remo was at his apartment yesterday."

"And made him choke on his own vomit?"

Haig nodded slowly. "A simple murder method," he

said, "and quite undetectable. It requires a victim who has had a lot to drink. When he has passed out or fallen asleep, one puts one's hand over his mouth and drives one's knee into the pit of his stomach. The victim regurgitates, cannot open his mouth, and the vomit is drawn into the lungs. One might find that Mr. Mallard's abdomen is bruised. This would still prove nothing. It's my guess that Miss Remo killed him, and it's virtually certain that she will never be charged with the crime."

"Nobody could make it stick," Leonard Danzig said.

"Quite so. But both she and Mr. Flatt will serve long sentences for the murder of Miss Abramowicz. Perhaps that is sufficient."

There was some more conversation, and then they left, a few at a time. Leonard Danzig took me aside on his way out and handed me two envelopes. "The other half of what I gave you last night," he said, "plus the bonus we agreed on. All in cash. If Haig wants to pay taxes on it that's his business, but it won't show up on my books so it's strictly up to him. Your boss is everything you said he was. It was worth four grand to watch him operate. It was worth more than that to find out that Gus Leemy hasn't been running as tight a ship as he should. No wonder the police were leaning on me. They thought I had a hand in a drug operation. I don't touch drugs." He smiled. "You're okay yourself. Anytime you drop by the club, there won't be any check."

Within half an hour they were all gone. Maeve O'Connor told me to hang onto her phone number even though the case was solved, and Rita Cubbage gave me her number, too. "In case you want to call me in the middle of the night," she said, "if something should suddenly come up." Simon Barckover asked Haig if he had ever thought of working up a nightclub routine. He started to sketch out what he had in mind but Haig glowered at him and he let it lie. Gus Leemy walked out looking very unhappy and Buddy Lippa trailed after him, looking very stupid. That left our client and her boyfriend, and I got rid of him myself.

I took old Haskell aside and told him he ought to divorce his wife, and he got into a riff about how he couldn't leave her because she would never be able to get another man, so I figured the hell with it and told him how nicely she had done in that department just that morning. This rattled him, and then I told him that I didn't think he should hang around Tulip anymore, and this rattled him a little too, and he went away.

So Tulip was the only one left, and she went home after Haig gave back her check for five hundred dollars. When she refused to take it he tore it up and threw it in the wastebasket.

"But that's not fair," she said. "I hired you to do a job and you did more than I hired you to do and now you won't let me pay you for it."

"I have been amply paid by someone else," he said. "And I am not refusing your payment. I am buying something in return. Use some of that five hundred to buy some good equipment and a group of breeder scats. Select a pair. Breed them. Then tell me exactly how you did it."

Nineteen

WE SPENT PART of the evening Scotch-taping hundred-dollar bills together. This would have been easier if we'd kept them in order but I dropped the second batch and they got all jumbled up. We had to match serial numbers. It didn't really take all that long, but the process kept getting interrupted by people calling from the newspapers and things like that.

Then Haig made me play a few games of chess with him, which I won, and then I played a game with Wong and lost in ten moves. And finally I stood up and said, "I'm going home."

"Very well."

"Oh, hell. You were beautiful today and I can't ruin things by not playing my part. I give up. How did you know to doctor the wheat germ?"

"I gave some of it to some fish while you were seating our guests. They lived to tell the tale." He examined a fingernail. "It was showmanship. I'll admit that. Without it, the police could still turn up enough evidence to con-

vict handily. Addicts who have bought drugs from Miss
Remo. Witnesses who could place her and Mr. Flatt in
various places at various times." He straightened in his
chair. "But I wanted to break them in public. The police
dig harder when they know they're digging for something
that exists."

"And you got a kick out of the performance."

He grunted.

"So how did you do it? I didn't know we had any
strychnine in the house."

"We don't."

"What did you use?"

"Those roach crystals Wong sprinkles around. I dissolved a handful in water and soaked the wheat germ with
it."

"How did you know it would kill fish?"

"I didn't. I fed some to some fish and they died."

"I probably should have figured that part out myself. I
guess I'm a little punchy. But that's not the main point.
How did you *know* they switched jars? How did you
know the strychnine was in the wheat germ in the first
place?"

He just smiled.

"Oh, hell," I said. "Actually I'm taking some of the
credit for this one. Do you remember the pipe dream I
was spinning about Haskell Henderson? How he poisoned
the fish because Tulip wouldn't eat the health foods but
gave them to the fish instead? And how he killed Cherry
because she was eating the crap instead of passing it on to
Tulip? Remember?"

"That piffle," he said. "How could I possibly forget
it?"

"Well, that's what put the idea in your head. And the
notion of Jan Remo stabbing Cherry with a pin, you even
said hatpin, and you got that idea because I told you how
Althea Henderson stuck a hatpin in her tit. For Pete's

sake, I'm the one who does all the work around here. Why is it that you get all the credit?"

He petted his beard. "Surely you can make yourself look somewhat more intelligent when you write up this case, Chip. It's only fair that you should have the opportunity."

"Thanks a lot."

"And don't forget what Miss Swann advised you this morning," he went on. "The book needs sex. Not nearly so much as you seem to need it, but it does need sex." He gazed past my shoulder and got a very innocent look on his face. "I see no reason why you couldn't embroider the truth somewhat in that department. In the interest of increasing the book's marketability. You might, oh, fabricate an incident in which you had sexual relations with our client, for example."

I glared at him.

"But that might not be enough in and of itself." He played with his beard some more. "Perhaps you could enlarge this morning's interview with Mrs. Henderson. Suggest that, after she bared her breast to you, you took her to bed. A bit farfetched, to be sure, but perhaps the circumstances warrant it."

Hell.

Was he just guessing? Did he know? Or was he really sincerely suggesting I make up something that he didn't know actually happened?

You tell me. I *still* can't make up my mind.

afterword

When Chip Harrison strode into view in *No Score* (1970), and then reappeared in *Chip Harrison Scores Again* (1971), some readers, remembering Hemingway's description of *Huckleberry Finn* as the book to which all American writers are indebted, wondered if the debt ceiling was not being raised into the vertigo zone. Like Huck, Chip was an invulnerable. Life had scathed him but he had healed and survived. Again like Huck, Chip had a curious kind of integrity, which, while it had nothing to do with ethics as the term is usually understood, seemed to put him on the side of the angels no matter what kind of trouble he got into. By ordinary standards of reckoning no one ever would measure Chip for a halo—for one thing, angels never are called on to do deputy duty at whorehouses. But Chip always imputed to others the best motives and his own were never skulking. If a piece of questionable luck came his way, he did not spurn it, yet he never schemed to bring it about. He merely let the zephyrs of fortune waft him along on a course of their own plotting.

Chip could never have shown up when he did without the suspicion arising that he was blood kin to another lineal descendent of Huck Finn, J. D. Salinger's Holden Caulfield, whose initials, in reverse order, are Chip's own. (Formerly his name had been Lee Harvey Harrison. He changed it shortly after 22 November 1963). If Holden is Huck Finn given a prep school education and set adrift in New York City on a winter weekend, in the post World War II era, Chip is Huck-Holden cast loose in the heyday of Viet Nam protest, when the world was in a state of tumultuous upheaval. But, however unsettled things were then, they were not so disordered that Chip, for sheer enjoyment, could not escape for reading pleasure into one of Rex Stout's Nero Wolfe novels, as in fact he does in *Chip Harrison Scores Again*. Stout fans liked that but none could have guessed that that was just the tip of the iceberg.

Chip, one surmises, identified not with the mountainous Nero Wolfe, but with Wolfe's lean and agile Dogsbody, Archie Goodwin, of whom Jacques Barzun has written: "Archie is one of the folk heroes in which the modern American temper can see itself transfigured. Archie is the lineal descendant of Huck Finn, with the additions that worldliness has brought to the figure of the young savior." It is fitting, then, that Chip, in the course of his wanderings, should fall in with Leo Haig, a man who not only hero-worships Nero Wolfe but patterns his behavior on his because he is convinced that Nero Wolfe exists in the flesh and will some day, when he learns how scrupulously Haig has emulated his methods, summon him into his presence.

With never a hint of disrespect toward Stout and his miraculous conceptions, his admiration for whom is never in question, Lawrence Block exquisitely caricatures not Wolfe and Archie but his two aspirants to their renown. Like Don Quixote and Sancho Panza in their naive usurpation of the chivalric mode, they, while striving for positive results, can only parody those standards of performance which they seek to replicate. In inviting us to laugh at their efforts, Block invites us to laugh at ourselves because no honest reader of detective stories can pretend that he has not, a thousand times in his imagination, tramped to the edge of the Grimpen Mire with Holmes and Watson, or, with Wolfe, trapped a murderer in the fumigation room.

Rumor has it, Fred Dannay relates, that Nero Wolfe took the name "Nero" because it has the same vowel arrangement as "Sherlock." "Leo" does also. Perhaps that was mere luck on Haig's part. But Leo means lion. Haig could not be that lucky. He must have adopted a theriomorphic name to identify closer with his idol. Lamentably not all his efforts to emulate the master have been so successful. He is not domiciled in a double-sized brownstone on West Thirty-fifth Street but lives at 311½ West Twentieth Street, down an alley, in half a converted carriage house, the other half of which is Madame Juana's Puerto Rican bordello. Instead of raising orchids, Haig raises exotic fish. He is authentically knowledgable about these and, in *The Topless Tulip Caper* (1975), they prove to be quite as essential to the plot as orchids are in such Nero Wolfe stories as *The Red Box,* "Black Orchids," and "Easter Parade." Wolfe surely would find this fish obsession revolting. He would loathe the floral wing chair Haig has in his office. And he would be appalled when Haig's personal chef, Wong Fat, in anticipation of Haig's wishes, serves coffee to Haig and Chip but serves none to Gregorio and Seidenwall, two obstreperous police detectives who have come uninvited to Haig's half-a-carriage-house. Wolfe would never discriminate against another man's palate, not even Jack the Ripper's. Haig has a lot to learn.

Haig's worst gaff—saying "Phooey" on three occasions when he meant to say "Pfui"—is so egregious a blunder it obviously ascribes neither to Haig nor Block but to the presumption of some underpaid and disgruntled typesetter who wanted to expose his employer to ridicule. It is best passed over in silence. Haig's permissiveness also strikes a discordant note. Wolfe would never invite Archie to cohabit at the brownstone with his current girlfriend or offer him the use of his own bed on that or any other occasion. He is no prude but his sense of what social usage will tolerate is unerring.

Despite Haig's gaucheries, Block succeeds so well in convincing us of his sincerity that we find his lapses almost endearing. No one can attain full parity with Wolfe. That Haig, even though he realizes this fact, points himself in that direction is laudable and we commend him for having a reach that exceeds his grasp. We are proud of him when he congratulates himself for his Neronian presence of mind in thinking to characterize the two policemen, to their faces, as "witlings." We approve when he patiently corrects Chip's solecisms. We are gratified to learn that he has a complete set of Stout's books, leather-bound, on his library shelves. And we rejoice with him when he concludes a case by staging a successful assembly of suspects in plausible simulation of the method of the master.

Left to himself, Chip would not presume, consciously, to emulate Archie Goodwin. But hired by Haig to transform himself into Archie he takes on the role with gusto. Since he likes Archie and is already a fledgling Archie, the strain on him is minimal. It is reassuring to hear him talk about such Stoutian props as Rabson locks and Rusterman's Restaurant, to have him dialing "the number I know best," and boasting, "Then I hit a name I knew, and then hit it again, and then I hit it a third time, and I cabbed to Haig's house with three pieces of paper in my pocket that would wrap up a murderer." No matter that he is premature in his expectations, he is establishing genuine rapport with his Goodwinian persona.

Chip's frequent boudoir calesthenics remind us, of course, that he is not Archie Goodwin, but that does not mean that Archie was an anchorite. Barzun says of Archie: "He is promiscuous with his eyes and his thoughts, and a woman must be past hope herself or else wanting in civility or human feeling, before Archie ceases to interweave his erotic fantasies with his shorthand notes on the case. . . ." Rex Stout estimated that, in the course of the stories, Archie slept with between fifteen and twenty women, but he airbrushed the details because he thought it would be tiresome to supply them. In *The Burglar in the Closet* (1978) Block indicates he has come to be of the same mind. His burglar is trapped in a closet in a bedroom where a couple, unaware of his presence, have come to make love. He is an audience to their cooings and gropings but supplies no details. A superior scene results.

Unlike Archie, Chip did not grow up on a sequestered Chillicothe farm, the son of Grade A farm folk. His parents were peripatetic con artists who had died in a suicide pact when the law overtook them. Before teaming up with Haig, Chip, despite his tender years, led a picaresque life such as Archie never knew. Haig's prospects for making Chip over into another Archie Goodwin are great but he has a broad stretch of turbulence to traverse before that destination is reached. A point in Chip's favor is his stead-fast refusal to move into the carriage house though Haig all but insists on it. He contends that any girl he brought home might feel compromised when she realized there was a brothel on the premises. If Haig cannot figure that out for himself then he, too, despite his leather bindings, his *Scatophagus argus,* and his verbal virtuosity still has a long way to go before he arrives at Nero Wolfe's powers of discernment.

The dedication page of the original edition of *Make Out with Murder* reads: "This is for REX STOUT, whoever he may be. . . ." Lawrence Block's readers did not need this announcement to know that Block had opened to Chip Harrison the gates of Nero Wolfe's world not as an act of vandalism but as an act of reverence. Block himself does not quibble on that point. He discloses: "The two Har-rison-and-Haig books were an obvious attempt at homage to Stout." He concedes, too, that even in his non-Harri-son-and-Haig books, "I occasionally find myself writing a sentence or a paragraph that echoes in my mind with a distinctly Goodwinian ring. . . ." And that is nothing to apologize for. Of Stout, Mark Van Doren said: "Rex is a perfect writer—economical, rapid, free of cliche, epigram-matic, intelligent, charming. What else? That's enough." Nor should we forget Harry Reasoner's remarks when Stout died, 27 October 1975: "The odds are overwhelming that when historians look at the bright blue late October of 1975 the only thing they will keep about the 27th is that it was the day Rex Stout died. . . . A lot of more pretentious writers have less claim on our culture and our allegiance."

I once asked Rex Stout if the picture of Sherlock Holmes hanging over Archie's desk was put there by Archie or

Wolfe. Rex professed to be stunned. "Did I say that?" he asked. "I was a damn fool to do it. Obviously it's always an artistic fault in any fiction to mention any other character in fiction. It should never be done." Ordinarily I would agree with Rex, but when the character is a truly created character who, for millions of readers—and non-readers—exists outside the pages of fiction (as Wolfe does for Haig), then I do not think that that rule holds. Holmes is an obvious exception. Huck Finn is another. Simon Legree, Tiny Tim, and Tarzan as well come to mind. Nor did I object when Graham Greene's Scobie was mentioned in Evelyn Waugh's *Men at Arms,* though the allusion startled me on first encounter.

Rex Stout knew that both Wolfe and Archie are created characters and he knew, also, that some impressive claim jumpers had taken cognizance of them in their own works—William Faulkner, John Steinbeck, P. G. Wodehouse, Georges Simenon, and Ian Fleming, to offer a random selection. He did not object. A breach of protocol is tolerable when it comes in the shape of a compliment. And when another writer writes two novels centering on a character whose ruling passion is his desire to win the approval of Nero Wolfe, that has to be an authentic compliment. Nor is such a character far-fetched. I have been to several Wolfe Pack dinners. The ballroom at the New York Sheraton is always filled wall-to-wall with gentle, admirable men who have eaten themselves into startling facsimiles of Nero Wolfe. There have been days when I have been tempted to jump into the competition myself, especially since, with the passing of the years, I have come to realize that my chances of being mistaken for Archie Goodwin are fading. Lawrence Block may have faced the same temptation. If so, he found an ingenious way to deal with it. He created a surrogate who could fantasize in his stead. A "little butterball" of a man, Leo Haig has longings perfectly comprehensible to all certified Neronians. We can only wish him well.

As to how Block proceeds when developing plots and building characters, he says: "My writing amounts to the answer to the question What would I do if I were this person in this situation?" He reflects further: "My characters are the people I would be were I clothed in their particular skins. I'm like an actor playing a role. I play that character's part, improvising his dialogue on the page, slipping into his role as I go along." Yet there is enough wit and brio in everything he writes to suggest that Archie Goodwin, Chip Harrison, and Lawrence Block would exhibit genuine camaraderie if they forgathered in some quiet alcove at Rusterman's to fraternize over select sirloins and a keg of Beck's.

That is not to say that Block does not play Leo Haig's part expertly too. He tells me: "I've found Rex Stout's books about Nero Wolfe endlessly rereadable. There's nothing ordinary about Wolfe and it's not only his corpulence that makes him larger than life. . . . Ordinary? Scarcely that. But so real that I sometimes have to remind myself that Wolfe and Goodwin are the creations of a writer's mind, that no matter how many doorbells I ring in the West Thirties, I'll never find the right house."

Perhaps so, but for many readers Leo Haig's faith is their faith. I know. I am one of them. I did not find it amusing when I heard that the wife of a college president, descending from a cab on West 34th Street, remarked to her husband, "Isn't this where Nero Wolfe lives?" only to be told by the cab driver, "No, lady. He lives on West Thoity-fifth Street." Maybe it was surprising that he knew, but, after all, he was right, and some day I expect to locate that house and when I do I shall not be surprised if I encounter Lawrence Block *and* Leo Haig on the front stoop. And I shall thank them both because *Make Out with Murder* and *The Topless Tulip Caper* have brought the dream several steps closer to reality.

John McAleer
Mount Independence, October 1982